D0251341

WITHDRAWN

ALSO BY BRANDON MULL

Series:

Fablehaven
The Candy Shop War
Beyonders
Five Kingdoms
Dragonwatch

Books:

The Caretaker's Guide to Fablehaven
Fablehaven Book of Imagination
Spirit Animals
Smarter Than a Monster

DRAGONWATCH
MASTER OF THE PHANTOM ISLE

BRANDON MULL

ILLUSTRATED BY
BRANDON DORMAN

SHADOW
MOUNTAIN

🦁 🦁 🦁

For Chase, forever my little pal

Library of Congress Cataloging-in-Publication Data

Names: Mull, Brandon, 1974– author. | Dorman, Brandon, illustrator. | Mull, Brandon, 1974– Dragonwatch (Series) ; bk. 3.
Title: Master of the phantom isle / Brandon Mull.
Description: Salt Lake City : Shadow Mountain, [2019] | Series: Dragonwatch; book 3 | Summary: As the evil Celebrant conquers more and more dragon sanctuaries, Kendra must raise an army of friends and allies on her own to fight him because her brother Seth and Bracken are missing.
Identifiers: LCCN 2019024701 | ISBN 9781629726045 (hardback)
Subjects: LCSH: Young adult fiction. | CYAC: Dragons—Fiction. | Brothers and sisters—Fiction. | Missing children—Fiction. | Magic—Fiction. | LCGFT: Fantasy fiction.
Classification: LCC PZ7.M9112 Mas 2019 | DDC [Fic]—dc23
LC record available at https://lccn.loc.gov/2019024701

Printed in the United States of America   6/2019
Publishers Printing, Salt Lake City, UT

10   9   8   7   6   5   4   3   2   1

Contents

CONTENTS

CHAPTER ONE

Under

Ronodin opened the door without knocking. "The Underking wishes to see you."

Startled, Seth looked up from the desk, where he had been making a coin spin by flicking it. Ronodin had assigned him to read a thick book about phantoms, which had sounded like an interesting topic until he encountered long-winded passages written in archaic language. Even skipping ahead a few times, he had failed to find an interesting part.

"Who is the Underking?" Seth asked.

"Our host," Ronodin said. "We're currently residing in a small section of his lair. You weren't reading."

"I tried," Seth said.

"For how long?"

"Every minute felt like an hour," Seth said. "You should be amazed that I'm still awake."

Ronodin scowled at the book. "It may take some time to reach the interesting parts."

"Maybe you could summarize?" Seth asked hopefully.

"Later," Ronodin said, folding his arms. A handsome young man dressed in black, Ronodin always seemed sure of himself. Seth hadn't known the guy very long. They had no history. In fact, Seth had no history with anyone. His memories went back less than a day, to a room in a castle with a girl named Kendra who claimed to be his sister. Ronodin had appeared shortly thereafter, as had some other people, including a magical dwarf. After a confusing confrontation, Seth had been teleported to another castle, where a big wooden puppet had grabbed him and brought him through a barrel to this underground location. He had been here for only a few hours.

"This matter of the Underking is a real problem," Ronodin continued. "I had hoped you could avoid the meeting entirely."

"He won't like me?" Seth asked.

Ronodin gave him a smirk. "He'll more than like you. He'll crave you. He hungers for all living creatures, let alone someone with dark powers."

"He's king of the underground?" Seth asked.

"King of the Under Realm," Ronodin said in a solemn tone. "He rules over all of the undead."

"Like zombies?" Seth asked. "And phantoms?" He glanced at the black book on the desk. "Maybe I should have read more."

"If it should be dead but isn't, the Underking probably

governs it," Ronodin said. "Entering his presence is incredibly dangerous. I have done so only five times, and I've known him for centuries."

"Then why should I risk it?" Seth asked.

"He asked for you," Ronodin said.

"What if I just slip out of here?" Seth asked.

Ronodin sighed. "For one, we couldn't sneak away. The Underking is enormously powerful here in his domain. His attention is already on you. In addition, we need access to his tunnels. The Under Realm connects to your world in many surprising places, simplifying travel."

Seth stared at Ronodin. How was he supposed to respond? Where could he even start? Apparently he was the hostage of an underground king. And what about Ronodin? Was he his ally or his captor? Seth sighed. Maybe he deserved this predicament. There was no way to be sure. Whoever he had been in his forgotten past, he must have led an interesting life.

"Don't look at me that way," Ronodin said. "Survival is uncomfortable sometimes. You've been through worse."

"I don't remember," Seth said.

"Sounds like a relief to me," Ronodin said. "Start over with a clean slate, unburdened by past mistakes."

"I could be anyone," Seth said.

"Not anyone," Ronodin corrected. "You are a shadow charmer. You wield arcane power. You can speak to wraiths and quench fire."

Seth knew he had the powers Ronodin was describing because, in their short time together, Ronodin had given him opportunities to use them. Supposedly Ronodin could help his powers increase.

"And you're a unicorn?" Seth asked.

"In human form," Ronodin said. "You mustn't keep the Underking waiting. It could make things worse for you."

Seth tried to calm himself. Without memories, it was hard to make sense of his circumstances. It felt unfair to be facing consequences he did not understand. How had he gotten into this mess? There didn't seem to be any way out. For now, his best chance was to learn what he could and try to stay alive.

"I have no choice," Seth said.

"In this matter, no," Ronodin said.

"I'm not a bad guy," Seth asserted.

"How do you know?" Ronodin asked.

"I just know," Seth said.

"I'm not a bad guy either," Ronodin said. "But we're both outsiders."

"Who live in the subterranean lair of the king of zombies?" Seth asked.

"We're visitors here," Ronodin said. "Follow me."

Ronodin walked out without looking back. Seth hesitated, then followed him, jogging to catch up. If this meeting needed to happen, he had better follow the unicorn's advice.

"You must not look at the Underking," Ronodin instructed. "To gaze upon him is to join the undead."

"I'd become a zombie?" Seth asked.

"Or worse," Ronodin said. "You will walk into the room

with your back to him. You will keep your eyes closed. You will never face him or open your eyes. Not for any reason. Understand?"

"What if he sneaks up on me?" Seth asked.

"We're in his domain," Ronodin said. "If the Underking wants you dead, you will die. If he wants you undead, little could stop him. Your job is to cause no unnecessary harm to yourself. Remember, don't look at him."

"What about in a mirror?" Seth asked.

"That might work with a gorgon," Ronodin said. "Not the Underking—eyes closed, back to him."

"You've never seen him?" Seth asked.

"I would be undead if I had," Ronodin said.

"What if he isn't there?" Seth asked. "What if it's just a sound system?"

"He could be a hamster for all I know," Ronodin said. "Or he could be a monster the size of a mountain. I suspect he looks somewhat like his subjects—he rules them because he is one of them."

"Why does he want to see me?"

"You are a guest in his domain," Ronodin said. "You are a shadow charmer in a time when that gift has become exceedingly rare. Beyond that, I cannot pretend to fathom his mind."

"Won't it seem rude if I walk in backwards?" Seth asked.

"He knows what is required to communicate with him and remain mortal," Ronodin said.

They turned a corner and moved down another subterranean corridor. Seth tried to imagine what it would feel like to become a zombie or a wraith. He had recently met a few wraiths with Ronodin, and they seemed like miserable creatures, cold and empty.

"Have I talked to the Underking before?" Seth asked.

"Never," Ronodin said. "Few have."

"I wish I could remember who I am," Seth said.

"It might prove better this way," Ronodin said, "at least for our present purposes. You'll be more of an enigma to him. Trust your instincts. You're not like other mortals. You know the basics about the magical world."

"I know magical creatures are real," Seth said. "Seeing the wraiths was no surprise. I generally remember them. In theory, I mean. I just don't recall having any experiences with them. I don't feel anything about them. I have a bunch of information but no opinions about it. There are no associations to rely on. How can I have reached this age with no connections to anything?"

"Seth, you lost your memories," Ronodin said. "If that erased your opinions too, find the benefit. Our assumptions often blind us. Now you have a chance to experience life through new eyes."

"I guess," Seth said. "What else should I know about the Underking?"

"Honestly, the less you know, the better," Ronodin said. "Be respectful. Be humble. Be meticulously honest. Don't make any foolish bargains. Agree to what you must. Don't look at him."

"That sounds awkward," Seth said. "Talking without looking."

"The Underking would be the last thing you beheld with mortal eyes," Ronodin warned. "Three of the great monarchs wear much of their power on the outside: the Dragon King, the Giant Queen, and the Demon King. The Fairy Queen and the Underking are more subtle, and all the more dangerous for it. If you want strategy, my advice is to be content. Desire nothing. Ask for nothing. The undead are full of insatiable cravings. More than with most, contentment looks like power to the Underking."

"Could he help me get my memory back?" Seth asked.

Ronodin stopped walking. "What did I just say? Desire nothing."

"Which makes me think about what I want," Seth said.

"Put that longing away," Ronodin said. "Pack all of your desires away, lock them up, and throw out the key. Portray yourself as a young shadow charmer whom I have offered to teach. You are here to learn from me. You do not desire accelerated learning. You don't desire anything. You are the simplest, most content boy in the world."

"I'll try," Seth said.

"Once he knows what you want, he'll figure out how to tempt you," Ronodin said. "Beguile you. Ensnare you. Destroy you."

"I do want to remember my identity," Seth said, "whether I admit it to him or not."

"Try to change your thoughts about that," Ronodin said, continuing along the corridor. "Your survival could depend on it."

"Can the Underking read my mind?" Seth asked.

"Possibly," Ronodin said. "But voicing a thought gives it added power. Makes it more deliberate. Deny all desires in his presence, and you may survive."

"Do you think I'll pull through?" Seth asked.

"Much of that depends on you," Ronodin said. He stopped at a large black door ornamented with bleached skulls of varying size, few of them human. "Ready?"

"No," Seth said. "Does that matter?"

"Not really," Ronodin said, extending a hand to rest a finger on the forehead of a small, narrow skull with pointy teeth. Ronodin closed his eyes for a moment, and, as he removed his finger, the door vanished. Cold darkness flowed from the doorway, washing over Seth and quickly blackening the hallway.

Pale blue light flared at the end of a short, gnarled wand, held by Ronodin, the tip bright enough to drive back the inky darkness, but not very far. Though it lacked any tangibility that Seth could discern, this particular darkness seemed especially resistant to light. Ronodin handed the holly wand to Seth.

"Why take a light if I don't want to see him?" Seth asked.

"Even without light," Ronodin said, "you would still see the Underking if you gazed in his direction. But you will need some light to stay on the tiled path. This holly wand can drive back even empowered darkness. Step gently, avoid the pits, and do not stray off into the bones."

"And I'm supposed to walk backward," Seth said. "Without looking up."

Ronodin shook his hand with formality. "You're

catching on. Off you go." Ronodin released his hand. "Remember, if something goes wrong, if you need anything at all, you're absolutely on your own."

Seth had no reply. It was possible Ronodin was trying to use humor to relax him, but Seth suspected he was simply apprenticed to a jerk. Ronodin gestured for him to proceed. Seth turned his back to the gaping doorway and passed through it in reverse with careful steps. Holding the wand low to better illuminate the ground, Seth kept his eyes downward to see where he was going without peering too far ahead. He had not taken many steps before darkness swallowed all view of Ronodin and the doorway.

The plain black tiles reflected little light. Seth backed along quietly. Jagged heaps of bones appeared off to one side of the floor, starkly white at the edge of the light from his wand. He reached a pit of impenetrable blackness, no bigger around than a hula hoop. No matter how close Seth brought the wand, no light brightened the pit.

Seth felt a creeping suspicion that something behind him was watching, perhaps even sneaking up on him, but he couldn't look in case he might accidentally see the Underking. There seemed to be movement in the darkness beyond his light, unseen, unheard, but convincingly present. Seth felt unsettled, then scared, and though part of him knew the impulse was irrational, it took an effort not to run off screaming in a random direction.

As he inched along the tile floor, messy piles of bones appeared off to one side. Seth wound around several smallish pits, wondering how long he would be traveling. Was he crossing a normal-sized room, or might this go on for miles?

Walking backward in a crouch was tedious. He felt entombed by the incredible quiet and stillness surrounding him. The shuffling of his feet seemed to desecrate an otherwise perfect silence. Seth resisted the mounting, suspenseful terror.

Occasionally he reached an individual bone, which he avoided in case it was cursed or diseased. The air was so cold that Seth could see his breath pluming in the wandlight.

Dry words reached Seth with no warning, slithering into his ears while chilling his nerves. "Who brings light into my darkness?" inquired a voice that seemed ancient, all rasp and whisper.

Goosebumps erupted all over Seth and his muscles tensed. The fear of anticipation was over—doom had arrived. Seth had to resist the urge to look over his shoulder toward that desiccated voice. Whoever had spoken was awaiting a response.

Seth stood up straighter, keeping his back to the speaker and his eyes closed. "I hardly know anymore," he said. "I'm told my name is Seth."

"You are warm and alive, young one," the voice observed. Each wheezy word carried the impression of skeletal hands reaching for him.

"I've been warmer," Seth said, trying to sound calm. "Alive for now, I guess. Who are you?"

"I am master here," the voice affirmed. "Ruler of all who dwell down below."

"The Underking," Seth said.

"What brings one so warm to such a cold place? Why does one who bears a light seek the shadows?"

"It wasn't my choice," Seth said. "Ronodin brought me here."

"The living who venture into my realm must join the undead," the Underking said.

"I don't want that," Seth said.

"What is it you want?" the Underking asked.

"Really?" Seth asked. "To leave."

The Underking laughed softly. "The moment you entered my domain, you belonged to me. Have you no purpose here?"

Seth decided he had better fall back on Ronodin's instructions. "I'm a shadow charmer. Ronodin is teaching me."

Seth waited in silence. There came a faint scraping sound from the direction of the voice, as if the speaker were stirring.

"I could teach you so much more," the Underking rasped softly.

"I bet," Seth said.

"The unicorn knows a type of darkness," the Underking said. "I dwell where the darkness deepens, Seth—where it continues for time immeasurable. All light is brief, Seth, so frail and fleeting, a feeble flash against the steady night."

"I just want to train with Ronodin," Seth said, sticking to the plan. "Can I stay here and do that?"

"Ah," the Underking said. "You speak the sacred words."

"I mean, stay temporarily, while I train," Seth said.

"You are alive," the Underking said. "Living is about change. Temporary states. You wish to remain under my protection for a season, like the unicorn. Are you brave?"

"I'm here," Seth said.

"Are you true?" the Underking asked.

"I think so," Seth replied.

"There are limits to what the unicorn can make of you," the Underking said. "What more do you want?"

"Just to learn from Ronodin," Seth said, remembering the warning to keep his needs simple. "I don't want anything else."

"Speak truly."

Seth sighed. "I'm trying to remember who I am. But I trust I'll figure it out."

"You are cursed," the Underking said. "My realm welcomes wayfarers such as you. And mortal shadow charmers have grown so very scarce. Turn and look at me."

"I better not," Seth said.

The Underking gave a hoarse chuckle. "Would some illumination help?"

Seth could feel new light through his closed lids. With his back to the Underking, was it safe to peek? By slitting his eyes, Seth glimpsed cold white radiance filling the room, revealing all without brightening anything too much. He squeezed his eyes tightly closed again just in case.

"If I look at you, I can never leave," Seth said.

"Gaze upon me and you will endure," the Underking

whispered, the words penetrating deeper than if he had shouted them. "You will outlast the stars."

"I just need a place to train with Ronodin," Seth said.

"What about my crown?" the Underking asked, the words reaching Seth as if whispered from close to his ears, private communication meant for him alone. "You could replace me, young one, and the splendors and powers of the night would be yours. You could be master over sightless reaches of virgin darkness undefiled by light, endless voids, lifeless and deathless, behind, beneath, and above the petty stages of the sunlit worlds."

"I'm just trying to keep out of the rain," Seth said. "I don't need more than a place to stay for a time."

"I will grant you sanctuary here," the Underking rasped. "All boons come at a price. I do you a favor by sparing the scant flicker of your life, and I do another by granting refuge. You will agree to two conditions in return, or your spark will be quenched here and now. You will not leave my domain until permission is granted by me, and you will assist Ronodin in freeing some of my captive subjects. Is that agreeable?"

Seth wasn't sure he had a choice, if he wanted to survive. "Will you ever give me permission to leave?"

"I will let you leave temporarily to perform errands for me," the Underking said. "Eventually, if you so desire, I will devise a task for you to perform that will grant you freedom."

"How long will I have to wait before you give me the task?" Seth asked.

"I shall devise it when I devise it," the Underking answered.

Seth felt sure he would get no better offer than this. "All right."

"Sealed," the Underking said.

Seth jumped as he felt something cold close around his wrist. Peeking, he saw a ghostly manacle clamped just beneath his hand, the translucent chain fading into invisibility after three links. The manacle was weightless, and the initial cold sensation quickly faded. Seth tried to touch the manacle with his free hand, but his fingers passed right through it. When he shook the arm to which the manacle was affixed, it refused to come loose.

"What's on my arm?" Seth asked.

"A reminder of our arrangement," the Underking said. "Ronodin will now represent my will to you. Follow his instructions as you would mine."

Seth knew some sort of trap was closing around him. But at least he was alive. Hopefully he could stay that way long enough to figure out what battle he was actually fighting. "I understand."

"Away with you then," the Underking rasped, the slithery words diminishing. "Take the light with you."

CHAPTER TWO

Restless

Despite the sunlight outlining the edges of the heavy curtains in her bedroom at Blackwell Keep, Kendra was supposed to be asleep. Everyone agreed she needed rest. After spending all night fighting for her life at Stormguard Castle, she had succeeded in breaking the enchantment imposed by the dwarf Humbuggle and at keeping the Wizenstone from the dragons. For much of the time the battle had not seemed winnable. Victory had felt like a miracle. A major threat to the safety of the world had been averted.

And her brother was gone.

Seth had sacrificed his identity to open a magical door. In the room beyond the door, Kendra had used a magical staff to send the Wizenstone away. Had Celebrant and his fellow dragons claimed the stone, they would have become too powerful to stop. Against staggering odds, she and Seth had done their duty as caretakers and protected Wyrmroost.

But her brother was gone.

After they had returned to Blackwell Keep, when the battle had seemed over, the animated limberjack Mendigo had snatched Seth and disappeared through a barrel. Originally, the barrel had been linked to another one at Fablehaven. The connected barrels had served as their portal to return home. Disturbingly, the barrel at Fablehaven had gone missing. The loss of that barrel meant her brother could be almost anywhere.

Kendra kicked off the covers. Her body felt weary, but her mind refused to rest. She had already shared all the clues she could think of with Grandma and Grandpa Sorenson. They had ordered her to go to bed, assuring her that they would keep pursuing all possible leads about Seth.

Kendra exited her room. Bleak stone walls kept the corridor cool and gloomy. Unsure of a destination, she walked to the door at the end of the hall. When she stepped out into the daylight, the heavy buildings and towers around her felt like ruins. Why not abandon this place? Should people sacrifice their lives to protect these dusty courtyards? Was it worth losing her brother?

Shuffling down a flight of stairs to the courtyard, Kendra wondered where she would go. Maybe to the farthest corner of the darkest dungeon. Or perhaps to the Blackwell—a deep pit teeming with the undead might match her mood.

Battle-ax resting on one shaggy shoulder, Brunwin the minotaur paced along the top of a nearby wall. Kendra averted her gaze—it was hard to imagine getting any real understanding from him. Up ahead, Newel was crossing the courtyard. The sight of the satyr lightened her mood instantly. He loved Seth. Though Newel wasn't the best at taking things seriously, he might be able to appreciate what she had lost.

She quickened her pace and called, "Newel."

The satyr glanced her way and stopped walking. "Hello."

"My grandparents want me to sleep, but I need to talk," she said.

"I've never believed in artificial bedtimes," the satyr said. "If you can't sleep, make the best of it—eat, revel with friends, watch a show."

"Can we go to your room?" Kendra asked.

"Proper concealment is an important aspect of taking control of your sleep," Newel said, waving her to follow him. "Cozying up to the quiet side of a haystack can help you snooze through an otherwise exhausting afternoon."

"But I don't want to sleep," Kendra said.

"Nobody wants to get stuck in bed wide awake by someone else's decree," Newel said as they reached his door. He used a key to open it. "I'll shelter you."

Kendra entered and Newel followed, closing the door behind them. She crossed to a couch and sat down.

"Hungry?" Newel asked.

"I can't stop worrying about Seth," Kendra said, tears squeezing from her eyes.

"Me too, Kendra," Newel said with concern. "He lost his memory?"

"He looked at me like a stranger," Kendra said. "Like he was meeting me for the first time."

"That's terrible."

"He was just . . . gone. He had been there a moment before. He was being so brave. And then he didn't know me. He's been taken someplace. We don't know where. What if Ronodin has him? Or some other evil person? What if Seth gets filled with lies? My brother is blank right now. Empty. How can he know what to believe?"

Newel crouched down in front of her. "Seth became who he is once. Can't we trust him to do it again?"

"I hope so," Kendra said. "And I hope we can find a way to reverse his memory loss. But what if we can't? And what if starting over with lots of bad examples and wrong information makes him regrow all crooked?" Kendra shied away from the next words—even unuttered, they produced horror. But she couldn't resist. "What if we've really lost him?"

Newel laid a hand on hers.

"What if we can't get him back?" Kendra went on, unable to stop herself. "What if by the time we find him, he doesn't want to come back?" The thought was too terrible for tears. Kendra felt numb and desolate.

"We can't let that happen," Newel said. "Do we have any leads on where he might be?"

"Grandpa says the wizard Vernaz who helped re-create Mendigo has a relationship with the Sphinx. Mendigo was revived from splinters of his former self, and he has needed additional work a few times since then as problems surfaced. Grandpa contacted Agad, who is trying to see what clues

he can uncover. But really, Seth could be anywhere. The Sphinx might be involved. Ronodin or Humbuggle could be part of it. Or maybe somebody else."

"Isn't the Sphinx on our side now?" Newel asked.

"They made him an Eternal," Kendra said. "Supposedly he has been playing nice since then. He would have to die for the demon prison to open, so he's probably not up to the same old mischief. But that doesn't mean he can't get involved with the dragons. Or help other private causes of his own. We know he has operated in secret before."

"The Sphinx has always been shifty," Newel said. "Did I hear correctly that Celebrant is no longer a caretaker?"

"The Somber Knight stripped him of that title after Celebrant declared war," Kendra said. "With Seth gone, I'm the only caretaker left for Wyrmroost. We went from three to one in a couple of days."

"It will be hard for you to look for Seth without leaving Wyrmroost," Newel said.

Tears blurred her vision. Could she tell Newel everything she felt? That her brother was more important to her than Wyrmroost? That part of her would rather all the preserves around the world fell into disarray if it meant she could have Seth back? And yes, that would probably mean the end of the world, with magical creatures running wild across the globe, in which case she would lose all of her family, Seth included, so maybe it wasn't what she really wanted, but it almost felt true right now.

She fingered her caretaker's medallion. "I wish this

wasn't my job. I want to go find Bracken and Seth, not babysit a bunch of dragons who want to kill me."

"You're doing an important service," Newel said. "You're protecting the people you love along with everyone else."

Kendra studied the goat-man and saw real concern in his eyes. "I know you really care about Seth."

He smiled. "Of course I do. Satyrs don't pretend. We do what we want when we want. No matter where you have to be, I'll not rest until Seth is safe and sound. But first I have to get back to Doren."

"Grandma mentioned that Doren and Tess are at Terrabelle," Kendra said.

"True," Newel said. "Before the drama at Stormguard Castle, we went looking for Seth with Knox and Tess. Maybe not our best idea . . . but we made it safely to Terrabelle. Knox left us with Tess when he took off with Seth to find you. After some deliberating, Doren and I realized your grandparents would be worried, so I ran back to Blackwell Keep with an update. I arrived right before Midsummer Eve began. Had I reached the gates ten minutes later, you would have one less half-goat friend."

Kendra looked him up and down. "I sometimes forget that you're half goat."

Newel shrugged. "We satyrs say it's the top half that counts." He leaned in and whispered conspiratorially, "Don't tell the minotaurs."

"I'm glad you're going back to help Tess," Kendra said. "We'll send extra help. Maybe Henrick. Seth may be out of

reach for now, but we can take care of those who are still here."

"What about Knox?" Newel said.

"We left him inside the Quiet Box at Stormguard Castle," Kendra said. "Tanu and Lomo were with him, and the stingbulb of Patton was nearby, along with Calvin. But we need to make sure Knox gets out. Grandma and Grandpa Sorenson are on it."

"They talked to me about retrieving Tess," Newel said, cracking his knuckles. "Shouldn't be hard. The roads are protected again. Celebrant has less authority after losing his caretaker status."

"Be careful not to underestimate the danger," Kendra said.

"Don't overestimate it either," Newel said, removing an apple from a bowl and taking a big bite. "Takes all the fun out of the adventure."

"Fun?" Kendra asked, incredulous.

"Sure," Newel said, wiping his lips on his forearm. "We have to make the best of things."

"Since when has this been fun?" Kendra asked. "Scary, and challenging, and maybe necessary, but not fun."

Newel scowled in confusion. "Adventuring is often fun. And profitable and thrilling and satisfying. It's what I like about it. Seth too."

Kendra felt anger rising inside of her. "Do you think Seth is having fun right now?"

"I hope so," Newel said.

"Fun as a prisoner?" Kendra asked. "Fun without his

identity? Fun becoming corrupted in ways that may never be undone?"

Newel raised his eyebrows. "Maybe you do need some sleep."

Kendra leaped to her feet. "Why did I think for one second that you might understand how it feels to lose somebody you love?"

"I miss Seth too," Newel said, almost taking another bite of his apple, then lowering the fruit. "What good does it do to get all worked up over it?"

Kendra clenched both hands into fists. "I'm not trying to do any good! I know I can't solve the problem right now! But I do have feelings! And none of this is fun!"

Newel reached back into the bowl and held out some fruit to Kendra. "Orange?"

"No, thank you!" Kendra replied icily.

Newel replaced the orange. "Banana?"

Kendra laughed a little, largely in disbelief. "I'm not hungry." She grabbed the sides of her head and started pacing. Newel probably wasn't trying to be rude or antagonistic. Seth found adventuring fun, and so did she—sometimes. But not right now. Not one bit. "I better go," she said.

"You can stay if you want," Newel said. "You don't have to eat."

"I shouldn't be around anyone right now," Kendra said, trying to speak calmly. "I am tired and hurting inside."

Newel gave a nod. "We'll get your brother back. Just you wait."

Kendra looked at the satyr. She hoped he was right. But

it didn't seem likely. This felt different from any problem they had ever faced. "We'll try."

She walked to the door, and Newel opened it.

"Can I give you some advice you may not want?" he asked.

"I guess," Kendra said, bracing herself.

"Find a haystack. You're exhausted."

She did feel stretched. But she doubted she could sleep. "We'll see."

"Your choice," Newel said. "Your grandparents weren't trying to punish you by sending you to bed. They were trying to help."

"I know," Kendra said.

"Where are you going to go?"

"Someplace I can be alone."

CHAPTER THREE

Hero

Knox had barely settled into the weightless nothingness within the Quiet Box, dimly wondering how long he would drift in stasis, vaguely relieved that he could no longer feel his shoulder turning to gold, when the door swung open. Instead of floating, he was suddenly standing, upholstered walls close at either side and behind him. His first reaction was to wonder what had prompted Kendra and Seth to remove him so quickly. His second reaction was to question how Patton was standing before him.

The real Patton Burgess had died many years ago. This was a replica created by a plant called a stingbulb. Supposedly, only mortals could enter Stormguard Castle, or creatures like dragons that could temporarily become mortal.

Behind Patton stood Lomo, a rebel member of the Fair Folk who had left the city of Terrabelle to assist them, and the potion master Tanu, who had reportedly been turned to silver. Knox looked to his formerly golden hand to find it was now entirely made of flesh. He gratefully flexed fingers that had lost most of their feeling moments before.

But it had not actually been a matter of moments. If his hand was healed, and Tanu was restored, and Patton was here, then the trials of the castle must be over. They had won!

"Where are Seth and Kendra?" Knox asked.

"No longer here," Patton said.

"They left me behind?" Knox asked.

"They were gone when I regained my senses," said a lean man with brown stubble on his chin. "I'm Lockland. I came out of that box when you went in."

"Who did you put inside to get me out?" Knox wondered.

"The same criminal who I removed when I entered," Lockland said. "A thief named Jasmine."

"She won't steal much in there," Knox said with a glance back at the Quiet Box. Several people in the dingy room laughed. Besides Tanu, Lomo, and Patton, there were a dozen attractive men and women assembled, dressed in courtly outfits—their finery incongruent with a dungeon cell. One breathtaking girl looked only a year or two older than Knox. "Kendra and Seth got away?" he checked.

"We're not sure," Tanu said. "We hope so."

"When we awoke from the spell, there was no sign of them," Lomo said.

"Nor Celebrant," Lockland said. "Nor Tregain."

"Good," Knox said.

"We hope Tregain is unharmed and simply missing for now," Lockland said. "He is my brother."

"And he was trying to turn us to silver," Knox said. "Who ended up with the Wizenstone?"

"We're not sure," Lomo said. "Perhaps the hunt has moved elsewhere."

"The dragon Jaleesa fled in human form," said a solid man with a glossy brown beard. "She was missing an arm."

"May I introduce my brother Heath," Lockland said.

"You were the one turning people to gold," Knox said.

"Yes, I possessed the golden glove for many years," Heath said. "After all that time, the challenge ended in a mess. We don't know what became of the prize."

"You were changed to gold before the end," Lockland said.

"I only hope Tregain managed to keep the prize in the family," Heath said. "Doom will soon follow should the dragons claim it."

Knox noticed a distinguished older man wearing a conspicuous crown. He stood beside an older woman with a jeweled tiara. "Wait, is that the king and queen?" Knox asked.

"My parents," Lockland said. "King Hollorix and Queen Satilla."

"I must congratulate you for your efforts undoing the curse," the king said to Knox. "We languished for years trying to break the stalemate."

"Just trying to help," Knox said with a glance at Tanu and Lomo.

"We wish to show our gratitude by throwing a feast in your honor," the king said, his gaze taking in Tanu and Lomo.

"Lockland gave essential help as well," Tanu said. "Along with Seth and Kendra Sorenson, the caretakers of Wyrmroost."

"It was Lockland's duty to help," the king said. "You three came to our rescue of your own accord."

"I don't want to rain on the parade," Knox said, "but most of your food might be spoiled."

The king gave a laugh. "We checked our stores. The spell held most of the castle in stasis. Our larders remain well provisioned with recommendable fare."

Knox smiled. "I *am* pretty hungry."

Many chuckled at the comment.

"Unfortunately, we must depart in a hurry," Tanu said. "We need to check in with Blackwell Keep and learn what happened to Kendra and Seth."

"Nonsense," King Hollorix said. "If you dine with us, this will have been a diplomatic mission, meaning our coach can take you back to the keep. There is no surer or faster way."

"He's right," Lomo said. "Their flying coach has full immunity. A reliable ride home is just what you need."

"I won't argue against that," Tanu said.

"The castle is still safe from dragons?" Knox asked.

"No location in Wyrmroost is more secure," Lockland

said. "It's why Jaleesa fled. She could not have transformed back into her dragon state until off this property. And once out, she would not be able to get back in without an invitation."

"Preparations for the feast are already under way," the king said. "You will have seats of honor."

"How about some help against the dragons?" Knox asked.

The atmosphere in the room grew more somber.

"Our neutrality policy stands as always, young man," King Hollorix said.

"But the dragons declared war," Knox said.

"Not on us," the king replied.

"The boy is right that the Fair Folk could make a difference in this fight," Lomo said.

"The last time the Fair Folk went to war, all who participated were lost," the king said. "And the world was no better for it."

"What if we had stayed neutral about your castle?" Knox asked. "You would still be cursed."

"Do not overstate your generosity," the king said. "We are grateful but we are not fools. Like the dragons, you came to this castle for the Wizenstone. My sons and I wanted it as well. The stone is evidently gone, and, as a happy accident, the curse is broken. Our gratitude is not an obligation. I recommend you accept it gracefully."

"Good food and a ride home," Tanu said. "I've had worse offers."

"There must be more comfortable rooms than this one," Knox said.

Friendly laughter greeted the statement. "Agreed," King Hollorix said. "We came here only to fetch you. Let us retire upstairs."

As they filed from the room into the dungeon hallway, Knox ended up beside the gorgeous girl. She was a little taller than him, with fine features, frosty blue eyes, and pale blonde hair.

"You were brave to come here," the girl said.

Knox shrugged. "I like saving people."

"I'm Regina," the girl said.

"Knox. Were you turned to metal?"

"Silver," she said.

"How was it?" Knox asked.

"Like a dream," Regina said. "Not a nice one. I faded in and out of awareness, but I always felt like a passenger in my body, everything muted and numbed. I think I was more aware on the festival nights, especially when in motion. My mother, Bethany, was turned to gold. She was the one who touched you."

"I'm sorry," said a woman from behind Knox. He recognized her as the human version of the golden figure who had started his transformation to gold.

"No problem," Knox said. "It helped get Lockland out of the Quiet Box."

"My brother," Bethany said.

"I'm just sad I missed the action," Knox said, stretching

his formerly golden arm. "Would have been nice to give those dragons some payback."

"I'm happy I got to dream away most of it," Regina said.

"I wish I knew what happened to my cousins," Knox said.

"The caretakers are your cousins?" Regina asked.

"Yeah," Knox said. "I think my grandparents want me to get more experience before I take over. I already saved Wyrmroost once. Went up against a bunch of dragons alone. In their dragon form, of course. Human form is a lot easier."

"You sound like quite a hero," Bethany said.

"I don't use that word," Knox said. "People around me do sometimes. I guess they think it fits."

"You are difficult to describe," Tanu said over his shoulder. "So many words fit."

Knox avoided meeting eyes with Tanu. He hadn't been aware the potion master was listening. Knox cleared his throat softly. "I couldn't have done any of it without my teammates."

"You performed bravely, Knox," Tanu said.

Knox glanced at Regina. "It's what I do."

CHAPTER FOUR

Innocent

"A re you sure nobody will see us?" Tess asked as she marched through the tall grass behind Eve.

"We made a clean getaway," Eve said, not looking back. "And we look like sheep to any onlookers."

Tess looked around. Woolly sheep grazed here and there, bright bells on their collars. No people were in view. Nearby, the sails of a large windmill slowly turned in the breeze.

"How far away are the fairies?" Tess asked.

"We're almost there," Eve said. "I can't promise we'll see any, but I usually find one or two."

Tess picked up her pace to stay near her new friend. Eve was one of the Fair Folk, the daughter of Lord Dalgorel. She was so pretty and nice, and Tess was delighted to be treated as an equal by a girl who looked a couple of years older than her. It had been Eve's idea to come see the fairies after Tess had shown her the cloak of innocence. Eve had been unfairly grounded by her father, so they had to sneak out of the castle. The escape hadn't been too difficult—Eve could disguise them with magic, and she knew lots of secret ways. Some climbing had been required, and a crawl through one low tunnel, but since they had left the town, the journey had been easy.

Eve led them into a stand of trees, where they found a trickling creek that in places became almost narrow enough to jump across. A small, ornate bridge spanned it at one point, and near the bridge fluttered a fairy with dragonfly wings.

"Hello!" Tess called, dashing ahead to the fairy. "I'm Tess! Am I glad to see you!"

The blue-skinned fairy zipped toward Tess and paused in front of her face, looking her up and down. "How did a little human like you get fairystruck?" the fairy asked.

"I love fairies," Tess said. "I never saw one with blue skin before."

"You're not one of the Folk," the fairy said.

"I'm a visitor," Tess said.

"You understand her?" Eve asked Tess.

"Don't you?" Tess asked. "Do you need to drink some milk?"

"I'm part of the magical world, silly," Eve said. "The milk makes no difference for me. But she's speaking a dialect of Silvian that I don't know."

"Why are you with her?" the fairy asked Tess, waving a hand at Eve. "She comes here a lot and pesters us."

"She means no harm," Tess assured the fairy.

"Ask her about the peaceful dragon," Eve said.

"What dragon?" Tess asked.

"Does she mean Raxtus?" the fairy asked.

"I understood that name," Eve said. "We're not looking for Raxtus. Seth met a peaceful dragon named Dromadus. He used to be the Dragon King."

"Ah," the fairy said. "Do you know Kendra?"

"She's my cousin," Tess said.

"She's my friend," Eve said.

"She is bossy!" the fairy said.

"You don't have to tell me," Tess said. "But I like her."

"Kendra asked some of us to keep an eye on Dromadus," the fairy said. "On all of the dragons, really."

Tess looked at Eve. "Did you understand?"

"No."

"Kendra asked her to watch that dragon, and the other dragons too," Tess said.

"The fairy knows where to find Dromadus?" Eve asked.

"I do," the fairy said.

"*Now* she speaks English," Eve said.

Tess did not hear the difference.

"Can you lead us to Dromadus?" Eve asked the fairy.

"I could," the fairy said.

"Won't we get in trouble?" Tess asked. "Tanu told me to stay put until they came for me. Is Dromadus far?"

"It would take some time," the fairy said.

"As long as you stay with me, you're following your instructions," Eve said. "They just didn't want you wandering off alone. Dromadus is a peaceful dragon. Now that the dragons declared war, maybe he'll help us. We should go ask him."

"I heard the dragons are all really dangerous," Tess said.

"Most are," Eve agreed. "This one is the exception. With your cloak of innocence, we can travel there without a problem. In a time of war, we need to do all we can to help."

"I heard something about a war," the fairy said.

"Don't you want to see a dragon?" Eve asked Tess. "A nice one, I mean?"

"Of course," Tess said. "It's what I want most of all." She turned her attention to the fairy. "Will you take us there?"

The fairy yawned, patting her dainty lips. "Wingless creatures are so slow."

"We can't help that," Tess said. "We'll walk fast and won't complain."

"I hope not," the fairy said. "I can't stand complainers."

"You'll take us?" Tess asked.

The fairy jerked a thumb at Eve. "For that one? No way! For you, though? I suppose."

Tess clapped her hands and grinned. "Thank you. How could fairies get any better?"

"It would be a challenge," the fairy said.

"Do you have a name?" Tess asked.

"Poza," the fairy said. "When would you like to go?"

Tess looked to Eve.

"Now, if possible," Eve said.

"Aha!" called a male voice. Tess turned to find Doren storming out of some bushes. "Oh no you don't, not under my watchful eye."

Eve covered her face with one hand and shook her head.

"Who is this?" Poza asked.

"Our goat-man friend," Tess said.

"More like your temporary guardian," Doren said.

"How did you find us?" Eve asked wearily.

"Followed you from the castle," Doren said. "Your illusions made my mind a little fuzzy, but I stuck with you."

"Why wait until now to interrupt?" Eve asked.

Doren blinked. "I thought you might be up to some innocent girlish mischief. I'm not out to spoil *all* your fun. But seeing this dragon would take you away from Terrabelle, and I can't have that. I was charged with watching over Tess."

"I didn't even notice you," Tess said.

"I'm stealthy," Doren said. "It's a talent. Not too hard to stay low in tall grass."

"This is a disaster," Eve said. "We need to talk to Dromadus. He might be able to help. With Wyrmroost at war, only the cloak of innocence gives us a realistic chance of getting to him."

Doren looked back and forth between the two girls. "Newel and I had planned to use the cloak to poke around a bit."

"This isn't just curiosity," Eve said. "This could be a chance to secure key help."

Doren looked in the direction of the castle. "It is kind of dull back that way. The Fair Folk women are so stuck up."

"Then you should come with us," Eve said. "Unlike those neutral cowards, we're actually trying to help. With a big, strong satyr like you helping us, what could go wrong?"

"You make a valid point," Doren said.

"A satyr was never part of the agreement," Poza said.

"Satyrs add to any group we join," Doren said, offended. "We're good luck! We're fun! And we appreciate beauty. You, my dear fairy, are absolutely exquisite."

"All right, I like him," the fairy said.

"Let's go," Eve said.

"I didn't agree to come," Doren said. "Or to let you go."

"But we're trying to save Wyrmroost," Eve said.

"I think you're more interested in going on an adventure," Doren said.

"What's wrong with an adventure?" Eve asked.

"The timing is wrong," Doren said. "We're at war. With dragons."

"We're going to a nice dragon," Tess said.

"Seth and Kendra visited him," Eve said. "Dromadus could help us in the war. He used to be the king of the dragons."

"You're telling me a former Dragon King is *nice?*" Doren clarified. "How is he even alive? How reliable are your sources?"

"Seth and Kendra got the scepter from Dromadus," Eve said. "Seth told me about it while we were walking away from Skyhold together. Dromadus is famously the only

Dragon King to renounce his position rather than lose it in combat. He got sick of all the fighting after he had killed his own nephew in a challenge."

"What makes you think he would help you?" Doren asked.

"It's common knowledge that Dromadus has become a hermit," Eve said. "Seth told me he is also a pacifist. I'm hoping he'll be displeased that the dragons needlessly declared war."

"Sounds like a long shot," Doren said.

"It will be fun to meet an actual dragon," Tess said. "He might even have treasure."

Doren folded his arms. "Treasure is always of interest. But making a dragon angry by taking his treasure might not be wise."

"We wouldn't steal anything," Eve said. "That would forfeit the power of the cloak. Don't forget the cloak. This will be safe."

"You three are exasperating," Poza said. "Are we going or not?"

Doren scratched his head. "I may get busted for this, but I do want to see more of the sanctuary, and I like your initiative. Let's do it."

"Hooray," Tess cheered. "Lead the way, Poza!"

Doren sidled nearer to Eve. "Think your dad will be angry?"

"He's already furious," Eve said. "I'd rather be punished for having met Dromadus than not."

"How long before he notices you're gone?" Doren asked.

"I'm sure he already has."

Doren glanced around nervously. "Will he come down hard on us?"

"Me, yes. Tess is too young. And satyrs, well, your kind have a reputation for frivolity."

"Play dumb. Got it."

"Or maybe skip the castle on the way back," Eve suggested.

Doren stroked his chin. "I prefer avoiding awkward conversations to having them. This is shaping into a good plan. Are you sure it's worth the trouble from your father?"

"To talk to a dragon?" Eve said. "My father can't take away that experience. I want to do my part to help Wyrmroost. I'm fascinated by dragons. And I'm a student of history."

"A punishment isn't so bad if accompanied by the right memories," Doren said.

Eve gave a nod. "Exactly."

"Lead on, fairy!" Doren called.

"There is nothing lucky about a satyr," the fairy muttered.

CHAPTER FIVE

Jibarro

Dark water sloshed against the rocky shore of the grotto, the churning surface rising and falling as it surged and splashed. Seth could smell salt in the moist air.

"Is this ocean water?" Seth asked. "Are we in a sea cave?"

Ronodin used his torch to light a trio of cressets, each one nearly as tall as Seth, the slender stands topped by metal bowls to hold the flames. "The domain of the Underking is large. Right now we're topside, not far from the sea, though the water here runs very deep."

"Does the Underking let you roam wherever you want?" Seth asked.

"I come and go as I please," Ronodin said. "There are areas of his domain that he keeps private, and regions where only a fool would venture, but otherwise I am without limits. It seems like your conversation with his majesty went well."

"How can you tell?"

"You're alive," Ronodin said.

"I had to promise to do things," Seth said, glancing at the spectral manacle on his wrist. He held it up. "Do you see that?"

"Your hand?"

"I'm cuffed to a ghost chain," Seth said.

"Some sort of bargain was bound to happen," Ronodin said. "Hard to get something for nothing."

"Why did you bring me here?"

"You need a place where you can regain your lost talents," Ronodin said. "Many would try to keep you from them."

"Why do you get to come and go as you please?" Seth asked.

"Because I earned the right."

"How?"

Ronodin grinned in the firelight. "We all have our trade secrets."

"The Underking assigned me to free some of the undead," Seth said.

"No big task," Ronodin said. "But you need to learn to manage your fear or they will devour you, body and soul."

"I wasn't afraid of the wraiths," Seth pointed out.

"The wraiths here are under orders not to harm you," Ronodin said. "And there are more dreadful beings than wraiths. Not all creatures who generate fear are undead. Few cause more paralyzing horror than dragons."

"I've heard that," Seth said.

"We need to learn how you fare against one," Ronodin said.

Seth looked around. "Here? Is it a baby?"

Ronodin gave a chuckle. "Hardly."

"This room isn't very big," Seth said.

"Not above the water," Ronodin said. He pointed with his torch toward an enormous drum. "Go strike that three times."

Seth reconsidered the turbulent water. "To call something?"

"Not all dragons dwell in the sky," Ronodin said.

"Can we handle a dragon?" Seth asked.

"In these close quarters?" Ronodin asked. "We would need an arrangement with the brute to survive."

"Do we have an arrangement?" Seth asked.

"Well, I do," Ronodin said. "Smite the drum."

Held in place on a wooden scaffold, the drum was shaped like a huge barrel tipped on its side. The circular drumhead was taller than Seth. Crossing to stand before the drum, he noticed a few bones scattered in front of it.

"That's right," Ronodin said. "Use a bone."

Seth picked up what looked like a large thigh bone. Holding it in both hands, he took a shortened practice swing. The prospect of hitting the drum was exciting. The thought of summoning a dragon was thrilling. The possibility of being devoured was less comfortable.

"Three times," Ronodin encouraged.

Seth could have asked more questions, but he had already learned that Ronodin did not stray from his intentions. Hitting the drum would bring answers soonest and was probably the inevitable outcome.

Seth did not believe that Ronodin wanted him dead. Still, his palms were sweaty as he swung the bone hard. The impact produced a satisfying boom that seemed to sink into the roots of the cavern. Seth hit the drum again, feeling the resultant vibrations in his teeth. After the final stroke, Seth stepped away from the thrumming drumhead and set down the bone, then looked up to find Ronodin backing out of the room.

"Go stand in the middle of the cressets," Ronodin called, pointing toward them.

"Where are you going?" Seth asked, panicked.

"See how they form a triangle?" Ronodin asked. "Stand at the center."

"Nice try," Seth said, hurrying away from the water toward Ronodin. "I'm coming with you."

"Do as you're told if you want to live," Ronodin said. "You have only seconds. You're safe within the triangle."

Seth hesitated. "Why aren't you in there?"

"The cressets can protect only one person," Ronodin said. "Face the water."

Seth ran over to the triangle of cressets. "What now?" he cried.

"Talk to him," Ronodin called.

The brine foamed and roiled as never before, and the ground trembled. Gritty dust sprinkled down from the stalactites overhead. Mouth dry, Seth glanced back at Ronodin, who waited a couple of steps from the exit. Seth wondered how much he could rely on what Ronodin told him. Was it too late to run for it?

Water fountained up and outward as a shape erupted from its surface, dousing Seth. Cressets still burning, Seth wiped saltwater from his eyes and beheld what looked like the gargantuan head of a lumpy, diseased lizard, infested with barnacles. Knobby horns projected in various shapes and directions, like the buds of malformed antlers, and the jaws gaped open to reveal a funnel of hooked teeth.

Seth found he could no longer move. The sea dragon roared, and though Seth's bones seemed to quake and the entire cavern shuddered, he could not cover his ears. Supported by a purple, shell-encrusted neck, the head drew nearer, misshapen nostrils flexing as they sniffed.

"Speak to him," Ronodin encouraged.

Despite his terror, Seth fought to move his lips. They refused to budge. Summoning all his strength, he tried to muster a hello, but his voice would not operate.

"This is no shadow charmer," the dragon said in a voice like the hulls of great ships grinding against rocky shores.

"His talents are still emerging," Ronodin said.

Yawning his jaws open, the dragon breathed out a warm, humid exhalation that reeked strongly of old fish. Seth stared past the uneven ranks of teeth to the leathery tunnel beyond, slimy brown surfaces wrinkled and clenching. He wanted to lean away from the stench but couldn't.

The dragon pulled back a bit, eyeing him with a flat gaze. "He is crab food."

"Give the boy time," Ronodin said. "Seth, now would be a good time to speak."

Seth tried to turn his head to Ronodin. He wanted to clench his fists and yell in frustration. His body refused to respond.

"He makes kelp look clever," the dragon said. "Why not present him as an offering?"

"You don't need a boy," Ronodin said. "You eat whales."

"I have not tasted human in a good while," the dragon said. "Admittedly, they are bony and stringy, but they fear deliciously. The terror makes a fine seasoning."

Seth wrestled with the accusation. He definitely didn't want to die, and the dragon scared him, but the fear was not smothering him. Ronodin had said he was safe within the triangle of cressets, and that appeared to be true. Although Seth was a helpless target, the dragon had not attacked. Seth wanted to show his courage, because his apparent fear seemed to make the dragon lose all respect for him. But his body would not comply.

"Please, Jibarro, give the boy a moment to compose himself," Ronodin said.

"Do not summon me for such dull entertainment," the dragon said; then his head plunged beneath the water, splashing Seth.

A moment later, Seth could move. Ronodin approached briskly.

"What went wrong?" Ronodin asked.

"That dragon could have eaten me," Seth said.

"Easily," Ronodin replied. "You would have been mostly digested before reaching the stomach."

"Why couldn't I move?" Seth asked.

"You tell me," Ronodin said.

"I tried to say hello," Seth said. "I was keeping it simple."

"I sensed that your mind remained lucid," Ronodin said.

"Yes, I could think just fine," Seth said.

"Normally an inability to think is what stops a shadow charmer when faced by a dragon," Ronodin said.

"I could definitely think," Seth said. "I just couldn't move."

"You have the power to overcome all magical fear," Ronodin said. "You simply have to claim it."

"How?" Seth asked.

Ronodin folded his arms. "Evidently, when you are bombarded by extreme fear, the signals from your mind are not reaching your body. There is a disconnect between the mental and the physical."

"I knew what I wanted to say, where I wanted to move, but nothing would respond," Seth said.

"Look inside yourself, Seth," Ronodin said. "Look deep. Can you find the darkness within you?"

"I don't understand," Seth said.

"A demon called Graulas granted you a gift," Ronodin said. "You have perceived the darkness and cold within a wraith. You have darkness in you as well. It establishes a degree of kinship with the undead. You can use it to hide, to extinguish fire, and to center yourself against fear."

Seth tried to focus inward but wasn't sure what he was looking for. "What should the darkness feel like?"

Ronodin sighed. "I'll give you a rare opportunity." He held out a hand. "Take my hand and look into me. I was once a vessel of light. See what you find within me now."

Seth took the offered hand, and his mind immediately perceived a void so startling, he worried he might lose himself in it. The vast darkness seemed sure and still. It took Seth a moment to remember to speak. "The darkness is everywhere."

"Good," Ronodin said. "You have similar power within you, though less developed. Close your eyes, and get curious about your center. Where is your essence housed? Behind your eyes? In your gut? Within your fingers?"

"I don't get it," Seth said. "I'm all me."

"Think harder," Ronodin challenged. "Where is your core? Look for the part of you that feels and chooses and holds you together."

Seth thought about it. "Maybe in my chest? Maybe behind my eyes?"

"What if it's an emergency, and you need to survive?" Ronodin said. "What takes over?"

"It's in my chest," Seth said.

"There is a part of you that is in charge," Ronodin said. "A part of you that insists no external influence is going to govern you."

"Yes, okay," Seth said. "In my chest."

"Look for the darkness near there," Ronodin said. "It is not yet throughout."

"I think I feel what you mean," Seth said. "Almost like a cloud around my heart. Is that supposed to mean I'm evil?"

"We're not talking about evil," Ronodin said. "We're talking about darkness as a power source. Is day good and night evil? No. That distinction is ridiculous. Night is better for seeing the stars. Is not the cool of night preferable for traveling in the desert? Probably. Is sleeping in a dark room evil and sleeping in a bright one good? No, and I would argue that darkness is better suited to the purpose of sleep. The darkness you draw from is a resource. You can use it for good or evil."

"I guess so," Seth said.

"You sense the darkness within you?" Ronodin asked. "The gift you were given?"

"I think so," Seth said.

"Good enough," Ronodin said. "Tap into that darkness. Anchor yourself there. It can enable you to remain in charge of yourself, even against potent influences. The power there can be drawn upon to accomplish many things. Use it to extinguish this cresset."

Seth opened his eyes to see Ronodin indicating one of the flaming cressets. Seth drew on the dark place Ronodin had helped him find and focused on the cresset, pushing coldness and darkness into it. The flames resisted.

"It's hot," Seth murmured.

"The heat is nothing compared to how cold and dark you can go," Ronodin said.

Seth gritted his teeth and pushed with all that he had. The fire in the cresset shrank, dimmed, and went out with a puff of smoke. Seth found that he was panting, and his jaw hurt. Droplets of sweat beaded his brow.

"Very well done," Ronodin said richly, releasing Seth's hand. "That cresset is magically waterproof. Not easy to put out." He used a torch to relight it.

"You can do this too?" Seth asked.

"I draw on darkness in many ways," Ronodin said. "Most unicorns are beings of light. It grew tedious to me. I traded my light to access darkness, making me unique. The dark unicorn."

"What does this have to do with talking to the dragon?" Seth asked.

"Go to that same power source when Jibarro appears," Ronodin said. "Draw on the strength there. Demand to stay in charge. Don't let any other stimulus suppress you."

Seth nodded.

Ronodin walked over to the drum and picked up the thigh bone. "Ready for another try?"

"Shouldn't I rest?" Seth asked. "Train? What if I fail?"

"Rules or no rules, this time he might eat you." Ronodin struck the drum three times.

Seth wanted to protest. He didn't feel ready! He considered fleeing but decided it was too cowardly. At least he knew what to expect this time. Steeling himself, Seth turned and confronted the agitated water. The cavern shuddered. A geyser announced the arrival of Jibarro, his knobby horns grazing the top of the chamber.

"You again?" the dragon asked, glaring. He drew near with a snarl. "Don't tell me you suddenly grew a backbone?"

Seth could not move or reply. As he searched the dark place near his center, calm sureness spread through him.

"Hello," Seth said.

He suspected he could move, then gave a little wave to prove it.

The dragon looked to Ronodin. "You're good."

"That's not news," Ronodin said. "But I'm not doing this. The boy is talented."

Jibarro sniffed Seth, nostrils not quite touching his shirt. "How is it done? Wires? A spell?"

Seth held his nose. "What do you eat? Pollution?"

Jibarro jerked away, eyes flashing. "Was that disrespect?"

"Independence," Ronodin said. "Thank you, Jibarro. Your offering is already in place."

The head disappeared below the surface with a tremendous splash. Seth was absolutely soaked but didn't care. "What offering?"

"A large quantity of pickled squid," Ronodin said.

"Might explain the breath," Seth said, sitting down unsteadily on the rocky floor. He felt shaken but relieved. "I did it!"

"Lucky for you," Ronodin said. "Otherwise you would not survive tomorrow night."

"What happens tomorrow?"

The dark unicorn smiled. "You have some captives to liberate."

CHAPTER SIX

Defenses

Kendra did not realize she had fallen asleep until she was gently shaken awake. For a moment she felt disoriented. Then she recalled having come to Glory's stall to hide and think. Her favorite horse was gone, so the stall provided a cozy place where she could be alone.

Except she was no longer alone.

Agad the wizard crouched before her. His smile looked strained. Seeing him brought Kendra fully awake.

"You're back!" Kendra said. "Any word about Seth?"

Agad started to rise, then, after a pause, went and sat on the opposite side of the stall from Kendra, back to the wall. "Nothing definitive yet. I'm sorry. After the message from your grandparents, I went right to work. I'm still piecing it together."

"What are the pieces?"

"I examined the barrel," Agad said. "Its counterpart is now deep underwater."

"Where?" Kendra asked.

"In the ocean, I believe," Agad said. "Deep."

"What ocean?"

Agad shook his head sadly. "I can't get a read on it. There is magical interference."

"Can we send somebody from our barrel to that one?" Kendra asked.

Agad shook his head. "Not without someone to help them out on the other side. And I believe the barrel is extremely deep. I suspect the pressure alone would kill a person."

"They sank it instead of destroying it?" Kendra asked.

"Meaning they may hope to use it again," Agad said. "We should consider destroying the one we have."

"It might be our only link to Seth," Kendra said. "Can't we lock it up? Make sure nobody can come through?"

"We could," Agad said. "You realize they may have scuttled the barrel someplace far from your brother. It may never serve as much of a clue."

"I know," Kendra said. She looked at the wizard. "Do you have any idea who did this?"

Agad dropped his eyes. In that moment, Kendra realized how weary and haggard the old wizard looked, his skin tinged with gray that darkened around the eyes, his beard more matted and tangled than usual, his robes rumpled and stained.

"The Sphinx was involved," Agad whispered.

"You're sure?" Kendra asked. Grandpa and Grandma Sorenson had suspected his participation.

Agad nodded. "Your grandfather used a hearing stone to contact me, and he told me what happened to Seth. I dropped everything and followed my intuition to Goblin Town."

"Is that a real place?" Kendra asked.

"It's in Nevada," Agad said. "Not a standard sanctuary, mind you. No caretaker. Without the milk, it looks to humans like a large ghost town. In reality, the ramshackle settlement is infested primarily with goblins, along with a roguish assortment of hobgoblins, kobolds, gremlins, and imps."

"Sounds lovely," Kendra said.

"Wonderful place to lose an eye," Agad said. "Or a tooth. Or your life. Fortunately, goblins and their sort have a healthy respect for wizards."

"What did you find out?" Kendra asked.

"I found Slaggo," Agad said.

"He got there quickly," Kendra said.

"I'm sure the Sphinx helped him," Agad said. "The Sphinx didn't want anyone talking to Slaggo or Voorsh. It isn't his style to kill an accomplice. He wants those who aid him to be rewarded. I counted on the Sphinx deciding Slaggo and Voorsh could blend in better in Goblin Town than anywhere else."

"How did Slaggo escape Fablehaven?" Kendra asked.

"I suspect the wizard Vernaz is helping the Sphinx," Agad said. "Vernaz helped reconstruct Mendigo, which explains why the puppet was following secret instructions.

Vernaz has the know-how and authority to take creatures across preserve boundaries, and also to transport individuals over great distances."

"Slaggo and Voorsh brought the barrel to the Sphinx?" Kendra asked.

"That much we know," Agad said. "When Knox inadvertently left them the keys, the goblins fled the dungeon with the barrel and exited Fablehaven through the front gate. Apparently some time ago the Sphinx gave Voorsh means to contact him. When the Sphinx heard about the barrel, he came immediately."

"The Sphinx has been to Fablehaven before," Kendra said. "It never crossed my mind he might have made a deal with the goblins in the dungeon."

"He is a dangerous opportunist," Agad said. "I fear it was a mistake to make him an Eternal."

"He has to die for anyone to open the new demon prison," Kendra said. "He's good at staying alive. It makes sense for him to be part of the lock."

"And it preserves him," Agad said. "Keeps him around, perhaps for centuries more, unless he is killed."

"Did you track him down?" Kendra asked.

Agad shook his head. "I tried. I checked with insiders. But the Sphinx has disappeared. So has Vernaz."

"Did Slaggo see Vernaz?" Kendra asked.

"A hooded figure was with the Sphinx," Agad said. "There was no confirmation on the identity. But based on the description and the circumstances, it was very likely Vernaz."

Kendra knocked her head back against the wall of the

stall a few times, hard enough to sting a little. "What would the Sphinx want with Seth?"

Agad raised his eyebrows and spread his hands. "I can only guess. Obviously, they are both shadow charmers. Or the Sphinx may have been working with somebody else who has an interest in your brother."

"Celebrant?" Kendra asked. "Ronodin?"

"It's guesswork at this point," Agad said.

Kendra picked up a brittle piece of straw from the floor of the stall and twisted it between her fingers. "The Sphinx originally allied himself with the demons. That door is closed, so now he might be scheming with the dragons?"

"Maybe," Agad said.

"Or does he think he can train Seth as a sidekick?" Kendra asked. "Could he have known Seth lost his memories? He had barely lost them when he was kidnapped."

"I don't know," Agad said.

"That plan could work," Kendra said bleakly, straw crunching in her grasp. "Whoever is behind it. Seth doesn't know who he is. He could be retrained from scratch. Reprogrammed by our enemies." Her eyes stung. "Agad, we could end up fighting my little brother."

"We'll try to recover him before it comes to that," Agad said.

"But we don't know where to look," Kendra said.

"Not yet," Agad replied.

"Didn't you have a tracker on the Sphinx?" Kendra asked.

"As part of becoming an Eternal, the Sphinx has the right to move and hide where he chooses," Agad said. "He had two minders—one we told him about and one we didn't. This is the first time we know of that he eluded both."

Kendra squeezed her eyes shut. This just kept getting worse. Would there ever be good news?

"I'm sorry that you kids were drawn into this crisis," Agad said.

"If this keeps up, the whole world will be drawn in," Kendra said.

"There is uncertainty and devastation all around," Agad said. "All of Dragonwatch is working overtime on problems across the globe. We managed to win back a portion of Crescent Lagoon. It seemed the whole archipelago had fallen, but the caretaker reestablished a foothold on one island. Your friends Warren and Vanessa played a key role."

"Are they all right?" Kendra asked.

"Last I heard they were safe and healthy," Agad said.

"I guess one less fallen sanctuary is a relief," Kendra said.

"It's a desperate fight," Agad said. "We'll take what we can get."

"Are people looking for Bracken and Seth?" Kendra asked.

"All of our agents are on the lookout," Agad said. "And I am making it my personal mission to find your brother."

That brought Kendra some relief. At least Agad considered Seth a top priority.

"What about the sanctuary that completely fell?" Kendra asked.

"Soaring Cliffs?" Agad asked.

"Yes," Kendra said. "Where Bracken was held for a time. Are those dragons rampaging? Destroying cities?"

"Nothing like that yet," Agad said.

"Why not?" Kendra asked.

"It's complicated," Agad said.

"Isn't that why we're fighting to keep these sanctuaries from falling? So dragons won't run wild?"

Agad furrowed his brow. "I suppose as a caretaker you should know about our last lines of defense. Someday this knowledge may prove necessary. These secrets should not be repeated except to the most trusted ally at the greatest need."

"I know how to keep secrets," Kendra said.

"I would not share this otherwise," Agad said. "Three of the seven dragon sanctuaries contain Dragon Temples. Each temple houses numerous priceless artifacts, along with one talisman of extreme importance. Here at Wyrmroost, that item is the Sage's Gauntlets. A wizard who masters the gauntlets can gain control over dragons."

"That would be amazing," Kendra said.

"For our side," Agad said. "Do not forget that like all wizards, I was once a dragon. Using arts that are all but forgotten, I became mortal in exchange for greater magic. Though I have not been a dragon for a great while, I still remember how the existence of the Sage's Gauntlets offended me. All dragons feel likewise. There is also a shield that allows the bearer to repel dragons, and a harp that can soothe dragons to sleep. These talismans helped defeat the dragons long ago. As part of the treaty that brought the dragons to the sanctuaries, the dragons were allowed to guard these items in their temples. If we were to recover any of the three talismans, it would frighten and enrage the dragons, because the talismans make them vulnerable."

"Do we have any of the talismans?" Kendra asked.

"No," Agad said. "To pursue them would have been an act of war."

"But the dragons already declared war," Kendra said.

"Exactly," Agad said. "So now, getting the talismans has become a priority."

"How does that explain why dragons are not attacking cities?" Kendra asked.

"I'm getting there," Agad said. "Another line of defense is the legendary Dragon Slayers."

"Like the Somber Knight?" Kendra asked.

"Each sanctuary has a Dragon Slayer," Agad said. "But there are five legendary Dragon Slayers abroad in the world. They are lost at present, but when Celebrant declared war, the door was opened for us to recruit them."

"Do you know how to find them?" Kendra asked.

"We're working on it," Agad said. "Finding them may not be easy after such a prolonged retirement. Aside from the legendary Dragon Slayers, we have a final line of defense between dragons and the mortal world."

"What?" Kendra asked.

"The Sovereign Skull," Agad said. "The fabled skull of Abraxas, the first dragon."

"It's really a skull?" Kendra asked.

"Of the very first dragon," Agad said reverently. "A pristine relic of crystalline beauty, more heavily enchanted and ensorcelled than any physical object in the world."

"What does it do?" Kendra asked.

"Listen, the unbelief of humanity provides a degree of protection from the magical world," Agad said. "The skull amplifies that effect, making human unbelief toxic to dragons. As long as the skull exists, mortals ignorant to the magical world are difficult for dragons to target, and unbelieving communities are impossible to invade."

"Where is it kept?" Kendra asked.

"For the safety of the world, that must remain a secret," Agad said. "The place was created by wizards, and only a few of us know the location."

"Are you one of them?" Kendra asked.

"I should not say too much," Agad said.

"The dragons that escaped Soaring Cliffs can't attack the nonmagical world unless they destroy the skull," Kendra verified.

"Correct."

"But they can get up to other mischief?"

"That is a definite concern," Agad said. "The world has some defenses left as these preserves fall. But unless we defeat the dragons and get them back into sanctuaries, this will not end well. The longer the conflict rages, the more likely it becomes that the dragons will discover how to overthrow our last defenses."

"There is so much to do," Kendra said.

"We start by protecting the sanctuaries we still control," Agad said. "You have done a remarkable job here, against terrible odds. I must say that you and your brother performed beyond all expectations."

"I just hope we can get him back," Kendra said.

"We need him back," Agad affirmed. "Sentimentality aside, he is a caretaker of Wyrmroost. This sanctuary is safer with him here."

The long, low bellow of a horn reached Kendra's ears. "The proudhorn," Kendra said.

Agad stood. "A dragon approaches."

"I hope it's Raxtus," Kendra said, getting up as well. "Did you know he joined us?"

"I heard," Agad said, exiting the stall. "Not a moment too soon, from what I understand."

"He saved me," Kendra said.

They trotted out of the stable to see a gilded coach gliding through the air, pulled by a team of winged rams. Dragons flanked the coach to either side, flying a bit behind it.

"There is a sight Wyrmroost has not seen in centuries," Agad said.

"Flying rams?" Kendra asked.

"The coach of Stormguard Castle," Agad said. "After all this time, the curse is broken. Let's go see what they want."

Agad and Kendra hurried to the courtyard where the coach landed. The handsome driver reined the six rams to a halt.

"They just flew over the wall," Kendra said. "Did they have permission?"

"The Blackwell Keep defenses don't repel the coach," Agad said. "It's part of an ancient treaty."

Kendra noticed that the dragons tracking the coach had veered away. "Dragons can't attack the coach?" she asked.

"The coach of Stormguard Castle enjoys immunity on all diplomatic missions," Agad said. "Even in wartime. The neutral status of the Fair Folk has some serious advantages. I'm sure the dragons would have attacked if it were possible."

Grandpa and Grandma Sorenson were coming down stairs to the courtyard, as was Brunwin the minotaur. Marat and Henrick approached from a different direction.

The door to the coach opened and Tanu emerged, along with Knox and Lockland. Tanu and Knox looked tired but healthy, and no parts of them were silver or gold.

"Knox!" Kendra called. "Tanu! You're all right!"

"Kendra!" Knox called back, waving and hustling toward her. "We wondered where you were! Did you get the prize?"

"No," Kendra said.

"Did Tregain?" Lockland asked.

Kendra winced. "Tregain was killed while trying."

Lockland closed his eyes and pressed a fist to his forehead. Knox seemed to be resisting a grin.

"How did he fall?" Lockland asked.

"He touched the stone and turned to ashes," Kendra said. "Obregon too."

Lockland composed his features. "My family and all of Stormguard Castle will rue these tidings. But casualties were to be expected in such a contest. What of your brother?"

Kendra saw Knox and Tanu looking at her expectantly. She tried to tell them, but words wouldn't come. Only tears.

"Seth lost his memory and was kidnapped by the Sphinx," Agad said on her behalf. "We are working to find him."

"Kidnapped?" Knox asked.

"Taken away through the barrel," Grandpa Sorenson said, an edge to his voice.

Knox blanched. "Oh no."

"The goblins at Fablehaven gave the barrel to our enemies," Grandpa said, "who used it to abduct Seth."

"No!" Knox said, eyes staring wildly. "No, no, no. I gave them the keys to the dungeon."

"It's not entirely your fault," Grandpa Sorenson said. "You didn't take Seth, nor did you understand the risks of using the barrel."

"I'm an idiot," Knox said. "I'm the worst."

"We all make mistakes," Grandpa said.

"Not that cause kidnappings," Knox said.

"True," Kendra mumbled. Then she raised her voice. "I know you've been trying to help. Right now our focus is getting him back. Where are Lomo and Patton?"

"Lomo remains at Stormguard Castle against his wishes," Lockland said. "My father refused to let him come. I will return with the coach. As Fair Folk, we can't get directly involved in helping you."

"And Patton is helping the mounts return safely," Tanu said. "Calvin is with him. But we have another problem."

"Fabulous," Kendra said. "What?"

"We stopped by Terrabelle in the coach to pick up Tess and the satyrs," Knox said. "Tess was gone. The satyrs too. I guess Newel came here, but Doren, who was watching Tess, has disappeared. Along with Eve."

"Disappeared?" Grandpa asked. "Where did they go?"

Knox lowered his eyes. "Nobody knows."

CHAPTER SEVEN

Mortals and Magic

How could a dragon fit in there?" Tess asked, pointing at what looked like a pair of wooden cellar doors on the ground within the sequoia grove. "Is he tiny?"

"He should be huge," Eve said, climbing down from her horse. "I wonder if he has another way in."

"I guess one of us should stay with the animals," Doren said, swinging down from his gray mare.

"I thought you didn't like horses," Tess said.

Doren held up a finger. "I never bad-mouthed horses. I was a little hesitant to steal three of them."

"We borrowed them," Eve corrected.

"We borrowed them without permission," Doren amended. "In order to sneak away from Terrabelle against the wishes of everyone in charge."

"You complained nonstop," Poza said.

"I mentioned I had never ridden a horse before," Doren said. "And that I was worried I would feel like a centaur."

"Did you?" Tess asked.

"A little," Doren admitted. "Look, satyrs don't ride horses. I've never heard of it happening before. I broke protocol for you girls."

"Now you want to stay with the horses because you're afraid of the dragon," Eve said.

"I'm trying to be a good leader," Doren said. "We need smart strategy. A peaceful dragon might be nice to two little girls. Kendra did fine with her visit. But the dragon might not like a satyr. Some creatures are biased against us."

"He makes a convincing argument," Poza said.

"Plus, somebody really should watch these borrowed horses," Doren said. "It would be a long walk back. And it's getting dark."

"You'll be out here without the cloak of innocence," Eve told him.

Doren shrugged. "I'm still part of the group. It might still cover me."

"It might not," Eve said.

Doren scratched his elbow and glanced around the grove. "In an emergency, I could follow you in."

"And leave the horses?" Tess cried.

"The horses could get away faster without me," Doren said.

"We do need to hurry," Eve said. "And it probably makes sense to leave a guard for the horses."

"I brought you here," Poza said. "May I excuse myself?"

"What about finding our way back?" Tess asked.

"Simply return the way we came," Poza said.

"But we came here without a path," Eve said. "What if we get lost?"

"You'll be fine," Poza said. "That cloak works perfectly."

"Nothing would attack us, but we might starve," Tess said.

"And it will get dark," Eve added.

"Let the satyr find the way," Poza said. "As part animal, he should have some instincts."

Doren scratched his sideburn. "I probably could retrace our route. I don't know, Poza. Would you trust your life to me?"

"Absolutely not."

"What about the life of little Tess?" Doren said.

The fairy glanced at Tess, then tossed up her arms in defeat. "Fine, I'll stay. Don't take too long. I will not be assisting with the horses."

"Thank you," Tess said. She patted her horse, staring at the considerable drop to the ground. "How do I get down?"

Doren helped Tess out of the saddle.

"Where do I tie up the horses?" Doren asked.

"No need," Eve said. "We train our horses well. Come help us open these doors."

Doren walked over to the cellar doors. A pair of nearby stones had writing etched on them in both recognizable characters and mysterious glyphs. "The languages I can read say 'Welcome,'" he said. "Anything else?"

"I see the same," Eve said.

"What kind of dragon puts 'Welcome' on the door?" Doren asked.

"A nice one?" Tess asked.

"I get wary when something that could eat me wants company," Doren said. He bent down, grabbed a door handle, then paused. "Do we know what's behind here?"

"The way to the dragon," Tess said.

"Do you suppose this door is within his view?" Doren asked.

"I've never been here before," Eve said.

Taking a step back, Doren spat on his hands and rubbed them together. "I guess we're about to find out." He bent forward and heaved open one of the doors. A long, straight stairway stretched down into darkness.

"No dragon yet," Tess said, sounding a bit disappointed.

"Foreboding nonetheless," Doren said. "I wish you well. Keep that cloak handy."

"Come on," Eve said, after lighting a small lantern with a match. She took Tess by the hand and started down the stairs.

"See you soon, Poza," Tess said. "You too, Doren."

The satyr gave her a nod and a wave. "Maybe don't mention my name. I don't want to be overly known in dragon circles." The fairy flitted out of view as the door closed.

"I'm glad you brought a light," Tess said as they descended the stairs.

"Wouldn't be very smart to visit a dragon lair without one," Eve replied. "This should have enough oil to last a couple of hours."

"The steps look like they go down forever," Tess said.

"It's the longest stairway I've seen," Eve said.

Glancing back at intervals, Tess noticed when the doors to the surface receded into shadow. "We're going deep underground."

"Are you getting nervous?" Eve asked.

Tess looked ahead at the stairs descending into darkness beyond the lantern light. "A little."

"We'll be fine," Eve said. "I don't freeze in front of dragons. If you do, I can drag you out of there."

"I don't think I'll freeze up if it's a nice dragon," Tess said. "My legs might get tired on the way, though."

"Just don't trip," Eve said. "A fall down a stone staircase this long would break just about every bone you have."

Tess took extra care with the steps from that point downward. She was beginning to despair that the stairs would go on endlessly when a level place came into view.

"Finally," Eve said.

"I wonder how much farther to the dragon?" Tess asked.

"Let's go find out."

Beyond the stairs they followed a rounded tunnel to a heavy oaken door. "Should we knock?" Tess asked.

"We've come this far without permission," Eve said.

"It said 'Welcome' up top."

"True. Ready?"

Tess felt nervous and excited. "Do you think this is where the dragon is?"

"Could be more stairs," Eve said. "Or another hallway."

Eve opened the door, and they passed into a vast cavern. It took Tess a moment to spot the dragon's enormous shape, filling much of the room, but half-buried in stone rubble. For a moment she thought it might be a statue because the hide seemed so rocky. Then the craggy head raised up and swiveled in her direction, scattering masonry and flinging dust into the air.

"Two young girls," the dragon said in a startlingly genteel baritone. "After years with no outside contact besides the ogres bringing food, I am getting the oddest visitors of late."

Tess gave a little curtsy. "I'm Tess. This is Eve. I'm friends with the fairies. We heard you're a nice dragon."

The dragon shuddered and seemed to cough, making boulders shift and more dust take flight. "Is that the new reputation for Dromadus the Terrible?"

"Were you called that?" Tess asked.

"I have been called many things," Dromadus said. "Never nice."

"We heard you are a pacifist," Eve soothed.

"And who are you?" Dromadus asked.

"Eve of the Fair Folk," Eve said.

"The other girl is mortal," Dromadus said.

Tess raised a hand. "Tess."

"Tess is fairystruck but mortal," Dromadus said. "And cloaked by innocence."

"I believe so," Eve said.

"We know you could probably still eat us if you wanted," Tess said.

"A prudent thing to know," Dromadus said. "Yet do not underestimate the power of innocence. Many of the maladies that ruin the wise can be utterly confounded by innocence."

"Really?" Tess asked.

"Innocence has a difficult time appreciating itself," Dromadus said. "Though it has certain vulnerabilities, once lost, true innocence can never be regained. Anything both powerful and irrecoverable is most precious."

Tess gripped her cloak tightly. "I'll be careful."

The dragon coughed lightly.

"Are you laughing?" Eve asked.

"That would be a rarity," Dromadus said. "Where did you hear I was a nice pacifist? Kendra and Seth, I suppose?"

Worried about getting her cousins in trouble, Tess looked to Eve.

"Seth told me a little about you," Eve said. "He never called you nice. Everyone knows that no dragon is safe, even a peaceful one."

"Try not to spread any gossip about my gentle side," Dromadus said. "Too many fools at Wyrmroost might take that for weakness. Some could get hurt."

"I won't spread it," Eve said.

"Me neither," Tess promised.

"Tell me, what brings you here today?" Dromadus asked. "Or did you simply hope to witness the peaceful dragon?"

"That was part of it," Tess said.

"We're also hoping you can help us," Eve said. "The dragons declared war."

"I'm aware," Dromadus said.

"It was unprovoked," Eve said.

"Many of the dragons in sanctuaries around the world consider themselves captives," Dromadus said.

"Dragons went to the sanctuaries by treaty," Eve said. "It was part of the terms of their surrender."

"Many dragons born inside the sanctuaries never agreed to such terms," Dromadus replied. "The war against the dragons occurred centuries ago. Defeated nations often regroup and fight again after time goes by. The dragons have old grievances to settle."

"Dragons have been treated well in the sanctuaries," Eve insisted.

Dromadus yawned. "Dragons never belonged in close proximity to one another. By nature we are solitary."

"Then why do they have a king?" Tess asked.

"Dragons have always established dominance," Dromadus said. "But the king never really acted like a true leader until dragons began to be hunted and killed. As the fight against dragons swelled into a war, we needed to organize ourselves. A real king was required."

"Is a king needed now?" Tess asked.

"To mount a war?" Dromadus said. "Yes, if that is what the dragons want. But dragons residing in a castle? That is a ridiculous imitation of humanity. We do not belong in colonies except in emergencies."

"The dragons are causing the emergency," Eve said. "They have received humane treatment."

"You fail to understand dragons," Dromadus said. "We have a strong need for independence."

"They have plenty of room at Wyrmroost to be independent," Eve said.

"Knowing there are boundaries decreases the feeling of

independence," Dromadus said. "Boundaries imposed by defeat are even worse."

"If the dragons wage another war, they could destroy themselves," Eve said.

"Or they will destroy everybody else," Tess said.

Dromadus sighed. "That gets closer to the crux of the problem."

"Then you'll help us?" Eve asked.

"I can't solve the problem," Dromadus said.

"You could try," Tess said. "We're trying."

"She doesn't mean to be presumptuous," Eve said.

"I like her sincerity," Dromadus said. "I no longer fear honesty. I have learned that anything important accomplished through dishonest means eventually unravels. Facing unpleasant truths protects us from building on faulty foundations."

"Can you help us?" Eve asked.

Craning his stony neck, the dragon looked around, sniffing the dusty air. "I deliberately trapped myself in here, never to emerge, never to influence outside matters again. That intent has wavered of late. This is the danger of conversing with mortals."

"Danger?" Tess asked. "Are you afraid of us?"

"Any wise creature of magic would be," Dromadus said.

"But you're so big," Tess said.

"I could try to rely on my size and strength," Dromadus said. "I did for years. And I was a fool. I harmed and destroyed many I claimed to love. You are very dangerous, little one."

"Why?" Tess asked.

"There is a divide between the magical world and the mortal world," Dromadus said.

"My brother couldn't see the fairies until he drank the milk," Tess said.

"Very good," Dromadus said. "That is evidence of the divide. Magic is not for mortals. It is not inherent to their natures."

"But I can see fairies without milk," Tess said.

"Mortals can derive magic from magical sources. Some fairies took a liking to you and shared their powers. They changed you. But I wonder if they are aware that you also changed them?"

"Did I change them?"

"Just as magic is not for mortals, mortality is not for magical beings," Dromadus said. "Those of an eternal nature do not change. We magical beings are nearly eternal, and so change comes slowly if at all. To many of us, change is a type of magic we do not understand."

"I change all the time," Tess said.

"I expect you do," Dromadus said. "Such change feels as foreign to me as magic seems to you. Fairies do not typically appreciate mortals. They do not willingly reveal themselves to mortals. If fairies learned to like you, they have been changed in the process."

"That's a good change," Tess said.

"It depends on your perspective," Dromadus said. "If those fairies get too friendly with mortals, they could get killed or trapped. They could get changed into imps. I noticed a satyr with you as you approached."

"How did you know?" Tess asked.

"I have ways," Dromadus said. "He was riding a horse."

"He is helping us," Tess said.

"But satyrs don't typically help anyone," Eve said with interest.

"How long have you known that satyr?" Dromadus asked.

"Not long," Tess said. "A few days."

"Does the satyr know other mortals?" Dromadus asked.

"He is friends with Seth," Tess said.

"And that is how a satyr ends up riding a horse," Dromadus said. "And helping humans, instead of indulging his own capricious interests."

"Because he is friends with Seth?" Tess asked.

"Probably," Dromadus said. "Any relationship with a mortal exerts influence. The divide becomes even more starkly evident with love. A romance between a magical being and a mortal is ultimately incompatible and ill-fated unless one joins the realm of the other."

"I have heard stories," Eve said.

"They tend to be tragic," Dromadus replied.

"You claimed Tess is dangerous to you," Eve said.

"Her cousins are too," Dromadus said. "No matter how wise or powerful you are, no matter how fixed in your determinations, if you bring mortals around, you invite change. Think about yourself, Fair One. How long have you dreamed of an adventure like this?"

"All my life," Eve said. "That has been constant."

"Did you actually embark before or after interacting with mortals?"

Eve paused. "Wow. After."

"You begin to glimpse my peril," Dromadus said.

"You want to help us?" Tess asked.

The dragon's head swooped in close, staring with black eyes. "I never wanted to help mortals. I had vowed not to interact with the external world again. But when I met Seth and Kendra, the seeds of conflict were planted within me."

"What conflict?" Eve asked.

"I do not agree with this war," Dromadus said quietly. "I can see why the dragons feel it will benefit them. I can see why they suppose this war could right old wrongs and tear down boundaries and increase freedom. But I believe their aggression is wrong."

"Then you'll help us?" Tess asked.

"I want to deny you," Dromadus said. "I fear where this could end. But I will give you a bit of information that could help. If you appreciate the assistance, please do not make your source public."

"What do you know?" Eve asked.

"You must hasten to Blackwell Keep," Dromadus said. "Warn them that the dragons have an attack planned for tomorrow night. An attack they expect to succeed."

"How?" Eve asked. "Blackwell Keep is secure now."

"I truly have no more details," Dromadus said. "But Celebrant is no fool."

"Can't you come with us?" Tess asked.

"The aid I can offer is limited," Dromadus said. "But I can watch you, and maybe share information again, if you trust me."

"How would you send information?" Tess asked.

"Through trusted messengers, perhaps," Dromadus said. "I make no promises."

"How will you watch us?" Tess asked.

The head of the dragon swiveled away and rummaged in a rock pile. When the head returned, Dromadus opened his jaws and placed a jewel at her feet. "Take the sapphire. If you keep it with you, I will be able to see you."

"Careful," Eve said. "You'll be letting a dragon peer into Blackwell Keep."

Tess picked up the stone and held it up with the light of the lantern behind it, enjoying how the facets gleamed. "He's a peaceful dragon. And he is helping us." She put the sapphire in her pocket.

"I hope so," Eve muttered.

"Hasten to the keep," Dromadus said. "I do not know whether there is time to upset Celebrant's plan. The sooner you arrive, the better."

"We should go," Eve said.

"Wait, he gave me a present," Tess said. Facing the dragon, she dug into her pocket and pulled out a yo-yo. "A satyr gave this to me. It's a yo-yo." She set it on the ground.

"Thank you, child," Dromadus said.

"Tess," she reminded the dragon, backing to the door.

"Thank you, Tess," Dromadus said. "Travel swiftly and safely. Keep the cloak of innocence ever with you."

Eve took Tess by the hand and hurried her along.

"'Bye, Dromadus," Tess said. "Thanks for the tip."

CHAPTER EIGHT

Threat

Out behind the Blackwell Keep stable, Knox chucked a dirt clod at the wall, where it exploded in a puff of dust. He crouched to tear another clump from a chunky dirt pile, but the selected piece crumbled in his hand. Trying a different part of the pile, he dislodged a clod that held together.

Seth had been taken by enemies and Knox could only blame himself. His insides constricted at the thought. He winged the dirt clod sidearm as hard as he could. The chunk burst into dust, leaving a little patch of dirt on the wall to commemorate the impact.

Knox had enjoyed the feast at Stormguard Castle. Many official, fancy people had treated him like a celebrity. The food had been plentiful and delicious. When he had departed the castle, Knox had not worried that the praise might have been somewhat exaggerated. After all, he had taken a risk by going to Stormguard Castle, he had been part of the team that broke the curse, and if Seth and Kendra went off someplace else before the feast, then they chose to miss the victory party.

Knox heaved a large dirt clump at the wall. It was one thing to accept a little more credit than he really deserved. It was another to learn he was the cause of Seth getting kidnapped. His cousin was in the hands of evil people because Knox had left the dungeon keys with the goblins back at Fablehaven.

Now every word of praise came back to him like a hot knife. Every delicious bite of food seemed poisonous. Stan and some of the others had reminded Knox that his involvement had been indirect—evil people had carried out the plan, not him. But at the very least Knox knew he was like a guard who had fallen asleep on duty and let the enemy harm his allies. No, worse: he was a clumsy outsider who had sidetracked the guards—with disastrous consequences.

Knox threw another hunk of dirt. And another. It made him sick to think that while he had feasted and laughed and bragged, his cousin who had actually saved the day was in the hands of the bad guys, probably getting tortured.

It almost made it worse that people had been mostly kind to him about his actions, as if they knew what he had done was so terrible it could mess him up for life. Maybe it should. Ruth had reminded him that he had not understood the consequences of what he was doing. Which was true, but Knox had known that it was wrong to steal the keys from Dale. He had known he wasn't supposed to sneak to Wyrmroost. What had felt like minor mischief had turned into a deadly mistake.

Another dirt clod smashed against the wall in a gritty burst. And another. He could not throw them hard enough. Part of him wished somebody was throwing the dirt clods at him. Or beating him, or locking him in jail. He had no means to express how remorseful he felt, no way to pay for what he had done. And no way to fix the mistake.

Knox had not slept well the night before. This morning he had eaten a hasty breakfast and then slipped away to be alone. He crouched and tore off another hunk of dirt.

Brunwin the minotaur came around the corner of the stable, and Knox dropped the dirt clod, suddenly worried he might have been violating rules. He tried to subtly brush the dirt from his hands.

"There you are," Brunwin said. "Your sister has returned safely from Terrabelle."

"Good," Knox said. He didn't love showing too much interest in his sister, so he kept his reaction simple. Terrabelle was a safe place, but with all the trouble at the sanctuary, it was a relief to know Tess was all right.

"The Sorensons sent me to fetch you," Brunwin said.

"All right," Knox said, mildly relieved that the dirt clods did not appear to be an issue. "Lead the way."

Rather than walk beside the shaggy minotaur, Knox followed. He began regretting the decision as the smell of the brute wafted back at him. He considered asking whether minotaurs ever bathed, but managed to hold his tongue.

Knox was glad to know Tess was safe. He had assumed she would be. He could not imagine she had done anything truly daring with the cloak of innocence, but he could easily picture her creating commotion by wandering off.

Brunwin escorted Knox to a room where Tess, Kendra, Newel, Doren, Marat, Tanu, and Agad sat alongside Stan and Ruth Sorenson at a long conference table. Patton leaned against a wall, arms folded. Stan invited Knox in and thanked Brunwin. The minotaur snorted and departed.

"Knox!" Tess said. "I saw a dragon. Did you see any?"

"I saw some with you on the road," Knox said.

"I mean up close," Tess said. "I talked to one. He used to be their king. He looked really rocky."

"I saw some dragons in human form," Knox said. "And I got partway turned to gold." He looked to Patton. "You made it."

"Arrived not long ago," Patton said. "We took turns running along the road or flying just above it. The winged mounts made the trip much faster. Overall, smooth sailing. I'm not feeling so good, though. The life of a stingbulb is brief."

"I'm sorry," Knox said.

Patton waved a hand and shook his head. "Nothing to mourn. Plants bloom and then wilt. Just sorry I can't lend a hand much longer. I knew this was coming. I have maybe a day left."

"Calvin made it as well?" Knox asked.

"I'm right here," the nipsie called from his place on the table. Knox had not yet seen him.

"Sorry about Seth," Knox said.

"We'll find him," Calvin replied. "Just one more adventure to have."

Knox glanced at his sister. "Is Tess serious about seeing a dragon?"

"Your sister took a terrible risk," Stan said. "But it could work to our advantage."

Doren raised a hand. "And I rode a horse."

"I still can't believe it," Newel said in disgust.

"It wasn't as bad as you think," Doren said.

"Zero goat pride," Newel said.

"It was an emergency," Doren said. "I had to supervise the child."

Stan cleared his throat.

"Right," Newel said. "The task at hand. Stan has the floor."

Stan fixed his attention on Knox. "Your sister and the daughter of Lord Dalgorel visited Dromadus, a former Dragon King who resides at this sanctuary."

"Did he know something about Seth?" Knox asked hopefully.

"Not that he shared," Stan said. "But apparently the dragons are planning an attack against Blackwell Keep. Tonight. They are confident of success."

"We rode through the night to get back to Terrabelle," Tess said. "My friend Eve wanted to come here with me, but she got in trouble with her dad. I was so tired." She yawned. "At least I got some sleep before Newel came."

"Newel and Henrick brought Tess and Doren here just

now," Stan said. "They came quickly after hearing the news. We couldn't find you so we sent Brunwin to retrieve you."

"I was behind the stables," Knox said. "Thinking."

"Thinking?" Tess asked skeptically.

"You should try it," Knox said. "How are the dragons going to attack?"

"Dromadus didn't know," Tess said. "And don't tell anybody who told us about the dragons. It's a secret."

Knox looked around the room. "Your secret is spreading fast."

"Just so we can protect ourselves," Tess said. "Dromadus wanted me to warn the caretaker."

Knox glanced at Kendra, then looked to Stan. "Any idea how they are going to attack?"

"None so far," Stan said. "We were just discussing the possibilities when you entered."

"The defenses of the keep are in perfect order," Agad said. "Stronger than when I was caretaker here. With the scepter in our possession, the dragons should have no chance of breaching our defenses through force."

"And yet Celebrant is planning an attack that he expects to succeed," Ruth said.

"Perhaps Celebrant is letting anger cloud his judgment," Patton said.

"Or perhaps Dromadus is toying with us," Marat said. "His assistance is most unexpected."

"Eve heard the dragon too," Tess said. "She told Doren."

"Both of the girls seemed sure of the message," Doren confirmed.

"But the message itself could be false," Marat said. "Dromadus is extremely old, and little is known about him since he shut himself away from the world. He could simply be eccentric. Or he could be scheming."

"We have to treat it like a real threat," Kendra said.

"I fully agree," Marat replied. "Just be aware that all may not be as it seems with this warning."

"What would be the point of a fake warning?" Knox asked.

"Could it be a prank?" Tanu asked.

"Anything is possible," Agad said. "Maybe Dromadus is working with Celebrant. Perhaps Celebrant wants to see how we react if we think an attack is imminent. He might hope we will show him a vulnerability as we scramble to prepare."

"Or the attack could be real," Marat said. "There could be some defensive weakness we have overlooked. Or we might have a traitor among us."

Knox considered the others. Surely nobody in this room would side with the dragons! Hadn't everyone present proven themselves? He wondered if any of them might think *he* was a traitor. After he had delivered the Fablehaven barrel to the enemy, they had a right to think anything.

"What about the barrel?" Knox asked. "Could that be the weakness?"

"We should not ignore the possibility," Agad said. "We placed the barrel in a cell in the dungeon with a trusted minotaur standing guard. With nobody to help an intruder out of the barrel, entering the keep in that way should be impossible."

"We could destroy the barrel," Tanu said.

"No," Kendra said. "It's our only link to the people who took Seth."

"We can place an additional guard outside the cell with the barrel all night," Agad said. "Just to be safe."

"Are there other vulnerabilities?" Kendra asked.

"Betrayal might be the most viable," Stan said. "A strong defense is best dismantled from the inside. Then again, maybe the dragons want to make us mistrust each other. Suspicion could do that." Stan turned toward Newel. "You satyrs wanted to be in on this meeting."

"Seemed appropriate since Doren was involved directly," Newel said.

"What do you think about all of this?" Stan asked.

"It's a long meeting," Newel said.

"About the defenses," Stan clarified.

"You've been warned, so be vigilant tonight," Newel said. "Not much else to do. Can't run away."

"Some of you could flee," Kendra said. "Tess has the cloak of innocence. I'm the only one who really has to stay."

"If you want to send away the satyrs or the younger children, that is one thing," Agad said. "But Wyrmroost must not fall. The able defenders must stand and fight."

"We have to protect the keep, especially when the dragons might be bluffing," Patton said.

"Should we send Tess and Knox away from the sanctuary?" Ruth asked.

"They could flee into the wilderness beyond the borders," Stan said. "Wyrmroost is not in a convenient location. We would need to order a pickup to get them back to civilization."

"I'm not going anywhere," Knox said. "Not until we find Seth."

"I'm not leaving either," Tess said.

"Sending anyone away from the safety of Blackwell Keep while the dragons are plotting may not be wise," Marat said.

"I've seen a lot of trouble come and go in my time," Patton said. "I've made it through much of it by patiently staying in a secure place. Not letting myself get lured out. Choosing to face enemies on my terms."

Stan sighed. "I've had similar experiences. Our safest bet is to keep everyone in our stronghold and to keep it secure."

"I will check all entrances and exits," Marat said. "We'll post twice the normal watch."

"I will examine all magical defenses," Agad said.

"I'll brew up some special potions just in case," Tanu said.

"Let's take whatever reasonable precautions we can think of," Stan said. "We have all afternoon to help ensure a quiet night."

"Might be prudent to have a good meal," Doren said. "We don't want to face trouble on an empty stomach."

Ruth stood up. "Hopefully, if we're vigilant, we'll end up having a calm rest tonight while the dragons snarl in frustration."

Though Knox appreciated her attempt to be positive, he worried she wasn't giving the dragons enough credit. In his gut, he worried they were all missing something.

CHAPTER NINE

Liberation

"All right," Ronodin said, backing up to admire his handiwork. "That suffices. Free yourself, if you can."

Seth stood in a torchlit room, his back to a stone column, fastened in place by a chilly cocoon of chains and locks. Ronodin had just finished securing the final chain, but the weight and pressure of the bindings were already uncomfortable. "Where do I start?" Seth asked.

"The locks, of course," Ronodin said.

Seth squirmed, but the chains hugged him maddeningly. He could barely move. Breathing felt laborious. Closing his eyes, he reached for the locks with his power but could only vaguely sense their locations.

"I can't connect my power to the locks," Seth said. "I can barely feel them."

"They're not as easy to sense as the fire," Ronodin said.

"How am I supposed to pick them if I can't feel them?" Seth asked.

"Your thinking is muddled," Ronodin said. "You're not going to mechanically pick the locks any more than you physically doused the torch."

"Then how will they open?" Seth asked. "I don't see how cooling them will help."

"With the torch, you sought out the source of the flames," Ronodin said. "You brought cold to the source of the heat. Don't seek out the physical mechanism of the lock so much as reach for what is binding you. The dark power inside you does not like to be bound. It can undo all but the most powerful confinements. Let the power do the work."

Seth tried to focus on where he was bound. Weren't the chains all around him? He stared at one of the locks on the chains. He tried not to focus too much on the physical lock. It was just something binding him. Something his power could undo.

Seth searched for the darkness near his center and found it. He tried to draw upon it as he had to quench the torch, but he wasn't sure what exact part of the darkness he was moving to the lock. Cold had seemed easier to isolate.

In frustration, he strained against the heavy links with his strength, but there was no give. He tried to use his power again, to no avail.

A small bell rang in the distance.

"That is our signal," Ronodin said.

"What about the locks?" Seth asked.

"Opening locks is more subtle than dousing fire,"

Ronodin said. "It may take time." He snapped his fingers, and the chains fell away from Seth to pile around the base of the column. "I was mostly distracting you from worrying about your upcoming mission."

Seth stepped over the chains. "This was misdirection?"

Ronodin gave half a smile. "And it was fun chaining you up."

"Wait," Seth said. "The mission is now?"

"It can be hard to judge time down here," Ronodin said.

"Where are we going?"

"Follow me," Ronodin said, already walking.

"You're coming with me?" Seth asked, hurrying to catch up.

"You'll go alone," Ronodin replied.

"Am I ready?" Seth asked. "What do I need to know?"

"We'll judge your readiness by whether you survive," Ronodin said. "You're about to learn all you need to know."

Seth felt full of questions but didn't know where to start. They passed down a hall and into a dim room with only a wet barrel inside.

"Is that going to transport me?" Seth asked.

"A barrel like this could lead almost anywhere," Ronodin said. "One of my top operatives is on the other side to receive you. He will provide the help you need to succeed."

"Where exactly am I going?" Seth asked. "What will I have to do there?"

"You are going to a prison," Ronodin said. "You will free the captives there."

"Are they bad people?" Seth asked.

"They are undead," Ronodin said. "They were incarcerated because of their natures. They have been imprisoned for far too long."

"Will I have to open locks?" Seth asked nervously.

"Not with your power," Ronodin said. "The man who will receive you has the specifics. In short, you will go through the barrel and then do as you're told. Save your questions for him."

Seth stared at the barrel. Was this the sort of activity he had done in his forgotten past? Maybe. Ronodin had certainly helped Seth regain access to dark powers, including conversing with wraiths. It didn't require much of a leap for Seth to imagine that he might have freed undead captives before. Left to himself, would he choose to do so right now? No way. But Ronodin was an expert at springing tasks on him without leaving much time to think.

"We've been underground since I came here," Seth said. "At least I'll get to see the sky."

"Don't count on that," Ronodin said. "Where you are going there may not be many windows."

"Do I have to do this?" Seth asked.

"I suppose you could go tell the Underking you changed your mind," Ronodin said. "I suspect the conversation would not end well."

Seth glanced at the ephemeral manacle on his wrist. He wished he could make that binding come loose. For now, he was trapped. He had not chosen to come to this underworld, but to buy time he had made promises to the Underking.

Right now, staying alive might be the best he could manage. If he survived long enough, maybe he could eventually take control of his life. What he wanted more than anything was some time alone to figure things out for himself. He would stay vigilant. Maybe going through the barrel would lead to a chance to escape.

"This will take me away from the domain of the Underking?" Seth asked.

"Out of his domain, yes," Ronodin said. "But make no mistake, Seth—nowhere is out of his reach."

"I'll free his captives," Seth said.

Ronodin gave a nod. "Into the barrel. Stay quiet. Follow the instructions you get on the other side. Perform as required. I hope to see you soon."

Seth climbed into the barrel and faced Ronodin. "Wish me luck."

Ronodin shook his head. "Luck has no business where you are going. Your success will be decided by good planning and proper execution. Get it right. Crouch down."

Seth hunched down inside the barrel. A strong hand grabbed his wrist and stood him up, then helped him out of the barrel.

An upturned flashlight balanced on the floor revealed that Seth was in a dungeon cell with the door ajar. The man with him had dark skin and short, beaded dreadlocks, and he wore black clothes. He had a handsome face and at first glance looked about thirty, but something in his eyes and his bearing suggested he might be quite a bit older.

The man smiled. "Good to see you again, Seth," he whispered.

"Do I know you?" Seth asked.

"Hard to know me when you hardly know yourself," the man said. "We've had dealings in the past. I'm called the Sphinx."

"Half lion?" Seth asked.

"Just a nickname," the Sphinx said. "I'm a mortal like you. In fact, I'm more like you than you might expect."

"Did you lose your memory too?"

"No, I'm a shadow charmer," the Sphinx said. "I don't believe there are currently any others besides us."

"Only the two of us?" Seth asked.

"It's a small club."

"If you're a shadow charmer, why do you need me?"

"I was cursed by some wizards," the Sphinx said. "As a result, my life was prolonged, but the tampering interfered with my powers. I can no longer communicate with the undead. I have only my defensive skills: hiding in dimness, dousing fire, picking locks."

"I don't know much about the mission," Seth whispered. "We're freeing some of the undead?"

"Ronodin can be so secretive," the Sphinx said. "This shouldn't be too hard. This way. Don't trip on the minotaurs."

The Sphinx picked up the flashlight and covered the top with one hand so only a little light leaked out. He led Seth out of the cell. A pair of dead minotaurs were sprawled in the hallway near an ax and a mace.

"Did you do that?" Seth asked.

"Self-defense," the Sphinx whispered. "Minotaurs tend toward violence. It was my life or theirs. Come on."

The minotaurs were big, and their weapons looked impressive. Apparently the Sphinx knew how to fight.

"Where are we?" Seth asked.

"The dungeon of a fort that holds many undead prisoners," the Sphinx whispered. "Operated by cruel monsters. We don't want to get caught. Go silent for a few minutes. Follow the light."

The Sphinx faded out of view. Only the light seeping between his fingers remained visible. They passed down a hallway of rough stone with cell doors on either hand. Seth wondered what kind of prisoners might be hidden away down here. He smelled mildew and decay and heard the skittering of small creatures.

The flashlight paused at an iron door. Seth heard a click, and the door opened.

"I'm still trying to figure out locks," Seth whispered.

"I have my competencies," the Sphinx replied, coming back into view. "This way."

They passed through the doorway, and the Sphinx closed the door behind them. After winding around and descending some stairs, they reached another iron door, this one mottled with corrosion and shedding brownish flakes.

"This door has been reinforced, physically and magically," the Sphinx said. "Do you hear the voices?"

"No," Seth said.

"Close your eyes," the Sphinx said. "Concentrate."

Seth complied, reaching out with his mind and his senses, listening. He noticed pressure, as if his ears needed to pop. The pressure diminished, and then it returned again. The sensation wavered, building and receding. "I feel a throbbing. It's hard to explain."

"Perceptive," the Sphinx said. "You sense voices and wills pushing again the magical barrier. The blunted impact of their efforts."

"The undead?" Seth asked.

"Yes," the Sphinx said. "The captives of the Blackwell."

"We're here to free them," Seth said.

"*You're* here to free them," the Sphinx said. "I'm here to lend support and get you back to the Under Realm."

"You have more experience than me," Seth said. "Can't you just do it?"

"Not an option," the Sphinx said. "I can no longer reach the undead. I'm able to sense them, but I cannot interact with them."

"How do I free them?" Seth asked.

"Carefully," the Sphinx said. "With conditions. They want out. When you enter the chamber, they will call to you, make promises, offer to serve you. Do not let them set the terms. You set the terms."

"How?" Seth asked.

"Don't try to become their commander," the Sphinx said. "There are too many undead in that well, and many are too powerful for any shadow charmer to control for any length of time. Have you any experience with revenants?"

The word seemed familiar. He knew they were undead. "Not that I remember. I've heard of them."

"What about liches?" the Sphinx asked.

Seth shook his head.

"Most of the undead have no mortal spark," the Sphinx said. "A corpse may be involved, but the human lifespark has fled. What identity they have is alien. They are cursed to long for life without a chance to regain it. A revenant still has some of that lifespark trapped inside. And a lich deliberately retains some of its former human will. These creatures are more powerful and more pitiable because they have actually tasted life and are now imprisoned without it. I suspect most revenants and liches eventually long for release, though they have learned to cling to their contorted version of living. Until deliverance comes, they are most formidable."

"There are revenants in the well?" Seth asked.

"And a lich," the Sphinx said. "A former enchanter named Belrab. He transformed from dragon to wizard to lich. A horrible descent."

"He's powerful?" Seth asked.

"You will address him first," the Sphinx said. "And you will keep it brief."

"You can't help?" Seth asked.

"Only with advice," the Sphinx said. "I can hear them speaking, but it is gibberish to me. And I can't speak words that they can understand."

"But they will understand me?" Seth checked. "Even the revenants and the lich?"

"It is a natural part of your gift," the Sphinx said, "and a large portion of your power over them. Remember what they crave above all else?"

"Life," Seth said.

"Your ability to understand them and respond to them is a connection to life," the Sphinx said. "They are often feared, but seldom heard. If ever."

"They still might kill me," Seth said.

"If you get this wrong, we'll both die miserably," the Sphinx said. "They like communication with the living but will soon set their sights on the light of life inside you. They will try to take it, and you will perish."

"Do they keep what they take?" Seth asked.

"They only sample it for a moment," the Sphinx said. "They leech the life from you, basking briefly in your waning vitality. An objectively small pleasure that feels large to them. You will die painfully."

"Why are we releasing them?" Seth asked.

"Because they are unfairly trapped in ugly conditions," the Sphinx replied. "And because the Underking desires it. And because we will flee."

Seth bit his lip. Freeing such dangerous creatures seemed like it could have disastrous results. How had he gotten into this mess? Seth glanced at the spectral manacle on his arm. The Underking governed these creatures, and it made sense that he wanted them treated humanely. Unless Seth was ready to defy the Underking, he would have to support his causes for a time.

"Sounds like a terrible existence," Seth said.

"They are to be pitied," the Sphinx said. "Sharks do not attack people out of cruelty. It is their nature to hunt. The undead are only following their natural inclinations. Locking them up is the cruelty, especially in a tiny space. You will not give these beings unlimited freedom, but you will grant them a wider area to roam. Care must be taken in how you release them."

"Tell me what to do," Seth said.

"Ignore their offers," the Sphinx said. "The foolish will make absurd promises they can't really keep and the smart ones will deliberately attempt to entrap you."

"What offer do I make?"

"There is a chain beside the well," the Sphinx said. "Lowering the chain would allow some of the undead to exit. Others must be granted permission to use it. You must work out the details before dropping the chain."

"What terms do we want?"

"Speak with Belrab first. Offer for him to be master of this castle if he agrees to remain in this castle and to keep the other undead here as well. We must make all the undead pledge to remain in this castle."

"Won't they still be trapped?" Seth asked. "Like they are already? If they're stuck in the castle? We're mainly trying to make them more comfortable?"

"We'll also grant access to the connected roads," the Sphinx said. "Limits must be set for the undead. We can't have them everywhere. Giving them a full castle to roam and some roads to haunt is a significant upgrade from being trapped at the bottom of a well."

"The castle is run by minotaurs?" Seth asked.

"Along with an assortment of other monsters," the Sphinx said. "They will flee if they have any sense. Before you lower the chain, you must obtain promises that we will be immune from the wrath of the undead who emerge."

"Should we make them promise not to hurt anyone?" Seth asked.

"That would be like telling a shark not to hunt," the Sphinx said. "It would be cruel, and probably not an agreement they could obey. We just need the ability to get away."

Seth had no way to verify the truth of what the Sphinx was telling him, but the dead minotaurs supported the assertion that monsters controlled the castle. He didn't like the idea of loosing the undead in an occupied castle, but if the jailers were all monsters and could get away, he supposed they knew the risks associated with locking up powerful creatures. Did undead monsters deserve fewer rights than living monsters?

"You'll walk me through what to say?" Seth asked.

"I'll stay at your side," the Sphinx said. "I'll be able to understand the words you speak, but not what the undead say. We should hurry. If we're discovered, it will not go well for us."

"Lead the way," Seth said.

The Sphinx spread his palm against the corroded iron door. Multiple locks disengaged, the metallic clicks and clacks echoing in the stone hall. Hinges squealed as the Sphinx pushed the door open, making Seth cringe for fear of being heard.

A jumbled flood of voices reached Seth, overlapping and full of desperate longing. The Sphinx looked at Seth. "Hear them now?"

"There are so many," Seth said, unable to make much sense of the chaotic gibbering.

"Hurry," the Sphinx said, leading Seth down a short corridor. "The masters of this castle could discover us at any moment." They reached an oval chamber with a circular hole in the center. A thick chain snaked around one side of the room, each link with two holes—one connecting to the previous link, and the other to the next.

Seth peered over the brink of the circular pit. Roughly ten feet in diameter at the top, the bottom was out of view, lost in gloom. Boisterous pleas issued from the blackness, tangled cries for help mingling with inarticulate moans. Several voices mentioned the chain.

"There is little time," the Sphinx prompted. "Ask for Belrab."

"I need to speak to Belrab," Seth said.

The frenzied appeals ended abruptly, and a slithery voice spoke out of the silence. "You have my attention."

"I'll free you if you promise to remain in this castle and on the connected roads," Seth said, glancing at the Sphinx, who motioned for him to continue. "And if you will keep the rest of the undead within those boundaries as well."

"I cannot speak for all," Belrab said. "You seem to speak for others."

"Those are my terms," Seth said.

"You are with a cripple," Belrab said. "A weakling

shadow charmer putting words in your mouth that he has lost the competence to utter."

Seth looked at the Sphinx. "What is he saying?" the Sphinx asked.

Seth held up a finger for him to wait.

"You are young and powerful," Belrab said. "With me at your side, those who seek to rule you will kneel in shame."

"I don't want a partner," Seth said. "And you're going to miss your chance to get out."

Belrab responded promptly. "Very well. If you lower the chain and grant my freedom, I vow to remain in this castle and on the associated roads to rule over the rest of the undead here."

That was what Seth had been waiting to hear. At least with those limits, the undead couldn't just run wild.

"I need all of the undead to agree to remain in the castle and on the roads if I let them out of this pit," Seth said. "If all do not agree, you'll stay down there."

The Sphinx nodded at Seth as many voices assented.

"Ask Belrab if all have agreed," the Sphinx said.

"Belrab, have all agreed?" Seth asked.

"All save one wraith and two revenants," Belrab said.

"This is the last chance for that wraith and those revenants to agree," Seth said.

Three gruesome voices assented to the terms.

"Was that them, Belrab?" Seth asked.

"It was," the lich replied.

"Extra protection for us," the Sphinx prompted.

"You must all pledge to do me no harm," Seth said.

"And no harm to the crippled shadow charmer assisting me."

Hellish voices called out their agreement. Seth could feel their eagerness at the prospect of release.

"Crippled?" the Sphinx asked.

"It's how Belrab described you," Seth muttered. Then he raised his voice. "Belrab, have all agreed?"

"All have agreed," Belrab responded. "Send the chain."

"The chain, the chain," countless other voices cried.

Seth glanced at the Sphinx. "How many are down there?"

"A lot," the Sphinx said. "Uncounted."

"Before I send the chain, you must all pledge to always obey any commands I give," Seth said, "along with promising to mean no harm to me and to do no harm to me."

There was silence for a moment.

"Hungry," one voice whispered.

"Cold," another murmured.

"And with these vows you willingly free us?" Belrab verified.

"To remain in this castle, and on the connected roads, yes," Seth said.

"Very well," Belrab said. Other voices assented. "We all agree. Send the chain."

"They agree," Seth said.

"Lower the chain," the Sphinx said. "Quickly, I heard a door."

Seth picked up the end of the chain, the links thick enough that he dragged it more than carried it to the edge of the well. The thought of the creatures behind all those sinister voices climbing toward him gave him a shiver as he hurled it over the edge.

Once the chain started falling, it had enough momentum to keep going, and the entire length unspooled downward with an uproarious clatter. After some time, an echoey clang rose from the depths. The chain jerked taut, the near end fastened to the wall.

"Time to go," the Sphinx said, hurrying out of the chamber to the short corridor.

Seth followed, but they both stopped short as an aged man came through the iron door. His eyes went to Seth, then to the Sphinx. "You," he accused.

"Hello, Agad," the Sphinx said. "You have a containment problem on your hands."

The old man's eyes moved to Seth. "What have you done?"

The distressed sincerity of the question made Seth feel guilty. "You'll want to get out of the castle," Seth said.

The old man's expression softened to one of concern. And then Seth felt rather than saw the dark presence behind him. The temperature of the air plunged. The old man looked past him and began to haltingly step forward, as if the movement challenged him.

"Come on," the Sphinx said, dodging past the old man and through the corroded iron door. Seth followed.

"You've been fooled, Seth," the old man called, voice strained.

"Hurry," the Sphinx said, running full speed. "We need to get out of here."

"Who was that guy?" Seth asked. "He didn't look like a monster."

"One of the wizards who blocked my abilities," the Sphinx said. "Don't let appearances deceive you. He's a ringleader of the creatures here."

The old wizard had looked devastated. He hadn't tried to attack them. Seth looked back, but the wizard was out of view. What might the wizard have told him if he'd had more time?

They ran in silence until they reached the dead minotaurs. The barrel awaited in the nearby cell. "Well done, Seth," the Sphinx said. "Mission accomplished. You first."

Seth hopped into the barrel and crouched. Was he being fooled? It was entirely possible. As Ronodin's sure hands helped him out of the barrel, Seth tried to forget the look of grave disappointment on the old wizard's face.

CHAPTER TEN

Falling

On the long counter rested bottles and flasks of varying shape and size, some with fluid in them, some with sludge or dry matter, others empty. A cauldron bubbled on a fireplace in the corner, and several other pots and kettles were heating on makeshift burners, expelling pungent vapors. Other diverse containers held sundry ingredients.

"Kendra, could you pass me some bristle root?" Tanu asked.

She grabbed the leather pouch and hurried over to Tanu. He opened the flap and dropped two pinches of what looked vaguely like red pencil shavings into a simmering pan. "What are you working on there?" she asked.

"A new gaseous potion," Tanu said. "By the time we're done, I'll have a stockpile like never before."

Kendra looked at the potions on the counter. "A lot of those are courage potions."

"If we face dragons this evening, those could be essential," Tanu said.

Kendra nodded. It felt good to be helping Tanu brew potions. Since the dragons were supposed to attack tonight, she wanted to stay busy. So far, the night had been quiet.

"You look tired," Calvin said from where he stood on the counter. "Maybe you should sleep."

Kendra yawned. "In a little while," she replied. "I want to help finish this batch."

Marat burst into the room, eyes wide. "We have to go," he said urgently.

"What?" Kendra asked, turning toward him in alarm.

"Someone has unleashed the entities from the Blackwell," Marat said. "The attack is from within."

"Is Agad trying to put them back?" Tanu asked, already gathering items.

"He did not seem hopeful," Marat said. "It's either the road or the refuge."

Kendra could hardly believe what she was hearing. She had long known that if the undead emerged from the Blackwell, the whole sanctuary could be destroyed. Was that the threat they were suddenly facing?

She knew there was a fortified room at the heart of the keep called the refuge. Though the room was secure, there was no way out. But if they fled to the road, a lot would depend on whether the Fair Folk of Terrabelle would grant them sanctuary. If the Fair Folk strictly maintained their neutrality, the road would lead to a dead end. "Can't we fight?" Kendra asked.

"Not the denizens of the Blackwell," Marat said. "We have to leave now or all avenues may be cut off."

"One moment," Tanu said as he raced to the courage potions, adding ingredients. "These were tuned to dragons. We need them to protect against the undead as well. The dose might feel uncomfortable, but it beats getting petrified."

"How long?" Marat asked.

"Quick and dirty, I can make them functional in less than a minute," Tanu said, shaking a potion with his thumb over the top, then adding a small spoonful of beige powder. He shook the bottle again and handed it to Kendra. "Drink."

She took it from him, and he immediately began working on another. "The undead will take over the castle, and the dragons are outside," she said.

"Road or refuge," Marat said simply.

Kendra had dealt with emergencies before. Seth had usually been with her, and little seemed to daunt him. When there was a battle to be fought, though scary, the prospect could be energizing. This was different. She felt so doomed that she was strangely calm. The only option was to go forward and try to weather what came.

She raised the bottle to her lips and took a sip. The fluid burned her tongue, but she swallowed anyhow.

"All of it," Tanu said, shaking up another bottle.

Kendra guzzled the rest in a few painful swallows. The

searing liquid felt like it was stripping away the soft tissue in her mouth and throat. Tears streamed from her eyes, and she coughed after choking down the last mouthful.

"Sorry," Tanu said. "No time to adjust for taste." He up-ended a bottle of his own and swallowed the contents.

Warmth spread through Kendra's body, starting at her center and radiating out to her limbs. The doomed feeling melted away like a dispelled illusion. They still had a chance. This wasn't just up to fate. There was plenty to be done. "We need to get moving," she said.

Tanu grimaced and exhaled noisily. "That was fierce." He started shoving flasks and containers into his pack. "I'll catch up. These potions could prove important before the night is through."

"I'll come with you, Kendra," Calvin called from the countertop.

Kendra picked him up and put him in her pocket. "I'll keep you safe," she promised. She also collected her magical bow and her sack of gales.

"You must survive, Kendra," Marat said. "You are the sole remaining caretaker of Wyrmroost. Road or refuge?"

"What do you think?" Kendra asked.

"The refuge is more accessible," Marat said. "It also has stores of food and stronger defenses than the road. It is the fort within the fort."

"Let's go," Kendra said.

"I'll be right behind you," Tanu promised, still gathering ingredients and bottles.

Marat ran from the room, and Kendra sprinted to follow.

They raced down a corridor, turned a corner, then dashed down another hall.

"We have to cross this courtyard," Marat said.

"Okay," Kendra said.

"Brace yourself," Marat advised, opening a door.

They stepped out onto a walkway that overlooked the courtyard. A bright moon shed silver light onto the scene. The stone steps leading down to the courtyard were empty, but the courtyard was not.

Kendra had been feeling bold and hopeful in the corridor. Suddenly it was hard to breathe. Her throat was constricting, and her heart felt cold.

Shadowy figures prowled the courtyard below, shrouded in pockets of darkness. Indecipherable whispers burbled in her mind. The two slowest figures drew her gaze. One limped, somewhat dragging the weaker leg. The other moved more fluidly, but so slowly that Kendra could count to five between each footfall.

Marat gave her a light slap on the cheek. "Revenants," he said. "Accompanied by a few wraiths. We move now or never. Others are spreading through the keep."

The fear Kendra felt was different from the paralysis inflicted by the dragons. This fear made her insides feel like they were turning to ice. "Yes," she said with effort. Even with the help of the courage potion, movement required heavy concentration.

Marat led the way down the stairs. As Kendra's eyes adjusted to the moonlight, she saw that the limping revenant was approaching a dwarf. The little fellow looked up at the

oncoming threat, arms slack at his sides, his short sword loosely gripped in one hand. The dwarf was clearly immobilized. As the revenant reached toward him, Kendra held out her bow and pulled the string to her cheek.

"One," she murmured, and an arrow appeared.

She released, and the arrow streaked across the courtyard to lodge in the forehead of the revenant. The creature did not act bothered, and the revenant's skeletal hand covered the face of the dwarf. After violent convulsions, the small victim fell to the ground, hair, beard, and skin as white as snow.

"No conventional weapons," Marat scolded. "You're trying to kill what is not alive. Hurry."

Kendra followed Marat to the bottom of the stairs, and they started across the courtyard. The viscosity of the air seemed to increase, as if she were pushing through water. And the temperature was plunging. Gritting her teeth, Kendra pressed forward.

"Do not stop," Marat advised. "Stay with me."

"You can do it," Calvin said.

"It's cold," Kendra said.

"Those revenants are pointing at you," Calvin warned. "Wraiths are coming."

Kendra didn't want to look. Marat was nearing a door. She kept her legs churning forward. Glancing back, she found the ominous forms of three wraiths closing on her, moving much faster than the revenants. And faster than her.

Kendra tried to speed up. Her muscles and joints refused

to respond as desired. At least she was grinding forward. But the wraiths were gaining. Would it be like her dreams, where she couldn't outrun the monsters no matter how hard she tried?

With a snarl, the long body of a serpentine dragon coiled around her. The leonine head of the dragon roared at the wraiths, and they stopped advancing. Marat had reverted to his dragon shape—Camarat.

"Go," Camarat said, lifting a segment of his long body so she could duck underneath. "I can hold off the wraiths but not the revenants."

"You come too," Kendra said as she stumbled to the door.

"I will," Camarat said. "You first."

Kendra pushed through the door into a corridor, and most of the iciness left her body. Marat joined her, with no sign he had just been a dragon.

"Thanks," Kendra said.

"Hurry to the refuge," Marat replied. "Those were not the only undead on the prowl. Not nearly."

The hallways seemed foreign. Was it the darkness? She had not roamed much of the keep at night. Urgent whispers intruded on her thoughts, heard more with her mind than her ears. After passing through a gloomy room into another hall, Kendra saw Knox, Tess, and the satyrs up ahead. They were standing still, facing away from her. The cloak of innocence glowed with a silvery sheen.

"Trouble," Marat said, breaking into a full sprint.

Kendra was able to stay with him at first. But as she

reached her cousins, she started to slow. The air grew chilly again.

Beyond her cousins and the satyrs, coming toward them, was a gaunt woman dressed in the tattered remnants of what must once have been a beautiful gown. Her eyes were dark gray, without irises or pupils, and irregular open sores marred her skin. Her head tilted at an unnatural angle, and she was slowly jumping forward, feet bound together.

"Revenant," Marat said. "A strong one."

The revenant was not coming quickly but scooting a bit closer with each jump. Kendra focused on her cousins. "Knox, Tess, can you hear me?" Neither looked her way or blinked. They seemed insensible. Kendra turned to Marat. "Can I stop the revenant?"

"Revenants are under enchantments," Marat said. "I don't know how to break this one."

"Here," Tanu said, approaching from behind. He held up a bottle to Knox's lips and poured fluid into his mouth. "Drink."

"You found us," Kendra said.

"Barely," Tanu said. "It's like a festival night out there."

Knox was drinking the potion, then spat some up.

"Swallow it all," Tanu demanded.

"It's like lava," Knox said.

"You can move now," Tanu said. "And speak. So drink."

Marat ran forward, dodging around the revenant, and soon passed out of view. With his eyes squeezed shut, Knox finished the little bottle. Tanu brought a potion to Tess's lips. The revenant drew nearer, her expression bland, her tongue shriveled and dry behind her remaining teeth.

Kendra wrenched her gaze from the revenant. "We have to move," she said. "What about the satyrs?"

"These potions are for humans," Tanu said.

"Gross!" Tess exclaimed, potion leaking down her chin. "What is that?"

"It'll let you run from the monsters," Tanu said.

"You can do it!" Calvin cheered.

Coughing and sputtering, Tess finished the potion.

Marat returned, knifing past the revenant. "The refuge has been sealed," Marat reported. "Some of our people must have made it inside. The antechamber is swarming with the undead. We have no chance of getting in."

"The road?" Kendra asked.

Marat gave a nod.

Tanu hoisted Newel over one broad shoulder and Doren over the other. "Show us the way."

"That lady looks like a corpse," Knox said, staring at the revenant.

"Welcome to our night," Kendra said, taking Tess by the hand. "Stay together."

Marat led them back toward the courtyard. "Hopefully we'll find fewer undead upstairs." He opened the door to a stairway and led them up.

As they climbed, the satyrs began to squirm on Tanu's shoulders.

"Was it just me," Doren asked, "or was she jumping?"

"I was holding still on purpose," Newel said. "Weighing my options."

Kendra rolled her eyes.

Tanu set the satyrs down.

Kendra could not help noticing the narrowness of the stairway, and she immediately imagined their peril if revenants pinned them in from above and below. She was relieved when they found no undead in the hall at the top of the stairs.

"What about Grandma and Grandpa?" Kendra asked.

"I sent them and some others to the refuge before I went to fetch you and Tanu," Marat said. "I didn't see them when I checked outside the refuge, so I assume they're inside."

"Then they're trapped," Kendra said.

"Cornered, for now," Marat said. "But much safer than we are."

"What about the griffins?" Kendra asked. "And the horses?"

"Patton went to free the mounts," Marat said.

"Could we fly away?" Kendra asked.

"I expect many dragons would greet us in the sky," Marat said. "The road is a better option if we can make it."

"Is there a chance your courage potion could work on us?" Doren asked as they ran. "I don't like becoming paralyzed."

"Give it a try," Tanu said, handing over a bottle.

Doren took a sip and immediately began to cough wildly. With tears in his eyes, he passed the bottle back to Tanu. "Pretty sure it's deadly to satyrs," he said.

"It felt gross and hot to me too," Tess said.

Marat led them out onto a walkway atop one of the walls. Kendra felt her muscles seizing up again, and she saw dark entities patrolling the nearest courtyard. Marat stopped, one hand going to his temple.

"My brother Agad is reaching out to my mind," Marat said. "The road is already taken by wraiths and revenants. We will not find safety there."

"What options do we have left?" Tanu asked.

"We can try a little-used side door," Marat said. "I'd rather not go over the wall in dragon form and attract attention. There will be no protection besides the cloak of innocence once we pass outside."

"Can it hold off Celebrant?" Kendra asked.

"Possibly," Marat said. "All items have limits. But we lack other options. The inhabitants of the Blackwell are claiming the keep and the road. At least dragons would provide a clean death."

"Are we going to die?" Tess asked.

"Not if we hide behind your cloak," Doren said. "Are you clear about who is under your protection?"

"Kendra, Knox, the potion guy, you goat-men, the dragon person, and the little guy in Kendra's pocket," Tess said.

"There are wraiths ahead on the wall," Tanu warned.

"Then we must abandon subtlety," Marat said, his body elongating into a serpentine dragon. "Take hold of me."

Kendra leaped onto the back of the dragon, straddling him and gripping as best she could. Tanu, Knox, and Tess climbed on as well. The satyrs stood petrified.

Camarat shot into the air, body fluttering like a ribbon.

Kendra hung on tightly. The dragon used several sets of his many legs to grab Newel and Doren and then flew low and quick, soaring over a building, his tale dislodging shingles, then down into a courtyard, where he skidded to a stop near a door in the wall. Kendra noticed half a dozen undead in the courtyard. A pair of emaciated men, one with a scraggly beard, the other wearing a helmet and dented breastplate, stood in front of the door.

"Revenants are barring the way out," Marat said after reverting to human shape.

"And wraiths are coming our way," Tanu said.

Fighting against the frozen feeling slowing her muscles, Kendra raised her bow. "Maybe lots of arrows are better than one," Kendra said, hauling the bowstring to her cheek and aiming at the revenants blocking the door. "Ninety."

She released the string, and ninety arrows sprang from her bow and turned the two revenants into pincushions, piercing flesh and armor. Many near misses thunked into the door as well. Neither revenant looked particularly bothered by the dozens of protruding arrows.

"No!" Marat cried.

"What?" Kendra asked.

"The cloak," Marat said, pointing.

Kendra saw that the cloak of innocence had lost its silvery glow. Her stomach dropped.

"None in the group can attack anything while under the protection of the cloak," Marat said, "or the protection is lost to all."

CHAPTER ELEVEN

Execution

As several wraiths, dark and almost translucent in the moonlight, drew nearer from across the courtyard, Kendra stared at Marat, her understanding catching up to his words.

They needed to leave the keep.

She had shot arrows at the revenants.

Arrows that had done no good.

Their only hope of survival when they left the keep was the cloak of innocence.

By shooting the revenants, she had negated that protection.

Without accomplishing anything, she had just ensured that she and all of those with her would die.

"I didn't understand," Kendra said numbly. "Couldn't you have stopped me?"

"I didn't make the connection until too late," Marat said. "My first reaction was regret that the arrows would be futile. Only once you let them fly did I realize that, futile or not, it was an attack. None under the protection of the cloak can try to harm another without breaking the spell."

"We can all go gaseous and try to escape that way," Tanu said. "At least the mortals."

After glancing at Newel and Doren, who stood petrified, transfixed by the revenants, Kendra turned to Marat. "Maybe you can fly the satyrs away to safety."

"If Celebrant is as ready as I expect, he will track and destroy you, gaseous or not," Marat said. "And I cannot evade a host of dragons."

A flaming figure burst from a door on the far side of the courtyard. Sheathed from head to foot in white fire, the burning humanoid raced toward a wraith and cut him in half at the waist with a fiery blade. The flaming newcomer continued toward Kendra and her allies.

"My brother," Marat said, directing the others to step aside.

The blazing wizard rushed the revenants blocking the door through the wall. They offered little resistance as he struck down one and then the other with consecutive swipes. After the revenants collapsed, Kendra felt the icy chill inside of her thaw, and the satyrs could move again.

The white flames fluttered out and Agad turned to face Kendra and the others, dropping to one knee. His hair and beard were singed and his robe was charred in places. One arm looked withered down to almost nothing, and part of his nose was missing.

Marat ran to his brother and helped him up. The others gathered around them.

"I got there too late," Agad panted, his bloodshot eyes weary. "There were too many of them, and Belrab was too powerful to challenge with so much support behind him. I tried to force them back down the well, and it nearly destroyed me." His eyes went to Kendra. "It was Seth, assisted by the Sphinx."

"Seth was here?" Kendra asked, hardly able to believe what she was hearing. "With the Sphinx?"

Agad gave a nod. "I saw them, Kendra. The Sphinx must have come through the barrel and hidden before Mendigo escaped with Seth. Mendigo would have brought him through while the barrel was missing. The Sphinx hid here until he killed the minotaurs, brought Seth through, and finally sent Seth back."

"Wraiths," Tanu warned.

Staggering, Agad waved an arm, and a semicircular wall of white flame sprang up to block the wraiths from approaching the door. Marat supported his sagging brother.

"You're exerting yourself beyond your limits," Marat said.

"As is appropriate," Agad said. "Ultimately, this sanctuary is my responsibility. If it falls, I should fall with it."

"We will need you in the greater conflict," Marat said.

Agad frowned. "I can't be everywhere, do everything. Instead I am doing what I can."

"Seth did this?" Kendra asked, on the edge of hysteria, not wanting to believe it.

"He did not know me," Agad said. "I doubt he understood what he was doing."

Kendra felt sick. Her worst fears were already playing out. Not only did their enemies have her brother, but he appeared to be siding with them.

"I suspect only Seth, with his caretaker status, could have opened the roads to the undead," Agad said. "Who knows what fiction they told him to cajole his assistance? Seth did not fail us, Kendra. I failed to rescue him in time."

"You're sure Seth is gone?" Kendra asked.

"I'm sure," Agad said. "He and the Sphinx fled purposefully."

"We don't know where?" Kendra asked. Even with danger surrounding them, more than anything, she wanted to find her brother.

"Only how," Agad said. "Through the barrel, undoubtedly." The haggard wizard looked tiredly at the others. "We have our own troubles now. We cannot stay here with the full wrath of the Blackwell unleashed. And unless we are extremely fortunate, we will not survive long beyond these walls."

"The cloak of innocence is undone," Marat said.

"I saw," Agad said. "That was when I knew I must rush to your aid."

"Is there any chance left of getting away?" Kendra asked.

"Not if the dragons are ready for us," Agad said. "Which I expect they are."

"Should we try gaseous potions?" Tanu asked.

"Keep them handy," Agad said. "I would not use them yet. Flee as a gas and the dragons will destroy you with their breath weapons. We are defeated and trapped. The best chance we have left is to negotiate a surrender."

"We're giving up?" Kendra asked.

"Not on the war," Agad said. "But on Wyrmroost, perhaps. Without Blackwell Keep, we have lost. Simple as that."

The wall of white fire was beginning to dwindle. Wraiths were visible behind it, hesitant but near, their numbers growing.

"Maybe we can still sneak away," Newel said.

"I will cloak us in the best distracter spell I can muster," Agad said. "Through the door on my count. Three, two, one."

Tess looked terrified. Kendra took her hand. Knox didn't look so well either. When he caught Kendra's gaze, he tried to smile. "Are we going to be dragon food?"

"I hope not," Kendra said.

Marat held the door open as Agad and the satyrs exited. Kendra, Tanu, Knox, and Tess followed. Marat brought up the rear.

Kendra beheld an empty field, bordered on one side by the gray wall of the keep and on the others by trees, the stillness eerie after revenants and wraiths and fire. A soft breeze ruffled the tall grass. How did this quiet scenery exist so near the perils they had faced?

For a moment she felt hesitant relief.

But only for a moment.

As the door to Blackwell Keep shut, the colossal form of Celebrant landed in the field in front of Kendra, platinum scales glowing in the moonlight. Other dragons alighted all around them, quickly filling the field and cutting off any avenue of escape. The satyrs became immobilized with fear. The courage potions left Tanu, Knox, and Tess able to move.

"Pathetic concealment spell," Celebrant gloated in a voice like a boisterous choir of men speaking in unison. "Look who we have here. It seems we have caught the crab outside of its shell."

Agad stepped forward, stumbling a bit. "We have come to negotiate surrender."

Celebrant laughed darkly. "You have come to negotiate, have you? I never received an invitation. It appears to me you are fleeing your fallen stronghold."

"Nevertheless, we are prepared to negotiate," Agad maintained.

"I must admit I enjoy this talk of surrender from the mighty Agad," Celebrant said. "Are you still pleased to have traded your claws and fangs for robes?"

"I stand by my decisions," Agad said. "What are your terms?"

"My first demand is that before negotiations begin, you must die," Celebrant said.

"Very well," Agad said, straightening. "We will decide this by combat. You against me."

Kendra's eyes strayed to the damaged spot on Celebrant's chest where Madrigus had injured him in combat. Would the injury give Agad a chance?

"You misunderstand," Celebrant said. "I was not proposing combat. This is a war. You have already lost this battle. You have no privileges. I need grant you no quarter."

"You are asking for my life," Agad said.

"Asking, telling, taking," Celebrant said. "Take your pick."

"If I refuse?" Agad said.

"No negotiations with the others," Celebrant said. "And I take your life just the same."

"No," Marat said.

Agad raised his good hand to halt his brother. "I'm injured, Camarat. Deeply. Perhaps fatally already. I might have mustered one last grand attack. But this may accomplish more good."

"I grow impatient," Celebrant said.

"Very well," Agad said, striding unsteadily toward Celebrant. He fell to his knees before the dragon.

"After all of these years, it is pleasant to see you submit," Celebrant said. Jaws flexing open, his head snaked toward the old wizard.

Kendra turned her head and covered Tess's eyes. When she looked back, Celebrant jerked his head up, swallowing. Agad was gone.

"Subpar for a human," Celebrant said. "Almost no decent meat on those old bones. Who speaks for you now? The caretaker, I presume?"

"That's me," Kendra said, stepping forward.

"There you are," Celebrant said, eyes alight with triumph. "For one so young, you have been a nuisance, but you are finally out of tricks, allies, and hiding places. Would you care to hear my terms?"

"All right," Kendra said, trying to bury her grief for the moment. The others were counting on her. She glanced over at Knox and Tess. Hopefully the terms would allow some of them to survive.

"I invite you to formally surrender and trust my mercy," Celebrant said. "Give me the caretaker's medallion and I will consider whether to let you and your comrades depart in peace."

Kendra looked back at Marat. "Surrender and the sanctuary has officially fallen," he said.

"Or of course I could devour all of you now and claim the victory I have already won," Celebrant said.

Kendra wondered if there might be a reason he needed her official surrender. Would some barriers remain in place without it?

"I'll surrender if you promise to spare us," Kendra said.

"Were you absent for this discussion with Agad?" Celebrant asked. "You are in no position to haggle. I do not need your surrender. Make your choice or I destroy all of you this instant."

"Fine," Kendra said, angry as she took off the caretaker's medallion. She wished for the sword Vasilis. For a moment she considered her sack of gales, but she knew it was only effective against airborne dragons. "I surrender." She threw the medallion toward the feet of the towering dragon.

"We have reached our destined ending," Celebrant said. "I accept your surrender. And now all of you must die."

"What about mercy?" Kendra cried, thinking first of Tess.

"Mercy is for those who have not insulted me," Celebrant said. "Mercy is for those who surrender before they have been utterly abased. You were foolish to ever oppose me. I will delight in providing the exact ending you deserve."

"Enough!" boomed a voice like thunder.

From out of the sky, a man descended, landing beside Kendra. Clad in a dark robe, he had a short white beard and white hair. In one hand he carried a staff. Kendra had never seen him before.

Snarling, Celebrant lunged at the newcomer but was repelled with a flash of red light when his face struck an invisible barrier. Celebrant opened his mouth and released a stream of white energy, but it splashed harmlessly against the barrier, brightening the night with a harsh glare.

At last Celebrant relented, glaring at the stranger. "Who are you and where have you come from?" the Dragon King asked.

"Had you simply shown mercy, you might never have met me," the newcomer said.

"Clearly you are a wizard, and not one that I know," Celebrant said.

"Right on the first count," the wizard said. "Half right on the second."

Celebrant's eyes widened. "No."

"Yes," the wizard said.

"Dromadus," Celebrant said.

"Not anymore," the wizard said. "I am Andromadus from now on."

"The art of becoming a wizard is lost," Celebrant declared.

"Not to me," Andromadus said. "Archadius, the first of this order, taught me long ago. I never expected to apply the knowledge."

"You were already an embarrassment and an outcast," Celebrant said. "You once wore my crown. Why would you further dishonor yourself and our kind?"

"You are the embarrassment," Andromadus said sternly, in a voice that shook the ground. "What honor is there in killing a young human girl who has surrendered? Such an execution is treatment for a worthy adversary. Do you consider her an enemy even now? A worthy opponent? Your better or your equal? Do you take pride in her defeat?"

The questions elicited a murmur from some of the dragons.

"She is an insect to be squashed," Celebrant said, his head bumping up against the unseen barrier again.

"If so, you would have squashed her," Andromadus said. "Instead, you had to drive her from Blackwell Keep with the aid of humans and unicorns. And then you solicit her surrender. Never have I begged an insect to submit."

The assertion was met with silence. Kendra noticed the other dragons staring at Celebrant intently. His status had been placed in question.

"I wanted to ensure no problems with the magical barriers of Wyrmroost," Celebrant said. "The treaty is strong.

With her surrender, our freedom is no longer in question. Dromadus, you have chosen an odd way to die."

"I will not die today," Andromadus said. "Neither will Kendra or her friends. You have forgotten your true nature, Celebrant. Dragons are not humans."

"Dragons will rule over humans," Celebrant vowed.

"A real dragon would not care to rule over humans!" Andromadus shouted. "A real dragon would not gather his people to a castle like some human lordling. A dragon hunts. A dragon hoards. A dragon assumes authority."

"Our authority was taken!" Celebrant cried.

"We lost our authority when we organized after human patterns and fought a war like mortals," Andromadus said. "We lost that war. And, despite our defeat, those humans gave us space to live like dragons. We were in their power. They could have exterminated us."

"They will regret their failure," Celebrant said. "We shall exterminate them."

"Where is the glory in that?" Andromadus challenged. "Some humans helped defeat us, alongside several of our kind who became wizards. But most humans do not even know there was a fight. You wanting to rule humans, to defeat humans, is like a human wanting to rule rabbits or defeat squirrels. It is not dignified. It runs against our very nature. It is not dragonlike."

"You are not dragonlike!" Celebrant roared.

"I am true to my nature," Andromadus said. "I side with the humans on this matter. It is time for my form to match my sympathies. This war is bad for dragons, bad for humans, and bad for the world. I now stand against you."

"The greatest coward of all dragons opposes me," Celebrant scoffed. "The Dragon King who resigned!"

"There is a kind of courage that looks to fulfill the expectations of others," Andromadus said. "Some might call it duty. There is another kind that insists on being true to oneself."

"You cannot stand against us," Celebrant said harshly.

"I do not wish to fight you," Andromadus said. "I wish for this war to end. I am still a friend to all dragons. I implore you to turn from this ludicrous path."

"You fear our victory," Celebrant exclaimed. "You worry that after our triumph I would root out the decrepit old king and openly put him to shame."

"You could have attempted that long ago," Andromadus said.

"You have disgraced yourself more than I ever could," Celebrant said. "You have become mortal."

"And you have disgraced the crown," Andromadus said. "You are leading our kind toward folly and ruin."

"Not *our* kind anymore," Celebrant said. "My kind. And *my* kind does not want to live like docile pets in a cage. My kind wants the dominance we deserve. This is the dawn of a new and endless age of dragons. Attack!"

The dragons all around the field charged forward, slamming against the unseen barrier Andromadus had raised. The wizard held both hands high, trembling with effort.

Judging from the way the dragons pressed against the barrier, Kendra could tell it was curved like a dome.

"You must depart," Andromadus said to her. "Have I permission to send you?"

"Where?" Kendra asked.

"Away," Andromadus said. "I will rejoin you when I can. I do not expect you will get a better offer."

"You're Dromadus?" Tess asked.

"So I was," Andromadus said.

"You came!" Tess cheered.

"So I did," Andromadus said with a small smile.

"Send us," Kendra said.

"As you wish," Andromadus said.

Kendra felt her body lurch. Everything temporarily went black, and then she dropped to her knees on a marble floor in a huge room decorated with absurdly oversized furniture. Knox, Tess, Tanu, Marat, and the satyrs were beside her, and directly before her loomed the giant Thronis.

CHAPTER TWELVE

Questions

S eated alone at a stone table, Seth tried to spread butter across a hefty slice of wheat bread, but the room was too cold for the butter to smear well. Instead he did his best to shave the butter down to slivers and space them around the bread. He also had a broad bowl of various shellfish cooked in a tomato-based sauce, and a carafe of the kind of milk that allowed him to see magical creatures.

Ronodin and the Sphinx had started the meal with him, but they promptly departed together with a pair of wraiths toting the barrel, leaving Seth alone. The bread and butter tasted satisfying, and he generally liked most of the shellfish, though the black ones were too rubbery. Absently pushing the remaining tidbits around his bowl, Seth wondered what his favorite food might be. He could remember many different kinds of food, but he had no memory of how they tasted, or which he preferred. He had an abstract impression that many found pie delicious but could match it to no specific flavor.

Water dripped from the ceiling in one corner of the room. He could sense the undead wandering nearby.

Mostly he felt haunted by the wizard at the Blackwell and his warning.

"You've been fooled, Seth."

Though distressed by the problem of the emerging undead, the old man had seemed genuine. Seth had been told the castle was controlled by minotaurs and monsters, but the old wizard had seemed very human, and he had not attacked Seth or the Sphinx for what they had done.

And the old man had known his name—at least, the same name everyone else had been using.

Seth frowned. How might he have been fooled?

What if he had done something terrible? What if unleashing the undead from the well had brought horrors to a peaceful castle? He had seen dead minotaurs, but maybe monsters only worked down in the dungeon. He had granted the undead access to roads. What if those roads led to villages? Was unleashing the undead against anyone ever a fair option? Even if the only victims were monsters?

The old man hadn't looked like a monster. Could he have been the evil wizard who ruled the monsters? The Sphinx had said the old guy was one of the wizards who had stripped his shadow-charming powers. But if shadow charmers freed the undead to overrun inhabited castles, maybe the Sphinx had deserved some punishment.

Seth had no proof the wizard was honest. Did the wizard really know him? Maybe the wizard knew that Seth had lost his memory and had made the comment to confuse him. But the wizard could as easily have been a dear friend as a dangerous enemy.

For all Seth knew, Ronodin could also be an enemy. Seth still had little context to build from. Ronodin had brought him to the Under Realm and gotten him indentured to the Underking. Seth was having to perform tasks just to stay alive. But Ronodin would argue it was for his good so he could relearn his abilities. Could anyone be trusted? What if it was him against everyone?

Ronodin was vague about so much. He refused to tell Seth exactly how he had lost his memory. He would reveal nothing about where this Under Realm was located. And he avoided specifics about Seth's history. That seemed suspect, though Ronodin assured him he would learn all in time.

It seemed reasonable to Seth that he may have once belonged in this Under Realm. After all, he could speak with the undead and had other dark powers. Might there be light in him as well? Seth knew he didn't want to cause harm to anyone. Even though he had dark abilities, he wanted to do good with them, not evil. Had he always felt that way? Even back before he could remember?

However dark his history might be, did it have to define him? With his memory wiped clean, how much did it matter who he had been before? What if it turned out he didn't like who he had been? He wanted to know his history, but did he have to be a slave to it? Did he have to learn from somebody who kept secrets and acted like he owned him? In principle, Seth didn't mind freeing some of the undead, but not if people would get hurt.

Seth ate more shellfish and munched on bread. The meal seemed like another hint that he was close to the ocean. What would he find if he got to the surface?

He thought about the girl Kendra, the first person he had met, who claimed to be his sister. She had run after him when the puppet Mendigo carried him away. Her desperation had seemed sincere. He wished he knew more about her. Was she really related to him? Or was it just a clever way to win over a person who had lost his memory? Had she been working with his enemies? Or was she on his side?

These questions had answers.

He needed them.

Ronodin had left him alone in an underground domain full of the undead. And Seth could communicate with the undead.

He pushed back his chair from the table, took one last sip of milk, dabbed his lips with the linen napkin, picked up the little lantern off the table, and walked into a neighboring chamber. Two wraiths stood there. Left to themselves, the wraiths did not do much besides sedately lurk. They were not like the wraiths in the well who had seemed so desperate for freedom, perhaps because these wraiths were already free.

"We need to talk," Seth said, pointing to one of the wraiths.

As you wish, the wraith responded, the chilling words flowing directly into Seth's mind.

"Can you speak out loud?" Seth asked.

"If desired," the wraith replied in a slithery whisper.

"I like talking better," Seth said. "Who am I?"

"You are living," the wraith said.

"I mean specifically," Seth said.

The other wraith moved away. Seth saw no reason to stop it.

"You are untouchable," the wraith said.

The other wraith left the room. Seth wondered if it was deliberately avoiding the conversation.

"You can't touch me?" Seth asked. "Do you want to kill me?"

"I serve the Underking," the wraith replied.

"Do you know my name?" Seth asked.

"You are Seth."

"What else do you know about me?" Seth asked.

"You are living. You are untouchable."

"Where are we?" Seth asked.

"We are in the depths," the wraith whispered.

"If I went to the surface, where would we be?" Seth asked.

"At the surface."

Seth rolled his eyes. "Where in the world would we be at the surface?"

"The isle," the wraith said. "But there are many ways."

"Many ways to the isle?" Seth asked.

"Many ways to many places," the wraith said.

Seth sighed. It was hard to get a straight answer. "Does anyone here know more about who I am?"

"The prisoner knows."

"What prisoner?"

"You must not meet the prisoner," the wraith said.

"Why not?"

"Orders from Ronodin."

"Is Ronodin in charge of you?"

"I serve the Underking," the wraith said.

"But you follow orders from Ronodin?"

"I heed orders authorized by the Underking."

"Do you follow orders from me?" Seth asked.

"You are untouchable. I hear you. You hear me. I communicate."

"Where is the prison?" Seth asked.

"You are to be kept from the prisoner," the wraith said.

"Orders from Ronodin?"

"Orders," the wraith said.

"Okay," Seth said. "Thanks."

He walked back to the room where he had eaten. The bread, seafood dish, and milk remained where he had left them. He knew his way to his quarters and went in that direction, but paused at his door and then kept going. He could sense more wraiths up ahead. Maybe he could get more out of a new wraith.

Seth walked up to the next wraith he found. "Will you take me to the prison?"

The words of the wraith reached his mind. *You are not to go there.*

"Speak out loud." Seth wondered if he could use some cleverness to get an answer. "What direction should I avoid to keep away from the prison?"

"The wrong direction," the wraith said.

"Which way is that?"

"The wrong way."

Seth folded his arms. "Who could tell me about the prison?"

"Ezabar," the wraith said.

"Can you take me to Ezabar?"

The wraith gave a curt bow and started walking. Seth followed, wondering if he should be worried or excited to speak with Ezabar. He had not yet dared to wander far unescorted by Ronodin, and he felt curious to see more of the Under Realm. Whether by slope or by stairs, the way descended downward, some portions of the journey like a cave, others enclosed by crude masonry. Seth frequently sensed undead presences, several of them unfamiliar and more disquieting than he had felt before, but he saw none of them.

The air grew colder, and the little lantern seemed to have more difficulty pushing back the darkness. The wraith stopped outside an elaborately carved doorway with bones fused into the stonework.

"Is this where I go?" Seth asked.

"Ezabar," the wraith said.

"Are you coming in with me?" Seth asked.

"No," the wraith said.

"Will you wait to take me back up?" Seth asked.

"Yes," the wraith said.

Seth took a step toward the door and then stopped. "Is Ezabar dangerous?"

"Yes."

Seth walked up to the door, ancient wood bound in iron. If there was a prisoner he was not supposed to meet, Seth wanted to meet him. Or her. Or it. If talking to Ezabar was a loophole that could help the encounter happen, Seth figured it was worth the risk. He thought about knocking, then hauled the door open.

Coldness flowed from the open portal. In the tomblike room beyond, the lantern light penetrated the darkness to reveal a sinister figure at rest on a large marble slab. The apparent corpse wore a long chain-mail hauberk under a white tunic, hands folded on the hilt of the broadsword atop his chest. His faintly glowing skin had a blue tint and was translucent enough that Seth could make out the bones inside his hands and behind his face.

"Why do you disturb me?" the supine figure asked in a deep, hollow voice.

"I'm looking for Ezabar," Seth said.

"You have found him," the figure said, rising from the slab to stand with his feet hovering a few inches above the ground, the sword clutched in one semitransparent hand. "State your business."

Seth worried he had disturbed a being he should have left alone. Goosebumps now textured both of his arms. He tried to act confident. "I need to visit the prison."

"You are alive," Ezabar said.

"Don't hold that against me," Seth said. "I'm doing my best with what I've got."

"Tell me, shadow charmer, what business have you in my prison?" Ezabar asked.

"Your prison?" Seth checked.

Ezabar rested the blade of his sword on one armored shoulder. "I oversee all matters here."

"Are we at the prison?" Seth asked.

"Nearly," Ezabar said.

"Could you give me a tour? I'm new."

"The living who enter my prison seldom return," Ezabar said.

"Are some in your prison living?"

"All."

"No undead?"

"None."

"Why don't I just go have a look?"

"I must destroy any who enter the prison without permission," Ezabar said.

"But I'm untouchable," Seth said.

"No living being is untouchable here," Ezabar said.

"That's what I get for listening to wraiths," Seth muttered.

"Perhaps the wraiths were asked not to harm you," Ezabar allowed.

"Why not give me permission?" Seth asked. "Isn't my shadow charm working?"

"You have yet to provide evidence to justify a visit," Ezabar said.

"What kind of undead are you?" Seth asked. "Is that too personal? You hold a better conversation than a wraith. And revenants don't seem to talk at all."

"Revenants are focused so deeply inward it is a wonder they can move," Ezabar said.

"You're a lich," Seth guessed.

"That is one label, I suppose," Ezabar said.

"What label do you use?" Seth asked.

"You are either extraordinarily brave or exceedingly ignorant," Ezabar said. "Either way, you assume too much familiarity. Either provide a reason for intruding on my rest or face the consequences."

"I heard there is a prisoner who knows me," Seth said, hoping to earn some points for honesty.

"I fail to see the relevance," Ezabar said.

"The Underking invited me to stay here," Seth said. "I work with Ronodin. I just freed a bunch of undead from a well and gave them their own castle to haunt. But I've lost my memory. If one of your prisoners might know me, I want to have a talk."

"There is a prisoner who knows of you," Ezabar said. "He would attempt to poison your mind if given the chance. Ronodin would not like that conversation to occur, though the Underking has not forbidden it."

"Wait, do you know me?" Seth asked.

"I know enough," Ezabar said.

"If you lost your identity, wouldn't you want to gather information?" Seth asked. "Speak to anyone who knew you?"

"I would never be so foolish as to lose something so precious," Ezabar said.

"I don't even know how I lost it," Seth said. "Ronodin is teaching me. Why would he want to keep me away from a person from my past?"

"This prisoner has harmed many of our kind," Ezabar said. "He destroyed several who were close to me. He is a menace."

"I'm not going to blindly believe him," Seth said. "But it's important I hear from multiple sources if I'm going to put together the pieces of my past. Unless Ronodin has something to hide . . ."

"I do not care to guess at the mind of Ronodin," Ezabar said.

"Then why not let me interview the prisoner?" Seth asked.

"I do not oversee a social parlor," Ezabar said. "This is the prison of the Under Realm."

"I'm a guest here, and one of your prisoners could be useful to me," Seth said. "Should I ask Ronodin? Is he who really controls access?"

"Ronodin is a visitor here as well," Ezabar said. "Albeit an honored one."

"How does it usually work to talk to a prisoner?" Seth asked.

"Seldom is a prisoner interrogated," Ezabar said. "Such rare circumstances are almost uniformly at the behest of the Underking."

"Then what do you manage here? Sounds like there isn't much to do."

"The prisoners are all living," Ezabar said.

"You already explained that," Seth said.

"I primarily keep the other inhabitants of the Under Realm from feeding on them."

"Gross," Seth said, wrinkling his nose. "I guess that makes sense, though. Then why not just let me talk to the prisoner? I promise not to feed on him."

Ezabar gave a nod. "It is amusing to hold a conversation with a live person. Especially one who is not imprisoned. What would you be willing to do for me if I grant the access you seek?"

"I don't know," Seth said. "You've got a tomb over your head, a sword to hold, a marble bed, cool armor. What do you get for the guy who has it all?"

"What about a piece of information?" Ezabar asked.

"You know I lost my memory," Seth said.

"This is information you can obtain," Ezabar said. "Ages ago I dwelled in the country of Selona. Do you know it?"

"I'm not sure," Seth said. "I remember some places. I don't think I'm an expert with geography, and who knows how much I've forgotten. I'm not even sure where I'm from, though I would guess the United States, since a lot of the states and cities sound familiar."

"Selona is in Europe," Ezabar said. "There was a boy called Toleron, son of the Duke of Hester. The child's mother was called Ingrid. It would interest me to know what became of him."

"Like what he did with his life?" Seth asked.

"Share whatever you can learn," Ezabar said. "The topic is of enough interest that if you vow to do this, I will grant the access you seek."

"Can I get to Selona?" Seth asked.

"Not easily perhaps, or soon," Ezabar said. "If you survive long enough, there are ways to get you close. Time is on my side."

"Okay," Seth said. "I vow to do that."

"Very well," Ezabar said. "Wait here." He gestured toward his marble slab. "I must check on the prisoners before allowing you access. If you exit this chamber before I return, the offer is void."

"I'll wait right here," Seth said. "Do you mind if I sit on your slab?"

"I do not mind," Ezabar said. "I shall return."

The lich left the room, closing the door. Seth sat down on the cold, hard marble, wondering how long he would have to wait.

CHAPTER THIRTEEN

Giant

Kendra knew Thronis only by reputation. Standing up tall, she barely came halfway up his hairy shins. He loomed before her, clad in sandals and a sky-blue toga. Liver spots stippled a bald head fringed by the short bristles of graying hair. Except for his enormous proportions, he looked like a regular man approaching the age of sixty, with a paunchy belly and inquisitive eyes.

"That guy is freaky," Knox murmured.

The enormous room of fine marble and granite was sparsely furnished with divans the size of sailing ships and ottomans bigger than gazebos. A bonfire roared inside a gargantuan hearth. A colossal mural on one wall depicted a giantess seated on an elaborate chair that had been carved into a mountainside. Numerous tiny humans groveled at her feet. On the far side of the room, doors stood open to a balcony that overlooked the night sky.

"Is this Stormcrag?" Kendra called.

"I hear you just fine," the giant replied, his voice powerful but not deep. "No need to shout. Welcome to my mountaintop. You must be Kendra."

"These are my cousins, Knox and Tess," Kendra said. "And my friend, Tanu, along with the satyrs Newel and Doren."

"And I know Marat," Thronis said. "You are welcome here. The new wizard known as Andromadus obtained my permission to send you."

"Where is he?" Kendra asked, looking around.

"He pledged to return shortly," Thronis said. "You have endured a difficult night. Can I provide any refreshments?"

Kendra sagged. Were refreshments an option? It felt like a long time since she had found a chance to pause. Were they truly safe? Agad had just been devoured by Celebrant. It had looked like they would all die.

"I'm thirsty," Tess said.

"I wouldn't mind a drink," Doren said. "If you're offering."

The giant walked away, footfalls sending vibrations through the furniture, and returned with a golden bowl, which he placed on the floor near Kendra. It came higher than her waist and was full of clear liquid.

"I have some cups for small folk," Thronis said, walking from the room.

"Are you sure he isn't going to eat us?" Knox asked.

"Thronis always tells the truth," Kendra said.

"Not by rule anymore," Thronis said, returning to the room. "The spell Agad cast on me died with him. But I do believe in honesty, and it has become quite a meticulous habit over the years."

The giant placed a large drawstring bag on the floor, and Tanu tugged it open. "Plates and utensils too," Tanu announced as he withdrew several glass mugs and began handing them around.

When Kendra dipped her mug in the fragrant liquid, she could feel it was warm. She tried a sip and tasted tepid water suffused with subtle herbal flavors, including mint. The aroma, the taste, and the temperature combined to make each sip relaxing.

"This looks like what a fancy guy would use to wash his hands," Knox said. "But it tastes good."

"Thank you, Thronis," Kendra said.

"My pleasure," the giant replied. "I very rarely get visitors."

With a red flash, Patton appeared, along with the winged horses Glory and Noble and many griffins from the stable, including Tempest. A moment later, Andromadus arrived with another burst of light.

"So many mounts," Thronis said.

"You have facilities for such?" Andromadus asked.

Thronis gave a nod. "I am fond of griffins and keep many of my own here. These are all welcome. You will reinforce the protections on my manse?"

"Indeed," Andromadus said. Closing his eyes, the wizard raised his staff and began mumbling words, his free hand splayed. He lowered the staff. "It is done. Your home is now a bastion of the founders."

Thronis smiled. "The dragons would probably not try to attack us here, knowing the winds I could summon, but I don't mind my abode becoming more secure, especially now that the sanctuary has fallen and I have taken in fugitives."

Kendra turned to Andromadus. "Did you see any sign of my grandma and grandpa?"

"Your grandparents are safe inside the last refuge of the keep," Andromadus said. "I had means to spy on the events of the evening. Henrick and the other survivors of the castle staff are in there as well. The spells protecting the refuge leave me no chance of gaining admittance. But the undead should fare no better. Neither should the dragons."

"How will they get out?" Kendra asked.

"In time, a rescue could be planned," Andromadus said. "That is a matter for another day."

"Thank you for saving us," Marat said. "It was most unexpected."

"If you came earlier, you might have saved Agad," Knox said.

"I chose my moment deliberately," Andromadus said. "I knew Celebrant would slay all of you. But knowing was different from hearing the sentence declared. I stood by for the end of Agad because he was an old and worthy opponent. Had Celebrant shown you mercy, Kendra, I would not have intervened."

"Are you on our side now?" Kendra asked.

Andromadus bowed his head. "Against some of my

better judgment, I consider myself your ally until the end of this war with the dragons."

"The dragons may rue this day," Thronis said. "It has been many a year since the birth of a wizard. The arrival of a spellcaster of your stature is no small event."

"Time will reveal what impact I may have," Andromadus said.

"How could you hold off so many dragons?" Knox asked.

"It helped that I had so recently converted into a wizard," Andromadus said. "Archadius taught that my powers would spike for a time with my rebirth. He tried to coax me into this transformation long ago."

"You learned this technique from the first wizard?" Kendra asked.

Andromadus gave a nod.

"You were truly ancient," Thronis said. "The power of the wizard is generally proportionate to the age and power of the transformed dragon."

"May that hold true," Andromadus said, "for I am the oldest dragon to undergo this metamorphosis."

"Could you have taken out any of the dragons at the keep?" Knox asked.

"Perhaps," Andromadus said. "But I remain a pacifist. I do not intend to stop this war with violence."

Kendra felt her hopes sink a little. It would be more comforting if Andromadus was fully on their side and ready to fight. She sympathized with his disdain for war, but she felt certain fighting would be required if humanity was to survive.

"The preserve has fallen," Kendra said. "I am no longer the caretaker?"

"Correct," Andromadus said.

"Your obligation is fulfilled," Marat added. "The sanctuary has fallen. You did very well under grueling conditions."

"Then I am free to search for my brother?" Kendra asked.

"You are free to pursue whatever you wish," Marat said. "Though finding Seth may be easier said than done."

"Tell me what happened to Seth," Thronis said. "I found him both entertaining and useful when he fetched items from the Dragon Temple for me."

Resisting her sadness, Kendra summarized how Seth had lost his memory and was taken, along with how he had been used to open the Blackwell. Thronis listened with interest until she concluded.

"To think the Wizenstone was within the boundaries of this sanctuary," the giant mused.

"It is good that such unfathomable power has been sent away," Andromadus said. "This war already has plenty of weapons."

"The Wizenstone could have ended the war," Marat said.

"Whoever won using the Wizenstone, the rest of us would lose," Andromadus said. "The world would face a nearly invincible reign of terror."

Kendra hoped that wouldn't be the case if *she* had the Wizenstone, but she didn't want to argue the point. It was the sort of claim a person could prove only by doing.

"How can we escape Wyrmroost?" Kendra asked. "What about teleporting us out of here?"

"Now that the preserve has fallen, I could send you a short distance beyond the boundaries," Andromadus said. "At least for a time, before my power recedes to normal. But the dragons can also cross beyond the former boundaries of Wyrmroost. This mansion is the most fortified location within my reach. Anywhere else I send you could lead to a hasty demise."

"So we're trapped here?" Kendra asked.

"I'll find a way out," Andromadus said. "At present, I suggest you rest."

The wizard raised his staff and vanished with a red flash.

"Am I correct to understand that we are welcome guests here despite your enormity?" Newel called with a hand beside his mouth.

"That is correct," Thronis said. "And again, I have excellent hearing."

"Have you known many satyrs?" Newel asked in a more regular tone.

"I hesitate to confess that your kind has stayed somewhat beneath my notice," Thronis said. "I have heard of satyrs."

"Great," Doren murmured. "He wasn't onto us. Keep drawing attention."

Newel elbowed his friend. "Satyrs are famously hungry."

Thronis nodded.

"I see now," Doren muttered. "Clever stratagem."

"I have food in abundance for such tiny guests," Thronis said, striding out of the room.

Kendra turned to Tess. "Are you all right?"

"I don't like dragons anymore," Tess said. "The only nice one became a wizard."

"There is another nice one," Kendra said. "The rest are pretty dangerous. Worse now that we're at war with them."

"Can we go home?" Tess asked.

"We can't yet," Kendra said. "Soon, I hope."

Kendra walked over to Patton. "How are you?"

He was panting a little and looked flushed. "I've been better. My body is failing. I managed to free the Luvians before the undead reached the stables. They should be running free. I took the flying mounts to the top of the highest tower. I hoped to swoop in and rescue you, but those dragons were everywhere. I was about to try when Andromadus showed up. Told me to lay low. He went and helped you, then came back for me, the griffins, and the winged horses."

"Thanks for all you've done," Kendra said.

"Wish I could do more," the stingbulb replied.

Thronis returned. He laid a platter on the floor with various offerings, including some green grapes the size of bowling balls, a wedge of cheese that would have barely fit in a bathtub, slices of salami larger than manhole covers, some olives that rivaled the grapes, and several slices of bread that Tess could almost have used as a bed.

"Where did you find such big food?" Knox asked.

"Most of my food is magically augmented," Thronis said. "Staying fed is one of the challenges of being a giant. I keep a greenhouse full of enhanced produce. You'll find the grapes are perfect right now. Enjoy."

"Where should we sleep?" Kendra asked.

"I imagine the girls would prefer separate accommodations?" Thronis asked.

"Sure," Kendra said, deciding some privacy for her and Tess would be nice.

"I can lead you there now if you wish," Thronis said.

"Thank you," Kendra said. She looked at Tess. "You eat, and I'll be right back." Then Kendra jogged to follow the giant into a neighboring room.

Thronis laid out a comforter that looked big enough to cover a swimming pool, then folded it down to a smaller size and placed a sheet on top. "Will this work?"

"That will be great," Kendra said. Folded, the comforter was much thicker than any mattress she had ever rested on.

Thronis strolled out of the room, and Kendra was grateful for the moment alone. She would go eat in a moment, but for now she found herself holding back tears.

Even without his memory, why would Seth have unleashed the undead from the Blackwell? Wyrmroost had fallen. Agad and probably some others of the castle staff had been killed.

"Are you all right?" asked Calvin from her pocket.

"I almost forgot about you," Kendra said.

"I stayed quiet in case you didn't want the giant to know about me," he said.

"Probably smart," Kendra replied.

"Now you know a little more about how I feel," Calvin said. "Being tiny in such a huge world."

"True," Kendra said. "Thronis must look unbelievably big to you."

"Dragons are enormous," Calvin said. "But I've never seen a person more than a fraction of his size. Are you holding up all right?"

"I guess," Kendra said. "Seth and I failed as caretakers."

"You did great," Calvin said.

"We barely lasted a week," Kendra said. "And Seth played the key role in destroying Blackwell Keep."

"He didn't know what he was doing," Calvin said.

"At least now I can look for him," Kendra said. "And Bracken. I guess that is the bright side."

"That's the spirit," Calvin said. "You'll feel better after some food and rest."

"I feel terrible about Agad," Kendra said. "He was so brave. It seems like everything is falling apart."

"Not everything," Calvin said. "Just Wyrmroost. And maybe your family a little."

"I'm not sure if we can fix this," Kendra said. "For now I'm going to focus on finding Seth. It may not be possible, and I might not be able to win him back to our side, but I'll give it all I have."

"It starts with getting some sleep," Calvin said.

Kendra sighed. "I better grab a little food and bring Tess to bed."

"I'd like to try some of that cheese," Calvin said.

"I'm glad you're with me," Kendra said.

"I'm sworn to Seth," Calvin said. "I'm with you until we find him."

"Let's hope he stops freeing the undead."

Prisoner

S eth was making a shadow puppet on the wall when the temperature began to plunge. By the light of the single lantern, the edges of the shadow were crisp as it morphed between an alligator and a dragon depending on how flat he kept his hands. Curling one finger above the others produced an eye, and little changes in the size or shape of that small window of light significantly altered the personality of his creation.

Within a few minutes after the lich had departed, Seth had grown fidgety in the bleak room. He did not want to void their agreement by exiting the chamber, so he sat in sensory-deprived silence staring at bare stone surfaces while wishing he could bring himself to lie down and doze on the hard marble slab. It was just too creepy and uncomfortable for a nap.

Seth did not realize how much colder the lich made the

room until Ezabar returned, his grim skull visible behind the bluish skin of his face. Seth dropped his hands as the lich passed through the doorway, hoping the shadow puppetry hadn't made him look like a little kid.

"Come," Ezabar said.

Seth picked up his lantern and followed the lich, clenching his jaw in an effort to prevent his teeth from chattering. Outside the room, Seth noticed the wraith waiting at a distance and waved. The wraith raised a hand in reply.

"Does the prisoner have a name?" Seth asked.

"Any matters relating to the prisoner are yours to investigate," Ezabar said.

They reached an empty cylindrical cage fashioned from thick bands of intertwined iron. The sole occupant was a bedraggled cat that looked scrawny enough to slip between the bars. The cat's fur rose, back arching as it hissed.

"Is that a stray?" Seth asked. "Did the cat sneak in here?"

"Nothing is in my prison by accident," Ezabar said.

"Why would you lock up a cat?"

The lich gave no reply.

"Unless it isn't just a cat," Seth said.

"This way," Ezabar said.

The corridor expanded into a vast subterranean underscape. Dozens of iron cages stood among the rises and dips of the uneven floor. Many were square or rectangular, some cylindrical, a few almost spherical. The cages ranged from crude to ornate in design, and most looked empty. The few wretched figures Seth could see in cages looked human, but they were hunched on the floor with their backs to Ezabar, heads down, bodies still. Glancing at his lantern, Seth wondered how long it had been since any of the cowering inmates had seen light.

On the far side of a boulder, Ezabar gestured toward a broad cage with a circular base and a sloping, conical top. In the cage stood a young man with extremely fair skin and silver hair reaching his shoulders. His build was surprisingly lean and strong for a dungeon prisoner. Unlike the cringing figures Seth had seen, this prisoner regarded Ezabar defiantly. Then his gaze shifted to Seth.

"Seth?" the prisoner called in a familiar tone. "Could that really be you? Surely this is a ruse."

"This visitor wishes to speak with you," Ezabar said. "He is favored by the Underking, and you will show him the respect he deserves."

The lich turned and walked away, his feet not quite touching the ground. As Ezabar moved away, Seth felt the chill in the air lessening, and some of the anxiety inside of him began to untangle.

The prisoner regarded Seth warily. Seth stepped closer to the bars of the cage, careful to stay out of reach.

"Who are you?" the prisoner asked.

"That is the question," Seth said.

"The real Seth Sorenson would not be here," the prisoner said. "He is fulfilling an assignment far away and has no connection to the Underking. Show me your true form."

"What kind of assignment?" Seth asked.

"Are you an illusion?" the prisoner asked. "Or a replica, like a stingbulb? I can't get a read on you."

"I'm a real person," Seth said. "I'm a kid with no memory of his childhood. I have questions about myself. I was told a prisoner here might know me."

"You can't be the person you look like," the prisoner said. "How did you get here?"

"A wooden puppet put me in a barrel," Seth said.

"Mendigo?" the prisoner asked. "How would one of the barrels have gotten here?"

"You know about barrels that work like teleporters?" Seth asked.

"Dual manifestations of the same barrel," the prisoner said. "You can go into one and get pulled from the other."

"Sounds right," Seth said. "I have almost no memories before coming here. I was in a castle with a girl who called herself Kendra."

"This is an act," the prisoner said, backing away. "Are you telling me you forgot Kendra?"

"Should I remember more about her?" Seth asked. "She claimed to be my sister."

The prisoner stepped forward, stretching one arm out through the bars. "If you're serious, take my hand and grant me full permission to search your mind."

"That doesn't sound smart," Seth said. "Why are you in here?"

"You should know me well," the prisoner said.

"I can't remember anything," Seth said. "I don't know who I can trust."

"I'm in here because my cousin has a score to settle with me," the prisoner said.

"Who is your cousin?" Seth asked.

"Ronodin, the dark unicorn," the prisoner said.

"I know him," Seth said. "He has been tutoring me."

"This is sick," the prisoner said.

"Are you a dark unicorn too?" Seth asked.

"Ronodin is the only dark unicorn," the prisoner said. "I am his cousin, Bracken, a true unicorn, and a friend to you and your sister."

"You mean Kendra?" Seth asked.

"Yes, your only sister, Kendra," Bracken said. He stretched out his hand again. "I'm a unicorn; you can trust me. We don't lie. I'm not trying to trick you or harm you. Let me see your mind. Maybe I can help you remember."

The possibility of this prisoner being able to help him was so enticing that it made Seth wary. "How do I know you're really a unicorn?"

"Did you notice how the presence of the lich did not affect me?" Bracken asked.

"That might just mean you're powerful," Seth said. "Turn into a horse and show me."

"I need my third horn for that," Bracken said.

"Unicorns only have one horn," Seth said.

"You really have forgotten a lot," Bracken said. "We shed our first two horns, kind of like humans losing baby teeth. Kendra has my first horn. Ronodin overpowered me and took my second."

"Where is your third?" Seth asked.

"It is part of a talisman called the Font of Immortality," Bracken said. "Seth, you're searching right now. You came to me because this place doesn't feel right. Go with those instincts. Don't trust a dark unicorn. I'm not sure anyone in the world is less trustworthy than Ronodin."

"I have dark powers," Seth said.

"Of course he would use your powers as evidence," Bracken said. "You're a shadow charmer. You speak arcane languages, you can hide in shadows, you once had an ally who was a demon. But you never chose spiritual darkness, Seth. You fought it. Let me see if I can help you."

Seth looked at the offered hand. He had let Ronodin touch him. This guy seemed sincere. "I still don't know if you're really a unicorn."

"You're choosing the wrong time to be cautious," Bracken said. "I don't get visitors. You may not be allowed to stay long. Look around. Almost everyone in this realm wants to drain your life force. You may be able to communicate with the undead, but your best bet to find an actual friend here is among the prisoners."

"The prisoners are all safe?" Seth asked.

"Absolutely not," Bracken said. "But most of the poor individuals encaged down here are more likely to help you than liches or dark unicorns would be. I truly am a friend of yours, and I know many in your family—unless you are deceiving me. I'll speak more freely when I know you really are who you appear to be."

"Fine," Seth said, taking the outstretched hand. "You can look at my mind. But don't mess with it."

Bracken tightened his grip. His brow furrowed. "You're almost blank. Seth, this really is you."

Seth yanked his hand back. "What can you see?"

"You're not a phony," Bracken said. "You have a lot of general knowledge. But your identity is gone, along with all of your specific memories from before your mind was wiped. It's like you were born this week."

"That's how it feels," Seth said. "Who am I?"

"You're Seth Sorenson," Bracken said. "Co-caretaker of the dragon sanctuary Wyrmroost, alongside your sister, Kendra, and assisted by your grandparents."

"Caretaker of a dragon sanctuary?" Seth asked.

"That's right," Bracken said. "A weighty responsibility for one so young."

"What am I doing here?" Seth asked.

"I can only assume you have been kidnapped by your enemies," Bracken said.

"Ronodin acts like he rescued me," Seth said.

"Look around," Bracken said. "Do you feel rescued? Pay close attention. Do you really think he's your friend?"

"I don't know," Seth said. "Probably not a friend. Maybe a teacher. Or an ally. Either of you could be tricking me."

"It's funny," Bracken said, stepping back from the bars and stretching. "You and I first met in a prison."

"Was I the prisoner?" Seth asked.

"We both were," Bracken said. "Of the Sphinx."

"Wait a minute," Seth said, retreating a couple of paces. "You almost had me going, then you pushed it too far."

"What's so strange about meeting in a prison?" Bracken asked.

"I've only really talked to three people since losing my

memory," Seth said. "You happen to bring up all of them? Kendra, Ronodin, and the Sphinx? She's good, they're bad?"

"When did you see the Sphinx?" Bracken asked.

"Don't play dumb," Seth said. "You saw into my mind when I took your hand. That's why you worked the Sphinx into the conversation."

"I wasn't searching your recent memories," Bracken said. "I don't see everything in an instant. I was checking to see whether it was really you. When did you run into the Sphinx?"

"You're messing with me," Seth said.

"I'm not," Bracken said. "He is a shadow charmer and one of the most dangerous men alive. We fought him together when he tried to open the demon prison, Zzyzx."

"Playing dumb makes you less believable," Seth said. "You saw him helping me."

Bracken came back to the bars and held out a hand. "Take my hand again and I'll look."

"No way," Seth said. "I don't know what you might do to me this time, now that I'm onto you."

"How did the Sphinx help you?" Bracken asked.

"We released some undead from a well," Seth said.

Bracken looked stunned. The reaction seemed authentic. "Not the Blackwell."

"Yes," Seth said.

"Oh, Seth," Bracken said, both hands covering his mouth. "What have you done?"

"The undead were suffering down there," Seth said.

"Blackwell Keep is the central stronghold of Wyrmroost,"

Bracken said. "The sanctuary you swore to protect. Did you give the undead unlimited access?"

"Just the castle and the roads," Seth said.

Bracken flinched. "The roads? Did you see the results?"

"We left quickly," Seth said, feeling uncomfortable. "An old wizard saw us as we left. He told me I had been fooled."

"That is an understatement," Bracken said. "Seth, you cannot trust your captors. Who knows what else they may have you do? You have endangered your sister, your grandparents—all the innocents at Wyrmroost."

Seth hated the implications of what Bracken was telling him. He reminded himself that the supposed unicorn had lots of motivation to lie. His story fit the circumstances, but that would be easy to do after reading Seth's mind. "I see why Ronodin told me you're dangerous."

"Excellent conclusion," Ronodin said, pacing into view from behind the nearby boulder.

"What have you done?" Bracken asked with real anger in his voice.

"Don't be a sore loser, Bracky," Ronodin said. "Seth, it was unwise to come here. You are talking to one of the deadliest con men in the world."

"That's what he said about you," Seth said.

"No surprise," Ronodin said with a smirk. "Mister light-makes-right would purge the world of darkness if he could. He finds your powers disgusting. He'd crush us both like cockroaches, given the chance."

"Ronodin is the liar," Bracken said with intense calm.

Ronodin laughed. "You would tell whatever story might

free you in order to destroy me. I, on the other hand, have spared the life of this criminal, as you can see, Seth. Bound his wounds, locked him up safe and sound."

"You must find out who you are, Seth," Bracken said.

Ronodin raised his eyebrows. "Many voices will try to persuade you of your identity. Your memory loss has been widely publicized. All of your worst enemies will try to win you to their side—Kendra, Bracken, and the rest."

"You're not like Ronodin, Seth," Bracken said. "Watch him control what you see and hear. Study his maneuverings. He's putting on a show, and you are in grave danger of hurting yourself and others."

"Enough of this abusive manipulation," Ronodin said. "I'm not trying to blind or deafen Seth. To the contrary, I'm helping him hone his powers. I'm trying to protect him from liars while he reacquaints himself with his true nature. You are a shadow charmer, Seth. You are here among your kind. According to Bracken, if it waddles like a duck and quacks like a duck, it must be a horse."

"This is low, even for you, Ronodin," Bracken said, his tone furious.

"Few prisoners adore their captors," Ronodin said. "I hold Bracken down here for the good of the world. I hope the day arrives when it will be safe to free him. Come, Seth. You have already spent too much time ingesting this poison."

"Stay sane down here," Seth said, backing away.

"Remember what I told you," Bracken said earnestly.

Seth looked away and didn't look back. They walked around the boulder, and Bracken passed out of view.

"Am I in trouble for coming here?" Seth asked Ronodin.

"I'd rather you hadn't," the dark unicorn said. "I wanted to protect you from the confusion he creates. Bracken is very good at what he does. But you were inevitably going to encounter lies such as he is weaving. Perhaps it was useful to test your will against his make-believe."

"He told me I destroyed the dragon sanctuary that I was supposed to protect," Seth said, still unsettled.

Ronodin laughed. "Forgive me, Seth, but the idea of you as the caretaker of a dragon sanctuary is absurd. You are talented, but you are a young teen. Such positions are given to beings with extensive experience. If Bracken were determined to lie, he could have come up with something less far-fetched. All you did tonight was liberate some captive zombies."

"Bracken said that you're his cousin," Seth said.

"Don't you find it odd that all of these people you don't remember claim to be related to us?"

"Yes."

"I hope you didn't let him touch you," Ronodin said.

Seth scrunched his face. "I did."

"Then you gave him a wealth of information with which to manipulate you," Ronodin said. "At least he's locked up. Steer clear of him in the future."

Seth wasn't sure what to believe. What Bracken had shared sounded plausible. What Ronodin claimed could be true as well. For now, it was probably best to err on siding with the person who was in charge here.

"Avoiding Bracken sounds like good advice," Seth said.

CHAPTER FIFTEEN

Old Friends

When Kendra came into the room where the boys had slept, she found Knox standing on the arm of a divan as if about to jump. Below him on the floor awaited a huge, folded quilt and a plump cushion that would be hard to miss. Newel and Doren stood off to one side watching.

"Knox, don't!" Kendra called.

He looked at his cousin. "I already did one from almost this high."

"That's like a three-story roof!" Kendra called. "Maybe four."

"With a giant fluffy pillow to catch me," Knox said, stepping off and tilting in the air to land flat on his back. The striped cushion enfolded him. After landing, he slid off the cushion wearing a huge smile.

"Excellent form!" Doren called. He glanced at Kendra.

"Assuming you're going to foolishly ignore orders from the former caretaker."

"Knox, you're crazy," Kendra said, trying not to be won over by his smile. "We can't afford for you to get hurt."

"I built up to it," Knox said. "The jump might look dangerous, but it doesn't even hurt."

"What sports do you play?" Kendra asked.

"Basketball and soccer, mostly," Knox said.

"Imagine I'm your coach," Kendra said folding her arms. She raised her voice. "Knox, we can't afford sprained ankles at this point in the season. Cut out the dangerous recreation."

"I think my soccer coach would have jumped too," Knox said.

"Then I'm your basketball coach," Kendra said. "More importantly, I'm your survival coach."

"This is a survival skill," Knox complained, gesturing at the satyrs. "I'm bonding with the team."

"We're strictly bystanders," Newel said.

"We're staying near in case we need to put him back together again," Doren said.

"I'm sure you weren't encouraging him at all," Kendra said.

The satyrs glanced at each other.

"Can't blame a guy for watching a free show," Newel said.

"Hard to beat live entertainment," Doren said.

"Live unless he lands wrong," Kendra said.

"Point taken," Newel said. "Game over."

"But I want to jump off the back!" Knox complained. "It's not much higher than the arm."

"No way," Kendra said. "You're lucky you haven't gotten hurt already."

"As if you're in charge of me!" Knox challenged.

Tanu walked into the large room, toting a generous chunk of cheese. Knox pointed at the potion master. "Tanu didn't mind me jumping!"

"Is there a problem?" Tanu asked uncertainly.

Kendra took a deep breath. Was she just spoiling their fun? Seth would probably think so. Was she trying to force an issue that didn't matter? But the divan was so high! The back had to be at least the equivalent of a four-story building.

"He shouldn't jump from so high," Kendra said. "It's too risky."

"It's a rookie mistake to get hurt outside of real trouble," Calvin called out.

"Listen to Calvin and Kendra," Tanu said. "They have better sense than the rest of us."

"She's not in charge of me," Knox said.

Tanu's face grew grim. "If you want to continue with us in peace, you will listen to her."

Knox looked at Kendra awkwardly, then glanced at the divan. "I guess I can go back to suffering."

"Good idea," Tanu said.

With a flash of red, Andromadus appeared. Calvin ducked into Kendra's pocket. Kendra could hardly believe who materialized along with the wizard.

"Warren?" she cried in disbelief. "Vanessa?"

Warren wore a bowler-style shirt, beige shorts with lots of pockets, and sturdy sandals. He looked tired and lightly sunburned. Vanessa had a deeper tan than usual and wore sleek sportswear on her lithe frame, her hair an enviable tumble of dark curls. Behind them, a long, painted canoe rested on the floor.

"Hey, Kendra," Warren said, hustling over to her and wrapping her up in a tight hug.

"Seth," Kendra said, her voice catching.

"I know," Warren replied.

Kendra felt some of her tensions relax. Somebody who cared about Seth almost as much as she did had arrived. Somebody with experience as an adventurer.

Warren released Kendra, and Vanessa drew her near. Kendra leaned her head on Vanessa's shoulder.

"I'm sorry, Kendra," she said.

"You came," Kendra said.

"As quickly as we could," Vanessa assured her.

Kendra stepped away from the hug. Vanessa was a narcoblix, and she had once plotted against Kendra and her family. After biting people, she could control them in their sleep. At one point Vanessa had exercised control over Tanu, but Bracken had broken the connection.

"Bitten anyone lately?" Kendra asked.

"Only those who deserved it," Vanessa said with an enigmatic smile.

"Your hair is curlier," Kendra said.

Vanessa pinched a few strands. "Humidity does it every time."

"Tanu!" Warren called.

The big Samoan shuffled over and embraced him. "Good to see you're still in one piece," Tanu said.

"We've been through a lot," Warren admitted.

Tanu glanced at Vanessa. "I was referring to your choice of partner."

"Warren will never be safer than with me," Vanessa said.

"Hello, Miss Santoro," Newel said, extending a hand stiffly.

"You're looking well," Doren added, taking his turn to shake her hand.

Kendra couldn't help smiling. She knew the satyrs had massive crushes on Vanessa and often spoke in hushed wonder about her intoxicating beauty.

"Who's the kid?" Warren asked.

"My cousin Knox," Kendra said. "He and his sister, Tess, are with us."

"That's a surprise," Warren said. "Are they . . . seasoned?"

"I'm learning fast," Knox said. "I was partly turned to gold."

"Sounds like a good way to get your feet wet," Warren said.

"He was healed," Newel explained.

"We lost Agad," Kendra said. "Wyrmroost has fallen."

"Andromadus gave us the headlines," Vanessa said.

"I didn't make the headlines?" Knox complained.

Warren scratched his cheek. "It usually takes extreme tragedy. You healed."

"And I'm Calvin," came a voice from Kendra's pocket. "I sometimes lie low, but it looks like we're all friends here."

Warren stepped near and peered at Kendra's pocket. "A nipsie?"

"A giant nipsie, thanks to a spell," Calvin said. "I'm sworn to Seth, but I'm traveling with Kendra until we find him."

"We'll take all the help we can get," Warren said.

"How did you get here?" Kendra asked.

"Wasn't easy," Warren said. "We came from Crescent Lagoon."

"The island dragon sanctuary?" Kendra asked.

"It fell for a time," Vanessa said. "We helped restore a safe haven for the caretaker."

"Most of the archipelago remains fallen," Warren said. "There is still a lot of work to do."

"Can the dragons leave?" Knox asked.

"They could have, for a time," Warren said. "We're pretty sure none took advantage of the opportunity. When we reestablished a haven for the caretaker, the boundary barriers were restored."

"Will the protection hold?" Kendra asked.

"Hopefully until we can find a more permanent solution," Warren said.

"The dragons can leave Wyrmroost?" Knox asked.

"At their leisure," Andromadus said.

"Raxtus found us," Warren said. "He told us about the trouble at Wyrmroost."

"Last night," Vanessa said, "as your keep was falling."

"How did Raxtus get there?" Knox asked. "We're nowhere near the ocean."

"Raxtus was hatched by fairies," Warren said. "He can travel between fairy shrines. The shrines at Wyrmroost and Crescent Lagoon were some of the first to be reconnected to the fairy realm."

"Raxtus carried us and the canoe through to Wyrmroost," Vanessa said. "By the time we arrived, the keep had fallen. We hid at the fairy shrine until Andromadus found us."

"I was hoping to find a home for the refugees of Wyrmroost," Andromadus said. "Somebody to take them away. Turned out I just needed a little patience. They came to me."

"Is the canoe like the barrels?" Kendra asked.

"There is a matching canoe at Crescent Lagoon," Warren said. "We can use this canoe to go straight there."

"We're going to an island?" Kendra asked.

"Right now it's the only reasonable way out of here," Warren said.

"And we think you may be extra motivated to come," Vanessa said.

"Why?" Kendra asked.

"We believe Ronodin has recently visited Crescent Lagoon," Warren said. "The islands have ten sacred pools of pure water where pixies play and naiads dwell. Yesterday one was corrupted."

"And you think the most likely culprit is Ronodin," Tanu said.

"Why him?" Knox asked.

"Just as a regular unicorn has the power to purify, Ronodin has the ability to corrupt," Warren said. "Even though the preserve fell, the pools have power of their own to withstand tampering. There could be another explanation, but Ronodin is the top suspect."

"We know Ronodin has Bracken," Kendra said, "and maybe could tell us something about Seth as well."

"Seems like our only lead, based on what Andromadus told us," Warren said.

"The Crescent Lagoon sanctuary almost fell," Kendra said.

"It did fall," Vanessa said. "We reclaimed a small portion."

"How?" Kendra asked.

"Sanctuaries are organized in different ways," Warren said. "They were established by teams of wizards using various methods. The treaty at Crescent Lagoon is upheld by one hundred moai. Do you know that word?"

Kendra shook her head.

"Easter Island heads," Tanu said.

"Yes," Warren said. "Upright statues with huge noggins. On the island of Timbuli stands a ring of ten—the Grand Moai. They surround a stone altar where the Sunset Pearl once rested in a basin. We're talking a magic pearl the size of a softball. Despite its being guarded by three cyclopses and a bunch of magical protections, the dragons stole the pearl, and all the guardian moai went dormant."

"Did anyone find the pearl?" Kendra asked.

"I wish," Warren said. "Most of the sanctuary remains undefended. Other than the ten Grand Moai, ninety other moai populate the islands."

"It's an archipelago?" Kendra asked.

"What's that mean?" Newel muttered.

"I think it's a musical term," Doren replied.

"It's a chain of islands," Calvin said.

"There are more than fifty," Warren said. "Many of them are small, though several are quite large. The main stronghold was on the island Kusaka. I managed to reactivate a single moai on the island of Timbuli. It happens to be the moai overlooking Crescent Lagoon, for which the sanctuary is named."

"How did you reactivate the statue?" Kendra asked.

"The moai require the sacrifice of your most precious physical possession," Warren said. "A person or animal doesn't count. The offering doesn't need lots of intrinsic value, so long as it matters most to the giver."

"Some people don't have an item that clearly means more than all others," Vanessa said. "I couldn't think of one."

Knox faced Warren. "What did you use?"

"My Carson Sears rookie card," Warren said.

"Never heard of him," Knox said.

"He was my dad's friend," Warren said. "We called him Uncle Carson. He only played for three innings in the major leagues. His one at bat was supposed to be a sacrifice bunt, but he beat the throw and got a single, so he has a perfect career batting average. My dad had the card printed. I kept it with me as a good luck charm."

"But you gave it to a statue," Kendra said.

"Put it right in the mouth," Warren said. "The mouth closes if the offering is acceptable. Then it opens once the offering is consumed."

"So the preserve is okay now?" Knox asked.

"Warren's offering was a short-term solution," Vanessa said. "It temporarily appeased a single moai guarding a limited area. The Sunset Pearl is the object the moai consider most precious. When the pearl was on the altar, no other offerings were required."

"We have to find the pearl," Kendra said.

"We're working on it," Warren said. "And we wouldn't mind help. But we also need to figure out why Ronodin corrupted one of the sacred pools."

"And learn if Bracken or Seth might be nearby," Kendra said.

"Or at least catch Ronodin and make him divulge their location," Vanessa said.

"I like it," Tanu said. "When can we leave?"

"With the canoe here, we can go whenever you want," Warren said. "And if needed we can retreat back to Thronis."

"Great," Kendra said. "My vote is we leave now."

"Leave where?" Tess asked, coming into the room, her hair disheveled from sleeping. "What's going on?"

"We're going to the beach," Knox said.

Tess brightened. "Will Mom and Dad be there?"

"No," Knox said. "Just more danger and dragons."

Tess shrugged. "Still might be fun to make a sand castle."

CHAPTER SIXTEEN

Mission

Seth jumped and turned when the door to his room opened without warning. Ronodin wore a gray cloak, tall boots, and heavy gloves. A second cloak was draped over one arm.

"Want to see some daylight?" the dark unicorn asked.

"Yes," Seth said. "The sun was beginning to feel like a fable."

"Don't get too excited," Ronodin said. "It's gloomy out. But real daylight is filtering through the mist."

"Good enough," Seth said, catching the thrown cloak. He wrapped the heavy garment around his shoulders as he followed Ronodin from the room. "I wondered if I'd ever see the surface here. I thought it might always be a mystery."

"The entrance to the Under Realm is a secret known only to a select few," Ronodin said.

"We're by the ocean, right?"

"Wait and see," Ronodin said.

Their way wound upward until they reached a ladder of iron rungs that climbed a vertical shaft comparable to the inside of a chimney. Ronodin started upward and Seth came after, glancing up occasionally at the soles of his teacher's boots, but mostly keeping his face down to avoid the gritty particles the dark unicorn was dislodging.

Fifty rungs later, Ronodin paused and threw open a trapdoor overhead, admitting muted gray light. He pulled himself up, then turned and extended a hand to Seth, hauling him out of the murky shaft.

Seth now stood high atop an ancient fort composed of rough, ill-fitted stone, next to a thick parapet overlooking a coastline. Slow mist curled around angular rocks and encompassed crumbling, bulky fortifications. With each inhalation, Seth smelled the salty scents of the sea mingling with the fresh moisture of the mist. The gray ocean surged and growled below, sinking and receding only to return with new vigor, attacking tide-sculpted formations with explosions of foamy spray.

"An ocean," Seth confirmed.

"The Pacific," Ronodin replied. "This uncharted isle guards the entrance to a realm very few would deliberately seek."

"Lucky us," Seth said.

"Aren't we, though?" Ronodin said. "Striding with impunity where the brave dare not tread? This way."

He paced along the top of the fort and down some stone

steps that led to a projection of rock overhanging the tumultuous waves. Further along the cliff, Seth spotted a couple of figures shuffling toward them through the mist, coming into clearer focus with every step.

"There are people here?" Seth asked.

"Depends on your definition," Ronodin said. "The people of the deep help guard this isle. They are the Underking's elite zombies, more powerful and deliberate than others of their kind."

One of the men coming toward them wore homespun clothes and was partially tangled in a fishing net. Another wore the tattered remnants of a sailor's uniform. Both appeared to have drowned long ago.

"Will they bother us?" Seth asked.

"Not while we're guests of the Underking," Ronodin said. "Unlike wraiths or revenants, they lack the faculties to really communicate with us. They primarily hear their king. Their own primitive thoughts are dominated by hunger."

Ronodin sat down, resting his hands on his knees, studying the restless water. After a final wary glance at the sea zombies, Seth sat beside the dark unicorn.

"How big is this island?" Seth asked.

"Not very large, though you can seldom see all of it. The mist is a nearly permanent feature."

"Are you showing me I can't run away?" Seth asked.

"You think this ocean is a problem?" Ronodin exclaimed incredulously, waving a dismissive hand at the water. "You can't escape because of the Underking."

Seth glanced at the ghostly manacle on his wrist. "Why are we here?"

"That's a profound question. Some say to master our wills."

"On the surface," Seth clarified.

"I thought you could use a little time under the sky," Ronodin said. "I don't mind the dark, but it gets tiresome. We're not dead. Variety helps."

"Why did you lock up your cousin?" Seth asked. "What did he do?"

"Are you still dwelling on him?" Ronodin asked. "I tried to warn you that he is dangerous."

"He made some good arguments," Seth said.

"Many will have persuasive arguments," Ronodin said. "Pay attention to who you are and who you want to become. If you let other people run your life, you'll never have more identity than a puppet."

"Why did you imprison him?"

"Bracken is my enemy," Ronodin said. "He lives to eradicate darkness. He has destroyed many of my friends and allies. He is a talented killer. He has captured and imprisoned others whom I respect. He estranged me from my family. He vilifies me wherever he goes. What is the ultimate triumph when you have an enemy? Capture him. I didn't maim him or kill him. I simply took Bracken out of circulation."

"He wanted me to help him get free," Seth said. "He talked like he was an old friend of mine. Had an elaborate story."

"Bracken can be extremely convincing," Ronodin said.

"You chose to seek him out. Now you must sort through the information he planted in your mind."

"You plant information too," Seth said.

"All yours to weigh and categorize," Ronodin said. "The Underking has a mission for us."

"More wraiths to release?" Seth asked.

"This one is different," Ronodin said. "We'll do it together. On a nearby island."

"How will we get there?" Seth asked.

"By boat," Ronodin said.

"Do you know how to captain a boat?" Seth asked.

"I know how to do almost everything," Ronodin said. "I have been around for a very long time."

"Why are you helping the Underking?" Seth asked.

Ronodin looked around, then held up a hand, palm outward. "I'm shielding our conversation. Seth, I don't care one bit about the Underking. If I could dethrone him, I would in a heartbeat. I would laugh as I threw his crown in the ocean."

"Then why help him?" Seth asked.

"Favors are the main currency in the magical world," Ronodin said. "The Underking has been useful to me, so I owe him favors. If it ever became convenient for him to destroy me, or you, do you think he would hesitate? Not for a heartbeat."

"What are you really after?" Seth asked. "How is the Underking helping you?"

"I don't like the idea of anyone ruling over somebody else," Ronodin said. "No one should be oppressed."

"Aren't you oppressing Bracken?" Seth asked.

"Bracken works for the oppressors," Ronodin said. "He works to keep wide varieties of magical creatures imprisoned. I only have him locked up so I can free others."

"That's all you want?" Seth asked.

"It's all I ask for myself," Ronodin said. "Unconditional freedom to go where I want when I want and to do what I want. I use my freedom to grant freedom to others. Right now the long-oppressed dragons yearn for liberation, so I'm helping them. If they, in turn, oppress others, I will work against them."

"You're the friend of the underdog," Seth said. "I like that."

"It never ends, Seth," Ronodin said. "Most of the world craves power over others. One tyrant falls and ten clamor to replace him. Or her. Humans, dragons, demons, giants— you name the person or the creature, they are almost always working to control somebody else. I fight against that trend."

"That's why you wanted to free the undead from the Blackwell?" Seth asked.

"They had been pent up for centuries," Ronodin said. "They deserved freedom. It indirectly also helped free some dragons."

"Was I at a dragon sanctuary?" Seth asked.

"Depends on who you ask," Ronodin said. "I would call it a dragon prison."

"Are any of Bracken's statements true?" Seth asked.

"Was I supposed to protect that dragon prison? Did I have a role there? Is Kendra really my sister?"

"You have a complex history," Ronodin said. "You had been to that dragon prison before. There were times when it suited your purposes to work with Kendra and some of the humans. You also worked with the Sphinx and some demons, most notably Graulas, one of the most cunning demons in history."

"I partnered with a demon?" Seth asked.

"Until you double-crossed and killed him," Ronodin said.

"Are you serious?" Seth asked.

"Absolutely true," Ronodin said. "The demon hadn't dealt fairly with you either. But when do they? I don't blame you for it."

"My history sounds confusing," Seth said.

"So is your present," Ronodin said. "But your future doesn't have to be."

"What do you want from me?" Seth asked.

"I want you to learn all you can," Ronodin said. "Your powers mustn't go to waste. Or get muzzled by the light-makes-right brigade. I'd like to see you survive the Underking and earn your freedom. I'd appreciate your help with the coming adventures. But mostly I want you to develop to your highest potential."

"What's our mission on the island?" Seth said.

"We're looking for a flower," Ronodin said.

"Really?" Seth asked.

"Orders from our bloodless sovereign," Ronodin said. "He has requested a certain flower from the island."

"Why?"

Ronodin dropped his hand. "It's known as the Everbloom. This flower never dies. The Underking wants to feed off its vitality."

"Are there many of these flowers?" Seth asked.

"The Everbloom is singular," Ronodin said.

Seth leaned in. "When you lower your hand, can the Underking hear us?"

"I doubt it," Ronodin said. "He likely could if he cared to listen. I was just being cautious."

"How do we find the Everbloom?"

"I have unearthed an old crypt on the island," Ronodin said. "We need you to go inside, find a phantom called Dezia, and learn the location of the Everbloom. I tried to go in with the Sphinx but we couldn't get past the guards."

"You think I can?" Seth asked.

"I hope so," Ronodin said. "I'm not a shadow charmer, and the Sphinx has lost a lot of his power. I can only command the undead here on the isle because I have authority from the Underking. His power bridges the gap for me. Off this island, I can't communicate with the undead."

"This mission comes from the Underking?" Seth asked.

"Yes," Ronodin said. "In fact, he wanted me to once again offer you the chance to remain in the Under Realm. I know of no shadow charmer to have received that honor in more than a thousand years. It could be an opportunity to acquire tremendous power."

"I'm not sure I want the kind of power the Underking has to give," Seth said quietly. "Did you know he offered me his crown?"

Ronodin held up a hand, palm outward. "Are you serious?"

"Yeah."

"That is highly unusual," Ronodin said. "Almost unbelievable."

"He told me I could outlast the stars," Seth said. "But I think if I was like him, I would just want to die."

"You have touched on the problem with the undead," Ronodin said. "They're so intent on persisting, on enduring, it seems they forget to consider whether theirs is an existence worth having."

"Right," Seth said.

"You wouldn't *outlive* the stars, because you wouldn't be alive," Ronodin said. "Perhaps you could outlast them, and acquire staggering power. I believe those who are undead by choice are driven by fear. They are so afraid to stop existing that they cling to a nightmare."

"I'd rather take my chances with what might come next," Seth said.

"An offer to wear one of the five crowns would tempt anyone," Ronodin said.

"Not me," Seth replied.

"Probably wise," Ronodin said. He lowered his hand and stood. "You'll join me on the mission?"

Seth looked up at the dark unicorn. Ronodin seemed to have good reasons for how he lived, and he had taught Seth a lot already. He had also brought Seth to an island where the Underking had fastened a ghostly chain to him. Was that the action of somebody who wanted everyone free? Until Seth was liberated from the Underking, he wasn't sure he had much choice but to play along. At least it sounded like this latest mission wouldn't endanger others.

"Do I have much choice?" Seth asked.

"You could choose to die instead," Ronodin said. "You could choose to participate halfheartedly. Your best chance to succeed and survive is to perform these tasks enthusiastically and well."

"I'll come," Seth said, standing up and brushing off his backside.

"I'll appreciate the company," Ronodin said. "Ready to head back down? The mist is thickening."

"Aren't we going in a boat?"

"Later."

Seth looked around. The day was dimmer. He could see only half as far compared to earlier. Indistinct human shapes haunted the grayness at the limits of visibility.

"Let's go back under," Seth said with a last glance at the crashing waves. It might be dark underground, but at least he could look forward to a boat ride.

CHAPTER SEVENTEEN

Tree House

Strong hands helped Kendra to her feet and supported her as she stepped out of the canoe. In an instant, after lying flat as if in a coffin, she had gone from a mountaintop at Wyrmroost to a beach curving around a placid lagoon protected by a long reef. It had recently rained, so the sand beneath her boots was damp, but the heavy clouds were clearing, unveiling a bright sun, and the fronds of the palm trees sparkled with droplets. The fresh, salt-tinged air was humid and warm.

The hands belonged to a shirtless redhead with freckly shoulders and a white coral necklace who looked like he should have a surfboard stashed nearby. Vanessa had already come through, and she greeted Kendra with a grin.

"This is Grady," Vanessa said.

The young man gave Kendra a smile and shook her

hand with both of his. "Welcome to Crescent Lagoon," he said. Then he turned and started hoisting Knox from the canoe.

"It's a paradise," Kendra said, her eyes sweeping the turquoise lagoon and the distant waves breaking against the reef.

"Don't let the beauty fool you," Vanessa said.

"Is that the moai?" Knox asked, pointing.

Kendra turned to face the looming statue, a long, grim face of stone with a jutting brow, the head larger than the rest of the body. She had an eerie feeling that it was aware of her. From base to top it had to be almost three times her height.

"He's the last one awake on the island," Grady said. "This lagoon is safe thanks to him."

"Just the lagoon?" Kendra asked.

"Out to the reef," Grady said. "Beyond that, you're on your own. Same if you head up the beach and around the point in either direction. Or if you trek inland more than a few hundred yards."

Grady hauled Tess out of the canoe, holding her in the air with one hand, muscles clenching in his shoulder until he set her down on the sand. She spun around, eyes wide.

"Why didn't I bring my swimsuit?" she cried.

"You need to be careful swimming here," Vanessa warned.

"She would be fine with me watching," Grady said. "I've spent a lot of time in these waters." He reached into the canoe and helped Tanu out. "I caught a big one."

"Thanks," Tanu said. "I've always wanted to visit this sanctuary."

"Welcome," Grady said. He crouched and pulled out Newel. "A satyr?"

"This is nice," Newel said. "Like a resort on television. Do you have any lounge chairs?"

"We could probably find some," Grady said, giving Doren a hand out.

"Now we're talking," Doren said. "Where can I get a piña colada?"

"How many more satyrs are coming?" Grady asked.

"Just us," Newel said.

"Let me guess," Doren said. "Satyrs are not endemic to these islands."

"Correct," Grady said.

"We promise not to take over," Newel said.

"We'll leave plenty of space for the native species," Doren said.

"Especially if you keep us fed," Newel added.

Grady pulled Warren from the canoe.

"I'm the caboose," Warren said.

"I wish Marat was coming," Knox said. "Couldn't hurt to have at least one dragon on our side."

"He felt like he needed to watch over Wyrmroost," Kendra said. "It's been his home for centuries. He feels allegiance to the protected territories that sided with us. I'm glad he'll be there to help them against the dragons."

"The borders of the territories are still strong," Tanu said.

"Yes, but now they're surrounded and unconnected," Kendra said. "They need a strong ally who can bridge the gaps between them."

Warren grabbed one end of the painted canoe, and Grady lifted the other. They started trudging inland over the sand.

"You're going to love the tree house," Vanessa said to Kendra.

"Tree house?" Tess asked.

"Look," Vanessa said, pointing ahead.

As Kendra focused behind the moai, amid the treetops, she saw structures cunningly crafted to blend with the leaves and branches. She noted platforms with railings, some with roofs, and walkways between them, with rope ladders connecting different levels.

"It's big," Knox said. "And hidden."

"You have no idea," Grady said. "We call it the Monkey Maze. The tree house goes on and on. And there are no dead ends. Everything loops. If you think you reached a dead end, you're missing something."

"Wouldn't the structure get messed up as the trees grow?" Knox asked.

"That's why we work with hamadryads," Grady said. "Especially Azalea, the mistress of this grove. Over the years, the Monkey Maze has adapted to the shifting environment, endlessly refined by the menehune and hamadryads."

"Menehune?" Kendra asked.

"Hairy little dwarfs," Tanu said. "Surprisingly strong.

Sort of the island version of brownies. They specialize in building."

"I want to go up there so badly," Tess said.

The closer they got to the trees, the more platforms Kendra could discern. Several appeared to be isolated, unconnected to the others, but Kendra suspected there must be a way to reach them, based on what Grady had explained.

Under the trees, droplets from the recent rainfall continued to percolate downward. Thanks to the warm air, Kendra found the cool drippings more refreshing than bothersome. She appreciated the lush green smell beneath the leaf shade. Having never been to a real jungle before, she found the smooth, wide trunks and fancifully sprawling limbs captivating, along with the dangling vines and intricate ferns. A glossy yellow frog with wavy black markings sprang from a tree trunk into a bush.

"Here we are," Grady said, pointing out a platform on the ground with a waist-high pole at each corner. Taut ropes connected the tops of the poles around the perimeter of the platform, apparently for safety, and other ropes stretched up into the leafy heights from each corner pole and from the center of the floor. Green, leaflike patterns disguised the ropes, and the wood of the platform matched the surrounding tree trunks. "How about one adult and the three kids?"

"Come on," Vanessa said, stepping over one of the guard ropes. Kendra ducked onto the platform. Knox placed a hand on a pole and, kicking his legs out sideways, jumped the rope.

"Is it like an elevator?" Tess asked as she ducked the rope like Kendra.

"A primitive elevator," Grady said. "You'll feel more secure if you hold the central line."

They all placed a hand on the rope rising from the center. Then Tess added her second hand. Kendra considered adding her free hand, but Vanessa's casual stance convinced her to refrain.

"Now think of your favorite treat," Grady said.

"Hot fudge ice cream cake," Tess said.

Grady pulled a lever, and the platform started rising. After the initial lurch, Kendra was relieved to find the ascent smooth and steady. Soon the ground was only partially visible as limbs and leaves crowded them. As they got higher, Kendra noticed a rope moving through a series of pulleys off to one side, along with a metal counterweight that fell as they climbed. Kendra tried not to picture ropes snapping, and she squeezed the central line a little tighter.

After decelerating, the simple elevator jerked to a stop, level with a much larger platform shaded by a thatched roof and enclosed by a chest-high guardrail. A bright yellow and blue parrot roosted on a perch, and Kendra noticed two large hammocks among the wicker furnishings. Four walkways branched out from the platform, two of them sturdy, with wooden guardrails, the others flimsier and held together by ropes.

Once they stepped off the elevator, it started back down. Knox stood by the edge, watching its descent.

"I get how a counterweight could make it rise," Knox said. "But how is it going back down?"

"By releasing the counterweight?" Kendra guessed.

"Then they would need another counterweight to raise the next load," Knox said.

"Maybe they have one," Kendra said. "Or a bunch."

"Where is everyone?" Tess asked. "I see lots of tree houses but no people."

Kendra looked around. At least ten other major platforms were in view, some higher than theirs, some lower, but she saw no other inhabitants.

"It's mostly deserted," Vanessa said. "After the pearl was stolen, those living in Spring Fort, the Scarlet Tower, and the Monkey Maze fled to the villages."

"There are villages?" Knox asked.

"Ten," Vanessa said. "Though smaller, they operate like the protected territories at Wyrmroost."

"Hard to believe anything bad could happen here," Kendra said. "It feels like paradise."

"When the sanctuary fell, the dragons could have torched these tree houses," Vanessa said. "They seemed more interested in assembling. Many had been confined to separate islands. I think they wanted to size each other up and plot together. The majority gathered to Wanai, the northernmost isle."

The elevator reached the top again, carrying Newel and Doren. Both of the satyrs looked a bit pale and uncertain.

"Are you all right?" Kendra asked.

"We do our best work down on the ground," Newel said,

stepping off the elevator and moving toward the center of the platform, near the tree trunk.

"I've never minded a climb," Doren said, a step behind Newel. "But living like a bird in a lofty nest seems a bit unnatural."

"Heights get to me, too," Kendra said.

Tess flopped into a hammock and giggled as it rocked. Kendra wanted to try the other one, but Knox beat her to it, so she wandered over to the parrot. She was tempted to pet its bright feathers, but the hooked beak looked thick and strong.

The elevator returned one last time bearing Warren and Tanu. Not long after they appeared, Grady vaulted the railing onto the tree-house floor.

"How did you get up?" Knox asked.

"I have ways," Grady said. "The caretaker is eager to meet you."

Knox and Tess slid out of the hammocks, and the group followed Grady along walkways from one platform to another. He mostly used stable, level walkways, but one long rope bridge swayed and bounced beneath their feet enough that the satyrs wore grimaces the entire way.

At last they reached a conspicuously large tree with stairs winding up and around the mighty trunk. Kendra and the others spiraled higher until they came through a large hatch in a floor and entered the only completely enclosed platform Kendra had seen. Larger than most of the other living spaces, this one had shuttered windows, wooden furniture, and five lanterns.

A detailed map hung on one wall, almost from the floor to the ceiling, depicting a curved chain of islands. In front of the map stood a Polynesian woman of medium height, her back to them, dressed in a simple floral wrap that showed off her toned shoulders and calves. She turned and smiled as they entered, the striking ferocity in her eyes lending an aggressive edge to her beautiful face, a ring of woven leaves surrounding her head.

"Welcome to Crescent Lagoon," she said, the words clearly enunciated in a way that made her English sound particularly well-learned. "I am Savani. This is the hallowed island of Timbuli. Ordinarily I would have greeted you on Kusaka in the Spring Fort." She looked directly at Kendra. "You must be the former caretaker of Wyrmroost."

"Yes," Kendra said. "The sanctuary has fallen."

Savani gave a small bow. "This sanctuary had fallen until Warren and Vanessa awakened Taki, the moai who watches over our Monkey Maze and the Crescent Lagoon. As long as one moai remains active, the outer boundary of the sanctuary remains engaged. While Taki endures, no dragons can enter or exit our sanctuary."

"That should keep Celebrant away for now," Kendra said.

"You worry about the Dragon King," Savani said.

"He is waging a war," Kendra said. "I know he wants to destroy me. Right now my priority is finding my brother and helping your sanctuary survive."

"Warren used a baseball card to appease the moai," Knox interjected.

"So I understand," Savani replied. "The offering was consumed within hours, but it bought me time to prepare an offering of my own."

"What did you give?" Kendra asked.

"The tablets containing the history of my people," Savani said.

"You lost your history?" Kendra asked.

"The tablets have been copied many times," Savani said. "Our history is not gone. But the original tablets were my most precious possession. My people entrusted the sacred records to my care."

"Who are your people?" Tess asked.

"The firewalkers," Savani said. "We appease Baga Loa, the great volcano of these islands. She is hidden by the clouds today. Perhaps she will emerge later. My people have served her for generations, helping anticipate and moderate her eruptions. Though the tablets represent our past, it was not worth clinging to them if doing so jeopardized our future."

"Will the tablets satisfy the moai for long?" Kendra asked.

"I can read the moai to a degree," Savani said. "Taki will be content with my offering for at least another couple of weeks. The moai were never meant to be kept awake by individual offerings. That aspect is for emergencies. The only way to truly reclaim this sanctuary will be to find the Sunset Pearl and appease all of the moai."

"Have you any idea where to find the pearl?" Tanu asked.

"Our best efforts have yielded no leads," Savani said. "I lost many of my most trusted companions when the sanctuary fell. Some perished in the chaos when the boundaries disappeared. Others have vanished since then while hunting the pearl. I hold out hope that some of my friends may have taken refuge in the villages or found other secure hiding places."

"We've tried to help in the pearl hunt," Warren said. "So far we keep coming up empty."

"Are there fairies on the islands?" Kendra asked.

"You can find a fairy shrine right here on Timbuli," Savani said. "Many exotic varieties of sprites and fairies thrive in the tropics."

"Fairies listen to me," Kendra said. "I could have them help in the search."

"I see that you are fairykind," Savani said.

"How?" Kendra asked.

"Surely you have met others with eyes to recognize your splendor," Savani said. "You shine so brightly. You carry more magical energy than any mortal I have met."

Kendra knew that Bracken talked about her that way. "It sometimes surprises me to hear that. I can't see it."

"You are unique," Savani said. "Your aid is most appreciated. The shrine and Pixie Falls are reliable places to find fairies on this island. The fairies have not approached any of the fairy feeders near the Monkey Maze since the sanctuary fell."

"Isn't it dangerous to go beyond the area protected by the moai?" Knox asked. "Can't a dragon attack us?"

"Within the sanctuary, dragons are now free to roam everywhere except the little region Taki protects," Savani said. "The triclops drove the dragons from this island and killed at least five of them. Now the triclops is the menace."

"Was the triclops freed when the boundaries came down?" Kendra asked.

"Indirectly," Savani said. "Mombatu the triclops was the designated Dragon Slayer of Crescent Lagoon. He had been in hibernation for so long that many of us questioned whether he still lived. But once the dragons ran wild, Mombatu returned."

"Doesn't he protect you?" Kendra asked.

"He would attack a dragon before he would attack us," Savani said. "But Mombatu is savage, and a danger to anyone who comes near him, including me. Legend tells that the original caretaker of Crescent Lagoon could calm Mombatu with a flute, but the method has been lost."

"Newel and Doren play the flute," Knox said.

"Don't mind the boy," Newel said.

"His brain has gone soft with all the danger," Doren maintained.

"But I heard you talking about—" Knox complained.

"Satyrs speak nonsense at all hours of the day," Newel interrupted smoothly.

"Our boasts should seldom be taken seriously," Doren said.

"Calming Mombatu requires a magical flute," Savani said.

"That makes our rudimentary piping skills even less relevant," Newel said.

"We'll try to stop interrupting the conversation," Doren said, giving Knox a glare.

"You satyrs are a welcome novelty on our island," Savani said. "Tanu's reputation precedes him. And who is the young man?"

"I'm Knox, and this is my sister, Tess. We just barely learned about magical stuff."

"Welcome," Savani said. "Any other visitors I should know about?"

"Just me," Calvin said from Kendra's pocket. "Calvin the nipsie."

"A miniature surprise," Savani said. "May the island treat you kindly."

"We understand a sacred pool was corrupted," Kendra said. "Warren mentioned that Ronodin is a suspect."

"It appears to be his handiwork," Savani said. "A menehune spotted him in the area shortly after the pool was spoiled."

"My brother was abducted by enemies of Dragonwatch," Kendra said. "We know the Sphinx was involved, and Ronodin has worked with him in the past. Also, Ronodin was at Wyrmroost near the time my brother vanished. My brother had just lost his memories when he was taken. We want to find Ronodin to see what he knows."

"Few are more slippery than Ronodin," Savani said. "We still don't know why the pool was corrupted. Hako the hunter plans to visit the site this afternoon to see what he can learn."

"Who remains of your staff?" Tanu asked.

"You met Grady, and I just mentioned Hako, our game-keeper," Savani said. "Uma is frail and in a wheelchair, but she might interest you, potion master."

"Not Uma Stormbrewer," Tanu said.

"The same," Savani said. "She joined our staff after her legs gave out. She is quite old but remains sharp."

"The thought of meeting her makes me shy," Tanu said. "I'll need to brew myself a courage potion. She is one of the grand masters of potion making."

"There are also a handful of the menehune who interact with me," Savani said. "It took long years to cultivate their trust."

"This is a big tree house for four people," Tess said. "And a few dwarfs."

"More than a few dwarfs," Savani said. "The menehune are not often seen, but they quietly keep all in order here. Still, the Monkey Maze was designed for many more oc-cupants. Even at its peak, this tree community never ap-proached full capacity, but now it feels abandoned."

"I want to go with Hako to check out the sacred pool," Kendra said.

"Are you sure?" Vanessa asked.

"Definitely, if there is any chance it could help us find Seth," Kendra said.

"The dragons are gone from this island?" Knox asked.

"I suppose they could return," Savani said. "But the chances seem slight as long as the triclops is rampaging."

"The triclops must be really big," Tess said.

"He's almost a force of nature," Savani said. "Mombatu may prove more hazardous than the dragons."

"I understand the dragons here tend to be smaller," Tanu said.

"It depends where you go," Grady said.

"The islands host many smaller cliff-dwelling and tree-dwelling dragons," Savani said. "Some are small enough to hunt in groups. None of those rival the great dragons at a sanctuary like Wyrmroost. But do not forget the sea serpents and the sea dragons. Very few dragons can match some of those in scale."

"Sea serpents?" Knox asked.

"Some are longer than any dragon I have heard about," Savani said. "Over ninety-nine percent of this sanctuary is ocean. Our largest occupants are under the water, and those boundaries extend beyond sight of the islands."

"I don't want to swim anymore," Tess said.

"Crescent Lagoon is actually quite safe if you are supervised," Savani said. "I don't mean the entire sanctuary—I refer specifically to the lagoon for which the sanctuary is named. I learned to swim there, as have many others."

"I'll think about it," Tess said.

"Have you examined the site where the Sunset Pearl was kept?" Tanu asked.

"Hako went there with Warren," Savani said.

"We didn't find much," Warren said. "Ten really big

moai in a ring facing inward. An altar of piled stones at the center with a bowl on top. Supposedly three guardians protected the pearl, but there was no sign of them. There were tracks from the triclops, though."

"Who were the guardians?" Calvin asked. "Could they have taken the pearl?"

"They were secretive, with a reputation for being calm and wise," Savani said. "Losing the pearl may have destroyed them."

"Could the triclops have taken it?" Kendra asked.

Warren shook his head. "Mombatu didn't appear until after the pearl was long gone."

"Maybe we'll find some clues at the pool," Kendra said. "And maybe I'll find a few fairies along the way."

Tanu stretched and groaned. "I would like to consult with Uma before we go. I have dragon parts she may find interesting."

"I expect she will," Savani said.

"I'm coming too," Knox announced. "To the pool."

"Me too," Tess said. "I love pools."

"I think it would be safer if Tess stays here at the Monkey Maze," Savani said.

"We volunteer to watch her," Newell said, nudging Doren.

"We can play hide-and-seek," Doren added.

"That sounds fun," Tess clapped.

"Warren and I will join you as well, Kendra," Vanessa said. "I wonder if somebody could create a diversion to distract the triclops? Lure him elsewhere on the island. Perhaps prevent him from falling upon us."

"I could try," Grady said.

"I wonder if two satyrs are required to watch one girl," Vanessa mused. "Distracting the triclops would be very heroic."

Newel swallowed loudly. "I could come help, Grady. I have experience annoying lumbering brutes."

"That's true," Doren said.

"Don't underestimate Mombatu," Grady said. "He is big, but he is also agile and impossibly strong. His hide can resist dragon fire and his hands can crush boulders."

"Sounds like my kind of party," Newel said feebly.

"I can watch Tess," Savani offered. "I should remain here to make sure our last bastion on the islands remains secure."

"I guess that frees me up," Doren said without much enthusiasm.

"Let's get ready," Kendra said. "I'm tired of being out of the hunt for my brother."

CHAPTER EIGHTEEN

Landfall

The dark craft bounded forward over the choppy swells, swooping down into troughs only to rise again. Water occasionally sloshed over the sides but somehow drained after reaching the bottom of the boat. Though there was room for at least six more people, Seth and Ronodin had no companions, and neither worked an oar. Seth wondered if Ronodin really had to keep his hand on the tiller, or if he just liked feeling in control. Since they had untethered the craft from a sheltered dock inside the sea cave, the boat had propelled itself.

Beyond the mist surrounding the island, Seth had discovered a bright day, and he was enjoying the feeling of direct sunlight on his face for the first time in memory. Now the misty island was fading to a smudge behind them, and a new island was growing as they neared it. A towering volcano presided over several lesser mounts, slopes green with vegetation.

"Timbuli," Ronodin said. "Soon you will glimpse other islands. And there are many more beyond our sight. This is the largest undiscovered archipelago in the ocean, a former dragon prison called Crescent Lagoon."

"Why hasn't it been discovered?" Seth asked.

"These islands are shielded by distracter spells," Ronodin said. "If a ship comes near, all aboard feel a subtle urge to steer away, along with an irresistible impulse not to notice what they avoided. Even a pair of eyes studying a satellite photo will feel an unnamed compulsion to ignore these islands."

"I don't feel that urge," Seth said.

"We're already within the prison," Ronodin said. "From inside, the distractions lose their influence."

Seth looked over the gunwale at the rolling sea. "What's pushing the boat?"

"Magic, of course," Ronodin said. "It takes some magic to depart the Under Realm, and more to find it again. This vessel has enough to do both jobs."

"Can you do it without the boat?" Seth asked.

"Naturally," Ronodin said with a smirk. "But I'd rather work smart than hard."

"How does the water drain?" Seth asked.

"A clever blend of engineering and magic," Ronodin said. "You should ask about the bucket."

Seth had hardly noticed the old bucket, even though

it was the only gear in the boat besides a coiled line. "Tell me."

"It's called a sweet bucket," Ronodin said. "Not much to look at, but fill it with seawater, and the water turns fresh."

"Really?" Seth exclaimed. "Can I try?"

"Be my guest."

Though not terribly thirsty, Seth felt very curious. With the boat still bucking and diving, he leaned over the side and scooped some water into the bucket.

"No magic words?" Seth asked.

Ronodin handed him a tin dipper. "Try a sip."

Seth scooped the dipper into the bucket. He tested the fluid with his tongue, then sipped some. Sure enough, the water was cool and fresh, without a trace of salt. "I'm impressed."

"We all live to earn your approval," Ronodin said solemnly.

Seth gazed ahead at the approaching island. "We're going to the crypt during the day?"

"Know your quarry," Ronodin said. "This crypt is guarded by wraiths. And ultimately you will need to converse with a phantom. Shadow charmers sometimes prefer to operate at night because they hide so well in darkness, but daylight is no handicap to you. Wraiths and phantoms, however, are much less comfortable during the day. You do not want to confront them at the height of their powers."

"The wraiths will be hostile?" Seth asked.

"They kept me out," Ronodin said. "The Sphinx, too. Do you understand the nature of wraiths?"

"I know they're cold," Seth said. "And starving. It's nearly all they talk about unless you ask direct questions."

"Do you know how wraiths originate?" Ronodin asked.

"No," Seth said.

"The creation of a wraith relies on a cruel trick," Ronodin said.

"Who would create a wraith?"

"A powerful witch or wizard. A demon. A viviblix. Or one of the mightier undead, like a lich. Any of those prey upon individuals who want something desperately. The victims are eventually led to willingly cheat death until they receive what they desire."

"What happens if the people get what they want?" Seth asked.

"Then they don't become wraiths," Ronodin said. "The all-consuming lust for the unobtained prize is what fuels the transformation. If the desired reward is attained in life, the potential for a wraith is lost. The birth of a new wraith depends on the coveted prize remaining elusive. Once a being powerful in dark magic facilitates the change, the wraith can gain freedom only by receiving the desired object, which brings the postponed release of death."

"And if the person can't get what they want, they're trapped?"

"Sometimes the originator of the deal will deliberately hide, withhold, or destroy the desired object to ensure an undead servant. At other times the targeted victims crave something they can never win, like the love of a certain woman, the respect of someone they admire, or to hold an important title or position. In any event, if wraiths ever obtain what they most want, they find release."

"Can I find out what the wraiths want?"

"Easier said than done. By the time they are undead, wraiths are so miserable and dissatisfied that they avoid the topic. They rarely wish to discuss their agonizing disappointment. Wraiths seek distraction. They leech life and warmth. And if they find a master they can comprehend, wraiths like to surrender their wills by serving."

"The wraiths are serving the phantom?" Seth asked.

"Or somebody who wanted the phantom protected," Ronodin said.

"Can I talk them out of guarding Dezia?"

"You may fail, but you must try."

"Will I need to do favors for them?" Seth asked, remembering the favor he already owed Ezabar.

"Wraiths are not terribly interested in favors," Ronodin said. "Many wraiths think they want freedom, although their only real freedom would be finding the object of their desire. Their sole remaining pleasure is the fleeting rush of draining a life force. Most would be willing to serve a better master. If it were me, I would try to help them feel released from their duty of guarding the crypt. Offer them a better alternative. Uninfluenced by outside sources, wraiths routinely stay true to commands for decades or even centuries. But you can talk to them, meaning you have a chance to influence them."

"And if I make it to Dezia?" Seth asked.

"Phantoms are less predictable," Ronodin said. "I gave you a book on the subject."

"I may not have read every page," Seth said. "I need the summary."

"Phantoms are ethereal," Ronodin said. "They have no tangible body. Nobody knows exactly where they come from, but they are born out of deep tragedy."

"If a person lost everything, they could turn into a phantom?"

"Such a person could cause the birth of a phantom," Ronodin said.

"Maybe I'm a phantom," Seth mused. "I don't remember where I came from."

"You're very much a human boy," Ronodin said. "The afflicted person does not turn into a phantom. The phantom is what fills the footprint of the tragedy. After coming into being, phantoms develop an independent identity. The fundamental nature of a phantom is difficult to discern."

"They can think and speak?" Seth asked.

"You should be able to converse with the phantom," Ronodin said. "How you get the information you need is up to you."

"Brute force?"

Ronodin grinned. "You could try."

"Favors?" Seth asked.

"Whatever it takes," Ronodin said.

"This is starting to feel like quicksand," Seth said. "I owe the Underking favors, and to do his favors, I'll need to owe other favors. I keep piling up new debts."

Ronodin laughed heartily. "Welcome to the magical world!"

"When does it end?" Seth asked.

"Let me know if you figure that out," Ronodin said.

Seth had plenty to think about as the island drew nearer, the prow of the craft aimed at a black beach flanked by low, rocky cliffs. How could he prepare for threats that remained largely unknown? He would have to rely on his ability to improvise as he discovered how the wraiths and the phantom interacted with him.

At length the boat moved into breakers and was propelled to shore at the fastest speed yet, waves frothing around them until the craft ran aground on fine black sand. Ronodin and Seth exited the front of the boat.

"Come," Ronodin said, as if talking to a dog. He snapped his fingers. "Up. Up."

The boat surged forward in little scoots until it rested completely on dry sand. Ronodin scanned the waves. "That will do."

"Obedient boat," Seth said.

"You should see it roll over," Ronodin remarked. "This way."

They tromped off the sand and onto a path of hard mud that wound back into the trees. Ferns crowded the path, some lacy and delicate, others broad and shiny.

"Do you expect trouble?" Seth asked.

"Why not?" Ronodin said. "We have a rampaging triclops on the prowl, the possibility of dragons, and the undead unwittingly awaiting our arrival."

"Aren't you on good terms with the dragons?" Seth asked.

"I'm an expert at avoiding trouble," Ronodin said. "I'm more concerned about you."

"So if dragons show up, I'm on my own?"

"I want you safe. See the flowers over there?"

Seth looked where Ronodin was pointing and beheld huge blossoms the size of hula hoops, red and white petals pristine against the verdant backdrop, maybe fifteen paces off the path. "The big ones?"

"Yes," Ronodin said. "They are responsible for the fragrance."

Seth sniffed purposefully. A definite perfume mingled with the humid air. "Smells tasty."

"Exactly," Ronodin said. "Not just a pleasant aroma. The smell seems to promise you will be fed. See the green bulbs near the blossoms?"

They were bigger than watermelons. Seth assumed they simply had not blossomed yet. "Sure."

"They will hastily devour you if you come within range," Ronodin said.

"Carnivorous," Seth said, stepping away from the plant even though it was not near him.

"Aggressively carnivorous," Ronodin said. "Strikes fast. Can bite through bone. Some birds can't resist the aroma. A meaty kill like you would satisfy the plant for months."

"Message received," Seth said. "Don't stop and smell the roses."

"Not without expert guidance. If you want a rule of

thumb, big and bright isn't right. Such species tend to be poisonous or carnivorous. Works in the jungle and in the sea as well. Some very nasty fish inhabit these waters."

"I want to see that flower eat something," Seth said, lingering as Ronodin moved on.

"Me too," Ronodin said. "Sadly, we lack gullible children, and we have a schedule to keep."

Seth hoped Ronodin was kidding.

They continued through the jungle. When they reached an open meadow, Seth noticed a moai on a nearby hilltop. "Cool statue," he said.

"They once guarded this prison," Ronodin said. "I prefer them asleep. It is why the Underking has chosen the present hour to send us on this mission."

On the far side of the meadow, the path continued. Several plants about Seth's height looked to have green dreadlocks instead of leaves. He amused himself by appreciating the variety of shrubs, flowers, and trees. Ronodin pointed out a tree that could kill by using its vines as nooses, and on the other side of the path, a spiky bush with exploding fruit.

Where a splashing stream crossed their path, Ronodin held a finger to his lips and crouched. Following his gaze, Seth looked upstream to where a red boar the size of a car was drinking. The creature abruptly raised its head, wide snout sniffing, tusks the size of baseball bats curving sharply.

As the beast turned toward Ronodin and Seth, the dark unicorn arose, one arm outstretched toward the boar, the other clutching what looked like a short, black unicorn horn. "Depart in peace or meet your ruin," Ronodin said calmly.

With a squealing snort, the boar turned and ran, crashing through the foliage. Seth remained tense until it passed out of earshot.

"What if the pig had charged?" he asked.

"Pork chops and bacon," Ronodin said, putting away the horn.

"Huge bacon," Seth said. "Was that your horn?"

"You saw nothing," Ronodin said.

"Okay," Seth said. "Must have been my imagination."

"An attitude like that could take you far," Ronodin said.

"Should I have brought a weapon?" Seth asked.

Ronodin stared at Seth. "Would you have fought that boar with a sword?"

Seth smiled uncomfortably. "That might not have gone well."

"Didn't you have some weapons in that satchel of yours?" Ronodin asked. "The one you carried when Mendigo brought you here?"

"Random gear," Seth said. "Like one glove. I had a knife in there. Should I have brought that?"

"You used to always carry the satchel with you," Ronodin said. He produced a short sword. "A weapon isn't a bad idea in case of emergency."

Seth accepted the short sword. "Thanks."

"It's yours," Ronodin said. "Mendigo took it from its sheath when he grabbed you."

"It looks fancy," Seth said.

"I hope you don't have to use it," Ronodin said. "Let's avoid trouble. Especially boars. Fighting is a last resort. Any clumsy oaf can fight."

They crossed the stream and continued along the path, moving generally uphill. After coming over a little rise, they saw a wide, muddy crater gaping before them. A few murky puddles sulked in the slick, black mud. On the far side of the crater, near the bottom, a smooth boulder rested beside a stone doorway.

"Is that the crypt?" Seth asked, pointing at the open doorway with one hand while the other covered his nose.

"You guessed it," Ronodin said.

"Did you move the rock?" Seth asked.

"No small feat," Ronodin said. "It was enchanted. The Sphinx has a talent for opening things. The harder part was draining the pond."

"This was a pond?" Seth asked. "Of what? Sewage?"

"Foul water," Ronodin said. "This would give the sweet bucket a real test."

Seth peered at the doorway. "It looks like a cave. How far back does it go?"

Ronodin slapped Seth on the back. "That is for you to discover. We should hurry. If the triclops shows up, we might wish that boar had finished us."

"He's that tough?"

"You won't believe how savage," Ronodin said. "This way."

Ronodin led Seth down the least steep side of the empty pond. Tarlike mud sucked at each step, covering his shoes with squelchy gunk. Flies swirled above the squalid puddles. The stink was everywhere, but covering his nose and mouth reduced the impact.

Before long they stood before the stone frame of the doorway, gazing into the darkness beyond. "Time to prove your mettle as a shadow charmer," Ronodin said. "This will be a worthy test of your abilities."

"Pass-fail," Seth said.

"Exactly," Ronodin said. "Sink or swim. Survive or perish. Off you go."

"You'll be here when I get back?" Seth checked.

"Me or the triclops," Ronodin said. "Or some other hideous creature. The faster you go, the better."

Seth did not like the feel of the cool air wafting from the forbidding doorway. He had a hunch the cave stretched a long distance. "Do you have a light?"

Ronodin pulled out a holly wand. He snapped his fingers, and the tip lit up. He handed the wand to Seth.

"Smooth," Seth said, starting forward.

"Watch out for traps," Ronodin remarked.

Seth paused. "What kind of traps?"

Ronodin shrugged. "Anything you can imagine. It's a crypt that was hidden behind a boulder beneath a pond on an island full of monsters. There might be traps."

Seth took a final glance at the blue sky and the tall trees surrounding the empty pond. Sword in one hand, glowing wand in the other, he stepped through the stone doorway into the chilly darkness beyond.

CHAPTER NINETEEN

Crypt

Seth promptly realized that the cold inside the crypt came from more than just the absence of sunlight. The rough walls and ceiling of a natural cave led to a chamber lined with yellowed stone blocks. He could sense wraiths ahead in the dimness of the chamber, six of them, spread out in a loose semicircle.

The hostility from these wraiths was unmistakable, contrasting sharply with the neutral attention Seth received from the wraiths in the Under Realm. Seth paused at the entrance to the chamber. The darkness seemed thicker here, offering greater resistance to the modest light of his wand. Wraiths emerged from shallow niches in the walls around the room, slinking toward him. The malevolent cold emanating from the wraiths made the little hairs on his arms stand up. Seth felt like prey; it was time to act.

"Greetings," Seth said in the brightest voice he could muster. "I brought a message."

Dezia needs no messages, one of the wraiths thought to him.

You do not belong here, another maintained.

Take his warmth, a third expressed.

He is plump with life, another conveyed.

"Hold on," Seth said. "My message is for you, not Dezia. Stop for a second. What's the big hurry?"

The wraiths halted. Seth was poised to run away if necessary.

He speaks to us, one of the wraiths communicated.

"And I hear you," Seth said. "You don't want my warmth. It would be a waste. I can help you."

It's cold here, one of the wraiths expressed.

He is alive, a different wraith spoke to his mind. *He is warm.*

"You can speak," Seth said. "You don't have to think at me."

We commune as we choose, another wraith transmitted.

"Have you heard that this dragon prison fell?" Seth asked.

For a time, one wraith expressed. *Then one of the watchers revived.*

"The hour of Crescent Lagoon is over," Seth said. "I'm here to grant you freedom. You don't have to stay in a forgotten hole at a fallen prison. You can go where you want now."

He speaks pretty words, one of the wraiths put in.

Beguiler, another wraith accused.

"That one watcher won't last long," Seth said. "Besides,

very few people even remember you're here. The world has moved on. You're guarding nothing. Nobody cares anymore."

Drain him dry, one of the wraiths yearned, stepping forward.

Seth held up a hand. "I wouldn't do that. I'm the only friend you've got. The only voice of warning you're going to get."

Hear him, another wraith demanded.

The wraiths kept still.

Hungry, one of the wraiths expressed glumly.

"I come from the Underking," Seth said. "I'm on an errand for him."

There is truth in his language, a wraith conveyed.

"I'm here to offer you a deal," Seth said. "Are other wraiths guarding this crypt?"

We six, one wraith expressed.

"If one of you agrees to serve me, the other five can go free," Seth said, hoping the deal sounded enticing. He had no real authority to allow them to leave, but he hoped that they remained there largely because nobody had given them permission to go. He also hoped that asking one wraith to serve him would make the others feel lucky about the bargain.

Serve you how? a wraith asked.

"Whatever I need until I leave the crypt," Seth said. "The one who serves me will be released when I leave. You're never going to get what you really want by staying in this forsaken burrow. I have met tons of wraiths who live better than this. I freed some recently. Now I'm here to free you."

Who will serve you? a wraith asked.

"The best one," Seth said.

"That would be me," one of the wraiths vocalized. No others challenged him. "I accept your offer."

"Smart wraith," Seth said. "What about the rest of you?"

"Yes," a wraith said.

Yes, another conveyed.

Yes.

I wish freedom, but to remain here for a time, a wraith expressed timidly.

I wish the same, the final wraith added.

"If you promise not to harm me, you may stay here, free to leave when you choose," Seth said.

I agree.

As do I.

"You who will serve me," Seth said. "Do you promise me no harm during your service and afterward?"

"You have my pledge," the wraith assured him.

"Congratulations," Seth said. "The path to freedom begins now."

May we leave in the night? one of the wraiths asked.

"Sure," Seth said. "As long as you don't trouble me."

All but one of the wraiths withdrew to their niches in the walls. Seth felt tension leaving his muscles. He had not been sure if the invitation would work.

"Ready for your first task?" Seth asked the wraith who had agreed to serve him.

"Speak and I will serve," the wraith replied.

"Do you have a name?" Seth wondered.

"Call me what you will," the wraith said.

"How about Midnight?" Seth proposed.

"As you desire," Midnight replied.

"I need you to guide me safely to Dezia," Seth said.

"You claimed your message was for us," Midnight said.

"I have other business with her," Seth said.

"I shall escort you to her door," Midnight said. "I cannot cross the threshold."

"Lead the way," Seth said.

The wraith strode away from the chamber down a winding corridor of natural stone. Seth followed, aware that the other wraiths were now behind him. He hoped their agreement not to harm him was binding.

Before the end of the corridor, Midnight stopped. "If you look upon any of the idols in the next room, you will go blind. I can guide you."

Seth tucked his hand inside his sleeve and extended his arm. "All right."

Midnight took his sleeve, and Seth closed his eyes. Icy cold spread from the place where the wraith touched his clothing. The wraith led him smoothly forward along a serpentine route. Eyes squeezed shut, Seth took halting steps, worried about running into obstacles, but the wraith led him true.

"You may look again," Midnight said, releasing his sleeve.

"We're through the room?" Seth checked.

"Yes."

Seth opened his eyes to find himself in another natural corridor of the cave. He realized that if there had been no room containing idols, and Midnight had been fooling him, there was no way for him to know. Seth started rubbing warmth back into his arm as the wraith led him forward.

The temperature began to rise, and Seth saw a red glow ahead. Around the next bend, they came into view of a circular room with a floor of hot coals, mostly black, but with irregular veins of fiery red. The air shimmered with heat.

"Dezia dwells beyond," Midnight said. "I will wait here."

Seth saw an open door on the far side of the room. It would take four or five consecutive jumps to get across. Even from down the hall, the heat was intense.

The coals were burning too uniformly and with too much heat to have been recently lit. He suspected some magic kept them eternally smoldering.

He edged forward, stopping about ten feet away from the room, when the heat became unbearable. His hair starting to singe, Seth took a few steps back to where the temperature was endurable.

"Can you cool it down?" Seth asked Midnight.

"Alas, no. These coals mark the beginning of Dezia's dominion," the wraith replied.

Seth flexed his fingers. How would it go if he tried to sprint across, maybe jumping as needed? He strongly suspected his carcass would get added to the coals.

What if he cooled the coals? The room was orders of magnitude hotter than a torch. Seth closed his eyes and focused on the relentless heat. He turned his focus inward, searching for the darkness within and the associated reservoir of cold. He located the source and circled it, feeling for the coldest place from which to draw. Then he shifted his energy to project a steady flow toward the coals. The effort seemed futile against the intense heat, but as Seth poured out all the cold he could summon, he felt the temperature of the nearest coals wavering.

Good, a whispery female voice spoke to his mind, startling him. *Not the intended method of passage, but clever. Keep trying.*

Seth redoubled his efforts, trying to fully extinguish the coals the way he had doused the torch with Ronodin. The coals seemed to yield voluntarily to his power, and soon he had cooled a wide stripe of them across the center of the room. But the coals to either side continued to radiate significant heat.

In previous attempts, Seth had siphoned cold from himself to douse fire; now he wondered if perhaps he could call upon it to protect his body from heat. Drawing more gently from his power, Seth directed the cold to encompass his body, and the chill seeped over him until he was shivering.

Keeping the coldness close, Seth raced onto the path of neutralized coals across the center of the room, kicking up ashes with each crunchy step. Intense heat encroached on the cold cocoon he had summoned, and he drew on the cold more powerfully until he dashed through the far doorway. As he staggered down a short hall beyond, the heat receded, and he disengaged from the darkness within.

A few steps later, Seth found himself entering a domed cavern. Panting, he held up his holly wand. Crude pictograms decorated the smoother parts of the circular stone wall. Other than the archway he had used to enter, there appeared to be no other passages out of the room.

"Dezia!" Seth called.

I hear you, the phantom responded. It was the same susurrant voice that had aided him with the coals.

"Where are you?" Seth asked.

A short figure stepped into view through the far wall of the cavern, her dark form semitransparent, gauzy wrappings flowing as if in a strong breeze, although the air was still. The figure seemed to be wearing a wooden mask with crude holes cut for eyes, nose, and mouth, embellished by ornamental carvings. But when she spoke, the mouth of the mask moved.

"What business have you with me, shadow charmer?" Dezia inquired, her voice matching the one Seth had heard in his mind.

"I'm looking for a flower," Seth said.

"Tell me more," the phantom said.

"The Everbloom," Seth explained.

"And why shouldn't I kill you for your impudence?" Dezia asked. "You discharged my wraiths."

"I'm on an errand for the Underking," Seth said.

Dezia waved a dismissive hand. "What is that to me?"

"Isn't he your king?" Seth asked.

"The Underking is one of many powers in the darkness," Dezia said. "I have no obligations to him."

Seth had hoped his errand would carry more weight. Maybe she was posturing for bargaining power. "I'm sorry about the wraiths. I needed to reach you."

"You're a shadow charmer," Dezia said. "All you required was access. Dismissing them lacked elegance and courtesy. Had you left the wraiths in place, my secrets would have been better guarded from your rivals."

"I can ask if any of them want to stay," Seth said.

"Not likely after your invitation to freedom," Dezia said. "Blunt but effective. I see some entities of note have offered to train you. I also observe that you have destroyed some powerful demons."

"How can you tell?" Seth asked.

"The signs are there," Dezia said. "The records of your interactions. It is evident that you stood in the presence of the Underking. No small feat for a mortal."

"I was telling you the truth," Seth said.

"You may know some true things," Dezia said. "But no mortal possesses very much truth. A mortal telling the truth is like a blind woman painting a portrait."

"I know plenty of truth," Seth asserted.

"It can be difficult to perceive what one does not know," Dezia allowed. "If I had a mind to teach you, there is much I could share."

"I'm looking for the Everbloom," Seth said.

"Merely the Everbloom," Dezia said. "Do you understand what you are asking?"

"It's a flower that never dies," Seth said.

"It's the supreme source of power on these islands," Dezia said.

"The Underking wants it."

"Everyone wants it. What if I refuse to help? Am I to be your next victim?"

"I'm not looking for trouble," Seth said. "Just information."

"You found trouble the moment you entered my crypt,"

Dezia said. "You are either quite good at concealing your thoughts, or else your past is a fog."

"Do you know where I can find the bloom?" Seth asked.

"That was your best question so far," Dezia said. "There are limits to what I know about the location of the Everbloom."

"What can you tell me?" Seth asked.

"I know generally where the Everbloom grows," Dezia said. "Not specifically."

"Will you share what you know?"

"Why should I?"

"To help the Underking?"

"Are you here because you love the Underking, or because you owe him?"

Seth could think of no clever response. "I owe him."

"You want me to help you repay a debt to the Underking," Dezia said. "What will you do for me?"

"I'll let you teach me something," Seth tried.

"You'll let me do you a favor as payment for a favor?" Dezia verified.

"How about we play hot or cold," Seth proposed.

"Hot, I'll wager," Dezia said.

"What is that supposed to mean?" Seth asked. "Don't I have to guess first?"

"I won't help you that way," Dezia said.

"What do you want?" Seth asked. "What can I do for you?"

"We're back to useful questions," Dezia said. "I was

losing hope. Do you know anything about me? Or about phantoms?"

"You were created by a tragedy," Seth said.

"Are you deliberately explaining it poorly so I will correct you?" Dezia asked. "Not a bad tactic, but I will resist the urge."

"How were you created?" Seth asked.

"Did you actually come here this unprepared?"

"I rely on my charm," Seth said.

"Then you came to me unarmed. Many years ago, fifteen firewalkers lost their lives inside the volcano Baga Loa. They are buried here under those coals I helped you cross. Their demise opened my gateway to your world."

"Are firewalkers people?" Seth asked.

"You are a stranger to the islands," Dezia said. "As nereids are to the sea, and naiads are to fresh water, firewalkers are to volcanoes."

"Volcano nymphs?" Seth asked.

"The true volcano nymphs are lost," Dezia said. "The firewalkers are their descendants. They live more like mortals than proper nymphs. They wed and have offspring. And they tend to Baga Loa."

"Can they swim in lava?"

"Almost," Dezia said. "You asked what I want. Pledge to cast my token into the volcano, and I will reveal what I know about the Everbloom."

"What will the token do?" Seth asked.

"Your throwing it into Baga Loa will grant me greater freedom to roam," Dezia said.

"What does that mean?" Seth asked.

"If the sanctuary fully falls, I will be able to leave this place and find a new abode," Dezia said. "If it stands, on festival nights I will be able to explore the island."

"Will you come bother me if you can roam?" Seth asked.

"Only if you fail to cast the token into the volcano," Dezia said. "Such failure would enable me to haunt you."

"How long do I have to get it there?" Seth asked.

"One year from today," Dezia said.

"Where is the token?" Seth asked.

Dezia drifted to a low stone altar on one side of the room and gestured at a primitive wooden doll. It had reedy hair made from dried grass, divots for eyes, and a simple smile painted onto the smooth, dark wood.

"A doll?" Seth asked.

"My token," Dezia said. "Will you deliver it to the volcano within one year if I tell you what I know about the location of the Everbloom?"

Seth doubted he would get a better offer. "Sure."

"Then take custody of my token," Dezia said.

Seth picked up the doll.

"The Everbloom grows somewhere within Baga Loa," Dezia said.

"Inside the volcano?" Seth asked.

"A complex system of caves leaves portions of the mountain hollow," Dezia said. "The firewalkers know those paths better than anyone. I am only sure that one firewalker knows the exact location of the Everbloom within those secret windings. Her name is Savani, and she is the care-taker of this sanctuary."

"That's all you know?" Seth asked.

"Yes," Dezia said. "I gave you the general location of the Everbloom, and I told you who can pinpoint the exact location. Now take my token and go. Hurry. With the pool gone, I mean to collapse the outer areas of this crypt to prevent easy entry."

"Now?" Seth asked, looking toward the room full of hot coals.

"Summon your cold," Dezia said. "I will aid you. Then run."

Seth mustered all the cold he could and directed it toward the coals. Again, a central aisle of coals lost their heat. He wrapped cold around himself and ran, eyes squinting against the temperature and the particles in the air.

At the far side of the coals he found Midnight. "We have to go," Seth said. "This crypt is going to collapse."

"That poses no problem for me," Midnight said. "But I will help you."

Seth had almost forgotten about the room where he needed to close his eyes. "Yes, please."

He hurried along the corridor, again tucking his hand into his sleeve and allowing Midnight to lead him. As Seth blindly followed the wraith, he listened for the rumblings of a cave-in. By the time he opened his eyes, he felt the first tremors.

When Seth reached the chamber with the wraiths, the walls trembled, gently at first, then with greater vigor.

"Thank you," Seth called to Midnight, running for the entrance. "Depart when you want!"

Midnight stayed close behind him. "I am free when you emerge from the crypt?"

Seth lurched and stumbled as the quaking increased. Cracks were forming in the walls. Behind him, part of the ceiling collapsed.

"Yes," Seth said, pinballing off the walls of the corridor until he emerged from the crypt into the empty pond. Dust gushed from the opening behind him, accompanied by the thunder of falling rocks.

Facing away from Seth, on the far side of the pond, stood a gigantic creature shaped like a man, but with a tough, gray hide like a rhinoceros and lumpy muscles across his back, legs, and arms. The huge brute clutched a wooden club that might once have been the trunk of a palm tree. Even at a distance, Seth could tell he came no higher than the creature's thigh.

The monstrosity turned, revealing a broad face with a flat nose and a huge forehead that accommodated three eyes spaced roughly in the shape of a triangle. As Seth had begun to expect, it was the triclops.

"Run!" Ronodin called from somewhere beyond the triclops, and a rock struck the monster, turning its attention away.

More dust belched from the crypt, reminding Seth that the cave would offer no shelter, but also providing Seth with some cover. Keeping within the dust cloud as best he could, Seth raced up the side of the empty pond, away from the triclops.

Once out of the muddy crater, Seth crashed into the jungle, plowing through ferns and shrubs with reckless haste. By the time he looked back, vegetation impeded his view of the triclops.

While glancing back, Seth blundered into something spongy and sticky, which to his disgust turned out to be the bell-shaped cap of a colossal yellow mushroom. Supported by a short, thick stalk, the bulbous cap went from Seth's knees to well above his head. To his horror, Seth found that every part of his body that had touched it could not pull away—his right shoulder, right arm, right hand, right side, and right leg down to the knee were held fast as if by instant, perfect glue.

Hastily trying to wrench free, Seth made the mistake of pushing with his left palm, and that hand became immediately stuck to the adhesive surface. Seth struggled, hoping to tear off part of the mushroom or perhaps snap it free from the ground, but it was like trying to outpull a stubborn elephant.

Rather than succumb to his efforts, the mushroom, as if by some predatory instinct, leaned away from Seth just enough to lift him off the ground, causing more of his body to press against the sticky surface. Pathetically dangling from the tenacious mushroom, Seth kicked his free leg in frustration.

Behind him, the triclops roared with a primal fury that triggered enough panic to halt Seth's struggles. Holding his breath, he prayed the behemoth would not venture his way.

CHAPTER TWENTY

Triclops

K endra crouched in the bushes near the drained pond, hands over her ears to dampen the roar of the triclops. After throwing a few rocks, Warren had hit the creature near one of the eyes, and now it was charging him. But Kendra's attention was focused on the place nearly halfway around the pond where her brother had vanished into the jungle. She had come to the corrupted pool hoping for a clue to finding Seth. The possibility that he would actually be there had not entered her mind.

The journey to the pool had been relatively calm until the last few minutes. Hako, a grim Polynesian man with a broad chest and thick limbs, had led them along quiet paths toward their destination, pointing out hazards along the way. As they traveled, Kendra had found two fairies, Nia and Beruni, who had joined her.

The trouble began as they drew near the pool. Hako had raised a fist, bringing the group to a halt, and after a few moments Kendra heard distant branches snapping in the jungle behind them.

"Mombatu," Hako had whispered, crouching low to place one hand on the ground. "Scatter. Remember, he is drawn to motion. I will lure him past you."

Kendra had raced off the path beside Tanu, the two fairies flitting nearby. Warren, Vanessa, Doren, and Knox ran in the opposite direction. Hako had previously warned that if the triclops found them, their best chance for survival would be to separate and individually make their way back to the protected area around the Monkey Maze. When Kendra and Tanu reached some bushes near the edge of the vacant pond, Tanu had pointed to a fern that would conceal her and then scrambled off to find his own cover.

Shortly after Kendra took shelter beneath the lush fronds, she heard Hako taunting Mombatu. As Hako led the triclops from the jungle into the wide depression of the empty pond, to her surprise, Kendra saw Ronodin fleeing into the trees. Hako tumbled into the mud at the bottom of the empty pond and promptly disappeared. Whether the camouflage was through skill or magic, Kendra could not see him, and neither could Mombatu, who stomped around the muddy crater, brandishing his club in frustration.

After that, the ground had begun rumbling, and seconds later, to her complete shock, Seth had emerged from the mouth of a cave in the waterless pond. Kendra had seen him only briefly before dust billowed from the opening and obscured her view. It was so unexpected that she hardly believed her eyes, but it was his face, his expression, his stance. Was Seth really alive? Was he free? Was he involved in some sort of adventure here on the island? Had she gotten lucky enough to encounter him? Somebody yelled for Seth to run, Warren started throwing rocks at Mombatu, and her brother dashed out of view.

Now the triclops was pounding off into the jungle after Warren, and Hako emerged from the mud to chase Mombatu. According to the plan, if the triclops attacked, Kendra was supposed to withdraw immediately to the protections of Crescent Beach. But having glimpsed Seth, she knew retreat was no longer an option. Not until she caught up to him.

"Did you see the boy who came out of the cave?" Kendra asked the fairies.

"Not as well as the triclops did," Nia said with a giggle. "I only have two eyes."

"I saw him," Calvin said. "It was Seth."

"I took some small notice of him," Beruni said.

"Can you fairies lead us to the boy?" Kendra said. "Going around the pond? To avoid being seen by Mombatu?"

"This way," Nia said, fluttering ahead.

Advancing in a crouch, Kendra followed. Both fairies were hard to miss with their elaborate butterfly wings. She could hear Mombatu bulldozing through the jungle behind her, thankfully, not in her direction.

"Kendra!" Tanu called in a stage whisper, appearing out

of hiding. "Where are you going? The lagoon is the other way."

"Seth is here," Kendra said. "I saw him."

"He's here?" Tanu exclaimed.

Kendra realized he must not have been in a position to view the empty pond when Seth had emerged. "The fairies are leading me to him. I have to go."

"Be careful," Tanu urged. "I'll check on Knox and the others. We'll draw the triclops away from you."

Kendra picked up her pace. If Seth had kept running, he had a big head start. Hopefully he was hiding. Either way, she wasn't going to give up until she found him. If he ran faster, she would run longer.

"Beruni," Kendra said, "fly ahead and find Seth, then come report."

Beruni darted out of view.

Kendra forced her way through the dense undergrowth, stumbling over creepers and roots, pushing aside fronds, rustling through ivy, trying to be swift and silent, with little success at either. Mombatu roared again, the naked rage of the bellow making Kendra fear for Knox and her friends.

"Nia, remember I can't fly," Kendra said. "Lead me the best way for a clumsy human to go. And help me avoid anything dangerous."

"Don't drink from those," Nia replied, indicating a creeping vine with leaves shaped like cups. "You'll hallucinate for hours."

Beruni flew back into sight. "He's not far ahead."

"Is he all right?" Kendra asked.

"He won't be, without help," Beruni said.

Breaking into a run, Kendra jumped a small trench, shoved through a curtain of vines, and wove among ferns until her brother came into view, his feet off the ground, most of his body affixed to the side of a huge mushroom the color of Dijon mustard. He was facing away from her as she approached, his free leg kicking halfheartedly. Part of her had worried she might never see him again, or that he would run from her, so finding him immobilized was a relief. But immediately she remembered the way he had looked at her like a stranger back at Stormguard Castle, and she wondered whether he would accept her help.

"Seth!" Kendra ventured in a loud whisper. "Are you okay?"

"Do I look okay?" he replied quietly. "Who are you? I can't turn my head."

Kendra walked around to where Seth could see her. Even with one cheek mashed against the side of the mushroom, it was amazing to see his face. For a moment she was speechless. It was her brother, frustrated, dangling helplessly. She really had found him!

"Kendra?" Seth asked.

"Do you remember me?" Kendra asked.

"Sure, from the castle," Seth said. "The first person I can remember. My sister, according to you. What are you doing here?"

Kendra tried to resist feeling deflated by his continued lack of recognition. "Looking for you," she said.

"Congrats," Seth said. "I could use some help."

"A local warned me about these mushrooms," Kendra said. "It will slowly absorb you."

"Unless the triclops decides I make a great topping for a fungal appetizer," Seth said.

"I can hardly believe it's really you," Kendra said.

"Please get me down," Seth said.

"Can you free him?" Kendra asked Nia.

"No problem," Nia said. "We have experience with death knells."

"Is that the name of this type of mushroom?" Kendra asked.

"Because of the bell shape," Nia said. "And the deadliness."

"Do fairies get stuck to them?" Kendra asked.

"No self-respecting fairy," Beruni said with a sniff.

"Maybe in a windstorm," Nia said. "Sometimes friendly animals get trapped. We help when we can. Should we free him?"

Kendra considered the situation. Seth might do anything if he were free. He might turn on her. Physically, this was her brother, but mentally, who knew? Right now, the triclops was grunting and growling somewhere on the far side of the empty pond. If she wanted to convince Seth he was helping the wrong side, she needed him to listen. It might not be smart to immediately end his captive-audience status.

"Leave him for the moment," Kendra said, careful to speak in the language the fairies were using. "Keep watch for the triclops. If Mombatu comes this way, free Seth immediately."

"Not you too!" Seth complained. "Not understanding the fairies was bad enough. What are you plotting?"

"I wanted to make sure they understood me," Kendra said.

"Can they get me down?" Seth asked.

"Probably," Kendra said.

"Then maybe we should hurry before I end up as a pizza topping."

"First I want to know where you have been."

Seth sighed heavily. "I get it. This is an interrogation."

"I want to help you," Kendra said. "But you have been working against us."

"You shouldn't even be here," Seth said. "Aren't you supposed to be watching over the dragon prison called Wyrmroost?"

"I was the caretaker of that dragon sanctuary," Kendra said. "So were you. Until you released the undead at our main fort and the sanctuary fell. Now I'm not caretaker of anything."

Mombatu roared loud enough to make Kendra flinch, though the triclops remained a fair distance away. Seth looked at her with startled eyes.

"Get me down," Seth said. "My skin is tingling where it's touching the mushroom. I think it's already digesting me."

"Where have you been, Seth?"

"You know."

"I really don't."

"The Under Realm."

"Where is that?"

"It's the realm of the Underking."

"And now you're here?" Kendra asked.

"For the moment," Seth said. "We'll go back to the Under Realm."

"Is it nearby?"

"It wouldn't be fair to say too much."

"Do you have to go back?" Kendra asked. "Could you stay? If you wanted?"

"Not really," Seth said. "I'm trying to earn my freedom from the Underking."

"Sounds like a great situation. Who took you there? The Sphinx?"

"The guy from the castle. Well, a puppet he sent."

"Ronodin sent Mendigo? Seth, you were kidnapped."

"He called it a rescue. Meanwhile, you're keeping me stuck to a mushroom."

"I'm on your side," Kendra said. "I'm your sister. You were taken from your family by an evil unicorn."

"And now you're risking me getting eaten by a triclops," Seth said.

"I'll get you down if the triclops comes this way," Kendra said.

"Are you daring me to call it?" Seth asked.

"Stop being dumb," Kendra said.

"Stop holding me prisoner," Seth said.

"The dark unicorn is holding you prisoner," Kendra said.

"According to you and the other unicorn," Seth said.

"What other unicorn?" Kendra asked urgently.

"That got your attention," Seth said. "Help me down and I'll tell you."

"You're infuriating," Kendra said. "We're on the same side. Stop making this hard."

"Everyone says I'm on their side," Seth said. "Everyone wants things from me."

"What do you want?" Kendra asked.

"Honestly? Some time on my own. Without anyone trying to control me."

"That could be good," Kendra said. "Can you get time alone?"

"Not yet," Seth said. "Soon, I hope."

"Ronodin won't let you go," Kendra said. "But if you're foolish enough to help him, he'll take advantage of you for as long as you allow it."

"If you're really my sister, get me down and let me work this out," Seth said.

"Of course I'm your sister," Kendra said. "Don't you see the family resemblance? What do you want to know about yourself?"

"Everything," Seth said. "But I don't trust anyone enough to tell me. I don't know what stories to believe."

"Is Bracken in the Under Realm?" Kendra asked.

"Good guess," Seth said. "All caged up."

"He's all right?" she asked, at first trying to hold back the tears, then almost glad for them, hoping they would show Seth her sincerity.

"He's not injured," Seth said. "I mean, he's locked up in the Under Realm, so he could be better."

Kendra nodded, trying to find words. This whole situation was so twisted, having her own brother not trust her, hearing him speak glibly about Bracken's incarceration. But it wasn't Seth's fault. He was doing his best with limited information. She had to try to reach him.

Kendra took a step closer to him and whispered, "You have to be curious about what happened. You have to wonder. You may not believe me, but here it is—we were racing against dragons to get a powerful talisman called the Wizenstone. You and I were running from the dragons, trying to get into the room where the Wizenstone was kept, but to open the door, the price was your identity. You knew that and volunteered to do it. You were so brave. After you opened the door, you looked at me like a stranger."

"My first memory," Seth said.

"Then Ronodin showed up and started manipulating you," Kendra went on hurriedly. "You saw what happened with Humbuggle and the stone. We got teleported away. And the Sphinx helped Ronodin kidnap you using the barrels. Before long he had you destroying the sanctuary you lost your memory to save."

"Sad story if it's true," Seth said. "You've had time to work on it."

Kendra struggled to ignore the crushing disappointment of his disbelief. "You're incredibly curious," she went on. "You're not great at obeying rules. But you're not bad, Seth. You're good. You've fought some of the most dangerous villains in the magical world. You held strong and beat them. You have a true heart. That has to win out in the end."

"I talk to wraiths and phantoms," Seth said.

"You have dark powers," Kendra said. "You never used them for evil. At least, not when I knew you."

"I'm not trying to do anything wrong," Seth said. "If you're so good, why were you holding all of those undead creatures prisoners in a well?"

"Because they're dangerous," Kendra said.

"You lock up anything you decide is dangerous?" Seth asked. "Dragons? What else?"

"These preserves protect magical creatures from the outside world," Kendra said. "They also protect the outside world from the creatures."

"Ronodin calls them prisons," Seth said.

"They may look that way," Kendra said. "But the creatures aren't in cells. The dragons hunt. The satyrs play. They just have boundaries."

"Imposed by you?" Seth asked.

"Imposed by treaties," Kendra said, "after wars that nearly destroyed the world."

"The wraiths were in a cell," Seth said. "A deep one."

"I guess some of the most dangerous creatures get treated like prisoners," Kendra said. "I didn't set up the system. It might not be perfect. But it's definitely better than the end of humanity."

"If I tell you I believe you, will you let me down?" Seth asked.

"I'm not trying to force you," Kendra said.

"Leaving me attached to a killer mushroom comes really close," Seth replied.

"You're different in some ways," Kendra said. "You're you, but some of the feel is different. Where is your satchel?"

"Back at the Under Realm," Seth said.

"You came without it?" Kendra asked. "That's hard to believe."

"I guess I always used to bring it," Seth said.

"It's full of your gear," Kendra said.

"Like a single glove?"

"The glove makes you invisible when you hold still," Kendra said.

"That would have been good to know. What else?"

"Lots of stuff," Kendra said. "A knife. You always have some rope. You have a little statue of a leviathan that turns into a real one if you put it in the sea and say the right words."

"What words?" Seth asked.

"I don't know," Kendra said. "You probably wrote them down."

"I can check," Seth said. "If I live."

"Would it convince you?"

"An enemy might know the same specifics about me as a friend does," Seth said. "In fact, an enemy might be more concerned with using little details to sway me to their side."

"A friend might do the same," Kendra said. "Or a sister who loves you."

"You seem sincere," Seth said. "I can tell you really

care. That's kindness, at least. I haven't seen that out of Ronodin."

"I just want to help you," Kendra said. "We grew up together."

"Can you understand how strange it is that you know me deeply, while for me, there is nothing familiar about you? My memory is fried. What you say could be true. If it is, I'm lucky to have such a kind sister."

"It's really frustrating that nothing seems to reach you."

"I hear your version of things," Seth said. "If you're telling the truth, I'm so sorry. If you're lying, shame on you. Trust me to sort it out."

"Why are you here, Seth?" Kendra said. "What are you doing?"

"I'm dangling from a mushroom," Seth said.

"Why did you come?"

"Back to interrogation," Seth said.

"Ronodin corrupted that sacred pool," Kendra said. "Why did you come here? What were you doing down there?"

"Pushy," Seth said.

"I want to help," Kendra said.

"Then help me down," Seth said.

"You really don't have time for this," said a hushed voice from behind.

Kendra whirled to find Ronodin approaching. She reached for her bow and put a hand on the string.

"I'm not looking for a fight, unless you insist," Ronodin

said. "We have a bigger concern right now. With three eyes."

"I'll never forgive you for what you've done to my brother," Kendra said.

"As if I want or need your forgiveness," Ronodin said. "You can be a convincing actress in a pinch—I'll grant that you deliver your lines with feeling."

"What are you doing here?" Kendra asked.

Ronodin went from whispering to yelling. "I'm wondering when that brainless, blundering triclops will find us!"

"Don't," Kendra whispered, wincing.

Ronodin lowered his voice again. "You better take that speed potion Tanu prepared. I saw some of the others using it. If you don't lure that triclops away, we're all doomed." He lit a string of firecrackers and threw them at the base of a nearby tree. They began to explode with a sound like machine-gun fire. Kendra flinched at the racket.

"Run along," Ronodin encouraged.

Kendra moved her hand from the bowstring to a little flask. The dark unicorn was right about the potion. It was her insurance if Mombatu got close.

"Free him," Kendra said to Nia as she slung her bow over her shoulder.

"In exchange for your help, I offer you a hint," Ronodin said. "Call it pity. You will simplify your problem if you lure Mombatu to the protected boundary."

The two fairies approached Seth. After several flashes of light, he dropped from the mushroom to the ground. Once the firecrackers stopped bursting, Kendra heard the rumble of Mombatu's approach.

"Will the boundary destroy him?" she asked.

"In a manner of speaking," Ronodin said. "Stop dawdling with the potion. I know how to avoid Mombatu. Your brother doesn't."

Kendra glanced at Seth. It hurt to think of losing him again. But Ronodin seemed willing to sacrifice him if Kendra didn't draw off the triclops. Seeing no alternative, she uncapped the flask and raised it to her lips. The fluid inside bubbled like soda and had a flavor like spicy grapes. She consumed it in three fizzy swallows.

And everything slowed down.

Nia's wings swished back and forth lazily. Seth inched toward Ronodin. And Mombatu came into view, his mouth opening to roar as his three eyes surveyed the scene.

Kendra crouched and picked up a stone as the roar began. She flung it at his eyes, and the rock struck his cheek. Raising his club above his head, the triclops swung it down at her slowly enough for her to lunge out of the way. The blow flattened part of the sticky mushroom.

After she hit Mombatu in the mouth with a second rock, he trained all three of his eyes on her. The snarling triclops ripped his club free and gave chase as she ran away. Behind Mombatu, Ronodin and Seth lay flat on the ground, silent and still, watching.

CHAPTER TWENTY-ONE

Cyclopses

Dodging around trees and the larger plants, Kendra dashed toward the empty pond. Tanu had warned that the effects of the speed potion would not last very long and would leave her exhausted when it wore off, so she decided to sprint across open ground to maximize her temporary advantage. Also, she figured that crossing the empty pond would more efficiently get her to friends who could help distract Mombatu.

It agonized her to be running away from Seth. After all her worries, having found him, she was fleeing, leaving her brother with their enemy. But with the triclops in pursuit, what else could she do?

Mombatu raced after her, his ferocious roar spurring her on. She rushed down into the drained area, mud accumulating on her shoes and spraying into the air with every sloppy step. Nia and Beruni flanked her, despite their wings seeming to flap slower than normal.

As Kendra reached the far side of the pond, exhaustion began to take hold. Each breath became laborious, and the muscles in her legs started to burn. A glance back showed the triclops pounding through the mud at the middle of the empty pond, huge feet sinking to well above the ankles, his three-eyed gaze locked on her. After a couple more steps, the underbrush screened her view of her pursuer.

Fighting the fatigue in her limbs, Kendra charged forward, wading through ferns and knifing through gaps in heavier vegetation. While the potion lasted she could stretch her lead, but after it failed, Mombatu would have the advantage.

Maintaining her top speed became increasingly hard. Breathing hurt, and no inhalation seemed to bring quite enough oxygen. Her legs began to feel wobbly, her head throbbed with each step, and her vision became hazy.

Behind her, she heard branches cracking as the triclops reached the jungle. Despite her best efforts, Kendra had slowed, but she dug deep to resist the rubbery fatigue in her legs. And then the effects of the potion ended abruptly. The fairy wings beside her fluttered like normal. She staggered and had to brace herself against the side of a tree to keep from falling. Her strength had all but disappeared.

There was a triclops chasing her. She had to keep going. But she felt so light-headed that she wondered whether she would faint if she remained standing any longer, let alone if she tried to advance.

Strong arms scooped her up and started running. Dreamily she realized that with somebody carrying her, she could relax for a moment. She glanced to see who held her and smiled. It was Warren.

"It's Vanessa's turn to distract Mombatu," Warren whispered. "Sorry he came your way. We couldn't compete with those fireworks."

Warren set her down and fell flat beside her.

"Stay low," he whispered. "Hako was right that the triclops ignores stationary targets."

Heart beating rapidly, Kendra rested her head against the forest floor. No bed ever felt so comfortable.

"The mental fog will clear in a moment," Warren said. "Rest and let it pass."

Kendra heard Vanessa taunting the triclops amid raucous sounds of wood splintering. One good thing about Mombatu—he was not subtle. His movements could be heard from a great distance.

Footsteps approached; then Tanu crouched beside Kendra and waved something under her nose. The piquant tang of his custom smelling salts made her head snap up. Suddenly her mind was alert again, and she wondered how she could have paused to rest with a triclops in pursuit. Nostrils tingling, Kendra hopped to her feet.

"Quietly," Warren instructed.

He and Tanu led her through the lush foliage. The fairies orbited Kendra from a greater distance now that human companions had joined her. Kendra's body felt tired but functional. She was no longer near the verge of collapse.

"The speed potion wipes out your strength," Tanu said. "I can't figure out how to get rid of that effect. But your vitality should return fairly quickly."

"The potion saved my life," Kendra whispered.

"That remains to be seen," Warren said. "Hopefully we can lose Mombatu."

"Ronodin claimed that luring Mombatu to the border of the protected area would be our best move," Kendra said.

"I caught a glimpse of Ronodin," Tanu said. "Why lead Mombatu to the border?"

"He acted like it would neutralize Mombatu," Kendra said.

"How would a boundary kill him?" Warren asked. "It should only repel him."

"Ronodin didn't say it would kill him," Kendra said. "He was being all smug, as if sharing a brilliant secret."

"Do you think he was telling the truth?" Tanu asked.

"Ronodin has been an enemy to us," Kendra said. "But the hint felt genuine to me."

"He may want Mombatu out of the way for his own reasons," Warren said. "Ronodin is obviously up to mischief on the island."

"Do we think leading Mombatu to the border would work?" Tanu asked.

Kendra considered it. "I can't be certain, but I believe him."

"We have our own work to do on this island," Warren said. "If taking the triclops to the border did neutralize him, it would free us up a lot."

"I'll catch up with Hako and talk to him," Tanu said, veering away from them.

"Where is Knox?" Kendra asked.

"With Doren," Warren said. "I sent them back. Knox used a speed potion. I used one also, and now Vanessa has too. Hako seems able to manage without one. Helps that he can disappear. He's like a chameleon."

"Is that a magic power?" Kendra asked.

"I think so," Warren said. "He tried to explain it to me. Something about becoming one with the island so he doesn't stand out. The reasoning sounded sketchy, but it seems to work."

Kendra noticed her strength returning. "I think I can run again."

"Let's just walk quickly," Warren said. "We have a lot of distance to cover, and moving quietly might be better right now than going fast."

Walking behind Warren, Kendra trusted him to go the right way and avoid hazards. It was a relief to let somebody else worry about how to avoid getting eaten by a plant. "Nia?" she whispered.

The fairy drifted closer.

"Would you watch Mombatu?" she asked. "Warn us if he gets close."

Nia darted out of view.

"This is degrading work," Beruni said. "Helping clumsy humans avoid getting crushed by a superior predator."

"It's my command that you help," Kendra said.

"Somehow you were authorized by the Fairy Queen,"

Beruni said. "It must have been an act of pity. I have no choice but to do my part."

Kendra heard some rustling off to one side, and Vanessa emerged from tangled branches, her face scratched and damp with perspiration. She gave Kendra a weary nod.

"Any body parts missing?" Warren asked.

"Hako diverted Mombatu after I ran out of steam," Vanessa said. "Tanu revived me with the salts, though I'm still unsteady."

"Do you think if you bit Mombatu, you could control him in his sleep?" Kendra asked.

"In theory," Vanessa said. "His hide looks really thick, though."

"Mombatu would be a seriously powerful puppet to manage," Warren said.

"Would you still love me if I was ugly and over twenty feet tall?" Vanessa asked.

"From a safe distance," Warren replied.

A roar from Mombatu ended the chitchat and made them all flinch. Feathery fronds brushed by Kendra, rustling gently.

Tanu reappeared, flushed and gasping for air. "Hako thought your plan was worth a try. We're going to lure Mombatu to Crescent Lagoon. Hako is getting tired, though. This will have to be a group effort."

"I'll take a turn baiting the triclops," Warren said. "Want me to use another speed potion? We still have a couple."

"Maybe," Tanu said. "Wait as long as you can." He pointed. "Go that way."

"I'll just follow the sound of trees being uprooted," Warren said, hurrying away.

"I should do more cardio," Tanu panted, face shiny with perspiration.

"You're fast for a big man," Vanessa said.

"Not over long distances," Tanu said.

"I hope Newel and Grady are all right," Kendra said.

"I wish they could have occupied the triclops a little longer," Vanessa said.

"We suspected Mombatu would be a threat today," Tanu said. "At least we didn't have to deal with him until we reached the sacred pool."

Kendra plodded forward, wondering how long this forced marathon would last. Tanu left to retrieve Warren. When they returned, Warren was leaning on the big potion master, looking pale and depleted. Mombatu continued to tirelessly trample through the jungle, roaring and growling. There seemed to be no end to his energy.

Vanessa went to distract the monster, and a short time later Hako caught up with the group. "We're getting close," Hako reported. "Mombatu is learning our tricks. Pausing more. Listening more. Hesitating before attacking the most obvious target. He isn't used to tracking small, evasive prey. He's more at home going head-to-head with dragons."

"Any bright ideas?" Warren asked.

"Let's hope we can string him along a little while longer," Hako said.

"Look out!" Vanessa yelled urgently from a distance.

Kendra heard the triclops plowing toward them.

"He didn't follow Vanessa," Hako said. "He heard us. I'll try to redirect him." He pointed ahead. "Hurry that way. About five hundred yards."

Warren and Tanu broke into a full run, and Kendra followed. Hako raced off on a course to intercept Mombatu. The fairies zoomed up to Kendra and reported that Mombatu was coming.

"Slow him down," she said.

The fairies zipped away. Hako was shouting. Vanessa heckled Mombatu from farther away, but the triclops did not change course.

A moment later the triclops shouldered aside a tree a little taller than himself and rumbled into view, eyes glaring, body lathered with foamy sweat. Bellowing in triumph, he charged.

"Split up," Tanu ordered, tossing Kendra a small flask.

She bobbled it but managed to hold on. "Another one?"

"Last one," Tanu said. "Insurance if he gets too close. It should work again—might wipe you out a little more than last time. Vanessa just took her second."

Warren swerved left, Tanu cut to the right, and Kendra continued straight. She could run five hundred yards at high speed, couldn't she? Hadn't she run at least that far last time? Tanu had trusted her with the last potion. Shouldn't she help the others?

Kendra uncapped the flask and guzzled the fizzy contents. The world slowed down around her. Holding his club high, Mombatu pounded his blocky chest with his free hand as he ran. His lips peeled back, revealing blocky teeth designed for mashing.

Glaring at Tanu, the triclops turned his way.

Kendra unslung her bow, pulled the string back, and muttered, "Two hundred."

As she released the string, a swarm of arrows streaked toward the triclops. With shockingly quick reflexes, Mombatu covered his eyes with his free arm before the arrows arrived. They stuck better to his wooden club than to his thick hide, but the message was received. Mombatu flung his club at Kendra so hard that, even perceiving it at reduced speed, she barely managed to duck in time.

With a guttural grunt, Mombatu gave chase.

The race was on.

Kendra dashed ahead with everything she had. The exhaustion hadn't set in yet, and she added to her lead. A glance back showed the triclops running hard, arms and legs pumping, humps of muscle clenching and releasing, strings of saliva unfurling from his mouth.

Kendra focused on the route ahead. She couldn't waste time by tripping or getting caught in a thicket. She crashed through a stand of bamboo, poles rattling behind her. When she emerged from the bamboo, the exhaustion started. Muscling onward, she knew she had a little more time before she reached her limit again.

Scanning ahead for the Monkey Maze or the beach, Kendra saw no landmark to hint at the location of the border. She would just have to keep going until the border

stopped the triclops. Or killed him. Or whatever was going to happen.

Her breathing sped up and her lungs ached. The fire in her legs made her cry out. Her heart felt like it would burst. But her pace still resembled a sprint.

Behind her, the stand of bamboo seemed to explode as Mombatu reached it. He wasn't brushing it aside—he was blasting straight through. Glancing back, she saw that the triclops had gained on her. She didn't intend to run slower, but it hurt so much, and the thick vegetation was grasping at her.

Her legs were becoming unreliable. Her vision was blurring.

And then the effects of the potion ended.

Kendra stumbled forward, trying to maintain enough desperation to keep moving, willing herself not to pass out. She lumbered drunkenly ahead, the ground seeming to tilt back and forth beneath her feet.

Where were those smelling salts?

She heard Mombatu gaining quickly, roaring exultantly.

She reached a clearing. Up ahead, in the distance beyond the clearing, she saw some platforms in the trees.

"Send help," she mumbled incoherently, tottering out into the field.

Kendra didn't remember falling, but she noticed when she hit the ground, landing on her side. Woozy, gasping, she pushed up onto her hands and knees and crawled forward. She had to keep moving.

Her arms gave out and she twisted onto her side,

looking back as the colossal triclops stormed into the clearing. Raising his balled fists high, Mombatu closed in.

Before he reached her, with a dazzling flash, Mombatu split into three smaller creatures.

Kendra blinked her eyes and shook her head. Surely she was hallucinating. Was she seeing triple? The world was seesawing, and she was imagining the triclops had divided into smaller components.

She couldn't blink it away. The three beings remained separate. They gathered around her, looming over her, perhaps ten feet tall.

Kendra closed her eyes.

"Are you all right?" a calm, deep voice asked.

"Tired," Kendra said. "I took a speed potion."

"You're safe now," said another voice, deep and melodious. "At least safe from us."

"I just need a minute," Kendra said, unsure if she could remain conscious. "Who is talking? Did you really just split into three?"

"Within areas protected by the watchers, we are the guardians of the Sunset Pearl," a third voice said, less deep than the other two, but perhaps the richest.

Kendra tried to sit up, but she slumped back down.

"Let yourself recover," the first voice said.

"I'm going to sleep well tonight," Kendra said, her mind cloudy. "I got all my wiggles out."

She heard footsteps coming nearer, accompanied by ragged panting. Somebody dropped down beside her, and she smelled Tanu's salts.

"Yikes!" she exclaimed, sitting up, eyes watering.

"I assume you're peaceful?" Tanu checked with the guardians.

"We mean you no harm," the third voice answered.

After rubbing her eyes clear, Kendra looked up. These three hulking humanoids had light gray bodies. Leaner than Mombatu, they had more defined muscles. Each was bald except for a long ponytail, and none of them had eyes—just a big blank forehead above the nose.

"You must be Himalayan cyclopses," Tanu said.

"Correct," the second voice said.

"Your only eye is a third eye," Kendra said, remembering a conversation with Eve.

"We see you with the eyes of our minds," the third voice said.

"I'm Kendra. This is Tanu."

"I am Baroi," the third voice said.

"Hobar," the second voice said.

"Tal," the first voice said.

Kendra stood up, still tired but recovering. Tanu rose as well. Warren caught up to them.

"I thought I had seen everything," Warren said.

"Himalayan cyclopses," Kendra explained.

"Who merge into a triclops," Warren said. "You boys almost killed us."

"Our memories of our other form are a blur of rage," Tal said calmly. "We apologize for any harm done. That vicious state is a defense mechanism for the sanctuary. In times of peace, we are peaceful. When the protections go down, we merge into a form more appropriate for war."

"It was the design from the beginning," Hobar said.

Despite the imposing size of the cyclopses, their polite demeanor and soothing voices set Kendra at ease. "You were the guardians of the pearl."

They nodded.

Kendra considered them. "If you walk away from this protected area, you will combine into the triclops again."

"We will not deliberately do so," Baroi said.

Kendra waved a hand experimentally. "Do you see me doing that?"

"I not only see you waving," Tal said, "I saw you were going to do it."

"I can see you stopping," Hobar said.

"You see into the future?" Kendra asked.

"The true eye of the mind has fewer limits than a sensory organ," Baroi said. "We see in all directions. We see some things far off, across space or even time."

"Not all," Hobar added. "Not nearly all."

"But we see much," Tal said. "That which is nearby tends to be easiest to discern."

"Do you see the pearl?" Kendra asked.

"We don't see it," Baroi said. "But we can feel that it passed into the Under Realm."

"That's where my brother has been held," Kendra said. "And my . . . friend."

"Do not be shy about how much you care for your friend," Hobar said.

"Can you help me get there?" Kendra asked.

"We cannot go beyond the boundaries of this protected region without uniting into the Enforcer," Tal said. "We certainly cannot go to the Under Realm."

"The Under Realm is near and far," Hobar said. "The entrance shifts."

"To go there you must find the Phantom Isle," Baroi said. "No small task."

"The Underking is there?" Kendra asked.

"Ruling over a domain outside of this world," Tal said. "The island is the gateway."

"The Phantom Isle appears and disappears," Hobar said. "The location is ever changing."

Vanessa and Hako approached. Vanessa looked thrashed.

"I guess these guys no longer want to eat us," Warren said. "They're bonding with Kendra."

"She radiates light," Baroi said. "Perhaps she can retrieve the Sunset Pearl."

"But you don't know where to find the Phantom Isle," Kendra said.

"We do not know," Tal said.

"The isle can be located," Hobar said.

"You must recover the fool's treasure," Baroi said.

"At Desperation Beach?" Hako asked.

"Sounds like a lousy place to vacation," Warren murmured.

"Obtaining the fool's treasure might be harder than finding the Phantom Isle," Hako said.

"Not harder," Baroi said. "Necessary. The treasure begins the journey to the Phantom Isle."

"You must complete the journey, Kendra," Tal said.

"We foresee it," Hobar declared.

"Will I succeed?" Kendra asked.

They remained silent, heads bowed.

"Unknowable," Baroi said finally.

"Is that the consensus?" Warren asked.

"What one of us sees, all of us see," Tal said.

"With rare exceptions," Hobar said.

"We three are one," Baroi explained. "Even when separate."

"Kendra, if you are willing to try, you might succeed," Tal said.

"And if you fail, others will try, building on what you left behind," Hobar said.

"Until there are no others willing to try, and darkness consumes the light," Baroi said.

"We're going to succeed," Warren said bracingly.

Kendra looked over her shoulder at Warren, then at Tanu, Vanessa, and Hako. "I'll do my best," she said. "But first, I'm really thirsty."

CHAPTER TWENTY-TWO

Heartstone

Seth looked back at the island of Timbuli receding behind the boat and wondered if Kendra had survived the triclops. She had been moving like a blur when she raced out of sight. Seth hoped no harm had come to her—especially because she might actually be his sister. It was annoying that she had left him stuck to the mushroom for so long, but in the end, she had distracted the triclops as if she really cared about him.

The stories Kendra and Bracken had told him combined to form a plausible scenario, except his dark powers didn't fit with their version very well. What role would his powers have had among people who fought and imprisoned dark creatures? Seth worried he might never sort out the truth about his past. How many different versions would he encounter?

The boat advanced purposefully over the swells, Ronodin at the rudder. Seth took a sip of water from the sweet bucket. The western horizon warmed to gold as the sun sank.

"We're leaving in a different direction than we came from," Seth noted.

"Nearly the opposite," Ronodin said.

"Are we going back to the Under Realm?"

"Yes."

"By a different route?"

"We're going directly back to the island we came from."

"How?"

"Think," Ronodin said. "If we're returning to the island by going in the opposite direction . . ."

"The island moves?"

Ronodin gave a small smile. "It's why they call it the Phantom Isle."

"Also, a bunch of phantoms live there," Seth said. "Wraiths, too. I got some information from Dezia."

"That's a relief," Ronodin said, "since you collapsed the crypt and blocked access to her."

"I didn't collapse it."

"Was the cave-in a coincidence?"

"Dezia collapsed the crypt as I was leaving."

"You learned where to find the Everbloom?"

"Not exactly."

Ronodin furrowed his brow. "That's distressing."

"I'm the one who should be frustrated," Seth said. "I was

the person risking my life! Going to Dezia wasn't my idea. She only knew the general location."

"What did you learn?"

"The Everbloom is inside the volcano," Seth said. "Baga Loa. In a cave. But there are lots of caves. It will be hard to find."

"Did Dezia share thoughts on how to pinpoint the exact location?"

"She said a firewalker named Savani should know."

"I suspected *she* would know," Ronodin said. "But Savani will not divulge the site."

"She is the caretaker of this dragon prison?" Seth asked.

"Yes," Ronodin said. "Seeking the location from her would be a dead end. Why did the phantom help you?"

"I agreed to throw her token into the volcano," Seth said.

"Interesting," Ronodin said. "What token?"

"Some doll," Seth said.

"May I see it?"

Seth took the little doll from his pocket and handed it over. Ronodin released the tiller to examine the primitive doll with both hands. As Seth had suspected, the tiller seemed to manage just fine without Ronodin handling it.

Ronodin brought the doll to his face and smelled it deeply, then held the little figure of wood and woven grasses up against the sky, closing one eye to study it closely. "Dezia wants this in the volcano?"

"Yes, Dezia told me throwing the doll in there would allow her greater freedom to roam around on certain nights,"

Seth said. "And allow her to find a new lair if the preserve falls."

Ronodin handed the doll back to Seth with a sigh. "You did well enough."

"Thanks," Seth said, a little insulted by the paltry praise. "I wonder if you could have left me stuck to that flesh-eating mushroom for a little longer?"

"I had much to contend with," Ronodin said. "The triclops arrived, along with Kendra and her friends."

"At least you came back for me," Seth said. "I wondered if you would."

"Don't ever count on another," Ronodin said. "We save ourselves or we perish." He put a hand back on the tiller and raised his voice. "Take us to Bridge Cove."

The boat turned in a new direction.

"Change of plans?" Seth asked.

"We can work with what you uncovered," Ronodin said. "But we need an ointment brewed by the Pinaki people."

"Why?"

"It will render you immune to heat," Ronodin said.

"Me?"

"I'm not going into the volcano," Ronodin said.

"Wait, somebody has to go into the volcano?" Seth asked. "Is that even possible? That's going to take more than the right lotion."

"You won't go swimming in lava," Ronodin said. "But you need to get close enough to accomplish your mission."

"Where will I throw the token?" Seth asked. "Does it

have to be down the main shaft? Or would any pool of lava work?"

"You won't toss the token into the volcano," Ronodin said.

"Then why do we need the ointment?" Seth asked.

"So you can go get the Everbloom."

"I promised Dezia I would throw the token into the volcano," Seth said. "She'll haunt me if I don't."

"Not if we haunt her first," Ronodin said. "A token like she gave you shares a connection with her essence. We can exploit that connection."

"Do you mean we'll trick her?" Seth asked. "Is that fair?"

"Was it fair of the phantom to ask you to perform a perilous task?" Ronodin countered. "Especially when she didn't provide the information you were seeking."

"She told me what she knew," Seth said.

"Did she?" Ronodin said. "Are you sure? The information she shared is of questionable value. I already assumed Savani knew the location of the Everbloom. And the volcano is a likely hiding place. In the absence of specifics, Dezia would be getting something for nothing. I can use the token to bind Dezia and ensure the phantom gave you the whole story."

"You're positive she won't end up haunting me?" Seth asked.

"The phantom will learn that you are more formidable than you appear," Ronodin said. "If she crosses you, she crosses your allies."

Seth nodded, but inside he still felt like using the token

to harass the phantom was a betrayal. How long before Ronodin did something similar to him?

The sun had fallen below the horizon when the little boat approached an island smaller than Timbuli, leaving the western clouds and sky smeared with pink, red, and purple. Seth watched the colors change and fade.

"Are sunsets typically this pretty?" Seth asked.

"It's always a pleasure to watch light diminish," Ronodin said. "Behold the island of Tiba Tiba. One of the lesser islands, but home to some interesting beasts and birds, along with the tribe we seek."

Bare projections of rock interrupted the jungle on this island. The low, jagged mountains complemented the rocky coast. The boat had to weave between inhospitable reefs to get in close.

"An arch," Seth pointed out, noticing a natural stone bridge ahead of them.

"The entrance to Bridge Cove," Ronodin said. "I wouldn't recommend coming here without an enchanted vessel. The currents in the cove are merciless."

After threading between contorted rocks, the boat passed between stone walls beneath the natural arch. Hemmed in by steep sides, the cove was not spacious. The water level rose and fell dramatically with the ebb and flow of the waves.

"How do we land the boat?" Seth asked, looking up at the sheer walls of the cove.

"I'll stay with the boat," Ronodin said, indicating a wet,

knotted rope hanging down the far wall of the cove. "You're going to climb. Don't slip."

"I'm going alone?" Seth asked as the boat bobbed toward the rope.

"I don't believe the Pinaki will deal with me," Ronodin said. "As a mortal youth, you should be fine. Tell them of your need, and offer a royal kingfisher in the morning as payment."

"Is that a bird?" Seth asked.

"A rare and magical bird," Ronodin said.

"Where am I going to get one?"

"You won't," Ronodin said. "It's what I'll do tonight as you enjoy their hospitality."

"Are they cannibals?" Seth asked.

"If they ate you, it wouldn't be cannibalism," Ronodin said. "You're a different species."

"What are they?" Seth asked.

"You'll see," Ronodin said. "Just be polite and explain your need for the ointment. Promise them the kingfisher."

"Are you sure you'll catch one?"

Ronodin grinned. "I'd bet your life on it."

"How will I get the bird from you?" Seth asked.

"Come back to the cove in the morning," Ronodin said. "You'll see it." He glanced upward. "Use the rope."

The rope was now within reach, stretching down into the water near the bow. "How will I find you again?" Seth asked.

"Come back here," Ronodin said. "The village isn't far."

"Where do I go after I climb the rope?" Seth asked.

"They'll find you," Ronodin said. "Off you go."

Sighing, Seth placed one foot on the gunwale, then reached out and caught hold of the rope. Leaving the boat behind, he hauled himself up one knot at a time, waiting until his feet were secure on a knot before reaching his hands higher.

By the time he reached the top, the little boat was out of the cove. In the dusk, Seth saw three little figures approaching, not much taller than his knee, two males and a female. They had big eyes, spindly limbs, and large, flat feet. Each carried a spear and moved over the rocks with agile ease, more leaping than walking.

"Are you the Pinaki?" Seth inquired.

"What brings a human to our shore?" said the little warrior in front, stouter than the other two.

"I need some fireproof ointment," Seth said.

"These are dangerous times to voyage," the stout one said. "Your need must be great."

"Yes," Seth said.

"You came alone?" the female asked.

"My friend dropped me off," Seth said. "He left with the boat. He'll be back."

"Do you mean us any harm?" the stout one asked.

"No," Seth said.

"We shall see," the stout one said. "We will take you to the elder, and you will be tried."

"Is that how you always greet guests?" Seth asked, not loving the idea of a trial.

"All strangers," the stout one affirmed.

"Follow us," the female said.

"I'm Seth, by the way."

"Call me Foamrider," the stout one said. "That is Stoneturner, and she is Starbreaker."

They led him away from the cliffs over rocky terrain interspersed with sparse succulents. Ahead, at the edge of the jungle, Seth saw a wooden palisade just a little taller than he could reach. To the Pinaki people, the timber fencing must have seemed incredibly high.

"We have a human guest!" Foamrider called.

Small doors opened at the base of the palisade. The Pinaki could comfortably stroll through with room to spare, but Seth had to get down and crawl. On the far side, Seth stood up in a bustling village crisscrossed by cords strung from house to house. Some cords continued to the top of the palisade in places, and up into the trees beyond the wooden wall. Many of the Pinaki traveled along the cords like tightrope walkers, their feet partly wrapping around the slender lines. Framed with bamboo, the walls and roofs of the huts were composed of tightly woven leaves. Shin-high torches had been lit against the deepening dusk.

Foamrider guided Seth to a long hut on the left side of the village, forcing Seth to duck or step over a couple dozen lines to get there. It was by far the largest building in the community, the top of the roof almost reaching Seth's chin. The front doors opened, and an old man came out, his clothes brightened with shells and feathers.

"Elder!" Foamrider called. "A human guest is here to be tried."

The wizened elder looked up at Seth through squinted eyes framed by deep lines. "Hello up there. You're young. What brings you here with the sanctuary fallen?"

"Not all of it has fallen," Seth said.

"You should stay on protected ground," the elder said. "These islands are not safe. Neither is the ocean."

"I need your heat-proof ointment," Seth said.

"You risked getting devoured by dragons for our renowned ointment?" the elder asked. "It will not stop dragon fire."

"I still need it," Seth said.

"So it seems," the elder said. "Our village can shelter you for the night, but we cannot feed such a stomach as yours for long."

"Thank you," Seth said. "I don't need to stay long. I just need the ointment."

"You would need much ointment for a body as large as yours," the elder said. "Our supply is low, and lately the ingredients are scarce."

"I can give you a royal kingfisher for the ointment," Seth said.

The elder whistled. "Where are you hiding the bird?"

Several of the villagers laughed.

"My friend will bring it in the morning," Seth said.

"Your friend has a royal kingfisher?" the elder asked.

"He is retrieving it," Seth said. "He will bring it in the morning."

"If you supply such a bird, we can spare enough

ointment for you," the elder said. "Come inside the assembly hall so I can try you."

The villagers murmured with interest.

The elder withdrew into the hall, and Seth dropped down and slithered through the doorway. Most of the inside was bare ground, the loose dirt swept away, so Seth had plenty of room to sit, if not a high enough roof to stand. Five colorful birds roosted in the rafters.

"Nice birds," Seth said.

"We would be glad to add a royal kingfisher," the elder said. "We cannot renew our ointment supply until we have one."

"What do you use? The feathers?"

"Our methods are private," the elder said. "But the song of a royal kingfisher is essential. Place your hand on the heartstone." The elder tapped a large rock beside the hearth.

"Hearthstone?" Seth asked, thinking he might have heard wrong.

"Heartstone," the elder said, tapping his chest.

"All right," Seth said. The surface felt a little warm from its proximity to the fire, but otherwise the stone seemed ordinary.

"Keep your hand upon the stone," the elder said. "Do you intend to harm us?"

"No," Seth said, glancing at the heartstone. Would it work like a lie detector?

"Are you a shadow charmer?" the elder asked.

Seth hesitated. Would admitting to that disqualify him?

He decided getting caught in a lie would be much worse. "Yes. How can you tell?"

"Do you mean to cause mischief on our island with your shadow charming?"

"No."

The elder gave a nod. "You will pay for the ointment with a royal kingfisher?"

"Yes," Seth said.

"Given the life you have lived up until this point, are you a trustworthy person?" the elder asked.

Seth considered Ronodin's plot to use the token against the phantom. It hadn't been his plan, and it hadn't happened yet. He thought about releasing the undead at Blackwell Keep. If he had betrayed people who trusted him, he hadn't done it deliberately.

"I'm not perfect," Seth said. "But I do my best to be trustworthy."

The elder studied him for a moment. "You can remove your hand," he finally said.

Seth took his hand off the heartstone.

"You have a good heart," the elder said. "Not perfectly pure, but a pristine heart is so rare, I have never seen it. You will receive your ointment in the morning. Tonight, this room is yours. It is the only space large enough to contain you. Are you hungry?"

"Yeah," Seth admitted.

"Thirsty?"

"A little," Seth said. He had sipped a lot from the sweet bucket.

"We will serve you food and drink," the elder said. "I hope you like fruit and fish. Then you may rest here in peace. Our village remains secure."

"Thank you," Seth said.

"You realize the sanctuary is compromised? Nearly all protections and boundaries are down?"

"Yes," Seth said.

"Enjoy our hospitality tonight. But tomorrow, we ask that you depart at first light."

Seth nodded.

The elder smiled. "Provide a royal kingfisher, and we will celebrate the trade."

Seth hoped Ronodin wouldn't try to trick them. Was the heartstone why Ronodin had sent Seth in alone? Would the dark unicorn have failed the trial? Or did he already have a bad reputation among the Pinaki for some reason?

These little villagers seemed good and fair and hospitable. The evening meal they brought was fresh and flavorful even though the portions were small. After they left, Seth reclined on his back and gazed into the rafters, watching the movement of the birds.

Why had Ronodin avoided a village where the citizens seemed harmless and kind? Was breaking the deal with Dezia a smart idea? Ronodin had no problem with the betrayal. But it wasn't Ronodin's promise. Seth knew he was the person in danger if things went wrong, not the dark unicorn. Questions without clear answers kept Seth awake until long after the birds grew still.

CHAPTER TWENTY-THREE

Shipwreck Key

The pale color in the sky hinted at the coming dawn. Kendra approached the north side of Crescent Lagoon, where the Himalayan cyclopses had gathered. The ocean was the calmest Kendra had seen it, the lagoon a silver pond in the predawn twilight.

Inside, Kendra was not calm. Last night, after planning a treasure hunt to Desperation Beach with Savani and Tanu, Kendra had realized that Calvin was no longer with her. She had searched her clothes, called his name, rummaged through her room, and backtracked down to the seashore. Warren had taken her to the clearing where she had first met the cyclopses, but the Tiny Hero was nowhere to be seen and did not answer her cries.

Warren had sent her to bed with a promise that he would return to the corrupted pool. This morning he had informed her that he, Vanessa, and Hako had gone back there in the night, but the search yielded no success. He also told her that Savani had sent her trained parrot, Piharro, to look for him. Supposedly the bird was quite intelligent and had a knack for finding lost things. But Kendra still wanted to do more.

The cyclopses had wandered away from the Monkey Maze last night before the meeting with Savani. Kendra had looked for them in vain, hoping they could help her locate Calvin. This morning, as she and the others prepared to depart, she noticed them up on the high point to the north of the lagoon.

"Well met, Kendra," Tal said.

"Fair weather today," Hobar noted.

"You are glum," Baroi said.

"Hi, guys," Kendra said. "I was carrying a tiny person with me yesterday. A nipsie. His name is Calvin. I somehow lost him."

"You had no tiny person with you when we met yesterday," Tal said.

"We would have noticed," Hobar said.

"Really?" Kendra said. "I guess that narrows things down. I must have lost him when we were traveling to the corrupted pool. Or while running from Mombatu. He was with me when we set out."

"Our apologies for any inconvenience we caused in our other form," Baroi said.

"He's so little," Kendra said. "I have to find him. I looked for you three last night. Did you ever come inside the Monkey Maze? Hide out in one of the bigger tree houses?"

"We do not go indoors voluntarily," Tal said.

"Confined spaces cloud our vision," Hobar said.

"From inside, how would we chronicle the seasons?" Baroi asked.

"Or monitor the shapes of the clouds?" Tal said.

"Or read the dance of the stars?" Hobar said.

"We prefer the caress of the wind, the kisses of the rain, the reassurance of the earth," Baroi said.

"Here we stand now, to greet a new day dawning," Tal said.

"Can you see a nipsie anywhere?" Kendra asked. "With your special sight? He's a little bigger than normal. His people put a spell on him to make him tall. He's still miniature compared to us. About the size of my pinky."

"We're always looking," Hobar said. "We do not see a nipsie."

"We will watch for him," Baroi promised.

"Thanks," Kendra said, still worried about Calvin. Was it possible she had squashed him during the chase yesterday? She had fallen several times. Calvin had always seemed surprisingly durable. Might he simply have fallen out and gotten lost? That sounded plausible.

"If you wish to cross to Shipwreck Key before low tide, the hour to depart is at hand," Tal said.

"Travel swiftly and safely," Hobar said.

"The fate of these islands rests upon your shoulders," Baroi said.

"No pressure, right?" Kendra said.

"Vast amounts of pressure," Tal said.

"Like a congested volcano," Hobar added.

"Adapt and survive," Baroi said. "Command the situation."

"Thanks," Kendra said, hurrying to the seaside trail where Tanu, Warren, Vanessa, Knox, Newel, Doren, and Hako awaited. Tess was staying behind again, with Grady and Savani.

"How did it go?" Warren asked. "Had they seen him? In a vision or anything?"

"No," Kendra said. "I'm really worried."

"He'll turn up," Tanu said. "Calvin is very independent. He probably lassoed a bat and is touring the other islands."

"I bet those nonclopses are faking blindness," Knox said.

"Nonclopses?" Doren asked.

"No eyes," Knox said. "Why should imaginary eyes in their minds count?"

"Because they can see with them," Kendra said.

"No way," Knox said. "You know their eyes are hidden somewhere, sneaking peeks. Maybe on their palms. Or under their ponytails."

"They seem legitimate to me," Vanessa said.

"I bet they remember being Mombatu just fine," Knox said. "They play dumb to seem innocent. Avoid consequences."

"Just because you would do that," Kendra said.

"What if they combine and come at us from behind?" Knox asked.

"You have the wrong worries, young one," Hako said. "Look ahead for today's trouble, not behind. The triclops is gone, but there are many dangers at this sanctuary, and away from the Monkey Maze we'll be in fallen areas, where all protections have collapsed."

"Other dangers don't erase the problem of a triclops sneak attack," Knox said. "If it happens, I called it."

"We should hurry," Hako said. "Reaching Desperation Beach precisely at low tide gives us the best chance to succeed."

He established a brisk pace. Kendra walked beside Warren. "Should we have brought Knox?" she whispered.

"It wasn't my first choice," Warren whispered back. "He won't be denied. He wants to help find his cousin."

"We're now beyond the protection of the moai," Hako announced as the lagoon passed out of sight. "Stay watchful. Everyone has a shovel?"

Kendra's was more of a spade. Tanu wore his hefty shovel across his back. The satyrs used theirs like walking sticks.

"Yes," Warren replied for the group.

"I also brought chains and grapnels," Hako said. "We're fishing for a rare prize today."

"We dig it up at low tide?" Knox asked.

"In less than three hours," Hako said.

"We can get to the treasure that quickly?" Knox asked.

"Proximity is not the problem," Hako said. "Many have tried to retrieve this reward. Some claim to have seen the treasure box. But the tide always interferes before any can lay hold of it. And as the tide rises, the spider eels come."

Kendra took a little hop away from Hako, trying to banish the slithering, biting images that came to mind.

"Tell me these eels stay in the water," Newel said.

Hako shook his head. "They venture onto the sand to pursue prey. The eels are voracious and run on a hundred spindly legs."

"Spiders have eight," Knox said.

"The number is off, but the legs resemble those of a spider," Hako said. "We won't beat the eels in a fight. Once they show up, we leave. If we have the treasure, we run. If we don't, we also run."

"I have more speed potions," Tanu said. "Some other potions as well. A few gaseous potions. Five doses of courage. I'm working on some new concoctions with Uma. That woman has forgotten more about brewing than I will ever learn."

"We should use some of the speed potions to dig," Vanessa said.

"The challenge hinges on getting to the treasure quickly," Hako said. "So yes."

"I'm trying to remember the poem you told us last night," Doren said, twirling his shovel.

"Long ago, a wild boar was found with the map and the poem tattooed on it," Hako said. "The islanders who copied it down introduced us to the fool's treasure. Digging at the spot revealed by the map has led to glimpses of the prize."

"Can we hear the poem again?" Newel said.

Hako recited:

> *Sift deeply through the golden sand*
> *If you by chance should come to stand*
> *Beside the wheel with bold command*
> *You'll hold the treasure in your hand*

"Has anyone seen a wheel while digging?" Kendra asked.

"The traditions are old and confusing," Hako said. "Some report to have seen a stone wheel near the treasure box. Others believe the wheel is in the box, or they claim to have glimpsed an insignia on the box. One treasure hunter theorized the wheel might refer to a charm on a necklace lost along the beach. The only aspect the stories agree upon is that the treasure always slips out of reach. Seasoned adventurers have gone mad with frustration."

"We need to do something others haven't," Kendra said.

"To get inside the box, we need to think outside the box," Knox said.

Kendra rolled her eyes at the triteness.

"Has anyone dug for the treasure using a speed potion?" Warren asked.

"Not to my knowledge," Hako said.

"When the potion wears off, we might need stretchers to drag us away from the eels," Warren said.

"My salts will have to suffice," Tanu said.

"Have satyrs ever helped?" Newel asked.

"I'm almost sure satyrs are a first," Hako said.

"Satyrs have noses for treasure," Doren said. "Mark my words."

They mostly hiked in silence after that. The trail paralleled the sea, running alongside beaches, over rocky stretches, and across clifftops. Occasionally the path angled inland, through jungle or marshland, but it always returned to the seaside before long. The day brightened and warmed as the sun rose, reflecting off the water.

As they came to the end of a bluff, Hako pointed ahead to a narrow spit of sand, no wider than a sidewalk, extending from the coast to a low island perhaps a mile away. The relatively calm ocean lapped at the sandbar but never covered it.

"The crossing to Shipwreck Key will remain above water for less than two hours," Hako said.

"Twice a day?" Kendra asked.

"Yes," Hako said. "Low tide comes every twelve hours and twenty-five minutes."

"Lots of shipwrecks out there?" Knox asked.

"Many in the water, and a strange amount on the beaches," Hako said. "The formerly wooden vessels that ran aground are all petrified."

"Petrified ships?" Warren asked.

"We have no explanation for it," Hako said. "These islands harbor many mysteries."

"Hoofs are not designed for deep sand," Newel complained as they plodded out onto the strip flanked by the sea.

"Feet aren't perfect for it either," Knox said. "Especially in shoes."

"What if we get stuck out there?" Kendra asked.

"Shipwreck Key has a high point only thirty feet above sea level," Hako said. "Nearly half of the islet disappears during high tide. If we get trapped, we'll wait it out. But with the protections dormant everywhere but Crescent Lagoon, let's not get stuck."

Kendra scanned the water as they walked. Scattered starfish inhabited the shallows, and an occasional ray glided by, broad fins rippling. The sandbar subtly widened as they went, until it joined the shore of Shipwreck Key. Tall palm trees populated the center of the islet, with broad, white beaches at either hand.

Where was Seth right now? Could he be on one of the islands? It had sounded like he spent most of his time in the Under Realm. It saddened her to think of Ronodin mentoring him. The dark unicorn could be very persuasive. It was hard to imagine what it might be like dealing with him without her memories. It was easy to picture how Seth might feel very confused and slow to trust anyone. Hopefully the present mission would bring her a step closer to rescuing him.

Hako turned right upon reaching the key. Fine white sand eventually gave way to a rocky section where Kendra stepped carefully. Crabs scuttled into hiding as the group approached, none bigger than a bar of soap. Some of them walked with upraised claws, as if signaling a touchdown.

The beach beyond the rocks glittered with golden sand. Three slanted masts of a large sailing ship projected from the sand about halfway down the beach, along with a large section of the bow, as if the stone ship had been frozen in an attempt to surge up out of the sand. No sails or rigging survived, but one of the masts had a crow's nest intact. A few smaller stony masts jutted from the sand in other places, along with one end of a petrified canoe.

"This way," Hako said, jogging swiftly over the sand.

The increased pace brought them quickly to the edge of

the water, not far from the largest petrified ship. The waves lapped gently against the sand.

"Is it always this calm?" Knox asked.

"Offshore reefs absorb many of the waves here," Hako said. "But this is a very placid day. The spot where we want to dig is still too threatened by water. We'll start in about ten minutes."

"Did you ever think you would dig for buried treasure?" Kendra asked Knox.

"I figured I would get around to it sooner or later," Knox said. "The stone boats are weird."

"Yes," Kendra agreed.

"Think this beach has some sort of Medusa?" he asked.

"Maybe," Kendra said. "It is a magical preserve."

"A gorgon like Medusa wouldn't turn wood to stone," Warren said. "At least, no gorgon I know about."

"It's a mystery," Hako said.

"At least I don't see any stone people," Knox said.

"The eels don't leave much behind," Hako said.

Getting his chains and grapnels ready, Hako talked to Warren and Tanu about a strategy for pulling up the treasure box. Kendra practiced a little with her spade. The sand was fairly easy to scoop. She knelt down and pinched some damp sand between her fingers, feeling the fine grains. The sand was so golden that she wondered if it might be valuable.

"Is there real gold in the sand?" Kendra asked.

"A little, I suspect," Hako said. "The sand only looks golden here, though. Any you take away fades to a duller hue."

"Enchantment?" Vanessa asked.

"Perhaps," Hako said, holding his shovel ready. "Prepare your potions. We have only a limited time. Ready?"

Kendra reached for her flask.

"Kendra and Knox, save your flasks to escape the eels," Tanu ordered. "Warren and I will use ours first. Then Hako and Vanessa, if they choose. I have a few extra."

"You need to brew some for satyrs," Newel said.

"Someday, maybe," Tanu replied.

"Let's go," Hako said, jamming his shovel into the sand about ten feet from the nearest water. Kendra wondered why he had started so far from the water until she beheld how rapidly the hole widened.

Tanu and Warren began digging in fast motion. This was her first chance to calmly watch somebody else use a speed potion. Their incredible haste made her giggle. She and the others helped, and the hole grew quickly. By the time Tanu and Warren slowed, they were four feet below sea level, with heaps of moist sand surrounding the hole, forming a lumpy wall against the sea.

Hako, Newel, and Doren kept vigorously digging while Vanessa used smelling salts to revive Tanu and Warren. Kendra and Knox helped shape the barricade of sand around the hole, evening it out, making sure the side facing the ocean was piled highest.

Soon Warren and Tanu were digging again. Kendra kept her eyes squinted to help protect them from the moist sand flying everywhere.

"Should I use the potion?" Vanessa asked.

"Not yet," Hako said. "Wait until we see the treasure box. We'll want a burst of speed right then."

As they reached six feet below sea level, Doren called out, "I struck something!"

Everyone in the hole gathered to him, and together they scraped sand from the top of a petrified wooden box bound in iron. Hako crouched down, trying to fasten his grapnels to the box as the others dug deeper.

"Told you," Doren gloated. "Satyrs have a nose for treasure!"

"No!" Warren cried.

"What?" Kendra called. Too many bodies were crowded around the treasure box for her to see.

"It's sinking!" Vanessa shouted.

"I can't see it anymore!" Doren cried.

"Drink," Hako suggested, unstopping his potion.

He and Vanessa chugged the contents of their flasks and started digging frantically. The others moved back to give them room. The treasure box came back into view several times, but overall continued to sink. When the effects of the potion wore off, the deepest part of the hole was nearly nine feet below sea level. Hako and Vanessa slumped to the ground, and Tanu got out his smelling salts.

"This is like trying to dig a treasure out of quicksand!" Warren complained.

As Newel, Doren, and Warren kept digging, Kendra noticed water leaking from the wall of the hole about five feet down. As she watched, the flow increased from several trickles to steady streams.

"Water," Kendra warned.

"I feel the box again," Warren called, shovel clanging.

Water spouted into the hole from a dozen places. Hako and Vanessa struggled to stand. As they regained their balance, they found themselves up to their shins in seawater.

Warren dropped to his knees, a grapnel in each hand. "These won't hook on!" he shouted in frustration. "I can't get them to grip! No! It sank again!"

"Keep trying," Hako called. "The water is slowing down. I'll dig a channel to divert some of it."

"The tide isn't back in yet," Tanu complained. "Why all the water?"

"The fool's treasure is notoriously elusive," Hako said.

Frustrated and feeling useless, Kenda stared at the sea. There was no sign of eels, but the water seemed slightly higher than earlier. As she peered up the beach at the huge ship projecting out of the sand, she noticed it was farther inland than seemed natural. Had it gotten stuck there at high tide?

She looked down into the hole at everyone splashing around, scooping up more water than sand at this point. They were going to fail. She knew it. This was what everyone in the past had tried. Hako's map had been used many times. People had dug at this spot. And everyone had always failed.

Glancing back at the masts projecting from the sand, and thinking about the poem, Kendra had an idea. It might be ridiculous, but not much sillier than chasing a stone treasure box as it sank ever deeper into a watery pit.

"Guys," Kendra declared. "I want to try something."

CHAPTER TWENTY-FOUR

Desperation Beach

The ship has a wheel," Kendra said. "What if the treasure is by the wheel of the petrified ship?"

Still digging, Hako grunted out the poem:

> *Sift deeply through the golden sand*
> *If you by chance should come to stand*
> *Beside the wheel with bold command*
> *You'll hold the treasure in your hand*

"The map and the poem are as old as the treasure," Hako said. "The map shows that this is the correct place to dig. The treasure has been seen here, including by us."

"It's called the fool's treasure for a reason," Kendra said. "It has remained elusive because everyone has missed something. It's slipping away for a reason. The poem mentions a wheel. Have you seen one?"

"No wheel," Hako said gruffly. "Just a treasure box."

"I'll go investigate with Kendra," Vanessa volunteered. "We have too many people down here anyhow. Help me up?"

Newel and Doren gave her a boost.

"We'll come supervise," Newel said. "I know a cursed treasure when I see one."

"I'll watch for eels," Doren said.

Shovels in hand, Kendra and Vanessa ran toward the petrified ship. Charging across the deep, dry sand made Kendra feel slow and awkward.

"The wheel will be toward the stern," Vanessa panted. "If I know my ships, it will be just behind the third mast."

Three petrified masts jutted up from the sand, all at the same angle, the first almost uncovered toward the front of the stone ship. The bow of the ship faced seaward, as if the ship had backed in to the shore.

They reached the third mast. Kendra paused to marvel at how closely the stone mast mimicked the texture of the original wood.

"The sand looks pretty deep here," Kendra said.

"From the angle of the ship, it might be ten or twelve feet down to the deck," Vanessa said. "To reach the wheel we'll need a hole deeper than the one by the sea. But the water shouldn't bother us here for some time."

"The eels might," Kendra said.

"We'll deal with them when they come," Vanessa said.

"Thanks for backing me up," Kendra said.

"It made more sense than the frenzy in that mudhole," Vanessa said.

A couple of paces behind the mast, Vanessa started digging. Kendra began scooping sand as well. The satyrs caught up and lent their shovels to the effort. The hole did not take shape very well at first, where the sand was dry. But as they got deeper, the sand became damper and more manageable.

Not long after, Knox joined them. "Hako is really focused over there. I started to feel like I was getting in the way. I'm pretty sure he wants to take a bite out of the treasure box."

A minute later Warren came along, soaked clothing dusted with sand, hair wet. "The hole is totally flooded," Warren said. "Hako is still catching glimpses of the box, diving for it. Tanu is there to help lift in case Hako can get those grapnels attached. I can't be over there any longer. Hako is like a captain going down with the ship."

Warren drank his second speed potion and gave one to Vanessa as well. They worked furiously, causing a miniature sandstorm. The others turned away from them, still digging, backs getting steadily peppered with little clumps of sand. By the time Warren and Vanessa collapsed, they had the hole to almost six feet down.

Knox ran back to borrow smelling salts from Tanu. Hako and Tanu returned with him, looking half drowned. Tanu used his salts to revive Warren and Vanessa.

"I wish you guys had remained at the treasure," Hako said. "We could have used all hands there. I touched it several more times."

Kendra felt annoyed by his scolding. She didn't think her presence would have made any difference in reaching the petrified treasure box. They had all been there for several failed attempts before the hole got flooded.

"We're giving this a try," Vanessa said, picking up her shovel.

"Not for much longer," Hako said. "The beach is quite level. When the tide comes in, the water rises fast. The sea swallows the entire beach at high tide, clear back to the trees. And don't forget the eels."

"Help dig for now," Vanessa said.

Kendra wanted to hug Vanessa. Hako had clearly become fixated on the treasure box and saw no value in her idea of digging to the wheel of the ship. But what if they found the treasure here? And even if they didn't, they could at least dismiss the idea of the ship wheel being relevant to the poem.

Tanu took another potion to help them dig faster, but Hako declined. With many shovels working, the hole widened and deepened. Kendra went to work at the top with Knox and Newel, moving displaced sand away from the hole.

"I think I've reached the spokes of the wheel!" Warren called.

Kendra looked down as Warren dug away more sand, revealing the top of the stone steering wheel. Tanu sat off to the side as Vanessa revived him with smelling salts.

"Let's uncover it and get out of here," Hako said. "If this leads to anything, I will eat my shirt."

"What's that?" Knox called, pointing out to sea.

Kendra shifted her attention to the ocean. The sea had drawn closer since the last time she looked. The motion of something scuttling out of the water drew her eyes. The serpentine body slithered forward, assisted by dozens of legs that crooked up to the sides like those of a spider. The ugly head was larger than a basketball, the fierce mouth full of needle teeth.

"A spider eel!" Kendra called. "It's huge!"

"Keep a low profile," Hako said, scrambling up out of the hole. "It's a scout. When they spot us they will swarm."

The eel moved in bursts, first one way, then another, mouth opening wider in rhythmic pulses. After a few moments it returned to the sea. Farther down the beach, Kendra spotted another eel coming out of the water. Then two more.

When Kendra checked on the progress in the hole, she found the steering wheel mostly uncovered. Knox shoveled furiously around it, having taken his speed potion. Kendra still had hers. Should she use it to dig, or save it to run?

An eel with a head the size of a sports bag came farther out of the water than the others had ventured, about a hundred yards to the left of the ship. Its body had to be forty feet long. Kendra kept a careful eye on it. How big did these things get? How many were out there? In hunter mode, Hako sank close to the sand and seemed to almost vanish. Kendra held very still until the big eel turned back to the water.

"It will get bad soon," Hako whispered loudly enough for all to hear. "If we stay much longer, we will be devoured."

Kendra realized it was now or never, so she drank the potion and slid down the side of the hole. She started digging quickly while everyone else seemed to move in slow motion. As Tanu administered smelling salts to Knox, Kendra got down to the base of the steering wheel. Shovels scraping against the stone, she and the others began clearing the petrified deck.

Most of the deck around the wheel looked like wooden planks turned to stone, but right in front of the wheel was a sandstone block, perhaps to let whoever was steering stand a little taller. Kendra saw no sign of a treasure.

Her breathing was becoming labored and her vision swam. The shovelfuls of sand seemed to quadruple in weight. The muscles in her arms strained and burned. Kendra sat down as the others slowly expanded the clear area around the wheel. They were no longer digging a hole. They were excavating an archeological site.

"Widen the radius," Tanu said quietly.

Kendra's head was swimming. She wanted to lie down and sleep. The effects of the potion ended abruptly. Everyone seemed to be working faster.

"Help," Kendra murmured, her limbs exhausted. "Salt."

Tanu put the salts under her nostrils, and alertness returned. They had cleared several feet in all directions around the ship's wheel without revealing anything of note.

Except for the oddly placed sandstone block. Could it secretly be a box? Was it there by accident? It looked very plain.

"Here come the eels in force," Hako said. "Time's up. I'll run left, try to misdirect them. Give me a moment and then run right. It's now or never, people."

Hako moved out of view. Newel, Doren, and Knox started clambering out of the hole.

"If you by chance should come to stand," Kendra whispered, "beside the wheel with bold command."

She went right up to the wheel and laid a hand on it.

"Show me the treasure," she whispered, hoping nobody heard her. It was a long shot but seemed worth trying.

Her words had no discernible impact.

There had to be some trick to this. The poem asked for a wheel. They had found one. She was beside it. How was she supposed to make a bold command? According to the poem, that was the key to holding the treasure. Would a commander stand at the wheel? Or by the wheel? Where did she need to stand?

Vanessa and Warren climbed out of the hole.

"We're in trouble," Warren called down. "Hako wasn't kidding. Hurry."

"We better go," Tanu said.

"Wait," Kendra said, stepping onto the sandstone block and placing both hands on the stone wheel.

Something was suddenly different.

No, everything was different.

She could feel the waves against the beach. Feel the ships buried in the sand.

The experience reminded her of the time she had touched the Oculus. She was perceiving more than her senses ordinarily allowed. Much more.

"No joke," Warren said. "They're swarming. Hundreds of them."

Kendra could feel the eels slithering over the sand, their numberless feet scrambling.

"Come on," Tanu said, grabbing her arm.

She jerked out of his grasp. "No. This is it. Something is happening."

"We're out of time," Tanu said.

"We can go gaseous," Kendra said.

Tanu held up two flasks. "We might be cutting it close even for that."

While talking to Tanu, Kendra continued her extrasensory experience. It was like the beach had become part of her. She could feel how deep the sand went, perceive the encroaching sea, distinguish where shells were buried. She could sense the hole filled with water left by their digging, the mounds of sand around it, the location of the petrified chest. She felt the footfalls of her fleeing friends. The hoofs of the satyrs.

And the spider eels. So many spider eels.

She and her friends were in serious trouble.

Kendra brought her focus to the hole where she and Tanu were standing. She could feel the contours of the ship in the sand. Dozens of eels were squirming toward the ship. They would reach it momentarily. She reflexively wanted to raise the ship out of the way.

And suddenly the entire ship was thrust up by the sand. Kendra not only felt the motion through her sand senses but perceived it happening around her. The sand shoved the ship upward, and suddenly she and Tanu were no longer in a hole. Tons of grainy particles cascaded off the deck to either side. Kendra helped will the sand off the deck, pushing with her mind, and the particles went flying.

The petrified ship now rested as high on the beach as

it would upon water, leaving much of the vessel submerged in sand. The deck was now well beyond reach of the eels. Kendra could feel that if she used the sand to push the boat too high, it would tip.

"Did you do that?" Tanu asked, wide-eyed.

"Yes," Kendra said. "I can feel the sand. I can sense the whole beach. But I don't just feel it. I'm somehow connected to it. I can control the sand, almost like how I can control my hand."

"You're commanding it," Tanu said. "You were right about the poem. Can you help the others?"

From her new, higher vantage point, Kendra could see her friends fleeing to the left and Hako running to the right, all retreating away from the water toward the palm trees. The seaward half of the beach now teemed with eels. Kendra saw Hako stab one in the eye with a knife after dodging its strike. He was about to be overwhelmed.

Besides seeing Hako with her eyes, Kendra could feel his steps on the sand. She forced a wall of sand up around him, the beach immediately responding to her desire. She found that by compacting the sand, she could make it hold its shape nicely, protecting Hako within a tall, open-topped cylinder. Several eels flailed against the base of the cylinder, but none made a serious attempt to scale it.

Turning her attention to Knox, Warren, Vanessa, Newel, and Doren, Kendra envisioned the beach forming an enormous sand castle around them. The creation was simple in shape but massive in scale, with an outer wall more than twenty feet above the beach and a main tower nearly twice that height.

With her friends safely behind sandy barriers, Kendra focused on the top layer of sand beneath the eels and curled it up and away toward the sea, catapulting hundreds of eels into the air over the water. As the layer of sand flung outward into a cloud, Kendra could still feel every grain, and she pulled them back in, returning them to the beach.

"Whoa," Tanu said. "That was amazing."

"It isn't hard," Kendra said. The beach had somehow become an extension of herself. Controlling it seemed perfectly natural.

A few eels wormed back onto the beach, and Kendra raised a twelve-foot wall just shy of where the sea had encroached, compacting the grains of sand so tightly that no water could leak through. Then she bowed the center of the wall outward, pushing back the tide until there was more beach exposed than when they had first arrived, leaving the ends of the wall curved inland so the water couldn't slip around the sides.

"I can feel the treasure box under the original hole we dug," Kendra said.

"Can you raise it to the surface?" Tanu asked.

Kendra found it was a simple matter of pushing up the sand beneath the chest while gently squeezing the sand around it. A moment later the petrified treasure box erupted from the beach and rested in plain sight. Kendra reached out to the sand cylinder and created an archway for Hako to escape, then created a similar archway in the castle wall.

Hako emerged from his sandy confinement. A moment later the others exited the castle.

Tanu cupped his hands around his mouth. "Kendra has control of the beach. The treasure box is on the surface. Get it before the tide rises."

Kendra was impressed by how loudly Tanu could shout when he needed to be heard. Everyone ran toward the treasure chest. Some eels started trying to slip around the ends of the seawall she had raised, but Kendra ripped up more sand and hurled them back into the water.

Kendra could feel her friends' footsteps on the sand. She considered moving the sand beneath them to hasten their progress, but she wasn't sure if she could do it with enough finesse to avoid harming them. She did move the treasure box toward them, but she left it still once they got close.

"I'll eat my shirt with mustard!" Hako called out.

The group gathered around the petrified box. Warren and Tanu tried unsuccessfully to lift it.

"It's brutally heavy!" Warren cried.

"I'll try to pick the lock!" Hako called.

Even from up on the ship, Kendra could see the big iron lock holding the lid closed. Hako got out some gear and knelt in front of the chest. Kendra repelled more eels trying to worm around the wall.

"Got it!" Hako crowed.

He and Warren raised the lid together. Hako distributed the contents of the box to the others. Kendra could see gold and jewels.

"Mission accomplished!" Hako called. "Let's go!"

Warren closed the lid, and everyone started racing away from the water toward the palm trees. The satyrs flanked Knox.

"We should scram too," Tanu said.

"Let me finish up," Kendra said.

She let the petrified ship sink into the sand until the deck where she and Tanu stood was level with the beach. Kendra made sure the seawall was holding strong, flung away some encroaching eels one last time, and stepped off the sandstone block.

The instant Kendra moved off the sandstone, she lost all connection to the beach. Even after such a short time in sync with the sand, it felt a little like losing a limb. The sand was now separate and inert, no longer hers to command.

"Are you all right?" Tanu asked.

Kendra realized she wasn't moving. "I'm good. It was kind of a jolt losing the connection."

"We should hurry," Tanu said. "Without you guarding the beach, who knows how soon it will be flooded with water and eels?"

They leaped over the railing of the ship into the sand and followed the others into the palm trees. By the time Kendra reached the trees, she looked back to see water gushing around the ends of the seawall to fill the previously protected beach. Writhing eels came with the water.

"This way," Hako said, leading them deeper into the palms, angling back toward the crossing to the larger island. "We may have been fast enough to return without waiting twelve hours."

"What was in the box?" Kendra asked as they jogged.

Warren held up a slim stone tablet. "This has a map. And a lot of text. We'll sort through the rest later."

"The goal is to find the Phantom Isle," Hako said. "The map could be the key."

"We found some gold and jewels too," Newel mentioned.

"Quite a good haul," Doren said.

"You are a genius, Kendra," Hako said. "If we had relied on my instincts, that treasure would have gone unclaimed until the end of tides."

"That's why we're a team," Tanu said diplomatically. "Thank you for leading us here, Hako."

"I just hope the treasure guides us where we want to go," Hako said.

They reached the white sand beach and found the strip of sand back to the island covered by an inch or two of water. Hako splashed out onto the slightly submerged sandbar.

"What about the eels?" Knox cried.

"I never see them over here," Hako said. "Hurry."

Kendra and the others splashed along behind Hako. At its deepest the water barely came above her ankles. When they arrived at the opposite beach, everyone stopped to catch their breath.

Kendra moved to where Warren was studying the stone tablet. The others gathered to him as well.

"The map has lots of words," Kendra said, trying to get a good look.

"We'll try to translate them when we get back to Crescent Lagoon," Warren said.

"I can read them," Kendra said.

"Being fairykind comes with some skills," Warren said, handing the tablet to her.

Kendra noticed that the islands were simply identified as "land," but the ocean was full of details. She recognized the shape of Timbuli from the map in Savani's room. A trail from Crescent Lagoon ran down to an underwater settlement.

"This is a map to the merfolk village," Kendra said. "It's under the sea."

"Scuba gear," Knox said.

"Way under the sea, by the look of it," Kendra said.

"Submarine?" Knox asked.

"It says the demon Remulon holds the compass to the Phantom Isle," Kendra said. "The merfolk protect the secret of his lair."

"The merfolk are not easy to deal with," Hako said.

"There is a formula for a potion," Kendra said. "It's called the Elixir of Dry Depths."

"You're kidding," Tanu said. "Does it list the ingredients?"

"Looks like it," Kendra said.

"That potion is legendary," Tanu said. "If we can brew it, we won't need scuba gear or submarines."

"What does it do?" Knox asked.

"Under the influence of that potion, we could move through water as if it were air," Tanu said.

"Let me guess," Newel said. "It won't work on satyrs."

"Probably not," Tanu said.

Doren gave Newel a high five. "Nap time."

CHAPTER TWENTY-FIVE

Negotiations

In a quiet room in the Under Realm, Seth sat at a round, iron table with Ronodin and the Sphinx. The chairs were iron as well, cold and hard to the touch, and heavy enough that moving them was no small matter. On the table rested a lantern, a vial of ointment obtained from the Pinaki people, and Dezia's wooden token.

"May I?" asked the Sphinx, reaching for the doll.

"Sure," Seth said.

The Sphinx picked up the little doll, hefted it, and began examining it from various angles, tapping it here and there with his forefinger. Ronodin watched intently.

Seth glanced at the ointment. Earlier that day, he had found the royal kingfisher in a wooden cage at the appointed location and received the ointment as planned. Seth had met up with Ronodin at Bridge Cove without difficulty, and, after boating back to the Phantom Isle, Ronodin had gone off in private to summon the Sphinx.

"You want to use the phantom to help find the Everbloom?" the Sphinx verified.

"Exactly," Ronodin said.

"I know just the person to do this for us," the Sphinx said. "I'll need to keep the token."

"Can we destroy the token after we get the Everbloom?" Seth asked.

The Sphinx shook his head. "If you throw that token in the volcano after we use it to control the phantom, you invite retaliation. The token must be kept secure to hold Dezia bound."

Seth frowned. "I agreed to throw it in the volcano."

"The phantom took advantage of you," the Sphinx said. "She asked too much from you for too little in return. Fortunately, she underestimated your friends."

"Outsmarting a phantom is standard practice, Seth," Ronodin said. "If you're not in charge, you're getting played. The undead don't call the shots. Are you a shadow charmer or a shadow chump?"

"Of course I don't want to be played," Seth said. "I know I'm new at this. But I don't like going back on a promise."

"The phantom will not be pleased you broke the arrangement," the Sphinx said. "But she will be powerless to retaliate. We can make her very useful. An incorporeal being will have a much easier time searching those caverns for the Everbloom than we would. The heat-repelling ointment you retrieved has limits. After Dezia finds a route, you'll have a direct path to the Everbloom instead of needing to negotiate a convoluted labyrinth where some paths lead to molten lava or volcanic creatures."

Seth wasn't sure if he wanted to force Dezia to find a route. Yet both the Sphinx and Ronodin seemed to think this was the obvious move. Right now, they were his only allies. Did he want to risk throwing the token into the volcano even though they thought it would be foolish? Did he want to take sole responsibility for finding the Everbloom?

Ronodin folded his hands. "Destroying the token in the volcano gives Dezia a very long leash. The phantom will have more power to haunt you if you follow her plan. Don't let the undead set the terms. The Sphinx's way allows Dezia less freedom to roam. And it gives you more information."

"All right," Seth finally said, feeling outnumbered and not seeing another option. "Just try not to get me haunted."

"You'll see," the Sphinx assured him. "It will be better this way."

"We have some experience in these matters," Ronodin said.

The Sphinx raised his head to look down one of the passages diverging from the room. "Do you feel that?"

Seth reached out to mentally probe the darkness. A sinister presence was coming slowly toward them. "Revenant," he said.

"Bardox," Ronodin specified.

"You know him by feel?" Seth asked.

"He speaks for the Underking," Ronodin said.

"I cannot abide the company of a revenant," the Sphinx said. "Those days have passed for me. Can I take the doll?"

Ronodin looked to Seth.

The approach of the revenant was undeniable, but part of Seth wondered if they were using the situation as leverage to force him to quickly part with the phantom's token. There would be no going back after this. Was he really going to do this their way? How much did he know about phantoms anyway? "Sure, go," Seth said.

The Sphinx grabbed the doll and marched away down a passage where Seth felt no dark presences. Ronodin put a finger against his lips and turned to watch the revenant approach.

"Remember how to interact with the Underking," Ronodin whispered. "He is ancient and incredibly powerful. Be careful about sharing any desires. He'll exploit your wants and needs. Be careful what you agree to do for him."

"You make it sound like I'll be speaking directly to him," Seth whispered back.

"You will," Ronodin said. "Bardox is just a mouthpiece. Almost like a telephone."

A moment later, an emaciated ruin of a man hobbled into view, cradling a metal weight that was shackled to one ankle. He was hairless and pale, the tendons in his neck stood out, and his ribs jutted grotesquely. The thickest part of his arms were his elbows, and the thickest part of his legs were the knees.

"Bardox," Ronodin greeted. "You're looking trim!"

"I must confer with Seth alone," Bardox said, somehow shaping a strangled croak into words.

"That is my cue to exit," Ronodin said. He patted Seth's shoulder. "Have a productive discussion. You can do this."

Seth gave a nod.

Ronodin left.

Seth waited.

Bardox stared emptily.

"I'm Seth."

Bardox offered no reply.

After another moment, Bardox opened his mouth so wide it looked like he was screaming. The whispery voice of the Underking emerged, just as Seth remembered it.

"Have you given thought to my offer to remain here in the Under Realm?" the Underking asked. Seth heard the words with his ears, but they also seemed to burrow into his mind. He felt a pull to obey whatever was asked and had to shake himself in order to resist.

"I don't want to stay here permanently," Seth said.

"You are in your element here," the Underking said. "You could do very well."

"I'm content learning from Ronodin," Seth said.

"What do you really want?" the Underking pressed, the whispery words squirming into Seth's psyche.

"I told you. I just want to study with Ronodin."

"Is that all? Look deeper and speak true. I have sensed questions growing within you. Dispense with false pretenses."

Seth paused. Ronodin had warned him against sharing

desires. But how much could it matter if the Underking already knew? Was there a chance the Underking could help?

"I want my memories back," Seth said.

"A mortal life is but a flicker," the Underking said.

"It's what I have," Seth said. "I want to make sense of it."

"Very little lies beyond my reach," the Underking said. "I could learn who took your identity and how it was accomplished. Pledge to serve me, and your memories will be restored."

"Aren't I already helping you?" Seth asked.

"Thus far, you have proven useful," the Underking said. "You would benefit infinitely more from a permanent arrangement. I do not make this offer casually or often. You have the potential to become as endless as night and shadow."

The suggestion tugged at him. The words felt compelling, as if only a fool would ignore such an opportunity. Seth felt as if he were treading water in a persistent current that was drawing him toward an undesired destination. If he drifted, if he stopped resisting, he would end up doing the will of the Underking. With effort, Seth held up the hand affixed to the ghostly manacle. "I want this gone. I want to be free."

"Bring me the Everbloom," the Underking said.

"If I bring you the Everbloom, can I go free?" Seth asked.

"After bringing me the Everbloom, if you still want freedom, I will grant it," the Underking said.

"What about my memories?"

"Pledge to join me, and I will help you regain your memories," the Underking said.

"That's asking too much," Seth said.

"What do you expect these memories to do?" the Underking said. "Most mortals are lost and wandering. The more information they have, the more confused they become. Your memories are as likely to haunt and disappoint you as they are to provide comfort and clarity."

"They might do both," Seth said. "But I deserve to know my past. I've heard conflicting versions. Is there a reason you don't want me to remember?"

"Why should such a trifling matter concern me?"

"Forget about helping me," Seth said. "If it doesn't concern you, and since I've been helping you, can you allow me some time to investigate my past? As soon as possible? Ronodin comes and goes. Could I have some of that leniency?"

"Ronodin has no obligation to me," the Underking said. "He has worked off his debts. After you are free, you can go where you will."

"We may have the Everbloom before long," Seth said. "Ronodin and the Sphinx came up with a trick that could work."

"Beware of your mentors," the Underking said. "They are not wholly loyal to me."

"I'm not sure they're wholly loyal to anyone," Seth said.

"You have loyalty to give," the Underking said. "They do not."

"They work for you, though," Seth said.

"Ronodin has his uses," the Underking said. "But beware—either the Sphinx or Ronodin may try to keep the Everbloom for himself."

"Why would they want it?" Seth asked.

"The power, Seth," the Underking said, hunger in his tone. "The Everbloom generates a vast amount of power. It is a nearly endless source of new life and magic. If your comrades are foolish enough to cross me, do not join them. Keep the Everbloom from them and bring it to me."

"Ronodin is my teacher," Seth said.

"And you have all agreed to fetch the Everbloom for me," the Underking said. "Unless you would prefer to side against me?"

The ghostly manacle burned coldly on Seth's wrist. He winced.

"I won't betray you," Seth said.

"Very wise," the Underking said. "Pledge to resist Ronodin and the Sphinx if they try to claim the Everbloom."

"Aren't you demanding more than the original arrangement?" Seth asked.

"This broadens our agreement," the Underking said.

"What do I get for promising more?" Seth asked.

"Do not try my patience," the Underking said.

Seth felt a tug to just agree. But his situation was bad enough already. He couldn't miss opportunities to maybe improve it. "I should get something."

"Very well," the Underking said. "The Hidden Sage resides upon the island of Omari, inside a small cave near the summit of Mount Dagaro. He has power to answer your questions regarding your memories."

"How will I get there?" Seth asked.

"You may take my clever boat on this single excursion," the Underking said.

"The one I took with Ronodin?" Seth checked.

"The same."

"When?" Seth asked.

"Tomorrow, I will inform Ronodin that you have been commissioned to fulfill a private task for me, and that you have leave to take my clever boat for the afternoon. The rest is up to you."

"I just tell the boat I want to go to the island of Omari?" Seth verified.

"Yes," the Underking said. "After your excursion, regardless of the result, I expect you to retrieve the Everbloom for me."

"I'll do my best," Seth said.

"We have an accord," the Underking said. The revenant Bardox twitched, reminding Seth that he was speaking to the Underking through the mouth of another being. The decrepit figure turned and started trudging from the room, mouth still open in the shape of a scream. "Remember our agreement," the Underking stressed. "Stray at your peril."

Seth cringed and drew air through his teeth as the manacle on his arm suddenly burned with coldness.

"Your debt is with me," the Underking said, the whispery voice slithering deep into Seth as Bardox withdrew. "Your obligation is to me. Do not forget who is master of the Phantom Isle."

CHAPTER TWENTY-SIX

Dry Depths

Withered down to a frail, wrinkly frame and confined to a wheelchair, Uma Stormbrewer had reached an age at which time had robbed much from her physically, but her gnarled hands worked with steady precision on the cap she was knitting. The shirtless, barefoot menehune who had pushed her chair to the front of the room had ropy muscles and long, wild hair. He looked too fierce to attend an old woman, but he treated her with reverence and care.

"Kendra, Knox, may I present Uma Stormbrewer," Tanu said to an audience that included Warren, Vanessa, Grady, Savani, and Hako. "She is a living legend among potion masters. Without her help, I would never have prepared the Elixir of Dry Depths so quickly. Her collection of ingredients was equally essential."

"Tanu is too modest," Uma said, knitting needles

clicking. "Some vital ingredients were among the dragon parts he brought here. I could not have concocted the potion without him."

Tanu looked pleased by the praise. "You're very kind," he said. "We produced enough of the elixir to allow six of us to make the journey."

"How long does it last?" Kendra asked.

"Three days," Tanu said. "Or until the potion is deactivated by the antidote. Uma will explain the dangers."

"Toby," Uma said, "fetch my coconut milk."

The menehune raced over to a counter cluttered by bottles and jars containing any number of objects and ingredients. At three feet tall, he had to stretch to reach the glass, muscles writhing across his brown back. He snatched a straw and brought the glass to Uma, who took a sip and handed it back to him.

"His name is Toby?" Knox murmured.

"His true name is a mouthful," Uma said. "For me, he goes by Toby."

"Take a good look," Tanu said. "You will seldom see a menehune interacting with humans."

"Now for the warnings," Uma said. "You must not imbibe any other potions while under the influence of the elixir. At best, you would end the effects of the elixir. At worst, you could eradicate all water from your body, essentially mummifying yourself. To be extra safe, you may wish to avoid food and drinks as well. The water in anything you ingest will react uncomfortably with your body."

"We won't be able to drink water?" Knox asked.

"Not without complications," Uma said.

"Explain how the elixir works," Tanu encouraged.

"Coconut milk," Uma said.

The menehune scurried to return the glass to Uma. She sipped again.

"It is called the Elixir of Dry Depths," Uma said. "Given the name, how do you imagine the potion works?"

"We won't get wet in the ocean?" Knox blurted.

"We'll be able to breathe water?" Kendra guessed.

"The effects are even more extreme than you describe," Uma said. "You won't sense the ocean water any more than you would sense air. You'll breathe and move freely, even down to extreme depths."

"That's incredible," Kendra said.

"Will we get salt in our eyes?" Knox asked.

"The magic will protect you from tiny particles in the water," Uma said. "The elixir does carry inherent dangers. For example, after taking it, if you jump out of a boat, you will fall straight to the bottom of the sea."

"Whoa," Knox said.

"Off the coast of this island, towering drop-offs and deep trenches await," Uma said. "While the elixir is active, great depths are as dangerous as great heights. If you do not take care, you will fall to your demise."

"I've never heard of a potion like this," Warren said.

"Until now, this elixir has not existed in the world for a long time," Uma said. "The making of it has been lost for ages. I am honored to have helped bring this miracle back into the world."

"Tell them how to cancel the effects," Tanu said.

"All who use the potion must carry an antidote," Uma said. "Make sure you don't cancel the effects while down deep. Not only would you get crushed by the pressure, but you could get trapped too far from the surface and drown."

"Could eating something cancel the effects of the elixir?" Knox asked.

"Probably not," Uma said. "But your body will not recognize the water in anything you consume. It will strain your system."

"What about the water in our bodies?" Knox asked. "We're largely made of water."

"The elixir will only change how you interact with outside sources of water," Uma said. "In a pinch, the best way to introduce water to your body while under the elixir's influence would be to suck on ice. After partaking of the elixir, you will still interact with ice like any other solid."

"What about when the ice melts?" Kendra asked.

"If you suck ice, some water will be assimilated before it moves out of phase with you," Uma said.

"What about our clothes?" Knox asked. "Will they get wet and all clingy?"

"This one is sharp," Uma said. "Coconut milk."

Toby brought her glass, and she took another long sip.

"The elixir is powerful enough to include your clothes as extensions of yourself," Uma said. "But not items you carry or clothes you add after taking the potion. Let's imagine you put on a life jacket after imbibing the elixir. The flotation device would not be very effective because your body will have no buoyancy. After you take the elixir, it becomes difficult to make your body float."

"Remember, after the elixir, relative to you, a boat is essentially an aircraft," Tanu said. "A life jacket capable of keeping you afloat would be like a jet pack, and without the ability to interact with the water, you would risk getting stranded as if in midair."

"Will there be side effects?" Kendra asked.

"The map you found had no information about side effects," Uma said. "This is an extraordinarily powerful potion. Elixirs of this caliber are often fine-tuned to minimize side effects. We'll find out if that holds true in this instance by trial and error."

"So if I encounter a shark, I'll be able to move as if on dry land," Warren said. "But the shark will be in water, as if suspended in the air, and move accordingly."

"Yes," Uma said. "Weapons or items you hold will react to the resistance of the water. But your body will feel no such constraints."

"Now the big question," Tanu said. "Who should go? The elixir won't work on the satyrs. We have six doses."

"I'm coming," Kendra said.

"Me too," Knox said.

"Will it work on blixes?" Vanessa asked.

"My other potions do," Tanu said. "From a physiological standpoint, narcoblixes are basically mortal."

"Then Warren and I will join you," Vanessa said.

"I would love to come," Savani said. "But our present situation requires a caretaker overseeing the sanctuary."

"I'll be your sixth man," Hako said.

Kendra glanced from Grady to Knox. "Is Grady an option?" she asked.

"The potion won't work on me," Grady said. "I'm not exactly mortal."

Kendra wanted more of the story, but nobody offered an explanation. "How friendly are the merfolk?" she asked instead.

"They tend to distrust surface dwellers," Savani said. "But the effects of the elixir will impress them. No mortal has walked freely in their sphere for many years. And I will provide you with an introduction—the merfolk have respect for firewalkers, and for the position of caretaker. If I explain that your mission could help restore the sanctuary, I believe they will cooperate."

"How will you introduce us?" Knox asked.

"We burn messages onto leather to send them underwater," Savani said. "We made a full copy of the map from the fool's treasure using that technique so you won't risk losing the original."

"When should we go?" Vanessa asked.

"We worked hard through the night to prepare the elixir by this morning," Tanu said. "I propose we eat a hearty meal, drink a lot of water, and then meet down at the beach. We still have most of the day."

"I will come see you off," Uma said. "It is a momentous hour."

Knox leaned close to Kendra. "Why do I suddenly feel like a guinea pig?"

"You could stay above water," Kendra whispered. "Nobody would blame you."

"What if you need somebody to stuff into a Quiet Box? Or to serve as eel bait?"

"I can't argue with that."

"We have to get Seth back," Knox said. "If that means being guinea pigs, oink oink."

"I don't think guinea pigs oink."

"Maybe the underwater kind do," Knox said. "We'll know soon enough."

🐦 🐦 🐦

Kendra ate quickly, filled up on water, and got to the beach before the others. She found the cyclopses wading in the shallows of the lagoon.

"Any sign of Calvin?" she asked.

"No nipsie sightings as of yet," Tal said.

"We are enjoying the lagoon until the rain comes," Hobar said.

"You are preparing to venture down to the depths," Baroi said. "But you will not feel the water as we do."

"Is a storm coming?" Kendra asked.

"A ten-minute downpour," Tal said. "Then some minor showers off and on."

Kendra looked at the sky. The only clouds were to the north.

"Not for two hours," Hobar said.

"Will we find the compass down there?" Kendra asked.

"The merfolk know how to guide you to the demon you seek," Baroi said. "Be courteous. And helpful."

"If you will excuse us, we are removing invasive sea slugs from the shallows," Tal said.

"Sure," Kendra said, taking the hint to leave. She felt disappointed they still had no view of Calvin. Maybe Tanu was right, and Calvin had convinced a bird to take him to another island. He had a way with animals, and he liked to scout around. Maybe he had gone too far for the cyclopses to see him. Or maybe he was just too small.

Knox came down to the beach and plopped on the sand beside Kendra. "I keep trying to imagine this elixir working. It's hard."

"We'll see soon enough," Kendra said, staring at the ocean, wondering what lurked beneath the choppy surface.

"I've been wanting to ask you something," Knox said. "I've been wondering this ever since I learned Fablehaven was magical."

"Okay," Kendra replied.

"Do you know what really happened to Grandma and Grandpa Larsen?" Knox asked. "When we all thought they died a few years back?"

"Oh, wow," Kendra said. "That's a good question. You wouldn't have known."

"The story we heard was almost unbelievable," Knox said. "Supposedly they had to go into the witness protection program until some trial was over, and so their funeral was staged with wax figures. Even after they got back in touch, we weren't allowed to know any specifics—for our protection, they said. At least they apologized for making us think they were dead."

"Their story isn't too far from the truth," Kendra said. "The bodies were fakes. Stingbulbs, like Patton. Staging their deaths helped with the cover they needed to work as spies against an evil group called the Society of the Evening Star."

"So it was magical stuff," Knox said.

"Yes," Kendra said.

"I wonder what they'll tell our parents?" Knox asked. "To explain us being gone."

"My parents know the truth about Fablehaven," Kendra said. "Maybe Grandma and Grandpa Larsen will have to let your parents in on the secret too. I guess it partly depends on how long we're gone."

"Also depends on if we survive," Knox said.

"I guess so," Kendra said. "I hope I can give them better news about Seth than we have right now." She felt tears coming but held them back.

"Me too," Knox said.

Tanu and the others had begun gathering on the beach. Two menehune struggled to push Uma's wheelchair through the sand, the wheels digging furrows more than rotating. A third menehune shaded her with an umbrella.

Tess came up to Kendra and Knox. "You're going in the water?" she asked.

"Yes," Kendra said. "Hiking, not swimming."

"I heard a rumor you'll see mermaids," Tess said.

"Yes," Kendra said. "We'll be visiting the merfolk."

"If you see Gracie or Lila, tell them hello," Tess said.

"What?" Kendra asked.

"They sometimes come up to those boulders by the shore," Tess said, pointing. "They sing me songs."

Kendra realized Tess had been spending a fair amount of time around Crescent Lagoon on her own. "Gracie and Lila?" Kendra asked.

"Lila is the blonde one," Tess said. "Be careful. Savani warned me not to let them touch me."

Tanu approached Kendra. He held a pouch on a belt. "I thought you might want your unicorn horn. And probably the sack of gales, in case it could be useful."

"Would it work underwater?" Kendra asked.

"It might," Tanu said. "That would be a lot of bubbles. Of course, if it isn't designed to function underwater, it could send you flying all over the sea. But the sack of gales is small, and precious, so I thought you might want to keep it with you, along with the horn."

Kendra belted on the pouch. She placed the sack of gales and the unicorn horn inside.

Tanu was handing out elixirs. With each he included a small capsule.

"The antidote is in the capsule," Tanu announced. "Only use it at the surface. Or very near. The capsule is waterproof. Carry it in a pocket."

Savani was passing out simple necklaces with a crystal attached to each. "These crystals draw light from sister crystals exposed to the sun. They will brighten your way in the deep."

"Should we drink?" Knox asked.

"Down the hatch," Tanu said, tipping his vial back into his mouth.

Kendra studied the little vial. It held a smaller dose than most of Tanu's potions, the fluid a pale purple. She raised the vial to her lips and drank. The liquid tasted of tropical fruits with a citrus tang and was a little salty, with a slightly bitter aftertaste.

"Did it work?" Knox asked.

"We'll know when we get in the water," Tanu said.

"I have some items for you," Savani said. "First, a message of introduction to the merfolk, along with a copy of the map you discovered at Desperation Beach."

"Thank you," Tanu said, accepting them.

"For Hako, the loyal harpoon," Savani said.

Grady stepped forward and presented Hako a seven-foot harpoon with a barbed tip. Hako accepted the weapon solemnly.

"We will also loan you Seaslayer," Savani said. "The blade moves unhindered in the water and has an edge sharp enough for a clean shave. Your best swordsman should wield it."

"Warren," Tanu said without hesitation.

"It might be Vanessa," Warren said.

"You take it," Vanessa told him.

Warren accepted the blade from Grady.

"We have extra harpoons for any who want them," Savani said.

Grady helped Kendra choose a harpoon, slim and light,

not quite as long as she was tall. Knox, Vanessa, and Tanu selected harpoons as well.

Warren swished his gleaming sword in the air. "This is a beautiful weapon," he said.

"May it serve you well," Savani said. "Our hopes go with you."

"Time to get wet?" Knox asked.

"Nope," Kendra said. "Time to stay dry."

Hako gave a nod. "I will take the lead. Tanu, perhaps you could stay near me with the map? Warren, I suggest you guard the rear. Keep your harpoons ready. Once we pass beyond the lagoon, we could encounter a wide variety of trouble. Remember, just as on land, the underwater boundaries are down. Provoke no creatures, but stay poised to defend yourselves."

The warnings helped remind Kendra that they were not just going into the ocean—they were descending into the sea at a sanctuary for magical creatures. Predators much larger and more dangerous than sharks might prowl the depths below.

Hako and Tanu stepped into the lagoon. It was strange to see the two men wading deep into the water without causing a ripple.

When Kendra entered the water, she felt nothing except the sandy bottom, as if the water were an illusion. That didn't change as she went deeper. In front of her, Tanu and Warren disappeared under the water, showing no propensity to float.

As the insubstantial water reached Kendra's neck, she

stared across the surface from a low angle, feeling a natural inclination to hold her breath. Then she crouched down, ducking her head under the water. The coloring looked like she was underwater, though the water seemed unusually clear—she could discern crisp outlines for a long distance in all directions. For a moment, all she could do was marvel at the panorama of sand, shells, kelp, coral reefs, sponges, sea fans, and brilliant tropical fish. It was weird not to feel like a clumsy intruder underwater. Though she could see water all around her, she felt no pressure from it, no hint of wetness. Breathing out produced no bubbles, and since exhaling felt normal, she took a small, experimental breath. Inhaling felt exactly like breathing air.

Closing her eyes and taking another breath, Kendra felt like she could have been anywhere. Her last guess would have been underwater. The only hint of dampness was the gumminess of the sand beneath her feet.

"Isn't this great?" Knox asked, grinning.

"Interesting," Kendra said. "I hear you just fine. It feels perfectly normal to speak. It shouldn't, but it does."

Knox ran over to a coral colony, scattering a school of yellow fish with dark blue stripes. He chased after some of the fish, and they darted in several directions to avoid him.

"If you want to indulge your curiosity, this is the place," Hako called back to the others. "Once we leave the lagoon, we will have to be on guard."

Kendra appreciated the permission to explore. Wandering into deeper water, she marveled at the fish floating around and above her. Her freedom of movement created the illusion that the fish were flying. After stooping to pick up a shell, Kendra found it lighter than she expected, but she could feel the resistance of the water as she moved it, letting her indirectly perceive that she was, in fact, underwater. Kendra released the shell and watched it slowly drop to the seabed.

Using the butt of her harpoon like a walking stick, Kendra caught up to Hako and Tanu. Hako pointed out an iridescent crab the size of a toaster.

"Charm crab," Hako said. "Don't stare too long or you might get mesmerized. Try to harm the crab and it will leave you stupefied."

"Stupefied?" Knox asked, joining them.

"In a state of deep confusion," Hako said. "In this lagoon, it's hard to predict what might be magical. Treat everything you encounter with extra respect."

"This is the best playground ever," Knox said.

"It's a wonderland," Hako said. "I've spent my life exploring these islands, but I've never experienced the water like this either. Unfortunately, we do have a mission."

Kendra nodded. First they needed to deal with the merfolk, then take a prize from a demon. All without getting devoured by sea dragons. "Lead the way," she said.

The lagoon was deeper toward the middle, then got shallower again as they marched toward the open ocean. Hako led them around a jagged barricade of reefs until they stood at the brink of a high cliff. Kendra stayed a few steps back from the edge, staring in amazement at how far the ocean descended and how dark the depths became.

"That would be a serious fall," Knox murmured.

"Keep still," Hako whispered, putting a finger to his lips.

Beyond the edge of the cliff, in the open ocean, a hammerhead shark the size of a school bus was swimming by, tail swishing smoothly. Kendra stared in awe as the tremendous shark traveled across her field of view, eventually swimming out of sight. She was relieved it had not turned toward them.

"That shark was unreal," Knox said. "Like megalodon huge."

"We're sharing this ocean with all sorts of aquatic monsters," Hako said. "The map indicates a trail this way." Hako started moving along the underwater cliff, parallel to its edge. "Keep those harpoons handy."

"I have a feeling I'm going to miss the kiddie pool," Knox said, glancing back toward the lagoon.

"Let's just try not to get eaten," Kendra replied. "Come on."

CHAPTER TWENTY-SEVEN

Merfolk

The longer Kendra walked, the more she appreciated that the island of Timbuli was merely the top of an underwater mountain, and that going deeper into the ocean meant climbing down it. Not all of the mountain was as steep as the cliffs just beyond the lagoon, and there really was something of a path that wound down the less precipitous slopes, occasionally twisting into switchbacks.

"Who makes a path underwater?" Knox asked quietly. "Fish with feet?"

"We're at an enchanted sanctuary," Kendra said. "Might be magic."

"Or left over from old times when our elixir was in greater use," Tanu said.

"Could also be the people of the deep," Hako said.

"Merfolk?" Knox asked.

"No," Hako said. "The people of the deep are the drowned undead who serve the Underking. I've explored underwater all around these islands, and I sometimes see paths. Occasionally on those paths I have spotted shambling wanderers."

"Like zombies?" Kendra asked.

"More powerful and deliberate than typical zombies," Hako said. "We'll keep watch for them—and for a thousand other dangers."

The path they followed curved and dipped and occasionally rose but mostly descended. The light dimmed the deeper they hiked, making the crystals they wore shine more distinctly. Noon faded to twilight as the shimmer of the sunlit surface passed out of view.

Reefs and fish became scarce as they descended deeper. When they reached a flat, sandy shelf crowded with clams the size of trampolines, Hako carefully led them around the huge bivalves.

"Shouldn't we check for pearls?" Knox asked.

"Never bother the grand clams," Hako said. "They summon predators when disturbed."

They all trod more lightly after the warning. The mountainside became less steep for a time, allowing for easier passage. Hako had them drop and hold still, then pointed out a long sea serpent swooping and corkscrewing in the distance. Without ever coming near, it fluttered away like a ribbon in the wind.

"Are sea serpents dragons?" Kendra asked.

"They are related to the serpentine dragons," Hako said.

"Sea serpents have no legs and no breath weapons, but the largest are the longest of all magical creatures."

The talk of dragons made Kendra think about Celebrant. Where was he now? What preserve was he trying to topple next? She hoped the members of Dragonwatch were finding ways to resist him. She really hoped they could find the Sunset Pearl. If she could help secure Crescent Lagoon from falling, it would be a measure of payback for losing Wyrmroost to him.

Just as the underwater half-light was fading to black because of the depth, the path came to the brink of a steep drop-off. The trail continued down in a series of switchbacks until it reached an underwater valley. Several dozen enormous shells rested on the sand, shedding luminance. The diverse shapes and colors made Kendra recall seeing Las Vegas from a distance at night on a family road trip.

"Shield your lights," Hako said, placing a hand over his chest as they peered off the brink.

Kendra hastily covered the crystal she wore around her neck.

"What's making those lights down there?" Knox asked quietly. "Glowing crabs?"

"Merfolk village," Hako said. "Their structures are grown rather than built."

"But they glow," Knox said.

"Bioluminescent microbes inhabit them," Hako said. "Enough to brighten the whole valley. If we dip much below the merfolk village, we enter the endless night of deep sea."

Kendra reconsidered the shells as buildings, impressed

by their organic design. She could see little swimming figures silhouetted against some of the luminous structures. "I see some merpeople," she said.

"You're looking at Alluvia Minor," Hako said. "One of the last known merfolk villages."

"Are there many unknown ones?" Knox asked.

"Hard to say for sure, if you consider the question," Warren said.

"We suspect that larger merfolk settlements survive in some unmapped depths," Hako said. "Over the years, a few of the merfolk have alluded to secret cities."

"What are those people doing on the outskirts of the village?" Vanessa asked.

"Sharp eyes," Hako said. "You'll notice they are all over the valley floor."

Now that Kendra focused her attention, she saw many figures milling about in the shadows beyond the vibrant illumination of the giant shells. "Dozens," Kendra said. "Maybe hundreds."

"People of the deep," Hako said. "Hundreds of them. A full horde of the zombies. Magical barriers protect the village, but it is besieged."

"Can we get through the barriers?" Knox asked.

"Mortals can cross any of the village barriers at this sanctuary," Hako said.

"Look at the whale," Tanu remarked, pointing.

Kendra followed his finger to see a half-devoured carcass of a whale in the shadows beyond the village, a large portion of the skeleton exposed. People of the deep swarmed the remains, tearing at the blubbery flesh with hands and teeth.

"How fast are these zombies?" Warren asked.

"Faster than you might think," Hako said. "They're more skilled and alert than most zombies."

"We didn't time this very well," Warren said. "Is it zombie season?"

"I wonder if the Underking is aware of our intent," Vanessa said.

"Who knows how long the siege has been going?" Hako said. "It may have started when the preserve fell."

"The village is surrounded," Tanu said. "How do we get past them?"

"It's too bad we can't swim," Hako said. "The people of the deep move on the ocean floor. They don't float."

"We could swim right over them?" Knox asked. "Are we too deep to cancel the elixir?"

"Almost certainly," Hako said. "Especially since we would have no way to breathe."

"Do we try to wait them out?" Vanessa asked. "Or consider returning another time?"

"The drowned ones could be here indefinitely," Hako said. "At least until we renew the protections of the sanctuary. If we want to get into the village, now might be as good a time as later."

"And we can't afford to wait too long," Kendra said. "The Underking has Bracken. And the Sunset Pearl. And Seth. Who knows what will happen to Bracken and Seth if we leave them there too long? And once we lose that last moai, the whole sanctuary falls."

"We have to succeed," Warren said. "And nobody gets helped if we're dead."

Hako looked around. "I don't see any of the people of the deep up here. If there were any behind us, traveling the switchbacks below us would leave us extremely vulnerable. Once we start down, we could get trapped."

"If those on the valley floor see us coming, we're in trouble too," Vanessa said. "If they come up after us, our only option will be to retreat."

"And once we're on their level, they could swarm us," Tanu said.

"I think there is only one chance," Hako said.

"A sea serpent attacks them?" Knox asked.

"Wouldn't that be nice?" Hako said. "We go down quietly. I will distract them. When they come after me, you run for the village."

"Is that your only move?" Knox asked. "Sacrificing yourself?"

"I should be able to get away," Hako said. "The loyal harpoon can carry a person through the water—even a Dry Depths Elixir drinker like me, though it may be slow."

"Doesn't have to be fast if you can get out of reach," Warren said.

"Those are my thoughts," Hako said. "It won't be easy. I may draw some of the zombies off, but you'll still have to fight your way through."

"Anyone have a better idea?" Tanu asked.

Nobody volunteered a plan.

"I'll take the lead," Warren said. "Vanessa will guard the rear. Tanu, cover Kendra and Knox."

"I wish I could use potions," Tanu said.

"I'd rather not be mummified," Knox said.

"So much depends on descending quietly and unseen," Hako whispered. "Hold the crystals in your hands. Don't let light leak between your fingers. Stay low, tread carefully, and keep away from the edge of the path. I'll hang back on the last switchback. You'll know when to charge. If a way doesn't open to the village, remember you can backtrack to the switchbacks and flee."

Kendra remembered running from zombies at Obsidian Waste. She was worried about tangling with zombies again, especially if these were more capable.

They started down the trail. It was dim, but there was enough light to see where to step. Hairpin turn after hairpin turn, Kendra stayed low, without a view of the sandy valley below. She hoped that since she could not see the undead, they could not see her.

After descending nine serpentine switchbacks, Hako hung back at the turn while the others descended the final stretch. Kendra kept as low as she could as the path joined the valley floor.

"If the zombies chase us up these switchbacks, I hope I'm not the slowest," Knox whispered.

Kendra glanced up. The top of the trail towered above them. She had to agree that an escape up the path was not appealing. What if she got eaten by zombies simply because she lacked better cardiovascular endurance?

Warren held a finger to his lips and motioned for them to stay down and wait. Looking toward the glowing village, Kendra could see the silhouettes of many shuffling figures. The near side of the village was little more than a hundred yards away.

"Who wants fresh meat?" Hako called to the multitude.

Kendra looked up the path to where he stood at the previous turn. Hako had uncovered his crystal and stood at the edge with his harpoon over his head. Leading with the harpoon, he leaped off the path at least sixty feet above the valley floor, but instead of falling, he was carried forward by the weapon, dangling from the shaft. He gradually lost altitude until he landed in the midst of the people of the deep. All of the sea zombies in view converged on Hako.

"Now," Warren said quietly, dashing forward.

Holding her harpoon ready, Kendra raced behind, with Knox and Tanu beside her. The sandiness of the seafloor kept her from reaching her top speed, but not by much. The people of the deep still strode toward Hako, allowing Kendra and her friends to advance several steps unnoticed. Kendra and her group dashed through the spaces between the unaware zombies. Hako yelled and swiped with his harpoon as the zombies swarmed around him.

The zombies looked bloated and otherworldly, their hair and clothes billowing because they were underwater. A crusty old guy with a limp and a tricornered hat noticed Warren coming and turned to face him, raising a corroded cutlass. Warren hacked his head off cleanly before the man could swing, Seaslayer a blur. But the action caught the attention of other sea zombies.

Waterlogged faces swung to face Kendra. Some of the zombies shifted course, leering and increasing their pace. Warren cut down another zombie, and Kendra felt more vacant eyes turning in their direction.

A woman with her head tightly wrapped in a scarf came at Knox with an upraised knife, apron flowing, and he stabbed her with his harpoon before she got near enough to strike. Her body twisted, wrenching the harpoon from his grasp. She dropped her knife, then gripped the harpoon with both hands and started pulling it out of her torso. On the other side of Kendra, Tanu used his harpoon to deflect the thrust of a gaff. Warren lopped the arms off a weaponless zombie coming at him.

Kendra and her group were moving faster than the people of the deep. Hampered by the water, the zombies stepped slower, but their reflexes were quick. Kendra was less than halfway to the village when she noticed the zombies massing ahead of them, blocking their route. Warren cut sideways to go around the mob, but zombies encroached from all directions, and the gaps between them were getting scarce.

"We may not make it to the village," Tanu said.

"Fall back," Warren called.

Though the zombies pressed from all sides, they were sparser behind the mortals. The group reversed direction, which put Vanessa in front. She turned her harpoon and used the blunt end to drive zombies back and deflect blows.

"We're in trouble," Knox said, dodging outstretched arms, weaponless.

Kendra handed him her harpoon, and he plunged it into a heavyset man reaching for them with bloated fingers, again losing his weapon as the man's hands closed around the shaft. Warren stepped up to fight beside Vanessa, carving space for them to move forward, but the way to the switchbacks closed off as more zombies crowded to block their retreat.

Kendra wondered if she should get out her sack of gales. If it didn't stabilize her underwater, she might end up like a failed rocket test. She also considered seeing if the unicorn horn would keep the zombies back, but she worried about losing it. She would save it to try as a last resort.

Slack, discolored faces approached from all sides, some clutching weapons, most without. Their numbers made weapons irrelevant. Each time Warren dispatched one zombie, three pressed forward to take its place.

"Above you," called a voice.

Kendra looked up to see several mermen and a few mermaids swimming about ten feet above the swarming zombies. Their long fishtails with wide fins undulated gracefully. Both men and women had long hair, but the females wore pearls and combs in their tresses. Their wide shoulders and impressive musculature reminded Kendra of Olympic swimmers.

"Take the line," a mermaid urged.

Kendra realized they were dangling slender ropes. Kendra grabbed one with both hands, and a pair of mermaids lifted her off her feet. Tails flailed and muscles strained as the women elevated Kendra above the zombies. Her full weight was evidently a lot for them to handle.

Her friends were being lifted above the zombies as well. Three powerful mermen were having a hard time with Tanu. The potion master kicked at people of the deep until a fourth merman joined and they hoisted him out of reach.

Kendra clung tightly to the line. The small knots in the slender rope helped Kendra just enough to support her weight. The people of the deep crowded beneath her, greedy hands reaching upward. The mermaids holding her line grimaced, tails sweeping vigorously, and began making slow progress toward the village.

"They feel full of iron," one of the mermen complained.

"These are depth walkers," another merman said. "Their great weight is legendary."

"She is too heavy," one of the mermaids holding Kendra complained. "Should we just feed her to the floorscrubbers?" She glanced down at the zombies.

"Please don't," Kendra said. "We were sent by the caretaker."

Tails still flailing, the mermaids looked down at Kendra in surprise.

"You speak Corilli?" the one with the orange tail asked.

"I speak many languages," Kendra replied.

"We'll try to save you," the one with the blue tail said.

She looked at her friend. "I've never missed the golems more."

"Golems?" Kendra asked.

"Four golems guarded our village until recently," the one with the orange tail explained, groaning, veins standing out in her neck.

"A lich came and drained their energy," the one with the blue tail said.

"Without the golems to ward them off, the floorscrubbers surrounded the village," the one with the orange tail said.

"Where are the golems now?" Kendra asked.

"Too many questions," the one with the blue tail said, short of breath. "Carrying you is harder than it looks."

"Try hauling the big one," one of the mermen holding Tanu grumbled.

"This is important," Kendra said. "Are the golems still in the area?"

"One is right over there," the mermaid with the orange tail said, jerking her head to one side. "They lie where they fell."

Kendra saw a jumble of large sea rocks where the mermaid had indicated. "What exactly was drained?" Kendra asked. "Magical energy?"

"How should we know?" the mermaid with the orange tail said.

"Magical energy," confirmed one of the mermen toting Tanu, muscles bulging, yellow tail swishing forcefully.

"These golems have turtle shells at their core that can store vast amounts of energy."

"Cyclonic turtles," another merman added.

"I think I can revive the golems," Kendra said. "I'm fairykind. I'm a well of magical energy."

"How would you revive them?" the mermaid with the blue tail asked.

"By touch," Kendra said. "If you can get me over to one."

"You might survive," the mermaid with the orange tail said. "The floorscrubbers don't climb on the golems."

"They might if they had a target," the mermaid with the blue tail said.

Kendra looked over at the heap of rubble that once was a golem. Would touching the stones be enough? Would direct contact with the shell be necessary? What if she was wrong? What if her energy didn't translate? If the golem didn't revive, she might be killed. Or zombified!

The mermaids jerked the line to the side and a harpoon glided past Kendra, thrown from below. Struggling, they lifted her higher. Kendra realized that if she fell, the impact alone would injure her.

More merfolk swam out from the village, several of them armed. Two mermen took Kendra's line from the mermaids. One of the mermen had red hair and a purple tail, the other, black hair and a green tail. Both bore spears, the heads shaped to imitate crab claws.

"I am Faro," the merman with the black hair said. "This is Lars."

"I'm Kendra."

"What took you so long?" the mermaid with the blue tail complained, rubbing the muscles in her arms.

"Word of this rescue is spreading," Lars said. "Some are debating whether we should help."

"Meanwhile they would die," the mermaid with the blue tail said.

"It's why we skipped the discussion," Faro said.

"Kendra believes she can revive the golems," the mermaid with the orange tail said.

"She is fairykind," the other mermaid added.

"How would you do it?" Faro asked.

"I just need to touch the golem," Kendra said. "Or maybe the turtle shell."

"Getting to the golem is no problem," Lars said.

"Once you reach the seafloor, your safety could be compromised," Faro said.

Looking down at the rioting zombies, Kendra wondered if she should just let the mermen carry her to the village. Getting dragged in by them would not be a very impressive arrival. However, if she could revive their golems, the merfolk might feel they owed her a favor. Plus, letting the golems clear out the people of the deep would make her departure a lot easier when the time came.

"I want to try," Kendra said.

The mermen veered away from the village toward the golem. They swam considerably faster than the mermaids with her weight, though they were straining as well. At least the golem was much closer to them than the village was.

They drew near the rock pile, sea zombies following below. "Remember," Kendra said, "I can't just drop. I fall like I'm in air, so lower me."

Faro and Lars gently let her down atop the rock pile. Weedy vegetation grew among the rocks, and small shells pimpled the rough surfaces. Touching the rocks had no effect, so Kendra scrambled around searching for the turtle shell.

After brief hesitation, one of the sea zombies stepped onto the rock pile, brandishing a large metal hook. Faro swooped down, stabbed him with his spear, and thrust him off the rocks. Lars joined the fight, skewering the next trespassing zombie.

Kendra moved from crack to crack, peering between the rocks. Deep inside one of the wider gaps, she caught sight of an iridescent turtle shell. Squirming in as far as she could, she stretched her arm forward until her fingertips brushed the shell. Upon contact, the shell blazed with light, and Kendra gasped as energy surged out of her. The rocks around her shifted, and she tumbled to the sandy seafloor.

Looking up, Kendra found herself overshadowed by a nine-foot-tall figure made of stone and sand. The robust golem had a large head with concave hollows for eyes, a thick torso, and outsized hands and feet. With two big sweeps of his long arms, the golem cleared away at least a dozen sea zombies.

Faro grabbed Kendra by one arm, Lars seized the other, and they swam her upward. The golem let them pass as they rose above the fight, then proceeded to punch and stomp sea zombies, crumpling bodies with every blow. For the first time, the people of the deep showed uncertainty, turning and trying to flee. Kendra heard shouts of relief from the merfolk carrying her friends, and cheering from the village.

"Are you all right, Kendra?" Faro asked.

"I'm okay," Kendra said.

"Think you could do that three more times?" Lars asked. "We can use this golem to clear the way to the others. Our mystics can give it instructions."

"Sure," Kendra said, "if you two come with me. You can help me find the shells and keep hold of me so I don't get dumped on the ground when the golems re-form."

"Consider it done," Lars said.

"We're in your debt," Faro said.

Kendra looked over at the rest of her group getting transported to the village, the golem hammering away at the zombies beneath them. Other merfolk were now streaming from the village to help.

"Let's wake up those sleeping golems," Kendra said.

CHAPTER TWENTY-EIGHT

Remulon

Lord Quintus of the merfolk had silver hair and the upper body of a prizefighter. Rather than a throne, he rested on spongy cushions fitted inside of a giant clam shell, lying flat, like a bed. Kendra had seen no chairs in the large room, and, looking around, she realized that since the merfolk could float and had the lower bodies of fish, chairs might not even make sense for them.

Outside the village, the four golems had the people of the deep on the run. With the help of Faro and Lars, re-energizing the golems had been relatively simple. Each golem they reanimated helped drive away the sea zombies so Kendra could revive the next. Once all four were in action, the sea zombies had no chance against the tireless onslaught.

After revitalizing the golems, Kendra learned, to her relief, that Hako had made it to the village using his loyal harpoon. Now he, Tanu, Knox, Warren, and Vanessa stood with her before the leader of the merfolk.

"You have done us a great service," Lord Quintus said. "Those floorscrubbers blocked access to many of the reefs and kelp forests where our foragers hunt and gather." He held up the document Tanu had given him. "I see that Savani endorsed your visit. You are on an errand to recover the Sunset Pearl?"

"We know the Phantom Isle is almost impossible to find," Kendra said. "But we have to go there. A map told us a demon called Remulon has a compass that will help us."

"You are brave," Quintus said. "The demon Remulon is more dangerous than almost any creature in the sea. I would never choose to visit his lair."

"We have to try," Kendra said.

"And the Phantom Isle is worse," Quintus said. "If you can find it, the isle is guarded by the sea dragon Jibarro. Beyond lies the entrance to the Under Realm. Most would exert great efforts to avoid such a destination."

"The land of the dead," Kendra said.

"No, much worse," Quintus said. "The domain of the neverdead."

The description made Kendra shiver. "One problem at a time. Can you help us find Remulon?"

"This demon is our neighbor," Quintus said. "I cannot jeopardize the uneasy truce we've established, especially now, with most of the sanctuary's protections down. We will not engage directly with the demon. But if you insist on seeking him, we will show you the way." Quintus raised his voice. "Who among our hunters will volunteer?"

"I will lead them," Faro said, swimming forward, spear in hand.

"You could have no finer guide," Quintus said. "Faro, show them to the lair of Remulon and then promptly return. How they fare with the demon is their concern."

"You know this demon," Kendra said. "What's our best approach?"

"Try not to let it come to a fight," Quintus said. "I wish I could convince you to avoid the demon entirely."

"Does he have any known weaknesses?" Kendra asked.

"He is frustratingly clever," Quintus said. "He is fierce in combat. His lair is well protected. But he does have a passion for collecting novelties."

"So we might be able to work out a trade?" Kendra asked.

"It is possible," Quintus said. "Though I fear his primary interest will be in acquiring you. Thank you for your service to our village. You will be remembered as a friend of the merfolk."

"Thank you," Kendra said, relieved that at least they had a guide to the demon. She withdrew from the glowing assembly hall with her group.

Faro swam up to her. "Shall we depart?"

"Sure," Kendra said.

He inclined his head. "It is my honor to escort you."

"Before we go," Kendra said, "do you know any mermaids named Gracie and Lila?"

"Those two are always into mischief," Faro said.

"They know my cousin," Kendra said.

He nodded. "That pair visits the surface more than most. Would you like me to look for them?"

"If you don't mind," Kendra said, hoping their relationship with Tess might win her some special treatment or information.

Faro swam away, and Knox approached her.

"We can be grateful for one thing," Knox said.

"What?" Kendra asked.

"We're not supposed to eat. I saw their food."

"Gross?"

"Squirmy," Knox said, pulling a disgusted face and shuddering.

"We get to negotiate with a demon instead," Kendra said.

"Think they would loan us some golems?" Knox asked.

"I wish," Kendra said. "They don't want trouble with the demon. Sending their golems to help us would probably be an act of war or something. We have a golem at Fablehaven—Hugo. It would be a relief if he were here."

"How did you bring those golems back to life?" Knox asked.

"They were out of magical energy," Kendra said. "Ever since I became fairykind, I have been like a magical battery recharger."

"How did that fairykind thing happen?" Knox asked.

"The power came from the Fairy Queen during an emergency at Fablehaven," Kendra said. "It's a long story."

"Can you use that power against the demon?" Knox asked.

"Not unless I have something to charge," Kendra said. "Otherwise the ability is fairly useless."

Faro returned with a pair of youthful mermaids, one with blonde hair, the other a brunette. "Lila is the blonde?" Kendra asked. "And Gracie?"

"Yes," Lila said. "You're Kendra."

"I think you met my sister," Knox said. "Tess."

"We did," Gracie said. "Up at the surface. Cute little thing."

"She's my cousin, and she wanted me to tell you hello," Kendra said.

"Give her our regards," Lila said. "We tried to coax her into the water, but she wouldn't come."

"Why invite her into the water?" Knox asked.

The mermaids giggled. "To bring her down deep with us," Lila said.

"You were going to drown her?" Knox exclaimed.

"Sure," Gracie said.

"Didn't you like her?" Knox asked.

"Of course," Lila said. "We talked and sang songs."

"Then why drown her?" Knox asked.

Gracie blinked as if surprised by the obvious question. "The sea claims all the unwary."

"We weren't going out of our way," Lila said. "No nets or traps."

"She was careful," Gracie said. "Stayed well out of reach."

"She wouldn't come examine the shell I tried to show her," Lila said.

"As a favor to me, please let her be," Kendra said. "She's part of our family."

Gracie shrugged. "If she's careless, and we don't claim her, it'll be something else."

Lila elbowed Gracie. "We're grateful to have the golems back," Lila said. "We won't tempt your little cousin anymore."

"Shall we go?" Faro asked.

"Sure," Kendra said. "Nice to meet you two."

"Likewise," Lila said, swimming off with Gracie.

Knox looked up at Faro. "Why did you come help us against the undead? Seems like merfolk would rather see us drown."

"You were not merely careless humans tempting fate," Faro said. "You were breathing water, as we do. It has been long years since we have seen humans walking the depths. There was some debate, but many of us wanted to meet you more than we wanted to let the floorscrubbers destroy you. I brought you gifts." He handed a slender spear to Kendra and another to Knox. "To replace what you lost."

"Thanks," Kendra said. The spear was a little longer than the harpoon she had used, and it felt lighter but no less sturdy.

"Is it far to Remulon?" Warren asked.

"Farther to walk than to swim," Faro said. "We should arrive just after midday. He's closer to the surface than our village is, but we'll have to start by going deeper to get there. Come."

As Faro led them out of Alluvia Minor, they received a warm farewell, with many of the merfolk waving and calling out good-byes. Kendra waved back, but she had a hard time feeling close to creatures who were willing to drown children. Hopefully they were not all as indifferent to human life as Gracie and Lila. At least the merfolk had helped them with their quest, and for that she was grateful.

Holding his spear in one hand and a lantern in the other, Faro led them across the sandy valley beyond the village, now clear of functioning sea zombies. The golems worked piling crushed corpses up against the valley wall and covering them with sand.

Faro led them up to the outward edge of the valley, where they could see that the village and the valley were like a balcony on the mountainside, with the slope dropping off farther below. "There are faster ways to go if you could swim," Faro said. "This path will have to do."

The trail wound down until the only light came from their crystals and the lantern Faro held. As Kendra saw the light of her crystal flash upon new rocks and shells along the path, she felt like an intruder in these depths. Had light ever touched this landscape? Did it even belong here?

"Will our lights make us targets?" Kendra asked.

"Most of the hunting down this deep is not done by sight," Faro said.

"Do you come down here a lot?" Knox wondered.

"There is not much reason to go this deep," Faro said. "We mostly forage higher than the village."

"Is that how you merfolk live?" Knox asked. "Foraging?"

"The sea provides what we need," Faro said. "We gather with gratitude."

"Have you ever been on land?" Knox asked.

"Few merfolk venture into the dryness," Faro said. "We leave the airy regions to your kind."

After some time, the way started to trend up more than down. At one point, Faro had them pause and cover their lights. Several bioluminescent jellyfish drifted in a group, clear and bulbous with glassy tentacles, bodies laced with squiggly patterns that glowed a light blue. When Faro had them uncover their lights, the jellyfish seemed to vanish.

As they climbed, Kendra felt relief to see a haze of light above. She began to notice more fish. Her legs grew tired from the upward incline. The light from the surface gradually increased until their crystals were needed less. Marine life reappeared in greater abundance, including plants and sponges. They reached a large iron bell, incongruously resting on the seafloor, corroded and lumpy with barnacles.

"We're getting close," Faro said quietly. "This bell marks the outskirts of the area claimed by Remulon, though he seldom leaves his cavernous lair. Does the water feel warmer to you?"

"Under the effect of the elixir we don't feel the water," Hako said. "But the temperature seems warmer."

"Thermal vents from the volcano heat certain pockets in this region," Faro said. "Stay near me."

They advanced, passing an ancient cannon and three human statues that looked more suited for a museum than the bottom of the sea. Ahead, a sheer cliff loomed lofty, partially masked by a dense kelp bed. As they neared the base of the cliff, the way forward was barred by a high reef of black coral, overshadowed by towers of kelp.

"This razor coral forms a protective barrier around Remulon's lair," Faro whispered. "Take great care—the edges are so keen you could lose fingers without even feeling the cut. The electric kelp above it can shock you with more power than a lightning strike."

"That seaweed could fry us?" Knox asked.

"Venture within range and it will electrocute you," Faro said. "We have reached your destination. This is where I depart."

Kendra stared from the barrier to their guide. Was he really leaving now that they needed him most? "Is there any way through?" she asked.

Faro jabbed at a low gap in the razor coral with his spear. "From what I understand, you can get through here. But do not brush against the coral. Keep your wits about you. Farewell. I hope you find what you seek."

As Faro swam away, Kendra could not help feeling a little jealous. The hike to this point had been pleasant. Faro had the luxury of leaving before the scary part began.

"Whoever goes first will have to take it especially slow," Hako said. "We don't know how the way might narrow or widen. Let's hope Faro was correct that it goes all the way through. Careful movements. Don't raise your head. Don't poke out your elbows. Stay aware of how much space you have on all sides. Watch out for unexpected protrusions. The good news is, the coral will remain stationary. Any damage we sustain will be our own fault."

"I'll go first," Warren said.

"Do we have a plan for dealing with the demon?" Vanessa asked.

"What can we do besides improvise?" Warren asked. "Try to bargain."

"And fight if we must," Hako said.

"Entering the lair of a demon is unwise," Vanessa said. "These creatures live to take advantage of others, to out-smart opponents. If not for our extreme need, I would not recommend going through with this. Don't let your guard down. Be wary of any agreement Remulon wants to make."

"Wish me luck," Warren said.

"Try to keep your fingers," Vanessa replied.

Warren got down on his stomach and started scooting into the gap beneath the razor coral. Hako crouched behind him.

"Should we announce ourselves?" Vanessa asked. "It might be more polite."

Warren stopped crawling. "If we catch him asleep, that could work to our advantage."

"He probably knows we're here," Vanessa said. "Anyone careful enough to have barriers like these will have systems in place to detect intruders. He might be listening to every word we say."

"Coming in!" Warren called. "Friends paying a neighborly call!"

"Charming," Vanessa said.

Warren wormed out of view, then Hako followed. Tanu gave a miserable sigh. "I'm not built for this," he muttered before scooting after Hako in an army crawl, keeping his body as close to the ground as possible.

Kendra winced as she watched Tanu slither forward. He had a lot less margin for error than the others. She got down and squirmed in behind Tanu, figuring that if he could fit, she should have no problem. The close tunnel through the coral twisted and turned unpredictably. Dark spikes and blades jutted above her and to either side. Kendra took care to keep her head down and to stay centered in the gap. It was easy to forget she was underwater and to imagine herself crawling through a thorny briar. She kept envisioning her skin getting mangled by a casual brush against dozens of tiny blades. The grisly imagery helped her proceed with caution.

At last Tanu rose to his feet ahead of her, and Kendra reached the end of the spiny tunnel. She crawled out and gratefully accepted a hand up from Warren. She turned to congratulate Tanu for making it through and noticed some blood misting into the water from his shoulder, but froze when she realized he and Hako were facing the mountainside as if transfixed.

A huge cavern hollowed out the base of the cliff, and in the opening awaited an octopus the size of a cement truck. The huge cephalopod was black with white suckers lining his tentacles, his intense red eyes fixed on them.

Knox exited the razor coral, trailed by Vanessa. She inspected Tanu's shoulder and looked relieved. Once they all stood together, Hako stepped forward.

"We come seeking Remulon," Hako said.

You have found him, gamekeeper. The penetrating words came directly into Kendra's mind, the telepathic voice methodical and resonant. *Step aside. My interest is in she who slayed our king.*

Hako backed away and Kendra stepped forward, summoning her courage as she had when speaking to Celebrant. Showing fear would only hurt their chances. Tentacles flowed in rubbery tangles as the octopus shifted, oblong head pulsing. Kendra did not think it looked like a creature that should speak.

"I guess you mean me," she said.

My, how you shine, Remulon spoke to her mind. *You come to me without Vasilis or any comparable armaments. Am I to understand you do not mean to destroy me?*

"I've come hoping for help," Kendra said.

You bear the mark of Jubaya, Remulon communicated. *I have a measure of respect for her, but she was no ally of mine.*

Kendra had not been thinking about the mark. In the fairy realm, the demon Jubaya had marked her by taking her hand, and then instructed her to seek help from the demons against the dragons. "We need your assistance," Kendra said.

The mark has never been used, Remulon conveyed. *It was especially meant for three others. Now you seek help? And from me? How did you fare at Wyrmroost?*

"The preserve has fallen," Kendra said.

I am aware. And you did not solicit aid from Talizar? He might have rescued you.

Kendra remembered that Jubaya had mentioned three other demons who might help her. Talizar was one, but she had never tried to find any of them. She had never intended to seek help from the demons. Now seemed like a poor time to bring that up. "It was a surprise attack," Kendra said.

You bring a peculiar test, Remulon mused. *You have achieved much. You found favor with the Fairy Queen. You are a dragon slayer. You vanquished Gorgrog the Vile. And yet you come to me apparently defenseless, announced by the mark of Jubaya, groveling for assistance. What aid do you desire?*

"We need to find the Phantom Isle," Kendra said.

His laughter filled her mind. *I wondered if you meant to approach another monarch. But the Underking? Truly? In his domain? How long do you expect to survive?*

"We have business there," Kendra said. "Friends to help, and the Sunset Pearl to recover. Don't you demons want to see the dragons fail? Without the pearl, Crescent Lagoon will not hold the dragons in much longer. They will be free to go conquer the world."

I know your methods are different from mine, Remulon expressed. *Perhaps you see different ways to leverage power than I do. But I feel compelled to wonder . . . has your success been luck? What am I missing? It's true that you shine, but you and any who enter the Under Realm with you will perish. The darkness is overpowering. You would face hordes of revenants, legions of liches, and the Underking himself. To gaze upon him is to join the ranks of his undead.*

Kendra ached to think of Seth and Bracken trapped in such a place. "Let me worry about how we will do what we need to do. We need to know where to find the isle. Will you help us?"

I could, Remulon assured her. *In my garden I have a nova song.*

"I was told you have a compass," Kendra said.

Less a compass, more a homing pigeon, Remulon explained. *You are fairykind. Are you not familiar with the storied nova song?*

Kendra looked back at Tanu. "Can you hear him?"

"I heard what he told Hako," Tanu said. "I feel telepathy coming from him, but I can't catch the meaning."

"Have you heard of a nova song?" Kendra asked.

"It's a legendary fairy," Tanu said. "Maddox would trade all he has for one."

A nova song is an amphibious fairy capable of extraordinary brightness, Remulon conveyed. *They live to light the darkest spaces they can access.*

"Your nova song can find the Phantom Isle?" Kendra asked.

It is telling to realize the nova song could dive to the emptiest cave in the deepest trench at the bottom of the sea. Instead she would seek out the Phantom Isle. The darkness there resists and even extinguishes light. It is thicker, richer than any natural darkness. A real challenge for her. And part of the reason nova songs are so rare.

"You hold a nova song captive?" Kendra asked. "Why isn't she an imp?"

My garden is protected within my caverns, but not behind any doors, Remulon explained. *None of my trophies are indoors.*

"Right," Kendra said. "Fairies only fall if kept indoors overnight. Remulon, will you loan us the nova song? That's all we need."

She is my most prized possession. Yours is a doomed errand from which none will return. To lend her would be to lose her.

"You're underestimating me," Kendra said. "I'll bring her back."

Impossible! Remulon exclaimed. *You would not make it past the sea dragon. If you did, you and anyone you bring would be overwhelmed by the undead. You will perish, paralyzed in the dark.*

"I can speak in the presence of dragons," Kendra said.

You fail to understand. Even uninvited dragons would be paralyzed by the power and darkness of the Under Realm. Orogoro himself would fall. No potion or trinket would make a difference.

"I'll find a way," Kendra said.

Your reckless optimism is instructive, Remulon expressed. *If you are baiting me for some sort of trap, I sincerely applaud you. I am convinced this is exactly what it looks like.*

"What do you mean?" Kendra asked.

Do you know who I am? Remulon asked.

"Kind of," Kendra said.

The demons of the deep are underappreciated by airbreathers, Remulon grumbled. *But even on the surface my name is renowned. I have never been captured. I have never been bested. I am feared by the most formidable of my kind. Each of my tentacles has different abilities.*

"You sound very impressive," Kendra said.

You came here unprepared. I believe you have a desperate need, and you visited me armed only with a mark from a demon and a vague hope I might help.

"We're willing to bargain," Kendra said.

How Gorgrog fell to you is incomprehensible. You have played this all wrong. What could you possibly offer me that would be more attractive than simply keeping you?

"Try me," Kendra said. "What do you want?"

Remulon fell silent. A few of his tentacles stretched and curled. *How much do your companions matter to you?*

"Very much," Kendra said.

Unconditionally bind yourself to me as my servant with an irrevocable oath. Fall on your knees and pledge to do my bidding for the rest of your days, and I will let you free your companions through your service, one by one.

Kendra stared at the octopus in disbelief. "No way!"

You solicited an offer, Remulon conveyed. *You wish to reject the opportunity I present? Under the circumstances, it is very generous. I will not make another offer.*

"You haven't captured us yet," Kendra said.

Remulon laughed again.

"Is he threatening to capture us?" Hako asked.

You are about to make the nova song my second most valued possession. The fairykind human who destroyed Gorgrog is an incomparable trophy. If your comrades posed a threat, I might consider slaying some of them. It will be a more pleasant novelty to keep all of you.

"He wants us," Kendra said, opening the small pouch on her waist and reaching for the unicorn horn.

With a yell, Hako flung the loyal harpoon at Remulon. It streaked through the water with supernatural speed, right on target, until a black tentacle lashed out, caught the harpoon, and snapped it like a toothpick.

"That was quick," Warren said in despair.

That tentacle is so quick I could kill you all before you understood what happened, Remulon conveyed. *I could kill you in so many ways, but this tentacle will put you to sleep.*

Kendra pulled out Bracken's first horn, accidentally dropping the sack of gales to the seafloor. Remulon raised a tentacle, showing the rows of white suckers on the underside. Dozens of dartlike spines fired from around the suckers, whizzing through the water toward Kendra and her friends. One pricked Kendra in the shoulder; another pierced her thigh.

She staggered, immediately drowsy. The unicorn horn fell from her hand, landing on the sack of gales. She pulled the slender spine from her thigh and stared at it blurrily. It was approximately the length of her hand.

Turning, Kendra regarded her companions. Warren had dropped his sword and sunk to his knees. Hako was already flat on his back, and Tanu was sprawled nearby. Knox had fallen right by the tunnel through the razor coral. Vanessa swayed, took a few steps sideways, and collapsed.

Kendra hit the ground before she realized she was falling. As consciousness slipped away, she felt large suckers puckering against her skin.

CHAPTER TWENTY-NINE

Sage

Puffy gray clouds shed a haze of rain to the west, and chaotic swells kept the boat rearing and plunging, but Seth was enjoying his time alone on the water. As he considered the solitude, Seth realized he had no memory of spending time on his own. Sure, he had been unchaperoned in the Under Realm before, but even in his room with the door closed, Seth could feel the undead around him and knew the Underking might be watching.

The clever boat maneuvered itself across the choppy water, leaving Seth free to ponder. Part of him wanted to tell the boat to take him to San Diego, but he had a hunch the Underking would override any command to flee. He rubbed at the ghostly manacle on his wrist, fingers passing through it. Was it absurd to think that if he delivered the Everbloom to the Underking, the manacle would come off and he could start living his own life? Was that too much to hope? Would there always be a catch? Another favor owed? More hoops to jump through?

The Sphinx and Ronodin had no intention of ever freeing the phantom Dezia. They would use her and then trap her as tightly as they could. Seth scowled. What would prevent them from doing the same to him?

Ronodin had brought Seth to the Under Realm knowing the Underking would strike a deal that bound him there. They might all be working together against him. Ronodin was teaching him the things he needed to know to serve as a useful tool. The dark unicorn spoke convincingly, but his actions didn't always add up. If he wanted to free everybody, why bind Dezia? Why lock up Bracken? Why force Seth into a situation in which the Underking could enslave him?

Seth used the dipper to sip fresh water from the sweet bucket. Were liches and wraiths more worthy of freedom than he was? Should liches and wraiths be free to roam where they might encounter innocent people? What about the freedom of their victims?

Seth knew he had dark powers. But did that mean he had to become like Ronodin? Or work for the Underking? The reality was, he didn't enjoy it, and his concerns about their practices and motives kept growing.

Hopefully the Hidden Sage could help him see more clearly. At minimum, Seth wanted to learn how to retrieve his past. He felt like he would do anything to get his memories back, no matter what they contained. He deserved to know who he had been. How much those memories influenced his future would be up to him to decide.

The tall, steep hills of Omari were rounded at the top, like colossal camel humps. Green with vegetation, they loomed larger as the clever boat neared the island, prompting Seth to wonder how such extreme formations took shape.

Seth approached a beach with pebbly sand and a few boulders. He had asked the clever boat to land him near Mount Dagaro. Gazing up at the many hills towering over the beach, Seth wondered which was his desired destination. If Mount Dagaro was toward the interior of the island, it might be none of the hills he currently saw. Identifying the right one to climb felt daunting.

As the boat eased into the breakers, Seth saw a huge white gorilla lumbering from the jungle onto the beach, muscles rolling in its broad shoulders as it supported its steps with its knuckles. The beast was at least twice the height of a normal gorilla, and it gave Seth a hard stare, baring sharp teeth. Behind the ape, Seth saw at least two other oversized white gorillas partly hidden by vegetation.

"Turn around," Seth ordered the boat. "We can't land here."

The boat halted, then backed away from the shore, angling expertly to avoid capsizing. The gorilla on the beach snarled and slapped its chest. Another hulking gorilla emerged from the foliage to join the first.

The Underking had not warned Seth about gorillas. What other dangers lurked on Omari? Though Seth had enjoyed the solitude in the boat, he now missed Ronodin's expertise and competence. Seth squeezed the gunwale. Was this why the Underking had let him venture to Omari? Did the Underking expect him to fail?

Bobbing on the swells, Seth tried to collect his thoughts. Those apes had guarded the beach as if they owned it, regarding him with open hostility. Even if he managed to get ashore, it would be foolish to wander a jungle patrolled by giant gorillas. They were way out of his weight class.

What were his options? What could he use to his advantage?

"Circle the island," Seth said. "Stay near the coast."

The boat complied.

As they made their way around the island, Seth reached out with his senses. If he could locate any undead, maybe he could gather information. Ideally he could charm some into becoming his bodyguards.

Seth perceived no dark presences at first. But as they rounded a rocky headland, a new promontory came into view on the far side of a bay. A squat stone lighthouse stood on the point, emanating a familiar dark energy.

"Go to the lighthouse," Seth directed, scanning the coastline for danger. He didn't see any gorillas. The dilapidated remains of a dock sagged at one end of the bay, but he saw no buildings besides the lighthouse. A few exotic birds added splashes of color, and he noticed a lone fairy twinkling over some blossoms near the dock.

The boat took a circuitous route to the lighthouse, instinctively avoiding rocks and reefs, many of them lurking just beneath the surface of the water. When the boat came alongside the stony promontory, the lighthouse looked abandoned on the deserted shoreline. But Seth could sense two wraiths inside.

"Wait here," he told the boat, hopping onto the rocks and climbing up to a grassy area beside the lighthouse. Built of rough stone blocks, a low tower rose from a broad, hexagonal base. Seth wondered how long it had been since the lamp atop the structure had been lit.

He walked up to the heavy wooden door and found it locked. Remembering what Ronodin had taught him, Seth closed his eyes. Drawing upon the darkness inside of him, Seth projected his power at the door and commanded it to open. To his delight, he heard a click. When he tried the door again, it swung inward. The success marked the first time he had used his power to undo a lock.

There was no ignoring the cold presence of the wraiths. "Hello?" Seth called. "Trick or treat. Anybody home?"

After stepping into a dusty room with webby furniture, Seth knew the lighthouse had a basement because he could sense the wraiths down there. They must have heard him enter—he could tell they were in motion, coming up the stairs. The temperature in the room plunged, and Seth felt the hair on his arms standing up.

Intruder, one wraith thought at him venomously.

"I can hear you," Seth said. "I came to help."

A door opened from the basement, and the wraiths entered the room. Seth stood firm against their icy malice.

You are young, one communicated.

You are warm, the other expressed.

"Tell me why you're here," Seth said.

We keep the lighthouse dark, one conveyed.

Ships crash on the reefs, the other volunteered.

"Seen many ships lately?" Seth asked.

They offered no reply.

"This place is abandoned," Seth said. "I bet the light stays out with or without your involvement. I've been helping wraiths around the islands, and now I need a hand. You know the boundaries are down?"

Yes, one of the wraiths acknowledged.

"I'm doing errands for the Underking," Seth said. "I need to climb Mount Dagaro. Do you know the way?"

Yes, the other wraith confirmed.

"Who put you here to keep the lighthouse dark?"

Nobody, one wraith expressed.

We found this purpose, the other conveyed.

"Want some variety?" Seth asked. "I need escorts."

Why should we aid you? one wraith asked.

"I'm a friend to wraiths," Seth said. "I freed wraiths from a prison at Wyrmroost. I freed wraiths on Timbuli. Someday I'll help you."

You pledge to help us? the same wraith asked.

"If you promise to help me get to Mount Dagaro safely," Seth said. "And then back to my boat. Someday, when you have a need, and I'm around, I'll help you. Maybe someday you'll want to get off this island. Maybe get recruited to the Phantom Isle, if that sounds good. Or else just find a really nice graveyard with some comfortable tombs. Until then, I can give you an exciting task, and I'm one of the few living people who can hear you. You've probably been cold? Hungry?"

I thirst, the other wraith communicated.

"I bet you thirst," Seth said. "Can you drive away those big apes? Are they scared of you?"

All animals flee us, one conveyed.

They flee or we bind them, the other expressed.

"That's what I need," Seth said. "Some powerful wraiths to keep the gorillas away. How about it? Will you promise to take me safely to Mount Dagaro? And then back to my boat?"

Yes.

Yes.

Seth smiled. "Do you want to start out traveling by boat? Or should we go over land?"

We do not cross the water, one of the wraiths stressed.

"We'll hike, then," Seth said. "I'll tell the boat to wait here. Should I give you names?"

If you wish, the other wraith allowed.

"How about lighthouse names?" Seth suggested. "You can be Lampy. And we'll call you Salty. And if you don't mind, I like when you speak out loud."

"As you desire," Lampy said.

"Great," Seth said, looking from one expressionless wraith to the other. "Let's go."

🦅 🦅 🦅

The hike to Mount Dagaro took more than two hours, and though Seth heard distant rustling on occasion, he saw no animals. The wraiths kept to the shadows when they could. They seemed taxed when crossing areas in direct sunlight, moving through the brightness with slower steps and bowed heads. Seth found their chilling presence both creepy and reassuring. If they kept the apes away and got him to the right mountain, he considered a little creepiness a small price to pay.

Mount Dagaro was one of the many soaring hills he had seen when approaching the island, taller than most. A faint, narrow trail spiraled up the mountain, sometimes steep enough that Seth had to use both hands and feet to climb. The sides of the hill were never quite straight down, but Seth suspected that if he started falling, he would not stop until he hit the bottom. The wraiths continued with him until the scant trail ended at a cave masked by a curtain of roots.

"We can proceed no farther," Salty said.

"We will await your return," Lampy said.

"Do you know anything about the Hidden Sage?" Seth asked.

"We cannot see into the cave," Lampy said.

"Nor can we enter the cave," Salty said.

Seth took their answers as a no. "Wait here. I'll be back."

Seth pushed through draperies of twisty roots that descended from the ceiling of the cave to the floor. It was hard to imagine a helpful sage living inside such a wild, secluded place. The cave looked more like a den for a monster. What if the Underking had sent him to his doom? Seth reminded himself that the Underking wanted the Everbloom. If he wanted Seth dead, why not have a bunch of liches gang up on him back in the Under Realm? There seemed to be no reason for the Underking to sabotage him, and that thought brought some consolation.

Beyond the curtains of roots, the cave opened up into a single room. Small, slender stalactites decorated the ceiling, and low stalagmites pointed up from the floor. Water dripped from some of the stalactites into a shallow pool. Seth saw no branching corridors—and no sign of life. He seemed to be alone at a dead end.

He was hoping to find the Hidden Sage. Maybe the sage was more hidden than just residing in an obscure cave on a mountaintop. Could there be a secret passage? Might the sage be invisible?

"I'm looking for the Hidden Sage," Seth tried. "If you are here, I need help."

"And why should I aid a shadow charmer who brought wraiths to my threshold?" answered a creaky little voice.

The words came from in front of him, but Seth couldn't see the speaker. "I brought the wraiths to avoid getting pounded to death by giant apes. Are you invisible?"

"To you I am, apparently," the voice answered, amused.

"Camouflage?" Seth asked. He took a few steps in the direction of the voice. It seemed to come from down low, so he studied the ground. "I lost my memory. I need advice."

"The world is in upheaval," the voice said. "I save my counsel for those who deserve it."

"Please help him," answered a tiny voice that made Seth jump. It came from the pocket of his pants.

"What is going on?" Seth asked, looking down.

"Sorry, Seth," the voice in his pocket apologized. "I can't stay quiet any longer. Mighty sage, Seth is lost right now, but he is a warrior for good with a noble character."

Seth saw a tiny head and a pair of arms poking out of his front pocket. They belonged to a handsome young man no bigger than his pinky finger. How long had he been in there? Was he a spy? Why did he sound so cheerful?

Seth reached for the little person in his pocket. The miniature young man crawled willingly onto his palm. "Amazing," Seth said. "You're a miniature person."

"His endorsement carries weight with me," the creaky voice said.

Seth glanced around. He still hadn't spotted the sage.

"When I say he's lost, I mean metaphorically," the little person said. "He came here on purpose."

"I understood," the creaky voice replied.

Seth finally identified the creaky speaker. Instead of rising to a point, one of the stalagmites ended with a little seat, and on it sat a small brown figure who, to a casual glance, looked like the top of the stalagmite.

Seth knelt in front of the tiny being. "Are you the Hidden Sage?"

"I am Gabrinko," the little figure said. The texture of his skin made Seth wonder if the shriveled little person was made of wood. Standing up, he would be about the height of Seth's pointer finger, only a little taller than the miniature person in his hand. "You may also refer to me as sage, or wise one."

Seth returned his attention to the tiny young man in his palm. "And who are you?" Seth asked him.

"I'm Calvin, the Tiny Hero," the young man said brightly. "I'm your only sworn vassal."

"My vassal?"

"Keeper of your secrets, protector of your honor, servant to your interests, and defender of your causes."

"His support speaks well for you," Gabrinko said.

Seth looked from Gabrinko to the Tiny Hero on his palm. "How long have you been with me?"

"I left Kendra and crossed to you the last time you talked to her," Calvin said. "When you were stuck to the mushroom."

"I'm not familiar with that expression," Gabrinko said.

"I was actually stuck to a mushroom," Seth explained.

"I've stayed quiet since," Calvin said. "A stowaway. A secret passenger. I heard you talking to Ronodin and to the Underking through that freaky undead puppet of his. Sorry to spy. I was worried that if I revealed myself, you might send me away."

"Or use you as fish bait," Gabrinko said.

"What kind of creature are you?" Seth asked.

"A nipsie," Calvin said. "Smallest of the fairy folk, though my people increased my size with a spell."

"And what are you?" Seth asked Gabrinko.

"A wood sprite," Gabrinko said. "We very rarely interact with big folk. My kind consider me an outcast, but the feeling is mutual."

"You live alone in a cave," Seth said.

"Keeps the rain off me," Gabrinko said. "And no neighbors bother me here. Just the occasional adventurer."

Seth returned his attention to Calvin. "You're friends with Kendra?" Seth asked.

"She's your sister," Calvin said. "I can't believe you don't see that yet."

"I know she might be," Seth said. "A lot of people tell me conflicting things."

"Some of those people kidnapped you to an island of the undead," Calvin said. "Use your brain."

"My brain is the problem," Seth said. "That's why I came here. I have a gaping hole where my memories should be. I can talk to the undead creatures on that island. My ability to recruit the help of two wraiths is the reason I made it to this cave alive. I can douse torches and hide in shadows. How can I be sure I don't belong there?"

"I see how that could get confusing," Calvin admitted.

Seth turned to Gabrinko. "The Underking told me you could help me."

"I don't think the Underking expected me to help you," Gabrinko said.

"Why not?" Seth asked.

"I suspect he did not believe you would reach me," Gabrinko said. "He also knows I don't approve of the undead, and that I don't waste good advice on those who will not heed it."

"I came here with an open mind," Seth said.

"Give me your finger," Gabrinko said.

"Why?" Seth asked.

"So I can read you," Gabrinko said. "It must be voluntary."

Seth held out his hand, pointer finger extended. Gabrinko laid a brown hand on his fingertip. Closing his eyes, the diminutive sage took some deep breaths.

"Calvin has done a service for you today," Gabrinko said. "Based on what I see in your mind, I would have chosen not to help you."

"Why not?" Seth asked.

"Your history is blank," Gabrinko said. "Instantly suspicious. What might you be hiding? The memories I can see do you no favors. You deal with darkness. You ignored the desecration of a sacred pool. You participated in the ruination of a dragon sanctuary. You consort with wraiths and evildoers. You intend to rob this island of a glorious treasure to appease your dark master."

"The Everbloom?" Seth asked.

"It imbues these islands with life and magic," Gabrinko said. "Calvin, may I take your hand?"

"Sure," Calvin said.

Seth held out his palm to Gabrinko. Calvin stepped forward, and Gabrinko took his hand.

"This provides a clearer picture of you, Seth Sorenson," Gabrinko said. He released Calvin's hand. "What do you wish to know?"

"Is Kendra really my sister?" Seth asked.

"Yes," Gabrinko said. "And you were a co-caretaker of Wyrmroost. Until recently, you always tried to stand against evil, though, like all mortals, you made mistakes."

Seth stared at Gabrinko. Did that mean Kendra was telling the truth about everything? What Bracken had told him matched Kendra's claims, so did that mean what Bracken said was true as well? The implications were too overwhelming to sort through right now. He needed to learn all he could from Gabrinko. "How do I know you're telling me the truth?"

"You don't," Gabrinko replied. "But I just read your history as Calvin witnessed it and understands it. I have no reason to lie."

"The Underking recommended you," Seth said.

"There are always reasons to doubt," Gabrinko said.

"How can I get my memories back?" Seth asked. "I want to know my history. I'm tired of trying to piece together who I was based on what other people tell me."

"This is a worthy desire," Gabrinko said.

"Can you help me?" Seth asked.

"You voluntarily surrendered your identity," Gabrinko said. "It is the only way so much of you could have been taken. I believe your motives were noble."

"Can I get it back?" Seth asked.

"Any magic that can be done can also be undone," Gabrinko said. "Anything with a beginning must have an end. Curses can be lifted, spells can be broken, bindings can be loosed. It may not be easy, but it can be accomplished."

"I would do anything," Seth said.

"You have an essence, Seth," Gabrinko said. "Call it a spirit, a soul, whatever you wish—you have an eternal component, a core self, that cannot be changed without your willing permission. You can be influenced, Seth. You can be encouraged, helped, fooled, misled. For good or ill, your essence evolves. But never against your will. To truly change your essence, you must be a fully willing participant."

Seth felt sick. "Did they take my essence?"

"No, Seth," Gabrinko said. "If you had lost your essence, you would be gone. There would be nothing left to worry or hope or ask questions. You are the victim of a sophisticated curse. No curse is perfectly executed, but this came close. It took your memories and all knowledge related to your identity, but it left your general knowledge. You remember facts, but you have lost your opinions about those facts. You remember procedures, but not what those procedures mean to you. You don't have to relearn how to eat with a knife and fork. But you have no idea what you most enjoy eating. You retain familiarity with prevailing opinions on various topics, without an awareness of where you personally stand. You can't specifically recall how you relate to anything or anyone."

"That sounds right," Seth said.

"I can't directly perceive your essence," Gabrinko said. "I suspect it remains largely unaltered. But it lacks context. You are trying to rebuild your convictions under the burden of considerable misinformation."

"What should I do?" Seth asked.

"How you resolve this dilemma is yours to decide."

"Do you know who cursed me?" Seth asked.

"Yes," Gabrinko said. "And I know how he took your memories. I can probably discover where he went."

"Who?" Calvin shouted.

"His name is Humbuggle," Gabrinko said. "He is an ancient and powerful demon. Very cunning. He used the

Wizenstone, a talisman of nearly incomprehensible power, to steal your identity."

"He was the little dwarf I saw?" Seth asked.

"Yes," Gabrinko said. "Near where your memories begin. The stone Kendra sent away was the Wizenstone."

"You can figure out where he went?" Seth asked.

"I need one of your hands again," Gabrinko said. "Palm up." Seth offered the hand without Calvin. Gabrinko sprang onto his hand and paced along some of the lines. Then he crouched and tapped Seth's wrist.

"Forgotten or not, your memories share a connection to you," Gabrinko said. He spat onto Seth's hand, crouched down, and rubbed it in. Eyes closed, one hand on Seth's palm, he raised the other. After a long moment, Gabrinko hopped to his feet.

"Any luck?" Seth asked.

"I should have known," Gabrinko said. "Humbuggle has gone to the Titan Valley dragon sanctuary."

"Where is Titan Valley?" Seth asked.

"New Zealand," Gabrinko said. "Near Australia."

Seth held up the wrist with the ghostly manacle. "Can you see this?"

"I know what you see," Gabrinko said.

"Can you break it?" Seth asked.

"I'm sorry, but I am not able," Gabrinko said. "And you will not be going anywhere until you are free from your obligation to the Underking."

"So I have to bring him the Everbloom," Seth said.

"It would harm these islands," Gabrinko said. "There

would be irreversible damage to the ecosystem. Some magical life forms here would go extinct."

"If I don't take it, somebody else will," Seth said.

"Perhaps," Gabrinko replied.

"And I'll stay a slave to the king of the undead," Seth continued.

"Perhaps," Gabrinko said.

"At least I know where to go once I'm free," Seth said.

"I have words for Calvin," Gabrinko said.

"In private?" Seth asked.

"Not necessary," Gabrinko said. He looked at Calvin. "You want to break a curse."

"What curse?" Seth asked.

"You don't remember," Calvin said. "My people, the nipsies, were cursed by Graulas."

"If they made you big, how small are they?" Seth asked.

"You would have a tough time seeing facial features with your naked eyes."

"Was I helping you try to break the curse?"

"You killed the demon Graulas," Calvin said. "Our curse came with a prophecy. All nipsies know it: *'The curse arose from the demon's blight; the lord who slays him will set it right. The slayer shall restore our pride, the Giant Hero at his side.'*"

"I promised to help?" Seth asked.

"And I vowed to serve you," Calvin said solemnly.

"And I have spoken with Serena," Gabrinko said.

Calvin whirled to face him. "You have? She came here?"

"I sent her to Titan Valley," Gabrinko said.

"Wait," Seth said. "Is that where you send everyone?"

"Depends on what the spit tells me," Gabrino said with a wink. "Humbuggle helped Graulas create the nipsie curse. Humbuggle lived for many years at Titan Valley. I told Serena she might find clues in his old castle. I did not know Humbuggle was ever at Wyrmroost. But now he has returned to his former home."

"So Serena might still be at Titan Valley?" Calvin asked.

"At present Humbuggle is there," Gabrinko said. "I know Serena meant to go there."

"How long ago?" Calvin asked.

"Less than a year," Gabrinko said.

"Who is Serena?" Seth asked.

"My true love," Calvin said. "She was selected to go study the curse before I was chosen. Some of my people fear she has perished. But I'm determined to find her."

Gabrinko stretched and yawned. "And our interview is at an end. Please take your wraiths far from here. And if you want to be wise, protect the Everbloom at all cost."

"Thank you for the information," Seth said. "Is there anything else you can tell us?"

"Many things, but my mouth grows dry," Gabrinko said. "You have your portion for now. Follow it, doubt it, ignore it—whatever you choose. If you want my advice, keep Calvin close, Seth, and distance yourself from the Underking as you are able. Farewell."

"Do I keep you in my hand?" Seth asked Calvin.

"That would get annoying for both of us," Calvin said. "Your pocket is perfect."

Seth pocketed Calvin and walked out of the cave.

CHAPTER THIRTY

Alone

Knox awoke with his cheek pressed against the sand. His mind felt foggy, and he had no idea why he had gone to sleep on the beach. His weary muscles complained when he shifted, and his joints felt a little sore. He had a mild headache. Opening his eyes, he stared at a complex network of black needles and razors.

A jolt of recognition went through him.

He remembered it all now—the giant demon octopus, the razor coral, the spine that grazed his shoulder. Drugged and drowsy, he had dragged himself into the little tunnel before collapsing. Looking around, he saw that he had made it around a corner. From his current position he could not see the cliff or the area where Kendra and the others had fallen.

Not wanting to turn around with razor coral on all sides, he carefully backed up until he could see out of the little tunnel. His limbs ached as if he had somehow slept wrong on all of them. The sandy expanse in front of the cavern was empty. Kendra's sack of gales still rested where it had fallen, the unicorn horn on top of it.

The others were gone. He was alone.

The light was dimmer than earlier, suggesting that somewhere above the surface of the ocean, the sun might be heading down. The light from the crystal he carried was more evident than it had been before.

Where was Kendra? Had the demon killed her? What about the others?

They were probably alive. Why would Remulon tranquilize them if he meant to kill them? It had sounded like the demon intended to capture them. Remulon had a reputation as a collector. Knox figured he had escaped the same fate as the others by getting far enough into the coral before passing out.

So what was he supposed to do?

He crawled deeper into the coral, around the corner, then a little beyond where he had awakened, just to be safe. If he was quick and quiet, he could probably slip away, go for help. And bring back who? The old lady in the wheelchair? The elixir wouldn't work on the satyrs, and who knew if there were ingredients to make more? At best, he might return with Savani and Grady. Could they somehow save the day? The merfolk had made it clear that they would not help.

Knox stared at the coral. Was it really as sharp as everyone claimed? He reached in his pocket and found a playing card. He pulled it out and saw it was the joker. He had shown the satyrs a card trick the night before. Having made the joker disappear, he had never removed it from his pocket. Apparently the elixir had included the card as part of his clothes, because it wasn't soggy.

Slowly, carefully, holding just the corner of the card, Knox brushed the joker against a dense snarl of keen edges. He felt no contact with the coral, not the faintest tug, but the card fell apart, shredded to ribbons that were diced smaller as they percolated through more coral to the sand.

He would look worse than that if he tried to take on Remulon. He knew it. He wouldn't last a second. The only way he would survive the encounter would be if the octopus chose to capture him. Did he want to spend the rest of his life as a prisoner?

Knox knew he needed to make a choice. Was he going to run away and be safe or try to save Kendra and the others? Maybe Remulon was asleep? Or out hunting? Knox fidgeted, rubbing his thumb against his fingers. What if he could sneak into the cavern and untie the others? Was it possible they could all make it out of this alive?

He knew his hope of saving them was not very realistic. If he ran away, at least he could report what had happened. Maybe Savani could send for help. Bring people to the island through the canoe. Expert demon hunters. Dudes with big muscles and magical weapons.

What if he fled and Remulon tracked him down before he could escape? Then he would be a dead coward instead of a dead hero. What if Remulon was just waiting for him to exit the coral? Those tentacles might be too big to reach into the tunnel. Maybe the instant he crawled out he would get snatched up.

Or maybe Remulon had forgotten about him. What if he could walk to the surface without any problem? He didn't want Tess to lose her brother. It wasn't fair for his parents to lose their son. He had school and sports and friends waiting back in Texas. He had a whole life to live.

Why had he even come on this expedition? This predicament was unfair. Even if there wasn't help to send back, he could act like he went for help. His intentions would look good. Wouldn't people say he had done the smart thing?

He could leave. Nobody would blame him.

There was only one major problem.

The thought of running away made him sick.

Could he live with leaving Kendra and the others behind? Without even checking if he could save them?

Nobody had made him come along.

They had invited him to stay behind.

So why had he come?

Because Seth had been captured. And it had been partly his fault. Largely his fault. Seth would not have been captured if Knox hadn't left the dungeon keys with the goblins back at Fablehaven. His cousin would still be a caretaker, and Wyrmroost would not have fallen.

Trying to save the island sanctuary was a noble purpose. But Knox was mainly here to try to save Seth. And if Kendra was trapped in that cavern, not only Seth was in trouble, but another cousin as well.

Knox grabbed a fistful of sand and squeezed it. Why had he come on this undersea adventure? He had thought maybe he could do something to help.

Everyone had been captured but him. When was he going to get a better chance to help? To do something that mattered? To make up for the trouble he had caused?

Was he really going to run away the first time nobody was watching? The first time everything depended on him? He remembered himself bragging about his bravery at the victory feast at Stormguard Castle. What if they could see him now?

It helped nobody for him to throw his life away. But he could at least check to see if there was a chance to free the others. If he freed them, he wouldn't be alone anymore. He would have their help. They might all escape.

He didn't have a weapon. He had dropped his spear when the spine pricked him. When he had looked a moment ago, the weapon was gone.

All the weapons were gone.

Unless you counted the unicorn horn and the sack of gales. He remembered Kendra explaining that unicorn horns couldn't be stolen. That had to be why Remulon had left it.

Knox wondered how it would work if he tried to pick it up. What if he wasn't trying to steal it? What if his intent was to return it to Kendra? The horn was the weapon Kendra had grabbed before Remulon attacked. Did she know it would hurt the demon?

With many glances over his shoulder, Knox started

crawling backward. If things stayed quiet, he would at least take a look inside the cavern. If the effort got him captured or killed, at least he would have done his best. But he needed to think positively. If he was quiet and smart, maybe he could save the others.

At the end of the coral tunnel, Knox paused, listening intently. If Remulon was waiting for him to exit, this could be the end of life as he knew it. He backed out and looked around, but he saw no sign of the octopus.

Knox rose cautiously to his feet. Stepping quietly, he walked over to the unicorn horn, crouched down, and gently touched the side of it, half expecting to get shocked. After he rubbed the pearly surface of the unicorn horn without any problem, he picked it up, along with the sack of gales beneath it.

The horn felt good in his hand, almost like a knife. If Remulon came out of the cavern at this moment, at least Knox had something to stab him with.

Except what if Remulon just shot more tentacle darts at him? There might not be a chance to poke the octopus. Kendra had carried the horn too, and it had done her no good.

What about the sack of gales? Would it even bother Remulon? It was hard to predict how the sack would work underwater. Knox knew if he opened it, he might get blown all over the ocean. If he opened it right now, the rush of air might thrust him straight back into the razor coral.

Knox walked into the wide mouth of the cavern. The cave didn't go far straight back from the entrance, but branched off to the left farther than he could see. The crystal he wore seemed brighter in the shade of the cavern. He covered it with his hand.

Progressing deeper into the cave felt forbidding. Was it smart to blunder onward? What if he ran into Remulon? He might find his friends. But would Remulon have left them unguarded?

Instead of turning left and going deeper into the cave, Knox tiptoed to the back wall of the entrance. There were enough large stones that he could easily hide. From where he stood, he could see out the mouth of the cavern to the razor coral and the electric kelp.

It might be best to meet Remulon on the most favorable ground he could find. With his back against the wall of the cave, maybe he could avoid getting blown around by the sack of gales. It would be risky, but so was any option at this point. If he found Kendra and the others and managed to free them, what were the chances of their escaping without the giant octopus hunting them down?

Maybe his best option would be to surprise Remulon. Hold the showdown where he would have the best chance. He wanted to control how the encounter happened. Knox decided to yell something, then paused. He needed to call from outside the cavern or the acoustics might give him away.

Knox ran out of the mouth of the cavern onto the sand. "Kendra?" he called loudly. "Can you hear me? Where are you?"

As he raced back to the rear wall of the cavern entrance,

he heard a faint reply. "Knox! Get out of here! Run!" Her voice was faint, but he could tell she was yelling. She probably thought he was so stupid! Maybe she was right. . . .

Knox reached the back wall and huddled down among the rocks, clutching his crystal tightly to conceal the light. Knox foresaw three possibilities: Remulon would either return from outside the cave, emerge from inside the cave, or not respond.

Knox didn't have to wait long to find out. The enormous black octopus came gliding out from deeper inside the cave, tentacles winding and rippling. Remulon passed where Knox was hiding and drifted out the entrance.

Where are you, frail human? Remulon called out mentally. *Deeper in the coral, perhaps. Imagining yourself secure? I see you took the horn. Do you think it frightens me? I am not diseased. It would be a minor irritant at worst.*

Knox tried to keep his cool. Was he really going to do this? He didn't have much choice left. By calling out, he had committed.

The giant black octopus glided closer to the coral. *Why so silent? Will you cower in there until your elixir wears off? I have a safe air pocket where you can survive. It is your only hope. Do not vex me by remaining hidden.*

Knox stood up, braced himself against the back wall, and opened the sack of gales. Some little sound he made caused Remulon to look back at him at the last second, red eyes intense. A storm of bubbles gushed from the mouth of the sack, astonishing in volume and velocity. The geyser of air blasted out of the cave mouth and into Remulon.

A single tentacle lashed out with blinding speed, clinging to a projection of stone at the mouth of the cave. The other tentacles flapped and flailed in the violent gust of bubbles, a couple getting sheared off as they hit the coral. The one tentacle anchoring Remulon looked tautly stretched to its limit.

Stop this at once! Remulon demanded, panic in his mentally projected words.

Knox remembered that the wind inside the sack of gales was a limited resource. If it ran out with Remulon still alive, Knox knew he was doomed.

Striding forward, Knox found he could walk while holding the sack. It fluttered in his grip, but it didn't blow him all over the place as he had worried! Keeping the airstream focused on the thrashing octopus, Knox approached the strained tentacle. With the sack of gales secured between one arm and his side, and one hand aiming the mouth of the sack, he raised the unicorn horn in his other hand.

I will destroy all of you for this! Remulon threatened. *I have never known defeat!*

Knox spoke through gritted teeth. "You've never gone up against a Texan!"

He brought the horn down, stabbing the tentacle as hard as he could. The meat of the tentacle sizzled and it released from the protuberance, wrenching the horn from Knox's hand. Driven by the underwater wind tunnel, Remulon flew helplessly into the coral.

Knox closed the sack in time to see shreds and scraps of the octopus fanning out from where Remulon had blown through the barrier of razors. Above the mess, the torrent of bubbles rose out of sight. Only the top of the demon's head remained intact, but it was being dazzlingly electrocuted by the kelp. After several blinding flashes, the scorched remains of the head drifted down into the coral, where it was minced into uncountable particles.

Knox sat down hard, tears streaming from his eyes as he laughed hysterically. It had actually worked! It had totally, perfectly worked! He wasn't going to die. The mighty aquatic demon had been grated into confetti!

Tears of shock and relief continued to fall. Knox felt the tears vanishing from his cheeks almost as soon as they were shed. His involuntary laughter finally started to subside.

He searched around on the floor of the cavern until he found the unicorn horn. He wondered if it might have octopus blood on it, but the horn looked pristine. Picking it up, he ventured deeper into the cave.

"Kendra?" he shouted. "Where are you?"

"Knox," her reply came, faint because of the distance. "Be quiet! Are you crazy?"

"Remulon is gone!" Knox called. "Lead me to you!"

"How is he gone?"

"He's sushi! He's dead. Where are you?"

It took some time calling back and forth, but Knox eventually heard her voice getting nearer. He was grateful for the light he wore as the cave got darker. After some time, he reached a large, fully lit chamber containing all sorts of strange items. The light came from bioluminescent fish and plants, no two of them alike. He paused to take in the bizarre variety of life and to admire the huge anchor, the suit of armor, the piles of gold and jewels, the statues, and the exotic shells.

"Knox?" Kendra called, her voice near.

"I'm almost to you," Knox replied.

He followed her voice to a ramp on the far side of the room that led up to a chamber full of air. He could see where the water stopped, held back by the air pocket, but he felt no difference as he passed into the air. The room was very bright because of a brilliant white fairy seated on a perch. She had wings like a bat's, but scaly, and her slender tail ended in a silky tuft. Her body was in the form of a human but covered in white, reptilian scales.

"Knox," Kendra said with relief.

She was lying on the ground beside Warren, Vanessa, Tanu, and Hako. Their bodies were completely cocooned in gooey gray strands, with only their heads showing. All the prisoners except Kendra were unconscious.

"What did Remulon do to you?" Knox asked.

"I'm not sure," Kendra said. "I woke up like this. Is he really dead?"

Knox smiled. "He finally met his match."

"You?"

"Well, yeah. I'm from Texas."

Kendra rolled her eyes. "I'm sure that was it."

"I attacked with your wind bag," Knox said. "I don't think Remulon ever dealt with wind before."

"The sack of gales?" Kendra asked. "Really?"

"I ambushed him," Knox said, unable to resist a big grin. "And blew him into the razor coral."

Kendra's eyes widened. "Knox, you're a genius!"

"I'm just happy it worked!"

"Knox, that was so clutch," Kendra said. "I can't believe he's really gone."

"He's not completely gone," Knox said. "He's in a million pieces. Part of him even got electrocuted."

"I was so worried about you," Kendra said.

"I dragged myself into the coral tunnel before I passed out," Knox said. "He left me there."

"I should have been worried about Remulon," Kendra said. "He had no idea who he was up against. I'm glad you got the horn."

"It came in handy," Knox said. "While I was trying to blow him into the coral, his fast tentacle grabbed a sturdy rock. A stab from the horn made him let go."

"That's incredible," Kendra said. "See if the horn works on this goo. I can hardly budge."

Knox knelt beside Kendra and touched the point of the unicorn horn to the cocoon around her. The gray strands melted away wherever the horn made contact.

"It works," Knox said.

"Get me out," Kendra said.

It took only a minute before her gray bindings were melted away enough for Kendra to squirm free. Knox did some touching up, dissolving most of the gray matter that still clung to her.

"What about the others?" Knox asked.

"I think they got hit with more octopus darts," Kendra said. "Only two poked me."

"I only got scratched by one," Knox said. "It was enough."

"My head hurts," Kendra said. "But I'm so happy!"

"Is that the fairy we want?" Knox asked, motioning to the brilliant white creature.

"Yes," Kendra said. "I've had a few words with the nova song. She speaks no English. She has been here for a long time. A little chain holds her to the perch."

"Will she fly away if we free her?"

"I don't think so," Kendra said. "I'll order her to stay with us. She technically has to obey me. But maybe we'll keep the chain attached just to be sure."

Warren let out a groan. "What is so bright?" he complained groggily. "Why can't I move?"

"Remember the octopus?" Kendra asked.

"Crud," Warren said. "I do now. Are we in his belly?"

"You're tied up in his lair," Kendra said. "And you'll never believe what happened to Remulon."

Craning his neck, Warren looked over at Kendra. "What?"

"Knox destroyed him," Kendra said.

"Wait, really?" Warren asked. "No offense, but did you say *Knox* destroyed him?"

"None taken," Knox said. "I showed him a little Texas hospitality."

"Meaning what?" Warren asked.

"Sack of gales into the razor coral," Kendra said.

Warren whistled.

"And we found the nova song," Knox said.

"I really wasn't looking forward to waking up," Warren said. "I mean, even as I was fading out, I was kind of hoping to just stay asleep. This feels like a miracle."

"What now?" Knox asked.

"You kids cut me loose," Warren said. "Then we wake the others and get out of here."

"There is gold out in his garden," Knox said.

"Add grab some gold to the list," Warren said. "Knox, we owe you, buddy. How did you keep it together and pull it off?"

"Honestly," Knox said, looking from Kendra to Warren, "I've never been more scared. I almost ran for it. But I couldn't leave without you guys." Tears sprang into his eyes again. "I thought we were so dead. This is the best day ever. But now we need to rescue Seth."

CHAPTER THIRTY-ONE

Assignment

On the floor of his private room within the Under Realm, Seth sat cross-legged with his satchel open, the contents spread in front of him. Having returned to the Phantom Isle just after nightfall, after dropping Lampy and Salty at their lighthouse and boating back from Omari, he had stolen quietly from the subterranean dock to his room, hoping to avoid interacting with Ronodin or the Sphinx.

"I was pretty smart," Seth said, approving of the contents laid out on the floor. He had first-aid equipment, string, duct tape, a compass, a matchbox, a magnifying glass, binoculars, a pocketknife, a dagger, a little mirror, a whistle, some beef jerky, hand sanitizer, vitamins, a flashlight, a small notepad, three pencils, a pen, some cash, a tightly folded rain slicker, a pouch of salt, several paper clips, a needle and thread, a pack of chewing gum, fingernail clippers, a bouncy ball, and a harmonica. An unlabeled bottle possibly held a potion.

He also had the single glove that could supposedly turn him invisible if he held still, as well as the leviathan carved from blue stone. He found a slip of paper with words to accompany the leviathan and also words for a tower. He didn't see a tower among the objects.

"I should have gone through this stuff earlier," Seth said. "I'm definitely bringing the satchel next time."

Calvin said nothing. He had suggested it would be best for him to remain silent while in the Under Realm, just in case the undead were listening.

Seth picked up the harmonica and gave a little blow, generating a wheezy, discordant sound. He figured he had once known how to play it, and he wondered if he was any good. On a whim, he took a vitamin, then started packing the items back into the satchel.

The door opened without warning, and Ronodin entered. "You're back late," he said. "How did your errand go?"

"Pretty well," Seth said.

Ronodin stared at him. "What did you learn?"

"What do you mean?" Seth deflected.

"You choose an interesting juncture to start hiding information from me," Ronodin said.

"Are you saying you've been open with me?" Seth asked.

"I've protected you from information that could confuse you," Ronodin said.

Seth stared at him. He knew Ronodin was an enemy.

But bringing that into the open right now would not be very strategic. "I guess that is one way to look at it."

"You're different," Ronodin said.

"What do you mean?"

"You look at me differently," Ronodin said. "Who did you speak with?"

"Don't I deserve a little private time? You take plenty."

"The Hidden Sage works with your enemies," Ronodin said.

"Who are you talking about?"

"Your lies reveal more than the truth would," Ronodin said. "You believe him. You've decided I'm your enemy and you must hide things from me."

"I'm confused," Seth said.

"At least you have that right," Ronodin said with an exasperated sigh. "Your determination to dig into your past is poorly timed."

"Why?"

"All is in place to retrieve the Everbloom," Ronodin said. "The Sphinx has the location. The phantom will lead you to it."

"I'll be with Dezia?" Seth asked.

"It's the most efficient way," Ronodin said. "She'll be compliant and docile. The Sphinx made sure of that. We'll go fetch the Everbloom tomorrow. Unless you no longer have the stomach for it."

"What other choice do I have?" Seth asked.

"I'd be fascinated to know," Ronodin said. "The

Everbloom is your ticket out of here. Hand that over to the Underking and you can go do whatever you want."

"The Underking would let me walk away," Seth said. "Would you?"

"Do you think the Underking is your friend?" Ronodin asked. "More than I am? Do you know what the Underking told me today?"

Seth wasn't sure he wanted to know. "What?"

"The Underking warned me to watch you," Ronodin said. "He thinks you might try to keep the Everbloom for yourself."

"Really?" Seth asked. "Why would I do that?"

"You tell me," Ronodin said. "It seems preposterous. The price of your freedom has been set. You can't escape with the Everbloom unless the Underking frees you."

Seth nodded.

"Unless you have some notion of being a hero," Ronodin said. "Handing the Everbloom over to somebody else."

"Who?" Seth asked.

"I don't know," Ronodin said. "But the Underking is no fool. He has suspicions for a reason. It's just a flower, Seth. It's beautiful and mystical, but just a flower. If the lord of the undead wants a flower in order to let you go, bring him the flower and move on."

"That makes sense," Seth said.

"You haven't had a chance to live your life," Ronodin said. "You could do a lot of good. But not bound here in the Under Realm. It isn't your fault that you're here. Pay the price and get free."

"I'm here because of you," Seth said. "You brought me here."

"I brought you here so you could learn, Seth," Ronodin said. "If not for me, your powers would have gone to waste. You think Kendra or any of those others would want you to regain dark abilities? They would be more than happy to leave you powerless, essentially lobotomized. I brought you where you could restore your potential."

"You brought me into slavery," Seth said.

"Not for long," Ronodin replied. "Not if you play this smart. You could be free by this time tomorrow."

"And you'll let me go?" Seth asked.

"Why would I want to keep you?" Ronodin asked. "I'd love to work with you in the future. But that is up to you. Can I get real with you?"

"Sure."

"The Underking isn't on your side," Ronodin said. "When he offered you his crown? That wasn't because he liked you."

"Why did he do it?"

Ronodin looked at Seth seriously. "To consume you. To utterly own you. Seth, you would have joined the undead not as their king, but as a puppet."

"I knew there had to be a catch," Seth said. "I wasn't regretting my choice."

"So much depends upon tomorrow," Ronodin said.

"I know," Seth replied. "We have the ointment to resist the heat. We know where to go. I'll do the job."

"You are saying words," Ronodin said. "Telling me what

you think I want to hear. I see the truth behind your assurances. You don't know what you're going to do."

"It makes sense to deliver the Everbloom and get free," Seth said.

"You're right about that. It would be the best choice. You didn't have to visit the Hidden Sage. You could have just come to me."

"What?"

"You didn't have to go to some sage to learn where to get your memories," Ronodin said.

"You never answer my questions," Seth said.

"Your memories were taken by a demon that looks like a dwarf," Ronodin said. "Humbuggle. You met him at the castle before he sent you away."

"Good to know," Seth said.

"He used the Wizenstone," Ronodin said. "You would have to defeat Humbuggle to get your memories back."

"How can I do that?" Seth asked.

"Nobody knows," Ronodin said. "Nobody has done it."

"Where is he?" Seth asked.

"Probably at a dragon sanctuary called Titan Valley."

Seth considered Ronodin. Did he know what the Hidden Sage had told him? Was he sharing this information because he knew it no longer mattered? How did he know so much?

"I've been in this game for a long time," Ronodin said. "I'm rarely a step behind. Don't try to outmaneuver me."

"Why are you doing all of this?" Seth asked. "What are you after?"

"The world is changing," Ronodin said. "The dragons are winning. There are going to be fewer prisons in the world. Magical sanctuaries are relics of the past. I celebrate this new era."

"What do you really want?" Seth asked. "It isn't just freedom for everybody."

"I want so many things," Ronodin said with relish. "But tomorrow I will settle for delivering the Everbloom to the Underking. Sleep well. Be smart." Ronodin walked to the door. "Goodnight, Seth."

"See you tomorrow."

Ronodin closed the door.

Seth left everything where it was and climbed into bed. He didn't want to think. He deserved some rest. He wanted to sleep. And he knew it might take a while for him to drop off.

Ronodin had been completely right about one thing: Seth had no idea what he was going to do tomorrow.

CHAPTER THIRTY-TWO

Wishing

Kendra snapped awake in the cool of the night, her hammock rocking as she sat up. White radiance shone through her window from the nova song chained to a perch outside the tree house.

The day before, Kendra, Knox, Warren, Vanessa, and Tanu had followed Hako on a long hike from the lair of Remulon out of the ocean, arriving at Crescent Lagoon just after dusk. They had taken their antidotes while standing in the shallows, and water became tangible to them again. Kendra had initially felt thirsty, noticing her hunger only after she had gotten enough to drink. They had eaten a big meal together before going to bed, too tired to plan for the next day.

Kendra had been full of worries as she climbed into her hammock. Remulon had warned that going to the Phantom

Isle meant certain death. Lord Quintus had also stressed that people ran away from the Phantom Isle rather than toward it. Yet it was their next step. Seth and Bracken were there. There was no hiding from it.

But she felt different now than she had been feeling when she went to bed. A few hours of rest had simplified the problem in her head. Suddenly the way forward seemed clear.

Feeling calm alertness, Kendra slid out of the hammock and got dressed. She quietly exited her tree house, then crossed a long rope bridge and a short stable one leading to the primitive elevator. There was no hint of dawn yet. After pulling a lever, she descended through the leafy canopy amid rustlings and dripping water until the elevator reached the jungle floor.

Kendra stepped off the little platform and walked to the lagoon. She gasped when she came through the trees to find the three eyeless cyclopses standing together on the sand, as if expecting her.

"You seek us," Tal said.

"You have awakened with a purpose," Hobar said.

"You wish to find the Fairy Queen's shrine," Baroi said.

"You guys are good," Kendra said.

"You sounded a clarion call," Tal said.

"We cannot escort you or we would revert to our more fearsome form," Hobar said.

"Instead we summoned a fairy to guide you," Baroi said.

"You can summon fairies?" Kendra asked.

"Come out, Andressa," Tal said.

A fairy bobbed out of hiding, tiger-striped butterfly wings sparkling. She fluttered near, allowing Kendra to appreciate her petite figure and playful elfin features.

"Most fairies do not perceive our summonings," Hobar said. "Or else they choose not to heed them."

"Andressa hears well," Baroi said. "We believe she is the most reliable fairy on the island."

"Pleased to meet you," Kendra said. "I'm Kendra."

"The pleasure is mine," Andressa said. "Are you certain you wish to visit the shrine? You shine brightly, but mortals who trespass there tend to die."

"I know it's never safe to visit a shrine of the Fairy Queen," Kendra said. "But I have great need—and a relationship with her majesty."

"I can show you the way and guide your return," Andressa said. "You don't want to get lost with so many dangerous creatures roaming the night."

"Go," Baroi said. "If you wish to return before dawn, you must hurry."

"You know what I intend?" Kendra asked.

"We cannot see your mind," Hobar said.

"But in the quiet of the night, we could see you coming to us," Tal said. "And we could see you on the trail to the shrine."

"Will I survive?" Kendra asked.

"That depends on you," Baroi said.

"I'll be back," Kendra said. She had to try. Too many people were counting on her for her to back down now.

The fairy conducted Kendra to a path, lighting the way

with her glow. Kendra didn't really need the illumination—ever since she had become fairykind, no natural darkness was complete to her. Even the deepest shadows under the trees looked dim, not dark. Still, with branches overhead screening the moon, and her line of sight limited by dense vegetation, Kendra wondered if it was wise to strike off across the island without any of her companions. It seemed like something her brother would do.

But she had to go to the fairy shrine—because to save Seth and Bracken, to restore the sanctuary, she and her companions had to go to the Under Realm. And if they went there without help, they were all going to die. The Fairy Queen was the most powerful being Kendra knew. Bracken was her son, and Kendra hoped a mission to rescue him would validate a claim to her assistance.

She would have been more comfortable if Warren or Vanessa were accompanying her. But none of her companions could risk approaching the Fairy Queen. Most mortals who dared invade the sacred terrain of the queen's shrine would be instantly struck down. Also, instinctively, Kendra knew she would better merit aid if she went alone.

"Keep up," Andressa said. "An ocelot is stalking this way, but we won't cross paths if we hurry."

Kendra increased her pace to a jog, her eyes searching the dappled moonlight to either side of the trail. The prospect of unseen creatures prowling the undergrowth kept her anxiously alert.

"You can slow down now," Andressa said. "You're much quieter at a walk."

Kendra settled into a comfortable walk. She decided that if she was going to invade the realm of the undead, she should try to enjoy the relative peace of strolling through a jungle teeming with dangerous magical creatures.

At least she knew where to find Bracken and her brother. That information had seemed unattainable a few days ago. She was closing in on her goal. There were still problems, though. Even if she managed to survive the Under Realm and find her brother, there was no guarantee Seth would come with her. That possibility made her ache inside.

She couldn't just force him to leave. That would do more harm than good. It would make her just like Ronodin. What she really hoped was that he would want to come with her.

As to surviving the Under Realm, Kendra needed the Fairy Queen to provide help. If not, she wasn't sure what to do.

Remulon had been right when he scoffed that they had arrived at his lair with no plan. If it hadn't been for some luck and some shocking heroics from Knox, they would still be his prisoners. The Under Realm was sure to be much less forgiving if they just showed up expecting to prevail. This was no time to fall back on improvisation.

Kendra followed the fairy through a dense jungle, across brushy fields, along the outskirts of a bamboo forest, and up into some hills. Andressa flitted close to Kendra.

"We're almost there," the tiger-striped fairy said. "I can't accompany you to the shrine or offer specific warnings. But be careful. Remember your true objective."

"Is it guarded by naiads?" Kendra asked, thinking of the Fablehaven shrine.

"Not naiads," Andressa said. "But the shrine is protected. If you are unworthy to be there, you will not survive."

Kendra had been to the Fairy Realm. But she had been escorted by Bracken, who was a rock star among the fairies. She felt sure her fairykind status rendered her worthy to visit the shrine, but she worried that its guardians might not agree.

"I'll await you here," Andressa said. "This path ends at the shrine."

Kendra could hear water splashing. "A waterfall?"

"Follow that sound," Andressa said. "I can say no more."

"Could I command you to tell me more?" Kendra asked.

"Your authority to issue commands comes from the Fairy Queen," Andressa said. "It was she who forbade us from revealing the secrets of this shrine."

"Fine," Kendra said. "Thanks for leading me here. I'll see you soon."

Alone, overshadowed by tall trees dripping with vines, Kendra proceeded along the path. She passed a few low, eroded ruins partially hidden by leafy creepers.

The steady churning of falling water grew in volume until Kendra entered a clearing open to the moon and stars. Ahead, water trickled and tumbled over the edge in several places along a low, curved wall of mossy rock, the largest waterfall at the center.

The incoming water spread over the clearing in a shallow pool. Carved tiki statues at least as tall as humans were spaced throughout the pond, heads disproportionately large, most submerged up to the shins. Little grassy islands poked above the water at random. Kendra could not see a stream flowing away from the pool, leaving her to wonder how water flowed in but not out. Perhaps it was escaping underground? Was the pool deeper in some places than it looked?

In Kendra's experience, though the area around a fairy shrine could be sizable, the shrine itself would be tiny. It was hard to guess where among the flooded statues she would locate the actual shrine.

Despite the backdrop of falling water, the moonlit pool felt still and sacred. Kendra stepped hesitantly forward, wading into the ankle-deep water with her shoes on. Immediately she felt like a trespasser. Looking up, she found the nearest tiki statue gazing right at her. Had the head been facing her way before?

As she took another few steps forward, Kendra again felt unwelcome. Were more of the statues looking her way? It had to be a coincidence.

Kendra held still. Should she come back another time? Something felt off.

No! She had no other time. This had to happen tonight.

Kendra sloshed onward, searching the surroundings for the fairy shrine. There was no escaping the sense that she was unwanted and in danger. She felt the message as if it were being silently transmitted from every direction. She stopped again and found that all of the heads of the tiki statues were facing her. One had a blowgun raised to stone lips. Another looked ready to throw a hatchet.

Something supernatural was happening. The positions were definitely new. Were the statues about to attack?

The only sound was the splash of falling water.

"I belong here," Kendra called out. "I'm fairykind, and I need help from the Fairy Queen. It's an emergency."

The impression that she was trespassing evaporated. Had the expressions of the tiki statues softened? She did not feel welcome, but she no longer felt rejected.

Kendra waded toward the main waterfall, the water never deeper than her shins. The tiki statues no longer seemed to follow her movements, and no weapons were aimed at her. As she neared the waterfall, Kendra noticed a golden necklace set with garnets arrayed on a stump. Her first impulse was to pick it up, but she realized it might be an offering to the Fairy Queen and decided to leave it alone. She also ignored an ivory scepter with a moonstone handle, which sat atop a little mound, and a silver javelin leaning against one of the tiki statues.

"I need to find the shrine," Kendra said, turning in a slow circle. "Can anyone help me?"

As she finished her rotation, she found one of the tiki statues pointing at the waterfall. She was almost positive the statue had not been positioned like that earlier.

Kendra approached the middle of the semicircular wall at the rear of the pool, where the water fell smooth and clear as glass in a curtain a little wider than her outstretched arms. She saw no fairy statue at the base of the waterfall, so she felt around underwater. After encountering nothing but slimy rocks, she looked up. Could the shrine be behind the falling water? It would be a shame to get wet for nothing.

Kendra scrutinized the area around the waterfall. She noted the occasional incongruous treasure, apparently unguarded, but still no fairy shrine. Three tiki statues now pointed at the waterfall.

"Thank you, I think," Kendra said. At least the night was warm; if she was going to get soaked, she probably wouldn't feel too chilled.

She walked up to the glassy cascade and tried to peer through it. She could see an alcove beyond. There was no space to go around. The waterfall shielded the alcove perfectly.

Reaching out a hand, she pushed a finger through the film of water and watched the curtain part a little beneath the intrusion. She liked how the water felt against her finger. It wasn't too cold.

Holding her breath, Kendra stepped through the waterfall, getting thoroughly drenched in the process. The churning water sounded different inside the small, humid alcove. The floor was submerged, the water to her ankles.

Delicately sculpted from white stone, a tiny statue of a fairy stood atop a small pedestal in a niche at the back of the alcove. A little bronze bowl rested near the statue. Kendra knelt in the water before the fairy figurine and pushed her rubbery wet hair away from her eyes.

"Hello, Fairy Queen," Kendra said. "This is Kendra Sorenson. Thanks for letting me come this far. I'm here because I have an emergency. You've saved me before, and I've never needed your help more. Your son Bracken is imprisoned in the Under Realm. My brother, Seth, is stuck there too. And I need to retrieve the Sunset Pearl from there to restore this dragon sanctuary. I found a nova song who will lead me to the Phantom Isle. I can get there. But the island is guarded by a sea dragon, and I need a way to survive the Under Realm."

The air stirred, and Kendra smelled freshly tilled earth, ripe bananas, frosty pine needles, sea spray, cave minerals, mint leaves, and dozens of other aromas, some more familiar than others, simultaneously distinct and jumbled. The room brightened as the fairy statue glowed.

Kendra, I fear for my son, came the familiar voice of the Fairy Queen in her mind. Feelings of grief and worry washed over her.

"So do I," Kendra said, tears in her eyes.

Alas, I cannot send anyone from my realm to help you, the Fairy Queen communicated. *If my astrids, fairies, or any other minions were to enter the Under Realm on my orders, it would constitute an act of war. We simply cannot afford a war with the Underking.*

"I'm willing to go," Kendra said. "Can you help me succeed?"

There is one way, the Fairy Queen expressed. *It involves great risk for both of us, and it would not protect any of your companions. Success will be hard-won. It will depend on your determination and courage.*

"I won't let you down," Kendra promised. "I won't fail Seth or Bracken, either. I'll do whatever it takes."

Kendra felt the warmth of approval. *Turn around and reach under the water.*

Still on her knees, Kendra turned and reached down, discovering that the water was inexplicably deep. She leaned forward until her face was just above the surface, both arms extended straight down without reaching the bottom. A hand brushed hers, passing her something metallic and circular.

Kendra lifted a beautiful circlet out of the water, wrought of a metal like radiant silver and inlaid with pristine gems, including a large white jewel in the front. The details were exquisite, the circlet formed by multiple strands in a perfect simulation of woven vines. Kendra knew instinctively that she had never held an object nearly as valuable.

My crown, the Fairy Queen explained.

In the emotion that accompanied the words, Kendra could feel the import of the gift. She got the feeling it was unprecedented. "You're giving me your crown?" Kendra asked.

Return it to me after you triumph, the Fairy Queen directed. *The crown will offer protection when you enter the darkness. You shine so brightly, Kendra, yet many lack eyes to see your light. As a mortal with a wellspring of energy inside, you can light this crown as no other. Use it when you enter the Under Realm.*

"Will it fit?" Kendra asked.

The crown always fits perfectly, the Fairy Queen conveyed. *The protection it provides depends upon you maintaining your courage. If the light within you dims, so will the crown.*

"The crown won't protect others?"

Any who join you will face much greater jeopardy, with little chance to alter the outcome.

Kendra considered the implications. Could she really walk into the Under Realm alone? She supposed it would be better than endangering anyone else, especially if having backup wouldn't change the outcome.

"I'll return with Bracken," Kendra said.

Do not lose my crown, the Fairy Queen admonished. *You would leave my kingdom vulnerable, and I would not long remain queen. Take nothing that belongs to the Underking, only that which he has stolen from the world above. You must prevail.*

The air stirred with uncountable aromas, and Kendra knew her connection to the Fairy Queen was severed. She stood up, holding the crown in one hand. She tested the depth where she had reached for the crown, only to discover the water was shallow again. After a final glance back at the inanimate figurine, she stepped out through the waterfall.

Inexplicably, passing back through the curtain of water dried her, except for her feet, which remained submerged. All of the tiki statues had their heads inclined toward her as if bowing. The moon and stars shone overhead. Kendra strode away from the pool determined to embark for the Phantom Isle before sunrise.

CHAPTER THIRTY-THREE

Phantom Isle

Kendra heard someone chopping wood as she approached the beach. Dawn was just beginning to color the sky, and birds had started to sing in the treetops. When Andressa led her into view of the lagoon, Kendra found six menehune hollowing out a tree trunk with axes and adzes. Two others were shaping outriggers.

Savani stood on the beach to greet her, accompanied by the Himalayan cyclopses. Kendra changed the way she was holding the crown so her body shielded it from view. Was it smart to carry something so precious in the open like this?

Savani approached Kendra and gave her a welcoming hug. Lips near her ear, the caretaker asked, "Is that what I suspect it is?"

"I can't believe she entrusted it to me," Kendra whispered back.

"Who *are* you?" Savani asked, clearly impressed. "Would you like a bag to conceal it?"

"Yes, please," Kendra said.

"Are you exhausted?" Savani asked.

"No," Kendra said. "I woke up energized. It was dark but I wasn't sleepy."

"One moment," Savani said. She went and gave orders to a menehune, who scampered off. Then she waved for Kendra to join her by the cyclopses.

"Greetings, Kendra," Tal said.

"You had rare success at the fairy shrine," Hobar said.

"You gained the respect of its protectors," Baroi said.

"They pointed the way for me," Kendra said.

"Tell us your plans," Savani invited.

Kendra looked over to where the menehune were now vigorously shaping the exterior of the dugout canoe. "Is that for me?"

"That depends on your intentions," Savani said.

"I'm going to the Phantom Isle," Kendra said. "Alone."

"You seek the Sunset Pearl," Tal said.

"You are prepared to venture into the dark," Hobar said.

"The way is fraught with peril," Baroi said. "There will be opportunities to fall."

"The cyclopses woke me," Savani explained. "They had a premonition of your intentions. You can journey into the Under Realm alone. But getting there is another matter. You will need assistance."

"I really don't want to drag others into this," Kendra said.

"I already have two volunteers," Savani said. "They will help you get to the Phantom Isle. You'll be on your own for the Under Realm."

"Thank you," Kendra said. The thought of having others to help her navigate the ocean was a relief.

Red hair tousled, Grady approached, holding the nova song by a slender chain with one hand and a burlap sack with the other. With the fairy above him straining against her tether, it looked like he was flying a small, beautiful kite. "Will this do?" Grady asked, holding out the sack.

Savani accepted the sack and handed it to Kendra. "Grady is one of the volunteers."

He smiled at Kendra. "A final voyage for me."

"Grady is a selkie," Savani said. "He was caught stealing from a village a couple of years ago and is working to earn his skin back."

"What does that mean?" Kendra asked.

"I can turn into a seal," Grady said. "But only if I have my skin."

"I'll entrust his sealskin to you, Kendra," Savani said. "Once you arrive at the Phantom Isle, it will be his payment. Receiving his skin back should give him a good chance to escape."

"Don't give it to me early," Grady said. "I won't be able to think straight. My instinct will be to go home to my people."

"You won't try to take it from me?" Kendra asked.

"There have been occasions when I wanted to steal it," Grady said. "Would have if I could have. But I believe in this mission to retrieve the Sunset Pearl. I vowed to Savani, and I vow to you, come what may, I won't take my skin until you offer it."

"All right," Kendra said. "Who is the other volunteer?"

"You'll join up with him after you embark," Savani said. "When I first arose, I sounded the conch to solicit help from the merfolk. They sent envoys to the surface, and I explained our need. Before long they sent a hunter called Faro to escort you."

"I know him," Kendra said.

Savani nodded. "He and Grady will help you reach your destination. After that, all will depend on you. Do you wish to bid anyone farewell?"

"I'd rather just slip away if I can," Kendra said. "While I feel good about it."

Savani issued a command in a language Kendra could not understand. A menehune approached and handed Savani a folded packet wrapped in banana leaves and tied with twine. She passed the bundle to Kendra.

"That contains the sealskin," Savani said. "Keep it at the front of the canoe with you. Down by your feet is fine. But Kendra, if I were you, I would never take my hands off that sack. What it contains should never be set aside or entrusted to another."

"I agree," Kendra said, holding the crown close.

"Your craft is ready," Grady said.

Kendra turned to see that the menehune had gone and the two-person canoe was complete, with an outrigger on each side. Handing the nova song's chain to Savani, Grady kicked his sandals off and cast his shirt aside, then grabbed the front end of the canoe and dragged it into the lagoon. Kendra liked the smell of the freshly cut wood.

"They asked if we wanted it painted," Savani said, returning the bright fairy to Grady. "I told them we had to hurry."

"They were fast," Kendra said.

"They placed their best enchantments on it," Savani said. "It's watertight. Shouldn't be splintery. The canoe will eagerly go in the direction paddled. It will normally be ignored by dangerous creatures and will gently summon the kind of fish you might want to catch."

"Will we be fishing?" Kendra asked.

"I hope not," Savani said. "It depends how far you have to go to find the Phantom Isle."

Grady stood in the water beside the dugout canoe. He had fastened the delicate chain of the nova song to the front. The scaly white fairy stood on the bow. Kendra realized it was time to depart.

"Tell my friends I love them and I'm sorry to sneak away," Kendra said. "I'll be back."

"I will help them understand," Savani said.

"You can expect fair weather," Tal said.

"Hold fast to your mission," Hobar admonished.

"Return with honor," Baroi said. "Many depend on you."

"I know," Kendra muttered. She wasn't sure how she could feel much more pressure.

Kendra waded out to the canoe, stashed the wrapped

sealskin in the front, and climbed in. Grady handed her a paddle, then pushed the canoe forward and climbed in the back with a paddle of his own.

Looking over her shoulder, Kendra waved. Savani and the cyclopses raised their hands in return. She helped Grady paddle out of the lagoon. What was she doing? Was she out of her mind? Was she really heading off to invade the Under Realm alone? Who did she think she was? Feeling the shape of the crown inside the sack on her lap gave her confidence.

As the canoe exited the lagoon, a familiar figure rose out of the water, clutching a spear that ended in the likeness of a crab claw. "Welcome, Kendra," he said. "Well met."

"Hi, Faro," Kendra said. "You're going to see us safely to the island?"

"When Savani sent her message, I knew I had to get involved," Faro said. "Not only did you get rid of the people of the deep and restore our golems, you eliminated a demon who has threatened our safety for centuries. Now you are on a quest to rescue this sanctuary. You will need help getting past Jibarro. If you are willing to venture into the Under Realm alone, I am determined to help you evade the great sea dragon."

"Does Savani call the merfolk often?" Kendra asked.

"Not often," Faro said. "And, truthfully, we do not always respond. Let's just say that after all of your help, our ears were more attuned to the needs of those on the surface."

"I'm Grady of the selkie," Grady announced from the stern. "We're grateful to have your assistance."

"It's my honor," Faro said. "We need a heading."

Kendra looked at the nova song, still standing on the bow. "Where do you want to go?" Kendra asked her.

"You ordered me not to go toward the darkness," the fairy replied. "I am repressing the urge."

"I promised you could follow your instincts before long," Kendra said. "You can now."

"Thank you," the nova song said. "And I promised that when you allowed me to obey my nature, I would share my name. Mizarine."

"Thanks, Mizarine," Kendra said.

"Thank you for not commanding me to share my name earlier than I preferred," Mizarine said. She flew until her chain pulled taut. "The darkness is this way."

"We have a heading," Grady said, paddling. "Ask her how far."

"Is it far?" Kendra asked.

"For me, unchained, less than two hours," Mizarine said. "At our present speed? Half a day, maybe more."

"Half a day will suffice," Grady said. "I can go faster than this, and I don't tire easily."

"You're fortunate," Faro said. "The Phantom Isle can range far and wide on the seas. It might have been many days away."

"What if it moves before we get there?" Kendra asked.

"Possible," Faro said. "Only one way to find out."

Kendra started paddling.

"Save your strength," Grady said. "I have this."

"I'll go underneath the stern and push," Faro said. "I can use the exercise."

A moment after Faro disappeared beneath the surface, the canoe sped up significantly, gliding more rapidly up and down the swells. Kendra looked ahead at the nova song fluttering on her tether.

"Mizarine, you can rest on the canoe," Kendra said. "Just correct us if we go off course."

"I have been bound to a perch for a long time," Mizarine said. "I want to stretch my wings."

"If you should get free, I command you not to ditch me," Kendra said. "Let me keep pace with you so we can find the Under Realm together."

"I will let you come to the darkness with me," Mizarine said, "if that is your wish."

"The darkness of the Under Realm is dangerous," Kendra said. "You don't have to go there."

"I must light the darkness," Mizarine said. "For me there is no choice. I must fulfill the purpose of my existence."

Kendra watched as Timbuli diminished in the distance. She enjoyed moving over the ocean in the canoe. It seemed like an activity a tourist might pay to do. A glorious sunrise led to a mild day, with a light breeze and scattered white clouds. Kendra felt in no hurry to reach her destination. Whenever they got there would be soon enough.

Kendra knew the realm of the Underking would be full of horrors. She remembered the terrible undead creatures that had attacked Blackwell Keep, the revenants and wraiths. The Under Realm was an entire domain packed with those kinds of beings and worse. There were no guarantees the crown would fully protect her. This could be her last day of her life.

But she had faced days like this before. Kendra was willing to do anything to save Bracken and Seth, and for a long time she had known no way to help, so it felt good to be able to take action, even if it was risky. She had been warned to keep the light inside of her burning bright, and part of that meant remaining hopeful. Kendra felt sure the Fairy Queen would not have lent her the crown unless she believed she would get it back.

Kendra glanced down at the packet wrapped in leaves and twine. "Grady, you have been a prisoner?" she asked.

"More an indentured servant," Grady said. "Working off my crimes."

"You were stealing?" Kendra asked.

"Being a selkie means having a dual nature," Grady said. "When we have spent enough time in the sea, we start longing for dry land. We always have the option of shedding our skin and walking about like a human. Occasionally we are coaxed out of the water by a pretty face. Other times we might crave a certain food or miss the experience of standing on a hilltop. Sometimes we get up to mischief."

"What were you trying to steal?" Kendra asked.

"A jade figure from a memorial to the oceanids," Grady said. "I took a fancy to it and decided it belonged in the water instead of on land. When we shed our skins, we take a risk. If somebody gets our sealskin, we can't return to the water except as a blundering human."

"Savani got hold of your sealskin," Kendra guessed.

"I have no hard feelings," Grady said. "She was within her rights. It has happened to me before and will probably happen again. After I spend enough time as a human, it begins to feel like my native state. But the longing for the sea grows over time."

"Your mind-set alters when you become a seal?" Kendra asked.

"Considerably, yes," Grady said. "Becoming a seal represents a different form of existence, complete with new abilities and instincts. Once I'm in my seal form, my human inclinations melt away until the next time I come up on land."

"Thanks for helping me," Kendra said. "I know this is dangerous."

"Whether I'm looking to my interests as a seal or a man, retrieving the Sunset Pearl would be good for the sanctuary," Grady said. "Anyway, I'm not doing the hardest part. I'm in awe that you're willing to go into the Under Realm alone. My role is minor compared to yours. And besides, I get my skin back early this way."

The sun was climbing high in the sky when a smudge appeared on the horizon directly ahead of them. As they drew nearer, Kendra saw it was a patch of gray mist, like a low, murky cloud.

"We're almost there," Mizarine said.

"It's in the fog?" Kendra asked.

"Yes," Mizarine said, batlike wings fluttering harder. "Isn't it thrilling?"

"We should pause and plan," Grady suggested, dragging

his paddle to slow the canoe. Mizarine redoubled her efforts to pull them forward.

Faro surfaced and rested a strong arm on one of the outriggers. "Once we cross into the mist, Jibarro will hunt us."

"What's the best strategy?" Grady asked.

"We should work together to propel the canoe to the island as fast as we can," Faro said. "If Jibarro appears, I will antagonize him, draw him away."

"You'll be killed," Grady said.

"I'm very quick in the water and accustomed to confrontations with big game," Faro said. "I'll make my escape. Just get Kendra to the shore without delay."

"We should free the nova song from the boat," Grady said. "Kendra can hold the chain. We may need to move in great haste."

Grady came forward, unfastened the slender chain from the front of the canoe, and handed it to Kendra. She noticed his eyes lingering for a moment on the wrapped sealskin. Then he returned to the stern and held his paddle ready.

"Are you going to push?" Grady asked the merman.

Ducking his head, Faro vanished beneath the swells with a flick of his tail. Kendra hoped he could see farther underwater than they could see through the mist.

"Ready, Kendra?" Grady asked.

She held her crown in one hand, the fairy chain in the other, and felt the sealskin in its leaf wrappings at her feet. She checked her sack of gales and the unicorn horn. The thought of perhaps presenting it to Bracken soon was encouraging. "Sure."

With a sweep of Grady's paddle, the canoe surged forward much faster than ever, making Kendra rock back. She could only imagine how hard Faro was pushing under the water.

Cool mist breezed against Kendra's face as the canoe entered the grayness. Kendra peered ahead, hoping to see land before she saw a dragon. The visibility within the patchy fog varied, allowing her to see sometimes a hundred yards before them, sometimes fifty.

When the island came into view up ahead, Kendra's relief was interrupted by a tremendous roar. Turning in the direction of the earsplitting bellow, Kendra saw the enormous head and neck of a dragon coming into view through the mist from off to one side.

"Get to shore," Faro said, surfacing and racing toward the dragon, spear upraised. "I am Faro of the merfolk!" he shouted in a surprisingly loud voice. "I have come to slay the sea tyrant Jibarro! You must be his little niece. Fetch him for me!"

The answering roar showed that the taunt had struck a nerve. Faro began to veer away from the island to lure the sea dragon away from the canoe. Grady paddled furiously.

"I always thought dragons belonged in the sky!" Faro yelled. "They look so majestic soaring against the clouds. Sea dragons are too fat and dull for such sport! They waddle like ducks and bob around like infants."

The island was coming into sharper focus. The ruins

of stone fortifications mingled with jagged rocks. The forbidding coastline offered no obvious place for the canoe to land.

Jibarro had taken the bait. The huge sea dragon was closing in on Faro, who looked tiny by comparison. Kendra squeezed the crown through the sack. What spectacular dodge was going to save him? Faro looked doomed.

"Choke on me!" Faro called, hurling his spear. It pinged harmlessly off the scales of Jibarro's neck. Jaws agape, the sea dragon launched forward.

In the last moment, Kendra saw Faro's eyes go to her. He seemed encouraging and at peace. Kendra realized the merman had never planned to avoid the sea dragon. Jibarro was too large and too fast. This had been a sacrifice from the start.

Her heart squeezed at Faro's heroism as he disappeared into Jibarro's mouth, maybe fifty yards away. Why had he done it? Maybe he understood how badly the sanctuary needed the Sunset Pearl. Maybe he believed in her. She would never know for sure.

Suddenly the canoe was catapulted into the air as an enormous tail rose up from beneath them. Flying out of her seat, Kendra let go of the nova song's chain but held tight to the crown. As Kendra soared through the air, she marveled that the dragon had kept track of the canoe even while moving away to devour Faro. She was also astounded at the size of the dragon—that his head could be so far away and his tail could still reach her.

Kendra hit the water and sank amid the bubbles of her

splash. Kicking her feet, feeling waterlogged in her clothes, Kendra rose to the surface. She saw Grady nearby.

Without the canoe they were mostly helpless. Neither she nor Grady had much chance of making it to shore ahead of the dragon. She saw no use in preventing Grady from becoming a seal. "The sealskin is yours," she yelled.

A thunderous roar announced that Jibarro was pivoting around to come her way. Grady dipped down under the water. Kendra started swimming toward the shore, hampered by her shoes and the sack in her hand. The unwelcoming shore wasn't far now, and Kendra realized she might get hurled against the rocks by the waves, but it seemed preferable to getting eaten.

Another roar told her that the sea dragon was closing in behind her. She was simply too slow. She would never reach the shore in time.

Something bulky nudged up against her under the water. After the initial surprise, Kendra recognized it was a chocolate brown seal. Assuming it had to be Grady, she threw her arms around the pinniped's neck and held her breath.

The large seal plunged down deep. Kendra had expected to get water in her face moving along the surface, but the seal had other ideas. Hoping the seal understood the limits of her lung capacity, she held on tightly.

They reached the underpinnings of the island and slipped into a little cave. The rocky walls brushed against Kendra as the seal darted forward, her clothes mostly insulating her against scrapes. Somewhere above and behind them, Jibarro was roaring. Kendra kept her eyes squeezed shut and held her breath.

As the seal swooped upward, Kendra fought the desperate urge to breathe. They finally broke through the surface of the water, and Kendra saw that the cave had widened as it curved upward into a large, landlocked pool, open to the sky. The water in the pool was turbulent, surging up and down, so she clung to the seal. The rocky walls of the pool extended at least twenty feet above the high point reached by the water, making Kendra feel like she was looking up from the bottom of a well. The sea dragon bellowed with a fury that made her ears buzz.

The seal towed Kendra near the wall of the pool and, when the surf was near the high point, helped boost her onto a shelf. Kendra released the seal and climbed to a higher shelf before the water surged up again. Panting, soaked, she covered her ears as the dragon roared again.

In that moment, with a hand over each ear, Kendra realized she no longer had the sack. She could hardly breathe as the implications sank in. She had deliberately kept hold of it when she fell into the ocean. She remembered feeling it in her grasp as she grabbed hold of the seal. That was her last sure memory of the sack in her hand.

Kendra watched the water in the salty pool rising and falling, almost reaching where she sat. The seal was gone.

The crown could be out in the ocean or in the cave. It might be directly beneath her. There was no way to be sure.

Kendra took a shuddering breath. Her insides felt hollowed out. Why had anyone trusted her? Why had she trusted herself? Bracken would stay captured. Seth would have no help. The Sunset Pearl would remain in the custody of the undead. Faro had died for nothing. The Fairy Queen had lost her crown. What would that mean for the Fairy Realm? And for fairies in general?

Jibarro roared again, sounding farther away. Part of Kendra wished the dragon had simply eaten her. It would have been a much cleaner death than what now awaited her.

The seal popped back into view, a sack in its mouth. Kendra felt an unexpected surge of hope. Could the crown still be in there? Was Grady really still helping her?

The next time the water surged high, the seal slid up onto the shelf where he had first deposited Kendra. She climbed down to that shelf and accepted the sack from the mouth of the seal. The crown was still inside.

Kendra flung her arms around the seal. "Thank you, Grady. I was about to lose my mind. I won't let you down. I promise." She ended the hug and started wiping away tears of relief.

When she looked back at the seal, he was Grady again, sealskin in his hands. "Good job, Kendra," he said quietly. "You can do this. Climb out of here and finish what you started."

"Okay," she said. "Thank you so much. You saved me twice."

"You're trying to save so many of us," Grady said. He then pointed out the route she could follow to climb out. Kendra appreciated the advice. It was impressive that Grady had rescued her. She wondered how much he had needed to wrestle with his seal instincts to do so.

"Was it hard to help me?" Kendra asked.

"A little," Grady said. "My instincts were to flee. And I always feel a strong urge to shake off my land memories. That will happen soon enough. Go. I want to see you make it to the top."

"All right," Kendra said, putting the wet sack in her mouth. Stepping carefully, taking care to find good handholds and stable places to set her feet, Kendra made her way up. It was easier higher up, where the rocks were dry. After scrambling up from the highest ledge to the top, she took the sack from her mouth, then turned and looked back.

Grady was a seal again. He barked once and then dove into the roiling water.

"You made it," a voice said behind Kendra.

She turned to find Mizarine fluttering nearby, shining white in the gray mist, the slender chain still dangling from her ankle. Kendra smiled. "You waited for me."

"Following orders," the nova song said. "The darkness is so close now."

"Let's go light it up."

CHAPTER THIRTY-FOUR

Everbloom

Just after midday, the keel of the clever boat scraped against sand, and Seth vaulted out onto the beach. He carried his satchel and had Calvin secreted in his pocket.

"Welcome back to Timbuli," Ronodin said, disembarking as well. "Consider this your final exam. If you pass the test, you can leave school and start living life."

Seth backed a few steps away as Ronodin called the boat up higher onto the beach. He still didn't have a clear plan, but he felt he should at least play along until he found the Everbloom. Otherwise Ronodin or the Sphinx might claim it without him, and he would lose the ability to influence the outcome.

"This way," Ronodin said. "These caves make up a complex system with several entrances. The opening we're looking for isn't far."

Seth followed Ronodin onto a trail between leafy philodendrons and fragrant anthuriums. The day was mild, less humid than normal, with a light breeze. It seemed like a strange day to confront the toughest choice he could remember facing.

Ronodin carried a duffel bag. Seth wondered what it might contain.

They branched left off the main path along a faint trail. After winding through trees and shrubs, they reached a grouping of boulders. In the ground between two of the largest boulders gaped a crack just large enough for a person to crawl down into.

"This isn't a cave," Seth complained.

"It leads into one of the largest cave systems on any island in the world," Ronodin said. He set down the duffel bag, unzipped it, and removed a garden trowel. "Dig up the flower with this. The Everbloom is resilient, but try to get as many of the roots as you can." Then he held up a ceramic flowerpot. "Keep the flower in here. Pack soil around it."

"Okay," Seth said.

"Time for your ointment," Ronodin said. "I'll give you some privacy."

After Ronodin walked out of view, Seth stripped down and took the broad stopper off the ointment jar. He gave a generous dollop of the ointment to Calvin, who went to work on himself inside a pocket.

"Need any help?" Seth whispered.

"I'll be fine," Calvin said. "You gave me enough to drown in. Your pocket might be a mess, though."

Seth slathered bluish jelly all over his skin, leaving him greasy but hopefully impervious to the heat he was about to encounter. More than three-quarters of the jar was empty by the time he finished and put his pants on.

"Ronodin," Seth called. "Can you get my back?"

"Absolutely," his answer came from a distance.

"I could reach most of it," Seth said. "I think I missed part of the middle, though."

Ronodin strode to him, picked up the jar, and began applying the ointment. "Is it a comfort to know I have your back?"

"At this moment?" Seth asked. "Sure. I'd rather not catch on fire. What about my clothes?"

"The contact of the material against the ointment on your skin should grant heat resistance to your clothing. You can smear a little extra onto your clothes to be sure. Your back is done."

"Thanks," Seth said, putting his shirt back on.

"Isn't a situation like ours interesting once trust has disintegrated?" Ronodin asked casually.

"Trust isn't gone," Seth said.

"No?" Ronodin asked.

"I'm going to get the Everbloom. You're letting me."

"I trust that you have compelling reasons to act in your own interest," Ronodin said. "I believe it is so sensible for you to fetch the flower and give it to the Underking that you might actually do it. And I'm also aware you might not."

"Giving the flower to the Underking is the key to my

freedom," Seth said. "You can trust I want this chain off me. But with you, I don't know what to trust."

"Probably wise," Ronodin replied. "It's clumsy to trust anyone. People are uniformly imperfect and erratic. But if you have to guess, bet on them serving their own interests."

"Is that why you're unclear about what you want?" Seth asked. "To make it hard for people to guess what you'll do?"

Ronodin grinned. "A penetrating insight. You could have been a great pupil."

"Could have been?"

"Had you really wanted to learn from me," Ronodin said.

"You're a very talented teacher," Seth said.

"Have you learned enough?" Ronodin asked.

"What do you mean?"

"Let's imagine everything you heard from the Hidden Sage is true," Ronodin said. "Kendra and Bracken have shared their perspectives. Maybe others have too. Given all you have heard, how much do you suppose you can trust the light-makes-right brigade? What do you presume they want from you?"

Seth considered a careful answer. "They act like they want to help me."

Ronodin laughed. "They want to do what they do best, Seth. They want to lock you up. They'll lure you with honey if you respond. But make no mistake: you have broken their laws. They see you as a threat who must be neutralized."

"Maybe," Seth said. He hadn't considered this possibility, and he found the suggestion disconcerting.

"You really don't understand. They lock up dark creatures. They will imprison you simply for who and what you are, the same way they might imprison a wraith or a dragon. You have committed crimes against them, Seth, of your own free will. You destroyed an entire dragon sanctuary. You got some of the people protecting Wyrmroost killed—I know this for a fact."

"You weren't honest about what I was doing," Seth said, distressed to hear that his actions had led to deaths. Hopefully Ronodin was lying about that.

"Really?" Ronodin asked. "You're going to tell them you released wraiths and revenants without knowing anyone might get hurt? Would you forgive a killer for not knowing how a gun functioned? How many would have to die before you stopped pardoning his ignorance?"

"You tricked me," Seth said. "I didn't understand what I was doing. I didn't have my memories. I still don't."

"You don't have to convince me," Ronodin said. "I'm on your side. Bracken and his allies were holding creatures captive. The only crime those wraiths and revenants had committed was following their natures. Jailers assume the risk of being harmed by their prisoners. I think you are a hero, Seth, a liberator of the oppressed. The problem is how Kendra and Bracken view your actions. It's their perspective, their laws, that condemn you."

"Why are you telling me this?"

"You might like to believe you once belonged among them," Ronodin said. "Let's imagine you did. Even if that were true, somewhere in your hypothetical past, you don't belong there anymore. It's too late for you. In their eyes, your crimes are too great. In their eyes, your nature is too dark. They'll lure you in, take what you offer, then zip you into a straitjacket and leave you in a cell."

"Maybe I belong locked up," Seth said. "Maybe you do too."

Ronodin gave Seth a sad smile. "You need to believe that if you want to rejoin them. You need to accept that you are a villain, a fiend. Because that is the treatment you will receive. In their camp, you'll always be an outcast. With me, you're a prized pupil. You have a great deal to offer. You mean well. You're only beginning to realize your potential. You could make a positive difference in this world. Or you can let them lock you up and throw away the key."

"Thanks for the advice," Seth said.

Ronodin grew grave. "I'm sure you're smart enough not to consider taking the Everbloom to them. I presume the sage advocated for you to leave the flower alone or to pass it to those who would guard it. Any who possess the Everbloom will use its power to serve their desires. Giving the flower to Kendra and her kind only increases their capacity to oppress you. Don't give them the rope they will use to hang you. And don't turn yourself into my enemy."

"I'd hate to do that," Seth said.

"So would I," Ronodin said. "We have been allies up until now. You don't want to see what I do to my enemies, Seth. Not firsthand. And what the Underking would do to you is a hundred times worse. Don't ruin your life so you can give a flower to people who hate you. They want you in chains. Don't let somebody else collect the flower for the Underking. Use the flower to buy your life back. You deserve to seek out your memories."

Seth glanced at the crack in the ground. "Maybe I'll die in hot lava."

"Save the dramatics," Ronodin said. "Bring the Everbloom to me. We'll give it to the Underking. Remember that I plan for all contingencies. Don't fight the inevitable."

"I hear you," Seth said. "I just climb in?"

"Chimney down using both sides," Ronodin said. He handed Seth a glowing holly wand. "The descent isn't too far. You'll meet Dezia at the bottom. She will guide you to the bloom. Tread carefully—Baga Loa is not a typical volcano. A cave system like this one would never form in the natural world. You may cross paths with some unusual creatures."

Nodding, Seth rubbed most of the remaining ointment onto his clothes and satchel. Then he squirmed down into the crack and started descending. Footholds abounded, and he reached the ground without much trouble. So far he noticed neither heat nor any glow of lava.

Dezia startled him when she came out of a wall, gauzy wrappings fluttering. "I will guide you to the Everbloom," she said with little expression. Seth saw accusation in her eyes.

She turned and started gliding forward. Seth followed, feeling awkward. "Sorry about the token," he said.

The phantom made no indication of having heard him.

"How are you?" Calvin asked.

"Truthfully?" Seth replied. "Shaken up."

"Ronodin was trying to make you ashamed," Calvin said.

"I might deserve to be ashamed," Seth said. "I've hurt people I should have protected. With or without my memories, there may be no way back to my old life."

"There never is," Calvin said. "We're always moving forward. All you have is the present. Here we are. Just think about your next step. Forget your past for now. Start today. Get your next step right."

"It sounds pretty," Seth said. "I'm not sure it fits what I've done."

"Kendra and the others know your memories were stripped," Calvin said. "They just want you home safe."

Seth stopped walking. "Phantom, you can wait for me, or you can let me tell the Sphinx how you left me behind."

The phantom halted.

"Calvin, don't you get it?" Seth said. "If what you say is true, if Kendra and the good guys would forgive me, it almost makes it worse. I know what I did, Calvin. I may have been manipulated, but I wasn't forced. If I was a traitor, if I caused destruction by releasing evil, if I got people killed and made a sanctuary fall, I have to live with that. I'm not sure how I can."

"You've been in an impossible situation, Seth," Calvin said. "You're trying to figure out who you are. I see it. And you'll make it. But not if you give up."

Seth heaved a sigh. "I might want to give up, but I

won't. I worry, though: what if everything I do just causes more harm?"

"Everyone causes harm," Calvin said. "Sometimes we hurt others, and sometimes we hurt ourselves. If you've caused a problem, you learn and do better. You become smarter for next time. And you undo what harm you can."

"What about the Everbloom?" Seth asked. "What should I do?"

"We've come this far," Calvin said. "Let's have a look."

Seth folded his arms and stared at the ground. What else was he supposed to do? Sit down and mope until Ronodin came looking for him? "Go ahead, phantom," he said.

Dezia drifted forward again.

"Besides, you might be right," Calvin said. "We may burn up in hot lava before we get there."

Seth followed the phantom through the labyrinthine cave. After a number of turns, Seth wasn't sure if he could find his way back. The air started to get hotter. In one room, steam wafted up from little fissures in the floor. In another, a bubbling pool of hot water in one corner saturated the room with a steamy, eggy odor.

Some passages narrowed so much, Seth had to turn sideways. Some wider chambers had room to spare, with stalagmites four or five times his height. The light from his wand did not always reach the ceiling, and it was hard to tell if some of the shadowy side passages went a long distance or ended after a few feet.

"Be extra quiet here," the phantom whispered.

Noticing a red glow up ahead, Seth shielded the light

of his wand with his hand and stepped carefully. In a neighboring chamber of the cave, Seth saw a blob of dark lava with molten redness glowing through the cracks. Fiery millipedes as long as Seth's arm skittered around the surface of the lava blob, some of them crawling into or out of the gaps to the red interior. He knew of no living creature that could handle such extreme temperature.

The air in the cave became increasingly hot and dry as Seth progressed. The stone around him smelled like it was baking. Seth crossed through one room where more than half the floor was a glowing pool of smoldering scarlet lava. He felt certain that without the ointment, his hair and clothes would burst into flame by proximity to such heat, but instead Seth discovered he could bear it. The air he breathed was somehow cooled by the ointment, and the ashy fumes did not clog his lungs.

Seth caught more glimpses of lava as he continued to follow Dezia. In a vast room where a goopy flow of lava ran down part of one wall and hissing geysers erupted on the far side, the phantom pointed to an arching stone footbridge that led to an island in the middle of a lava lake. The bridge marked the first evidence of masonry Seth had seen since entering the cave.

"You all right, Calvin?" Seth asked.

"I never imagined a place like this," the nipsie replied. "I'm fascinated. Wouldn't turn away a cool drink, though."

Seth walked over the bridge, feeling the heat of the stone through his shoes. In the center of the island, Seth spotted a single flower. He jogged to it and then stared in wonder.

The flower radiated light, almost like a stained-glass window with the sun behind it. Seth could not believe the complexity of the endless colors in the petals, tiny facets and slivers of every shade he knew and some he doubted he could ever describe. Like nature's finest kaleidoscope, the vibrant patterns shifted so that if he closed his eyes, he opened them to behold a new masterpiece.

"It's a miracle," Calvin said.

"It's beautiful," Seth said, kneeling down. The golden stem and leaves had a glow like heated metal. The blossom of the Everbloom was no bigger than Seth's fist, the stem barely a foot tall. Ronodin had done his homework. It would fit easily in the flowerpot Ronodin had prepared.

"We can't give this to the Underking," Seth said.

"I agree, boss," Calvin said.

"Which is a problem," Seth said, glancing at the ghostly manacle on his wrist. "You gave me smart advice. I can start by making a good choice right now. This flower helps fuel these islands. It's exquisite. I don't want to harm it—or the creatures that depend on it. I want to like myself, Calvin. I want to make choices I can live with."

"I like you already," Calvin said. "You're doing great."

"I'm going to do everything I can to protect this flower," Seth said. "That idea feels good. And maybe doing that will get me killed. But taking the flower to Ronodin might also lead to my death. I'd rather die liking myself than hating myself."

"I think the same way," Calvin said. "And I'll do everything I can to keep you alive."

"To protect the flower, we have to start with the phantom," Seth said. "Dezia, listen to me, I need to speak with you."

The phantom turned. "I have led you to the Everbloom," she said tightly.

"I'm sorry I gave away your token," Seth said. "I made a mistake."

The phantom did not answer.

"I want to fix this," Seth said. "How can I free you?"

The phantom stared at him. "I would need a new token. You would have to bind me to the new one and break the connection with the old."

"Can I do that?" Seth asked.

"As a shadow charmer, you have the power," Dezia said, a hint of hope in her voice.

"And then could I throw the new token into the lava?" Seth asked. "Keep my promise?"

Dezia took a step toward him. "You could, yes. Do you mean it?"

"Would you still lead us out of here?" Seth asked.

"Once my token was destroyed, you could no longer obligate me," Dezia said. "But I pledge to lead you out of these caves if you do this service for me. And I will speak of you with admiration ever after."

"What would work as the new token?" Seth asked.

"I must feel a connection with the object," Dezia said. "Pluck a leaf from the Everbloom."

"Would that empower you too much?" Seth asked.

"After being plucked, the leaf will lose the potential to greatly empower me," Dezia said. "But it will possess some inherent power, simplifying your task of transferring the connection."

"The leaf will grow back?" Seth asked.

"The Everbloom is alive," Dezia said. "It sheds leaves and petals as all plants do."

Seth crouched beside the Everbloom. One of the little leaves looked droopier than the others. "Sorry," Seth told the flower. "This is to protect you."

When Seth touched the leaf, his mind suddenly became more alert, his body felt stronger, and he could perceive his power more distinctly. For a moment, his best hopes about himself seemed possible. His hunger and thirst disappeared. With a tug he plucked off the leaf, and the influx of energy ceased, though many of the effects lingered.

"That will do nicely," Dezia said. "You know how to access your power?"

"Yes."

"Can you sense me?" Dezia asked.

"Yes," Seth said. Since touching the leaf of the Everbloom, Seth felt like his inner vision was clearer than ever. He could mentally sense the phantom in great detail.

"Can you feel my connection to the crypt?" Dezia asked. "And my connection to the token?"

Seth searched, studying the phantom with his mind. He closed his eyes and tried, then made another effort with them open. He discerned no connections.

"I'm sorry," Seth said.

"Keep trying," Dezia said. "Unless you can sense my connections, you can't break them. You need to establish a link between me and the new token, allow the new token to share my connection to the crypt, and break the bond with my current token, the doll."

Seth could not feel any hint of the connections she described. He had a sense of her presence, and that was all.

He glanced at the Everbloom. Holding the plucked leaf in one hand, Seth reached out with the other and rested a finger against the petals of the flower. Immediately he felt a powerful influx of energy, and his mind sharpened. He fixed his attention on the phantom. The dark umbilicus connecting her to the crypt was obvious, and so was the dark channel of power uniting her to the doll. The channel of power to the doll felt sullied. Somebody was tampering with it.

"I feel the connections," Seth said excitedly.

"Change them," Dezia said. "Link me to the leaf. I am willing it. Help it to happen. Break the bond with my current token. Be quick about it. If they catch on to what we are doing, they will try to pull me away."

Seth searched the power inside of him. The darkness he drew from to quench torches was enlivened by his contact with the Everbloom. Drawing on that power, Seth focused on creating a channel between Dezia and the leaf, but the connection to the current token blocked his effort.

Seth concentrated on her bond with the doll. He could not sense the location of the doll, only that it was far away.

He willed the phantom free of that bond, as he would when attempting to open a lock.

The bond with the current token resisted, gaining strength and trying to pull Dezia away. The phantom moaned. Forcing all of his effort into breaking the connection, Seth felt energy course through him from the Everbloom.

The bond with the doll broke. Suddenly it was easy to pour energy into the channel between Dezia and the leaf. When Seth felt that link solidify, he stopped touching the flower.

The instant his finger broke contact with the petals, Seth slumped forward, his body drenched in sweat. The struggle against the dark forces controlling the phantom had left him depleted. His heart hammered as if he had just run a mile at a brutal pace.

"Thank you, Seth," Dezia said. "That was clumsy work, but you are very strong, at least with the help of the Everbloom. Now dispose of the leaf and I vow to lead you out of here."

"Can we go out a different way than we came in?" Seth asked. "I'm not sure Ronodin will be glad to see me."

"Whatever you wish," Dezia said. "After a painful betrayal, you have done me an unexpected service."

"They have no hold on you now, right?" Seth asked.

"Correct," Dezia said.

"And you won't help them find the Everbloom?" he checked.

"Never," Dezia said. "They abused me."

"Do you promise?"

"I give my vow."

Seth nodded. "The flower is safer if I leave it here."

"What if Ronodin or the Sphinx get a new phantom to help them?" Calvin asked.

"They need the ointment to come in here," Seth said. "And they needed me to recruit the phantom. Neither of them can charm the undead."

"It would be a serious risk to remove the Everbloom," Calvin said. "I bet it could destabilize the volcano."

The phantom laughed darkly. "Any fool could see that much."

Seth shook his head. "Why am I not surprised they didn't warn me?"

"Ronodin is usually so helpful," Calvin said.

Seth walked over to the edge of the island, above the rich red lava. Even with the help of the ointment, the proximity made it almost unbearably hot. He could look at the lava directly for only a couple of seconds at a time.

"Is this as good a place as any to drop the token?" Seth asked.

"Yes," Dezia replied.

Seth released the leaf and watched it seesaw down onto the lava. A brief flame flared up, and it was gone.

"Thank you, Seth," Dezia said. "Follow me."

Seth gently patted the pocket with Calvin in it. "Ready to get out of here?"

"So soon?" Calvin asked. "I thought a sleepover could be fun. Another time, maybe. We can go . . . as long as you do the walking."

CHAPTER THIRTY-FIVE

Underking

There are foul beings in the mist," Mizarine warned. "I'll try to lead you around them."

Kendra glimpsed the fog-shrouded figures as she followed the nova song over and around decaying fortifications. She had taken the crown out of the sack and held it in her hand. She wondered if she should put it on. She decided she would if any of the zombies in the fog got too near.

"Is there a darkest place in the Under Realm?" Kendra whispered.

"Yes," Mizarine answered.

"Will you stay with me until we get there?" Kendra asked.

"I'll try," Mizarine said. "You may want to hold my chain. The pull of the darkness gets stronger as we get closer."

Kendra took hold of the chain. She heard waves

crashing against the rocks below. Off to one side, a peg-legged zombie in a long coat limped into view.

"Run," Mizarine said.

Kendra came as close as she could to running, trying to stay mindful of where she placed her feet on the uneven rocks. The nova song led her to the brink of a cliff above the sea. Kendra discovered stairs slanting diagonally down the face of the cliff, ending at a stone platform about halfway down to the turbulent water. A ladder descended from the platform to the surf below, and another set of stairs climbed to the clifftop in the opposite direction.

A glance back revealed several zombies in pursuit. More climbed the ladder from the sea, and others rushed down the stairs from the opposite side of the clifftop, trying to beat Kendra to the platform.

"Hurry," the nova song urged.

Kendra raced down the stone stairs two at a time. The steps were damp from the mist, but there was no time for caution. "The entrance is at the platform?" she asked.

"Yes," the nova song said.

Out of control, Kendra stumbled as she reached the platform several steps ahead of the oncoming zombies, but she managed to stay on her feet by catching herself against the cliff. At the rear of the platform yawned a large door-way framed in stone with no door. The dimness beyond was a shade most would see as black. With sea zombies on the stairs behind her, clambering up from the water and rapidly descending the opposite steps, Kendra had no time to hesitate.

Kendra followed Mizarine through the doorway, and the fairy began to sing. The high, trilling notes were calming and ethereal, music to inspire contemplation. As she sang, the fairy began to glow brighter, throwing light all over the wide hall extending from the doorway. The hall continued for a long way, with many passages branching off.

Glancing back, Kendra found the sea zombies congregating at the entrance, but none crossed the threshold. Mizarine kept tugging Kendra forward.

Wraiths began to emerge from side passages, moving smoothly and silently, bringing a supernatural chill. A revenant, blindfolded and gagged, shuffled toward them from farther down the hall. The temperature plunged. Kendra rubbed the goosebumps on her arms. The wraiths stalked toward her. Another revenant hobbled into view, body partially decomposed, arms bound to her sides.

Kendra knew it was time. Part of her was scared to put on the crown. If it didn't work, her fate would be sealed. But there was no time for hesitation. The undead were seconds away from claiming her. The nearest wraith was barely ten steps away and closing.

Holding Mizarine's chain in one hand, Kendra placed the Fairy Queen's circlet on her head. Immediately the crown flared to life, exponentially outshining the nova song. With her ears and mind, Kendra heard agonized shrieks as the wraiths fell back and the revenants halted. Looking at her hand, Kendra found her skin radiating light. Glancing back at the entryway, she saw the sea zombies recoiling, eyes averted.

Hope and confidence flooded into Kendra, more than a response to how brightly she gleamed and how the undead reacted. Resolve and strength flowed directly into her mind and heart from the crown. The crown glared brighter in response to her growing confidence. Tendrils of smoke wafted up from the retreating wraiths.

"I don't want to harm you," Kendra announced. "You have taken things that don't belong here. I have come to retrieve them."

The nova song kept pulling Kendra forward, and she followed. The revenants turned and started moving sedately into side passages. Kendra walked straight down the hall. Wraiths fled the beacon she had become.

They were right to flee. Kendra knew she possessed in abundance something these shadow creatures lacked and feared. She was full of life and light. She could feel it coursing through her, radiating from her. She felt regal, like a queen. With the crown on, maybe she was a queen. No, not maybe. The truth of it became plain, and the realization freed her to burn even brighter.

A door at the end of the hall opened, and an intimidating figure emerged. He was dressed in black armor, and his translucent face allowed Kendra to see his skull. A dark aura around him resisted her brightness.

The figure raised a hand toward her. *Halt, intruder,* he thundered in her mind. *I am Stavius the Obscure, door warden of the Under Realm, a captain among liches. Depart or suffer my wrath.*

Kendra imagined creatures like him tormenting Bracken. "Step aside," she commanded.

You have no authority here, Stavius warned. *This is the seat of our power.* He pointed at her. *Writhe.*

Kendra's muscles suddenly felt sore, as if they were trying to cramp, and her vision became blurry. Gritting her teeth, she pictured Seth being indoctrinated by these foul beings. Power emanated from her crown, and Stavius staggered back. Strength flooded into her muscles and her vision sharpened. Looking down at herself, Kendra found her entire body shedding such glorious light that it almost looked like she was being consumed by white flames.

Impossible, Stavius expressed in dismay. *Come no closer. My touch will stop your heart.*

Kendra sensed his uncertainty. "You don't get it. Warn your friends. Unlike you, I have a heart. I'm alive. And I'm not afraid of you."

Begone, Stavius demanded. *I had thought to show you mercy. No longer. I will drain you to the brink of death and hold you there for ages beyond counting.*

Kendra was drawing near. The lich was significantly taller than she was. In his heavy armor, normally he would have been very frightening. But under the bright light, Kendra could see right through him. He wasn't entirely tangible. The Fairy Queen had warned her to maintain her courage. If she backed down now, how would she save Bracken? How would she rescue Seth? How would she retrieve the Sunset Pearl? If this lich wanted to play chicken, he had picked the wrong girl on the wrong day.

"I wasn't half this strong when I killed Gorgrog," Kendra said. "Stand down, or there will be nothing left of you to cast a shadow."

The lich took a step toward her. His next step was hesitant, and for the third, he looked as if he were leaning against a heavy wind. It ended up being only half a step.

Kendra was almost to the lich. Even bolstered by the power of the crown, Kendra felt hesitant to touch the creature. As she closed in, his aura of darkness was swept away, and he became even less substantial.

Standing his ground, the lich stretched a trembling hand toward Kendra. She pitied him. He looked feeble, almost invisible.

You . . . will . . . perish.

Did he believe that? Was he just being stubborn?

Kendra stopped. "I didn't come here to harm you. I don't even know you. Move out of the way."

You . . . falter.

Kendra continued forward, barely able to see the dazzling flames consuming the lich because he had become so faint. But she heard the horrific scream in her mind. When she walked through the place where Stavius had stood, there was nothing left.

Pausing to look back, Kendra found the hallway bare. She wondered if the corridor had ever been so brightly lit.

"Hurry," Mizarine urged. "Not much farther now."

Kendra went through the door the lich had guarded and down a long flight of stairs. Though the nova song tugged her forward, Kendra did not hurry. What if going to the darkest place in the Under Realm led her to the Underking? Was she ready for that?

Then again, how was she supposed to find Seth, Bracken, and the Sunset Pearl without confronting the Underking? This was his domain. He would find her if he wanted. Judging by the splitting corridors and winding hallways, this place was a huge maze. Even if nobody attacked her, could she find what she was looking for amid all these twists and turns?

At least following the fairy to the darkest place in the Under Realm gave her a destination. She could make new plans from there. She found herself almost wanting to encounter the Underking. Confidence had worked against Stavius. She saw no advantage to fearfully avoiding the Underking.

The route wound onward, down inclines and stairs. At every junction, the nova song eagerly chose the next turn. Kendra was not simply lighting the halls—she was scorching them. Her own light reflected harshly off the rough stone walls, and though none of the brightness bothered her eyes, she could tell it was intense.

The lower they traveled, the more cavelike the corridors became, though the floor remained smooth and comfortable for walking. The entire complex seemed abandoned. Kendra assumed the undead were staying out of her way.

Coming around a corner, Kendra unexpectedly found a familiar face awaiting her. The Sphinx stood in the middle of the hall, wearing a leather overcoat.

"Wow, Kendra," the Sphinx said, shielding his squinted eyes with one hand. "Looking bright. Unbelievably bright."

"You betrayed us," Kendra accused, stopping. He wasn't undead, so she didn't know if her brightness would repel him. She grabbed the sack of gales just in case.

"You'll be glad to know Seth is alive and well," the Sphinx said.

"Where is he?" Kendra asked.

"I honestly don't know," the Sphinx replied. "I don't rank very high around here. Are you really wearing the crown of the Fairy Queen?"

"How can I find Bracken and Seth?"

"I see that you are," the Sphinx said. "You and the crown really light each other up. I can't believe she parted with it, even to help her son. That was quite a risk."

"I'm also looking for the Sunset Pearl," Kendra said.

"Why not?" the Sphinx said. "Might as well. You want it all. The risk was in coming. Take what you can, if you can. Why don't I show you to the boss around here? The guy with the answers."

"The Underking?" Kendra asked.

"He may not be happy to see you," the Sphinx said.

"I haven't seen anyone since leaving the entry hall," Kendra said.

"They're not used to light down here," the Sphinx said. "That works in your favor. No missteps, though. They are all aware of you, and they will swarm if you stumble."

"Don't you try anything either," Kendra said.

"I'm not your enemy, Kendra," the Sphinx said. "I never

set out to hurt Seth. Just to help him reach his potential. He's already a much more powerful shadow charmer than before he forgot everything."

"What have you done to him?"

"I didn't take his memory, Kendra," the Sphinx said. "He made that choice. Ronodin and I have simply taught him about his powers."

"After you kidnapped him."

"I may have played a role," the Sphinx said. "But you and I have different goals. You're working to save the sanctuaries. I'm working to save the world. Our methods might never match up."

"Was opening Zzyzx part of saving the world?" Kendra challenged.

"In fairness, you never got to see how that would have played out," the Sphinx said. "You interfered with the dragons, which is what led to them making their play for power."

"I don't have all day," Kendra said. "Where is the Underking?"

"You have a nova song," the Sphinx said. "Good find. She can lead you to the Underking. I can lend some help with the door."

"Lead the way," Kendra said. "Don't get close to me."

"Come," the Sphinx said.

Kendra followed the Sphinx, trying to restrain herself from blasting him with wind simply out of principle. He was as shameless as ever—unwilling to admit his crimes, quick to offer explanations. She decided evil was most dangerous when operating with a smile. She preferred creatures like

Stavius who looked and acted evil without apologies or excuses.

They did not go far before the Sphinx stopped at a large black door decorated with skulls that blazed white beneath the glare of Kendra and her crown. "He's in there. He generates the darkness your nova song is seeking. Take care—no darkness in the world can compete with his."

"How do I open the door?" Kendra asked.

The Sphinx brushed a finger against a small, narrow skull with pointy teeth, and the door disappeared. Inky blackness awaited beyond the entryway. From where Kendra stood, her light did not seem to touch it.

"I heard the Underking can turn people undead," Kendra said.

"Merely looking upon him will cause that transformation," the Sphinx verified. "Move cautiously. He has a lot of power here. You've been protected thus far. I think your only option is to rely on the crown."

The Fairy Queen had told her to be confident. So far that had gone well. The power from the crown filled her with surety, and her light grew brighter. Mizarine flapped her wings desperately, straining to pull Kendra forward.

Kendra stepped through the doorway into the darkness. The moment she entered, her light pressed the darkness back, forming a sphere around her. But the light did not extend to fill the room, and Kendra could feel the darkness squeezing the sphere of light smaller.

Beyond the bright sphere, the darkness seemed heavy,

like molten tar. As Kendra began to fear, she watched the sphere shrink inward.

She stamped her foot. No! Her light was brighter than a bunch of darkness. The sphere expanded with the thought, and Kendra felt power from the crown reinforcing the sentiment. The sphere of light around her grew bigger than it had been when she first entered. The nova song perched on Kendra's shoulder, singing softly and adding her light to the effort.

Whispered words burrowed into her mind, quiet but penetrating. *What feeble light intrudes upon my sanctum?*

"Feeble?" Kendra asked, insulted. As her light resisted the darkness, Kendra could feel the crown drawing upon her own energy. Focusing, Kendra forced more energy into the crown, and the sphere of light brightened and expanded.

You brought the crown of a rival into my presence, the voice observed. *A foolhardy risk.*

"We'll find out," Kendra said. "Are you the Underking?"

I am master of this realm, the voice responded.

"I'm not here to invade," Kendra said. "I'm here to retrieve some things you have that don't belong to you."

Everything in the Under Realm belongs to me, the voice responded, incensed.

"I don't," Kendra said.

The Underking gave a slow, delighted laugh. *You believe you can return to the surface?*

"Yes," Kendra said, trying not to entertain any uncertainty.

I lured you here. Removed all obstacles. Granted you access. Commanded the Sphinx to show you the way.

Kendra tried not to let the words frighten her, squeezing her eyes shut out of sheer anxiety. Should she keep them closed? If she saw the Underking would she become undead? Or would keeping them closed be more dangerous? When she opened her eyes, the sphere of light around her was smaller and still shrinking. "Where is Seth? Where is my brother?"

What does it matter? Worry about yourself. The Fairy Queen wields power, especially in her realm. I would not venture there. You, my dear, are not the Fairy Queen. You have strayed far from where you belong and are in grave danger. Would you rather be a lich or a revenant? A lich boasts more power and autonomy. It depends upon your willingness.

The whispered words were calm and certain, but also unclean, as if they were leaving stains on her mind. The sphere of light contracted a bit more. Kendra couldn't think of a worse fate than joining the undead—neither living nor able to rest, cursed to hunt and crave that which she could no longer enjoy herself. She pictured herself as a revenant, body degenerating as she listlessly wandered the world, forever unsatisfied.

The darkness constricted tighter. Seth needed her. Bracken needed her. If she failed, not only would she suffer a fate worse than death, but Crescent Lagoon would fall and the Fairy Queen would lose her crown. That would all contribute to the dragons winning their war against humanity.

When the darkness overtook her, she would have failed everyone.

If you kneel and remove that crown, I will show you mercy, the Underking offered.

The proposal struck Kendra like a slap. She remembered with a sharp pang how Celebrant had encouraged her to surrender Wyrmroost so that she and her loved ones could obtain mercy. It had been a lie. Agad had died believing a similar lie. She and her group would have been murdered had Andromadus not intervened.

Maybe the Underking *could* make her one of the undead. But if so, why talk about it? Why not take action? Confidence had brought her this far. Was she going to let him shake her? Why not doubt him instead of herself? If he was going to turn her into a revenant, he would have to fight for it. She wasn't going to surrender.

Resolve flared inside Kendra, and the light of her sphere swelled bigger and brighter than ever. Nobody would rescue her here. It was up to her to save Bracken and Seth. And to save herself. She already had all the help she was going to get. The Fairy Queen had given her the crown, which meant the Fairy Queen believed she could succeed.

"You have this all wrong," Kendra said, her light growing. "I didn't come here to ask you for anything. I came here to tell you what I am taking. I'll destroy anyone who gets in my way, including you. Show yourself!"

No answer came, and she started walking forward, her light growing. There were shallow pits in the black tile floor, and bones strewn off to the sides. She kicked a fragment of bone out of her path.

You are ensuring an eternity of suffering for yourself and those you love, the Underking threatened.

The voice seemed to be coming from up ahead. Kendra kept going. The darkness pressed more ferociously than ever, seeming to exert physical force against the sphere of brightness around her. Kendra had to lean forward to keep moving. Kendra pushed power into the crown and felt it feeding confidence back to her in return. After a moment of constricting, her sphere grew the largest it had been.

"You would know about an eternity of suffering," Kendra said boldly. "You're living it. That's your best-case scenario. You need to do more than threaten. Where are you?"

No answer came, but the darkness pressed frantically.

"Are you hiding from me?" Kendra asked. "Am I scaring you?"

Very well, the Underking answered coldly. *You have been warned. Come to me, and we will finish this.*

The darkness no longer pressed so hard against her light.

Follow my voice, the Underking invited. *Come and behold me.*

Kendra felt a chill as she took another step. Being invited was much creepier than forcing her way forward. What if she was playing right into his hands? What if she transformed the instant she saw him? She felt tempted to close her eyes. But the Underking lived in darkness. He wanted to hide. Wouldn't closing her eyes help him? If she wanted to beat him, it would be with light. He might be encouraging her forward because all else had failed, and he hoped it would scare her. She had bet on confidence so far, and it had brought her to this point, including right through Stavius. If she was betting on confidence, she had to be brave. She kept walking.

"Where?" Kendra asked.

Here. Yes. Come meet your fate.

He sounded near. The front edge of her sphere would illuminate him at any moment.

And then the darkness surged in as never before. Gasping, Kendra pushed back against it, but her sphere was shrinking fast. Soon it was scarcely lighting where she stood. Kendra resisted with all she had, barely holding the light steady.

The nova song sprang from her shoulder. With the sphere of light so small, there was enough slack on the chain for the fairy to cross into the darkness. Instantly the chain went limp, and the shriveled corpse of the fairy swung back into view, dangling lifelessly.

"No!" Kendra cried, angry and horrified.

You're next, the Underking jeered.

Outside the sphere of light, the nova song had instantly died. Kendra had to sustain her light. It was keeping her alive. And hopefully it could help her defeat the Underking. The chain dropped from her nervous fingers. Kendra took a step forward, walking over plain black tiles. One step. And then another.

The next step brought a skull into her circle of light. Browned with age, it was webbed with cracks and missing the jaw. Only two other bones rested beside it, also aged and discolored, an arm bone and a femur. A black crown rested on the brow of the skull. The crown reflected absolutely no light.

Suddenly Kendra's sphere broadened to fill the room. It was a large chamber with many bones. But the bones before her were different somehow. They had presence. And the skull was wearing a crown. Kendra could hardly believe the implications.

"Is that you?"

Look into my eyes, the Underking invited.

"You don't have eyes," Kendra said. "Just holes."

You're still alive, the Underking ranted. *This is impossible.*

"No wonder you prefer the dark," Kendra said.

Stop, the Underking demanded.

"No, you stop," Kendra said. "You're just a broken old skull. Unless those bones are part of you?"

Do not gaze upon me, the Underking said.

"Too late," Kendra replied. "Is that all you have left? A few corroded bones?"

I will never pardon this insolence, the Underking said.

"Why didn't you turn me into the undead?" Kendra asked. "Was that all just a lie?"

I have that power, the Underking said. *But not while you are protected by the light.*

"I get why you hide down here in the dark," Kendra said. "This is where you pretend you still matter."

I am appalled that you brought such resilient light into my sanctum, the Underking said. *I am also impressed. I admire power. You have passed my trial and shown your strength. My crown is now yours.*

Kendra looked at the crown. It looked like a void in the shape of a crown. The skull was pathetic. The crown was not.

Your crown knows, the Underking whispered. *Your crown recognizes the power it would wield united with mine. Light and shadow! You could rescue those you love. You could end the war with the dragons.*

Kendra could sense the truth of his words. A vision came to her of a new infusion of power, like what she felt from the Fairy Queen's crown, but rich and dark, providing contrast. She could comprehend light and dark, life and death, above and below. Kings would kneel to her. Dragons would eat from her hand.

These opposing powers could only be united in a mortal, the Underking said. *With these two crowns, you could go on to uncrown the other great monarchs. Nothing could escape your view. You would tower above all and penetrate the deep places. You would outlast this world. You would outlast the stars.*

Kendra swayed, and she had to steady herself. This was no bluff. But she had not come here for a crown. She had come here to help Seth and Bracken. She had been warned to take only what the Underking had stolen.

"Why are you offering so much?" Kendra asked.

I need not offer, the Underking whispered to her mind. *You have bested me. The crown is yours to claim.*

"And I would keep it until I look like you?" Kendra asked. "No thanks."

It is your only hope, the Underking insisted.

"Enough of your lies," Kendra said. "It would be an end to hope. I'm not interested. My fear is becoming like you. I'm not going to do that on purpose. I don't have to listen to you. I could completely shut you out of my mind."

Do not close our dialog, the Underking conveyed.

"What's the point of sitting in a dark room as a skull?" Kendra asked. "Wouldn't you rather die than exist this way?"

No, the Underking maintained.

"But you're not alive," Kendra said. "Not in any of the ways that matter. There might be something better than this life. I think it's likely. Why choose to remain stuck here? Why not move on?"

You do not understand, the Underking accused.

"I'm not going to wear your crown," Kendra said. "But I might take it to the Fairy Realm. Maybe the Fairy Queen can figure out how to destroy it."

My crown is infused with pure will, the Underking explained. *Will independent of life and death. Will cannot be taken or destroyed by another. It can only surrender. You cannot destroy my crown.*

"Then I can take it to the Fairy Realm and lock it away," Kendra said.

You could, the Underking said, a smile in his voice. *You would not be the first to attempt such a tactic. You may be resisting my crown now. Can you always? Can the Fairy Queen? Even when great need arises? What about her subjects? This was not always my domain. It once belonged to others. Any realm I inhabit eventually becomes the Under Realm. It only takes time. The Fairy Realm can become my new seat of power.*

"But it would take time," Kendra said. "Stopping you any amount of time is better than not stopping you at all."

And there we have my problem, the Underking said. *My crown would eventually corrupt the Fairy Queen or one of her minions. But it would take time, and I am comfortable here. I wonder if you have considered the chaos that would ensue were you to take my crown from this realm? No walls hold the undead here. They stay for me and for the darkness I provide. To remove my crown from here is to flood the world with darkness.*

"I'll let the Fairy Queen figure out what to do with the crown," Kendra said.

That outcome is unacceptable to me, the Underking said. *It is not worth the trouble. I prefer to remain where I am. I rarely make concessions, but today I am willing to bargain with you in exchange for your departure. What do you want?*

"First tell me why you want me to claim your crown," Kendra said.

We are not merely this skull, the Underking said. *We live on. We never end. There is surety in it. You could join us.*

"We?" Kendra asked.

We are every Underking. We endure. We increase. We never die.

"You want to add me," Kendra said. "You want me to become part of you. It's all a horrible trick. You don't die because you're not really alive."

Your life is a ridiculous spark, the Underking asserted. *A random flash. But you could become so much more. You could see back before the beginning and on past the end. You could know all we know. And combined with the crown you now wear, there would be unimagined horizons to pursue.*

"I like who I am," Kendra said. "I don't want to be anything else."

You will soon be gone.

"I know I'm not permanent in this world," Kendra said. "But guess what—neither is the sun. I get to live my life. Someday death will free me and I will go someplace new. I don't want to get stuck here. What if this life is just the beginning?"

What if death means the end?

"I don't believe that," Kendra said. "But I'd rather take that chance than become like you. Or like any of your servants. Being undead seems like a nightmare to me."

What are your terms?

"I just want Bracken. And Seth. And the Sunset Pearl. Give me those things, and I'll leave you alone."

The skull remained as inert as ever. The Underking gave no response.

"You can keep your Under Realm," Kendra said. "I don't want to stir up more trouble with you. I don't want to unleash the undead on the world. I'll leave, and I won't return unless you cross me again."

My identity cannot be known, the Underking finally expressed.

"I'll keep it a secret," Kendra said. "I'll say we reached an arrangement. It isn't my business to reveal your identity.

I can tell you think darkness is important. You can stay hidden."

I cannot risk—

"I give you permission to see my mind only to check if I am telling the truth," Kendra said. "I will keep your secret. I mean it."

Interesting. Yes, I see it is so.

"It will be the same as your darkness. The information will not spread. Give me what I want and I'll leave. And I'll leave you alone. If you leave me alone."

Your light desecrates my sanctum, the Underking expressed. *You have sufficient power to disturb my contemplations. I admit that you have placed me in a difficult situation. Existing for days without end includes learning certain lessons in practicality. What you ask is small compared to the relief of your absence. I grant your request.*

"Thank you."

Your brother is not here, the Underking conveyed. *He has gone on an errand for me.*

"Seth told me he is bound to you," Kendra said.

True.

"Free him," Kendra said. "And if he comes back, make sure he knows he is free, and send him away."

Done, the Underking pronounced. *What else?*

"I need Bracken and the Sunset Pearl," Kendra said. "And a way back to Timbuli."

I will indulge your request, the Underking asserted. *An assistant will take you to Bracken. He will be freed. The Sunset Pearl will be brought to you. None of my subjects will interfere with your departure. You will be escorted to my clever boat. It will take you to Timbuli.*

"Bracken needs to leave with all of his possessions," Kendra said. "Including his horn, if he had it."

Agreed, the Underking confirmed. *You have disturbed our environment long enough. You must promise to cause no harm to my subjects, to depart in peace, and never to return.*

"As long as you don't cross me," Kendra said.

Away with you, the Underking insisted. *Your light is tiresome.*

"You killed the nova song," Kendra accused, frustrated and sad.

Light has no place here, the Underking warned.

"Can I take her body?" Kendra asked, fighting the sting of tears. "I don't want her to become something unnatural."

Fairies cannot join the undead, the Underking expressed. *Leave her. She sought my darkness, and here she will remain. Depart.*

"Keep your bargain," Kendra said.

I hold to my vows.

Kendra turned and walked from the room.

CHAPTER THIRTY-SIX

Unicorns

The Sphinx was gone when Kendra exited the sanctum of the Underking. The door of skulls reappeared after she exited. Without Mizarine, Kendra was alone for the first time since embarking on this adventure.

She had survived her encounter with the Underking, and he had agreed to deliver what she had come for, but she would not be at peace until she was back on Timbuli with Bracken and the Sunset Pearl. She was disappointed by Seth's absence. Hopefully, wherever he was, he somehow knew he was free. Was there a chance he would come find her?

A robed figure glided into view, feet not quite touching the floor. She had long, dark tresses and was slightly translucent, leaving her skeleton somewhat visible beneath her skin. "Kendra Sorenson," she said.

Kendra found it unsettling that the lich knew her first and last name. "Are you a lich?"

"And your guide to the prison," the lich said. "Follow me."

Kendra considered asking for her name, then decided she didn't care to know. She wondered how much the brightness of her crown mattered, since the Underking had promised that his subjects would not harm her. She put no extra effort into increasing the output, but even so, it glared more on the scale of a lighthouse than a lantern.

There was no keeping track of all the twists and turns, but Kendra noticed that overall their route continued to descend. She saw no undead besides the female lich until they found a new lich waiting for them near the top of a stairway. He was dressed like a Viking, with a horned helm, leather armor, and a braided beard. He refrained from speaking but set down a sack before walking away.

"You will find the possessions you requested in the bag," the female lich said.

Kendra opened the large sack and was surprised to discover two sizable unicorn horns, one slightly longer and thicker than the other. She had Bracken's first horn, so these had to be the second and the third. But wasn't his third horn part of the Font of Immortality? Not anymore, apparently.

In addition to the horns, at the bottom of the sack she found a pearl the size of a softball with a silky, variegated sheen. In the bright luminance emanating from Kendra, she could imagine numerous little sunsets reflected on its surface.

"Looks like it's all here," Kendra said.

They continued until they reached a cylindrical iron cage with a cat inside. Another lich awaited them—a man wearing a white tunic and a chain-mail hauberk.

"I am Ezabar," he said. "Keeper of this prison. We seldom receive guests, and we almost never release prisoners. Must you shine so brightly?"

"It's who I am," Kendra said.

"Calumbra will await you here," Ezabar said. "This way."

The female lich remained behind as Kendra followed Ezabar into a subterranean junkyard of cages. Spaced haphazardly across the rocky terrain, only some contained prisoners. The occupants looked miserable. All flinched away from Kendra and her light. She searched for Bracken but did not see him.

As she followed Ezabar past numerous cages of varied shape and size, she wished she had asked the Underking to release all of his prisoners rather than only the people she knew. It just hadn't occurred to her. And she was getting weary. So much time in the dark was making it harder to stay bright.

As she rounded a boulder, Bracken came into view inside a circular cage with a conical top. Unlike the other prisoners, he did not turn away as she approached. Despite his ragged surroundings, he looked healthy and fairly clean and didn't even squint. He seemed at home in her light. Leaving Ezabar behind, Kendra ran to the cage.

"Please let this be real," Bracken said.

"It's me," Kendra said. "I have permission to let you out."

"What are you wearing?" Bracken asked. "Don't answer that. I'm fully aware, just astonished. Will you take my hand and give me permission to see your thoughts? This seems too good to be true."

"Sure," Kendra said. "But you can't look at my negotiation with the Underking. It was part of the deal." Kendra held out her hand, and Bracken took it. The contact made him light up, taking on some of her shine.

"I don't believe it," Bracken said. "How did you manage this?"

"I can't say too much," Kendra said. "But I was destroying liches with light, and they couldn't stop me."

Ezabar arrived at the cage with a key, unlocked the door, and opened it. He stepped aside.

"What's in the bag?" Bracken asked as he exited.

"None of your business," said a voice from behind them. Kendra turned. It was Ronodin.

"We got these from the Underking," Kendra said. "We have his permission to leave."

"Maybe," Ronodin said. "But you don't have mine. I wish I could say I like your little hat, Kendra, but it brings back unfortunate memories."

"The Underking told his subjects to stand down and let us go," Kendra said.

"Fortunately, I am not his subject," Ronodin said. "Those horns belong to me."

"Where is Seth?" Kendra asked.

Ronodin smiled. "Fulfilling his most treacherous mission thus far. I confess I left him behind when I got word the Under Realm had been invaded."

"Where?" Kendra demanded, her brightness intensifying.

"Don't shine at me," Ronodin said. "I may not like the light, but I also have no fear of it."

"I know what's in the bag," Bracken said. "And I know what you meant to do."

"I had your mature horns," Ronodin said. "I only lacked the first. Now they're all here."

"You should run away," Bracken said. He took the bag from Kendra and pulled out a horn.

"I came prepared," Ronodin said, raising a black horn into view.

"What?" Bracken cried. "Your horns were lost."

"I discarded them after they were corrupted," Ronodin said. "I wanted nothing to do with my heritage. It was my biggest mistake. Others used them as power sources. It was messy work getting them back."

"All of them?" Bracken asked.

"All three," Ronodin said with a grin. "The Underking helped with two, and Celebrant assisted with the third. I have already paid in full."

"What was the payment?" Kendra asked.

"You have no right to know," Ronodin said. "A smart girl would guess."

"The Sunset Pearl?" Kendra asked.

"That was one payment for the Underking," Ronodin said. "All right. I'm bored. The other was releasing the undead from the Blackwell. Your brother performed perfectly. And the payment for Celebrant was the information about the Wizenstone."

"What about causing the fall of Blackwell Keep?" Kendra asked.

Ronodin nodded. "He still owes me for that one. It dovetailed so nicely with releasing the denizens of the Blackwell, I wanted to make sure I got credit for the consequences."

"You're a monster," Kendra said.

"I'm much more than that," Ronodin said.

"You don't want to fight me," Bracken warned.

"I really do," Ronodin said. "Desperately. A duel might surpass what I had planned."

"He wanted to find out if he could taint me by corrupting my horns," Bracken said.

"Once I had all three of mine it might have worked," Ronodin said. "If I had all three of yours. But this is better. More manly."

"Another time," Bracken said. "Another place. Name it."

"Here," Ronodin demanded with more anger than Kendra had ever heard from him. "Now. What's the matter? Worried Kendra could get hurt?"

"I don't want to destroy you," Bracken said.

"Really?" Ronodin asked. "You could have fooled me."

"I discovered you were working with the demons," Bracken said. "But you committed the crimes."

"You share the same narrow view as all our kind," Ronodin accused.

"Because of you, my father fell prey to the demons,"

Bracken said. "He was trapped in Zzyzx for an unthinkable amount of time. Even after all that, unlike you, he never went dark."

"If he had, maybe he wouldn't have stayed chained up for so long," Ronodin said. "*En garde*, Bracken."

Ronodin raised his horn, and in a swirling cloud of dark vapors, a transformation took place. In his place stood a powerful stallion, dark grey, with a fiery mane and tail. The orange horn glowed as if superheated. The dark unicorn immediately charged.

"He has learned to take his old shape," Bracken said, raising his horn. In a burst of light, Bracken was no longer a man, but a pure white unicorn. Muscles clenched as he bounded forward to meet Ronodin's charge.

Horns lowered, the two unicorns converged as if jousting. Their horns clashed with a blazing flash, and the unicorns brushed past each other.

Kendra raced around to the far side of Bracken's cage, keeping it between herself and Ronodin. The dark unicorn showed no special interest in her, instead wheeling about to charge Bracken again. The white unicorn was doing the same.

Kendra tried to think of a way to help, but for the moment it seemed like staying out of the way might be the best idea. The unicorns galloped at each other again, their horns clashing brilliantly. After one pass, Bracked crashed against a tall, rusty cage, toppling it. After another, Ronodin glanced off a stone column and nearly fell.

As the fight progressed, they charged less and got in closer. Kendra soon realized the unicorns were using their horns less like lances and more like swords. Along with thrusting, they also slashed and parried. Both were giving as much attention to defending against the opponent's horn as to attacking.

The horns flashed each time they connected, highlighting the surreal landscape of cages with dazzling strobes. The unicorns circled in close, horns crossing and deflecting as each tried to gouge the other. Both unicorns reared, front hooves flailing, and Kendra saw a wound open on Bracken's shoulder, spilling silver blood. A new gash on Ronodin's neck bled reddish gold.

Yield, Ronodin commanded. *This is my day.*

You're flagging, Bracken replied. *Not accustomed to this form, are you?*

You haven't taken this shape in ages, Ronodin taunted.

You tarnished yourself, Bracken accused, lashing out with a strike that Ronodin deflected. *Your horns are abominations.*

Ronodin dove at Bracken with a lunging counterstrike. *Yours are for show. They are the ornaments of mindless conformity.*

They crossed horns, directly testing their strength. Neither unicorn moved to break the deadlock. Muscles straining, hooves shuffling, each strained to overpower the other.

You're weak, Ronodin mocked.

Your coloring is absurd, Bracken countered. *Gray and orange?*

Not as original as pearly white.

You look like a logo for a band.

I could do this all day.

How about you push me over?

Kendra started sneaking toward Bracken from behind the cage. The horns quivered with the pressure of mutual exertion. She knew they could break the pose at any moment, so she rushed forward and rested a hand against Bracken's side and pushed all the energy she could muster into him.

The light of her crown intensified, Bracken's hair glowed, and his horn glared a blinding white. With a loud crack, the deadlock broke as Ronodin's horn snapped off.

Back to human form, Ronodin stumbled and fell onto his side. Bracken touched his horn to the fallen one, and it turned an unblemished white.

"You'll pay for that," Ronodin muttered, upending a vial into his mouth.

Breaking contact with Kendra, Bracken bounded toward his cousin, but Ronodin flew away in a flurry of black feathers. He had become an enormous raven. Without a backward glance, Ronodin flapped out of sight.

Lowering his head, Bracken shed his horn and resumed human shape. Blood stained his shirt at the shoulder.

"You're hurt," Kendra said.

"It's nothing," Bracken replied. "I heal fast, and nothing gets infected. If I'm alive, I'll be fine."

"What happened with his horn?"

Bracken put an arm around Kendra. "You happened. That boost of energy you provided let me rip it from him.

The horn really was flawed. Once it was severed from him, I was able to purify it."

Kendra looked at the white horn on the ground. "His third horn is healed."

"As if it was never corrupted," Bracken said.

"Could that influence Ronodin?" Kendra asked.

"He won't be able to transform into his unicorn shape anymore," Bracken said. "The horns are connected to our identity, but they do not define who we are. I don't think I could heal him by purifying his horns any more than he could darken me by corrupting mine."

"His plan wouldn't have worked?" Kendra asked.

"It would have weakened me," Bracken said. "Made me less powerful. But my identity belongs to me. Only I can surrender that."

Kendra could not help thinking of her brother. "Do you think Ronodin will go to Seth?"

"Maybe," Bracken said. "If Seth can be of use to him."

"That potion transformed him into a bird?" Kendra asked.

"That magic was unfamiliar to me," Bracken said. "But Ronodin deals with many whose company I find distasteful."

Ezabar approached them, his feet just a little above the ground. "It appears your altercation with Ronodin has ended," he said.

"Yes," Bracken said. "I'm tired of marinating in darkness. No matter your strength, it becomes exhausting."

"It's draining," Kendra agreed. "Ezabar, get us out of here."

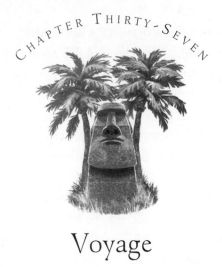

CHAPTER THIRTY-SEVEN

Voyage

When the ghostly manacle fell off with a sound like shattered glass, Seth was seated on a rock in the jungle near the mouth of a cave. "Did you hear that?" Seth asked.

"Hear what?" Calvin replied.

"Like something breaking?"

"No."

Seth rubbed his wrist. The spectral manacle that had adorned his wrist since he had struck the deal with the Underking was gone.

"I don't get it," Seth said. "I didn't deliver the Everbloom."

"What happened?" Calvin asked.

"I think I'm free," Seth said. "The ghost chain attached to my wrist disappeared."

"Could Dezia have done it?" Calvin asked.

"I don't think so," Seth said. "The Underking put it there."

Following the phantom had allowed Seth to exit the caves without any major problems. As promised, she had taken him to a different opening from the one he had used to enter. After a final expression of gratitude, the phantom had departed.

"Maybe touching the Everbloom weakened it," Calvin theorized.

"Possibly," Seth said. "That flower was incredibly powerful. I still feel energized."

"What now?" Calvin asked.

"That's the question," Seth said. "There's no reason to go back to the Phantom Isle. Eventually Ronodin will catch on that we're not returning and come looking for us."

"Do we go find Kendra?" Calvin asked. "I think I can lead us to the tree house."

"I'm not sure," Seth said.

"Why not? The tree house is still protected. They can help keep you safe from Ronodin and the Underking."

"I see why you like the option," Seth said. "I only really want two things, though. I want some time alone, without people telling me who I'm supposed to be. And I want my memories back."

"The tree house won't be good for time alone," Calvin said.

"And what if Ronodin had a point?" Seth asked. "What if they want me locked up? Even if they try to do it humanely. What if they don't trust me enough to let me track down Humbuggle?"

"You're thinking of going there on your own," Calvin surmised.

"Not completely on my own," Seth said. "With my Tiny Hero."

"I'll admit we're a formidable team," Calvin said.

"I don't want other people to decide who I am," Seth said. "I want to decide that for myself."

"You deserve to know your past," Calvin said.

"And after I know, I get to choose what comes next."

"How will we get there?"

"What do you know about leviathans?" Seth asked.

"Not a lot besides they're humongous," Calvin said.

"Some people carry snacks in their gear," Seth said. "I carry humongous leviathans. If Kendra is right, I just put a little statue in the water and say some magic words."

"You didn't happen to trade a cow for this statue?" Calvin asked.

"I'm not sure where I got it," Seth said.

"Let's say it works," Calvin said. "We ride it like a horse? Will it obey you? What if it just swims off?"

"We might end up needing a new plan," Seth admitted, rummaging in his satchel. He pulled out the little statue fashioned out of blue stone. "But why not try this first?"

"It looks like a whale," Calvin said.

"We'd definitely get style points," Seth said.

"I've never traveled by whale," Calvin said. "Why not try?"

"Think we can get to a beach without running into Ronodin?" Seth asked. "Or getting eaten by giant mushrooms?"

"Worth a try," Calvin said.

Seth stood up and followed the path leading away from the cave. It intersected another path, and Seth turned downhill. Before long they reached an overlook above a beach.

"This is the same beach where I arrived with Ronodin," Seth said.

"Are you sure?" Calvin asked. "I was mostly keeping my head down."

"I was just here," Seth said. "See that rock shaped kind of like a mitten? And the palm trees on that little peninsula? I can even still see where the boat was on the sand."

"No boat?"

"No boat."

Seth stared up and down the coast and out to sea. The clever boat was nowhere in sight.

"What's Ronodin up to?" Calvin asked.

"He might have hidden the boat to lure me down to the beach," Seth said. "Make it look safe. But why would he expect me to go to the beach? If I was escaping with the Everbloom without a boat, I'd take off through the jungle. Maybe he left. But why would he leave without the Everbloom?"

"You freed the phantom from her old token," Calvin said. "Ronodin might have gotten word and figured you betrayed him."

"Wouldn't that make him hunt me down?" Seth asked. "The boat is gone. He might have really left."

"Maybe there was an emergency," Calvin guessed.

"I don't need the beach," Seth said. "I want the tip of the peninsula."

"The beach might be too shallow for a humongous whale," Calvin said.

"We'll go carefully," Seth said. "If Ronodin left, he may come back. If we can swing it, I want to be gone before he does."

With Calvin in his pocket, Seth continued down the trail to the beach. He walked quietly, watching and listening, but saw no sign of trouble. The beach lacked much cover, so once he reached it, Seth ran to the peninsula and out to the tip.

"Still no sign of Ronodin," Calvin said. "There's a yellow fairy over by those rocks."

"I'll take her over a wild boar," Seth said. Looking out at the swells, he passed the stone whale back and forth between his hands. "I'm supposed to toss this in the water and say the magic words." He fished the paper with the words out of his satchel. "Do you think this could possibly work?"

"I think we should find out," Calvin said.

Seth threw the little stone whale out into the water. Then he read the words.

Water exploded into the air as a gigantic whale expanded into existence. Seth ducked his head as water showered down, then marveled at the size of the beast before him. The water was clearly too shallow, because all but the belly was above it. The titanic creature had to be at least a hundred yards long.

What is your request?

The words, ancient and slow, came into Seth's mind, surprising him. The leviathan did not seem distressed to be in shallow water. One eye the size of a hula hoop regarded him patiently.

"I can make requests?" Seth asked.

You brought me back. I am yours to command.

Seth laughed uncomfortably. "Do you give rides?"

Where would you care to go?

"New Zealand? As close to the Titan Valley dragon sanctuary as you can get me?"

Making the beach rumble, the leviathan swiveled until its mouth was even with the tip of the peninsula. The mouth opened, and Seth felt like he was staring into a huge, fleshy cave fringed by teeth larger than traffic cones.

"Inside?" Seth asked. "Will I be able to breathe?"

The forward void within me remains full of air. Do not proceed deeper than that.

"Should we go?" Seth murmured to Calvin.

"Isn't this exactly what you wanted?" Calvin asked.

"I pictured us riding up top," Seth said. "But I guess this way we won't fall off."

"Should we leave a message for Kendra?" Calvin asked.

"Ronodin will find it," Seth said.

"I suspect Ronodin already knows where you're going anyway," Calvin said. "But my friends will be worried. They don't know where I am. Your sister could come in handy if we need help."

"Is there a good way to tell her?" Seth asked.

"Let me think."

Come. I desire deeper water.

"I'm coming," Seth said.

"Write it in the sand with a stick," Calvin said. "At least it gives them a chance."

Seth picked up a stick and made big block letters where the sand was a little wet:

CALVIN LIVES
TITAN VALLEY

"Better than nothing," Calvin said.

Come, the leviathan insisted.

"Okay," Seth returned, stepping into the vast mouth. The whale kept still as Seth walked back through the moist, spongy surface of the throat into a large room with curved walls that moved as the leviathan breathed. The water in the room came up to Seth's knees. It smelled like a mix of wet blubber and old fish.

In the room there were a pair of battered rowboats, a desk, a table, and several crates and barrels. A squat, ugly creature sat in one of the rowboats. It had greenish skin, an oversized head, pointed ears, and a wide, lipless mouth.

"No!" the creature cried. "Not visitors."

The leviathan's mouth closed. A lantern glowed in each rowboat, so the interior of the leviathan did not become dark.

"This is my leviathan," Seth said.

The creature laughed. "You no own leviathan. I be here when you dead."

"It's a hermit troll," Calvin whispered. "They're squatters. They move from home to home."

"I've heard of them," Seth replied. He raised his voice to address the troll. "We're here until we get to New Zealand. Can we share the leviathan for now?"

The leviathan lurched, and Seth fell to his hands and knees in the slimy water. Everything kept shaking and jerking. He decided to stay down while the leviathan flopped toward deeper water.

Are you at ease? came the leviathan's voice in his mind.

"I'm okay," Seth said. "Just talking to a hermit troll."

"Me no hermit troll. Me fishy king."

The stores are meant to be shared. Let me know if you need a break on land.

"Those barrels have food?" Seth asked. "Thanks!"

"Who you talk to?" the hermit troll asked.

"The leviathan."

"You crazy."

"The leviathan said we have to share the stores."

The hermit troll shook his head emphatically. "You get own stores."

Seth stared. "I'm pretty sure I could have the leviathan spit you out."

"We share," the hermit troll replied quickly.

"I'm Seth."

"Me Hermo."

"How long have you been in here, Hermo?" Seth asked.

"Big long time."

"He was probably in stasis while the leviathan was a statue," Calvin said.

"Who that?" Hermo asked.

"My secret friend," Seth said. "We might as well be friends too, since we're sharing this space."

"No friend unless play game," Hermo said.

"What games do you like?" Seth asked.

"You know Old Maid?"

"Yeah. Do you have cards?"

"No."

"Do you have any games?"

"Mancala." The troll rummaged around in the boat, then held up a board full of divots and stones.

"I don't know how to play," Seth said, "but I'll give it a try."

"I teach. You learn."

"Sure."

"Teacher always win."

Seth sighed. "I have a feeling this is going to be a long ride."

CHAPTER THIRTY-EIGHT

Victories

Walking along the path to the fairy shrine was different under the light of day, with Bracken at her side. The cyclopses had replaced the Sunset Pearl the night before, which meant this path was perfectly protected all the way to the shrine. And with the Fairy Queen's son at her side, Kendra didn't worry about problems at the shrine, either.

"How is your shoulder?" Kendra asked.

Bracken pulled back his loose shirt far enough for her to see the slightly raised scar.

"It's already a scar?" Kendra asked. "No scab?"

"It will be faint by tomorrow morning," Bracken said. "Gone by the afternoon."

The Underking's boat had left them at Crescent Lagoon yesterday evening, then had departed unmanned. Warren and Knox had complained the most about Kendra going to the Phantom Isle without them, but since she had returned with Bracken and the Sunset Pearl, they were left with little room for chastisement. The cyclopses had thanked her profusely and departed immediately to replace the pearl on the altar. The party at the tree house had lasted long into the night, but Kendra couldn't stop worrying about the unsolved mystery of Seth.

"Thinking about him again?" Bracken asked.

"I don't know how to think about much else," Kendra said. "It was the same with you."

"The cyclopses sensed the appearance of a leviathan here at Timbuli," Bracken said. "That had to be Seth's doing."

"I'm sure," Kendra said. "But where did he go?"

"We'll find him," Bracken said.

"If he was on this island, why didn't he come find me?"

"He was confused when I saw him," Bracken said. "But he was still Seth. He'll figure it out. If he doesn't, we'll help him."

Kendra held up the crown. "Think your mom will be happy to see this?"

"I still can't believe she gave it to you," Bracken said. "I don't even think it was the right choice."

"You thought I would blow it?"

"No," Bracken said. "But it was not a risk she should have taken for me or anyone."

"Even though it worked?"

"Of course it seems brilliant now," Bracken said. "But

it embarrasses me that my mother took such a risk on my behalf. She endangered our entire realm."

"It wasn't just for you," Kendra said. "We're fighting a war against the dragons. Celebrant is free now. Who knows what he is doing? She didn't want Crescent Lagoon to fall."

"I know her," Bracken said. "It was mostly about me. Kendra, I can still hardly believe you came for me. I barely know what to say. I owe you my life."

Kendra smiled. "Anytime."

When they reached the pool with the tiki statues, Kendra was surprised to find Baroi waiting. He raised a hand in greeting. "Hail, Kendra. Hail, Bracken."

"Hi, Baroi," Kendra said. "I thought you three never left the Grand Moai."

"We are adjusting that stance," Baroi said. "Our presence did not prevent the theft of the Sunset Pearl last time. We want to take more complete care of Timbuli."

"Sounds good to me," Kendra said.

"I came with a request for Bracken," Baroi said.

"What do you need?"

"You are a unicorn."

"Yes," Bracken said.

"Ronodin corrupted one of the island's sacred pools," Baroi said. "We hope you will purify it."

"That would be my honor," Bracken said.

"Thank you," Baroi said. "And Kendra, we have good news for you."

"Tell me," Kendra said.

"The pearl augments our sight," Baroi said. "We reached

out to see if anyone had knowledge of whether Seth may have left with the leviathan. His departure is confirmed."

"That's a relief," Kendra said.

"A fairy witnessed the events," Baroi said. "Seth had a tiny person in his pocket who matches the description of your missing nipsie."

Kendra bumped the heel of her hand against her forehead. "Of course. Calvin must have gone to Seth when he was stuck to the mushroom! Why didn't I see that?"

"The fairy also had a sense for where they might be going," Baroi said.

"Really?" Kendra asked.

"Seth wrote four words in the sand before entering the leviathan," Baroi explained.

"Entering?" Kendra asked.

"Leviathans are enormous," Bracken said. "If a leviathan is friendly, large groups can travel comfortably inside of it."

"What were the words?" Kendra asked.

"Calvin lives," Baroi said. "Titan Valley."

"The dragon sanctuary?" Kendra asked.

"Perhaps," Baroi said. "Only those words were provided."

"Titan Valley is one of the big three," Bracken said. "Like Wyrmroost, it has a Dragon Temple."

"I don't remember where it is," Kendra said.

"New Zealand," Bracken said. "It is probably the most secure of all the dragon sanctuaries. Titan Valley has an extremely unconventional caretaker."

"Who?" Kendra asked.

"The Giant Queen," Bracken said.

"She's one of the five monarchs," Kendra said.

"We cyclopses acknowledge her as our sovereign," Baroi said.

"And she is in charge?" Kendra asked.

"It is the largest of the preserves," Bracken said, "serving as a dragon sanctuary and as the homeland of the giants."

"That settles it," Kendra said. "Let's get this crown back to your mother. Then we need to figure out how to beat a leviathan to New Zealand."

"That shouldn't be hard," Bracken said with a wink. "Titan Valley has a fairy shrine."

"Another adventure," Kendra said, steadying herself. "I can do this. I can't rest until Seth is safe."

"None of us will get much rest until we end this war with the dragons," Bracken said.

Kendra shuddered. It was daunting to consider what could be happening out in the world, beyond the boundaries of Crescent Lagoon. What progress might Celebrant be making in his war? "We should consult with Andromadus before we go," Kendra said. "And a member of Dragonwatch."

"We'll do all that," Bracken said. "But it will take the leviathan time to reach New Zealand. You've been through so much. You've won some difficult victories. Crescent Lagoon is a fully functioning sanctuary, thanks to you. Seth is free from the Underking, and so am I. Today, we get to relax."

"Speak for yourself," Kendra said. "I get nervous around your mom."

"Look what you're holding," Bracken said. "I think you can expect the royal treatment."

Acknowledgments

I will never master writing a novel. Every new story presents unique problems to solve. This is my nineteenth novel, and, as usual, I faced several challenges I hadn't encountered, including trying to inhabit the point of view of a character who has lost his memories. With two books left to write, I have a grand plan for Dragonwatch, and discovering how to best tell this tale will be an adventure. I am grateful to those who helped me improve this book.

My agent, Simon Lipskar, lent keen insight, and the brilliant editors Chris Schoebinger, Liesa Abrams Mignogna, and Emily Watts helped with much of the heavy lifting. I had intensive assistance from Erlyn Madsen, who gave me the most thorough and useful editing I ever received from a friend. I also got great ideas and reactions from Cherie Mull, Jason and Natalie Conforto, and Pamela Mull. Even though he is battling cancer, my uncle Tucker Davis offered lots of thoughtful feedback. I failed to mention in the previous book that Tuck made up the Wizenstone when my siblings and I were kids. It was kind of him to let me use the name in the story.

I owe a debt to Brandon Dorman for once again creating outstanding illustrations for the cover and interior, and to art director Richard Erickson from Shadow Mountain for working to get the look of everything just right. I also owe thanks to many others at Shadow Mountain for helping produce and market the book, including Ilise Levine, Rachael Ward, Troy Butcher, Callie Hansen, and Ali Nelson, and to the good team at Simon and Schuster, including Mara Anastas, Cassie Malmo, Caitlin Sweeny, Michelle Leo, Elizabeth Mims, and Alissa Nigro.

I also need to thank my assistant Rene Lindsey for her invaluable support, and my kids, who are understanding when Daddy has deadlines and events. My friends and family make me a fortunate man.

And, of course, I must thank you, the reader. When you purchase one of my books or recommend my stories to friends, teachers, and librarians, you help keep me employed and increase the chances for sequels to be written and for movies to be made. Also, when I meet you at events, it increases my motivation to share my stories. Thank you for your enthusiasm.

Concurrent with *Master of the Phantom Isle*, I am releasing a picture book called *Smarter Than a Monster: A Survival Guide for Young People*, illustrated by the incredibly talented Mike Walton. The next novel I release will be Dragonwatch Book 4. If you are enjoying this series, I hope you already know that it is a sequel series to the Fablehaven books. Some of my other series would probably appeal to you as well, like Five Kingdoms and Candy Shop War.

I'm happy to have completed three of the five Dragonwatch books. I've already started work on the fourth, and I can't wait to share the rest of the story!

Reading Guide

1. At the start of this book, Seth has lost his identity. If you knew you would lose your identity in a week, how might you try to prepare?

2. In this story, magical barrels are used to transport people instantly from one place to another. If you had a pair of magical barrels that could transport you back and forth between two locations, where would you place them? Why?

3. Tess received protection from magical creatures with the cloak of innocence. Name some ways innocence can be a protection in real life.

4. Why do you think Agad chose to surrender to Celebrant? Why did Kendra surrender? What else might they have done? Could any other option have yielded better results? Why or why not?

5. Andromadus taught Tess and Eve that mortals could cause magical creatures to change. What examples from this series or the Fablehaven books show magical creatures changing because they interacted with mortals? Have you ever been changed because you interacted with somebody else? Share an example.

6. After the Sunset Pearl was lost, the moai could be awakened by people offering the material possession they

most treasured. What might you offer to revive a moai? Why do you treasure it?

7. The cyclopses were known to glimpse the future. If you could have them look into your future and see only one of three options—whom you will marry, how you will die, or who will win the next Super Bowl—which would you choose? Why?

8. What pressures kept Seth working with Ronodin? Why did Seth decide to rebel against the orders of the Underking? Could he have reached that conclusion earlier? If so, when?

9. If you had the Elixir of Dry Depths, where would you explore? What would be the dangers?

10. Why did Knox almost run away after he woke up in the razor coral? Why did he help Kendra instead? What would you have done in his circumstances? Explain.

11. Kendra used light to fight the Underking. Why do you think the Underking preferred to remain in darkness? What would be the advantages of wearing the Underking's crown? What would be the disadvantages?

12. Why do you think Seth decided to set off alone (with Calvin) at the end of the story? What else could he have done?

13. Is this question unlucky to answer? Why or why not? Try this game of luck: Roll a die. Even number, your light beat the Underking. Odd number, the darkness overcame you. Now, try it five times in a row. How lucky or unlucky were you?